Dear Future Husband

Dear Reader,

Hey friend, thank you for being here. Before you dive into this story, I wanted to talk to you about the serious themes you may experience in this book.

This story, while full of hope and love, does explore themes such:

- Death of a loved one
- Abuse
- Trauma
- Depression
- Physical Violence
- It does briefly reference topics like SA but is not detailed.

Overall, as you read, I hope you find joy in the dark and find the desire to "live like Maybelle". Happy reading.

Love,
Taryn

"Of all the things trauma takes away from us, the worst is our willingness, or even our ability, to be vulnerable. There's a reclaiming that has to happen."

- **Rising Strong: The Reckoning. The Rumble. The Revolution.** By Brené Brown

"Traumatized people chronically feel unsafe inside their bodies: The past is alive in the form of gnawing interior discomfort…"

\-   **The Body Keeps The Score: Brain Mind and Body in the Healing of Trauma**. By Bessel Van Der Kolk, M.D.

1

Mayhem

Maybelle

*D*ear Future Husband,

I stared at those three words. Words I'd written a hundred times. Words I cherished and words I cried to. Pulling my blanket up over my shoulders, I glanced at my bedroom windows. Bruise-colored evening light stained the blinds. I twisted back to the book spread out on my lap as I clicked my pen once, then twice.

Sucking in, holding and then letting out a deep breath, I put my pen to the paper.

The only time I ever truly feel alive is when I imagine escaping. Running away from the pain, the memories, and the fears. It makes sense that running away is why I often have this dream.

I've told you about this dream before.

A vivid dream that is full of so many conflicting wants. A dream that's always so intense. Intense enough that I can feel the sand beneath my bare feet threaten to rub my skin raw. But I don't let up my efforts—I relish in the feeling.

In this dream, I am racing, flying down a beach bathed in morning light, away from the past, the dark corners of the world. The salty sea air is a welcome aroma to my senses and a delight as it combs through my curly hair, whipping and tangling as I press forward.

The dream is always on a beach, and it always leads to a fork in the road. A choice.

Growing up, when I found myself faced with the choice of one way or the other, I often let my gaze dance to the path on my left. The one that would lead me to you.

I mean—at least—I think it's you.

My being feels drawn to the path where you stand. I hesitate, looking out at you while you watch me from where the waves brush up on land. Then I turn my attention to the right.

That way is empty, a clear path to the end that lures me away. Through the years, I've veered left, running with all my might. My breathing is labored. My heart is scarred. I'm weary with a soul-deep exhaustion, but you are the fantasy I chased after.

As I've gotten older, the image of what I believe is you on that beach has blurred. It's becoming more of an illusion than a hopeful dream. And the lonely, short path to my right is one I find myself often stepping toward. I never get far enough to see what the other path offers; I usually wake before I can. Finding myself in my small bed alone, trapped, stuck, tangled up in the confines of my comforter and sheets—

Just as I did now.

"Maybelle! You up? We gotta go."

I rolled to the right. My blue alarm clock stood smugly on my nightstand. It looked down on me with a disdainful time face that informed me just how late I was to start another day.

"Maybelle," the familiar holler of my name rushed out from some place down the hall. "If you aren't out here and ready to go in the next five minutes, I'm leaving your ass to walk to school!"

Lovely.

"Go ahead," I drawled back as I accepted defeat and buried myself back under my bedcovers.

As much as I wished I could skip, Mom wouldn't let

me miss the last days of school—no matter how pointless attendance was.

Peeking out from under my bedsheets, I rubbed a hand over my sleep-riddled eyes. I shifted to look at the nightstand to my left. The journal I fell asleep writing in sat atop the table surface. It didn't look down on me condescendingly like the alarm clock. It smiled at me, giving me the motivation I needed to keep breathing.

Today marked the last official Monday and week of our high school careers—mine and my brother's.

Today's spectacle was the rally. It was a whole ordeal—one that Liam, my twin brother, the student body president, and varsity football captain, was in charge of. And currently the one threatening me with the shame of walking the five miles to school alone.

Jerk.

It may have taken every drop of my diminishing motivation to pour myself out of bed, but I picked up a pair of jeans from my bedroom floor and slipped on my favorite, fitted grey shirt.

"T-minus two minutes!" Liam shouted from what I guessed was the kitchen. Which meant he was on the move, nearing the exit, my abandonment and impending long walk to the school.

I didn't bother answering him as I brushed my teeth. Sliding a pair of strappy sandals on, I tied my long curls into a loose knot on top of my head. Then I stumbled out the door behind Liam, with about thirty seconds of his patience to spare.

Regaining my balance, I approached our short driveway and the tiny family car we shared with our mom.

"We aren't taking the car today. Mom needs it to get to work," Liam said as he swung his backpack over an arm. He adjusted his football jersey, so it laid straight on his bulky shoulders.

"Did you order a ride, or were you planning on

walking to school with me?" I asked, bending over to fix the strap of my sandal that meandered off the back of my heel in my rush out of the house.

"No, Trey's on his way to pick us up."

I paused, mid-rise; palms suddenly sweaty in the sixty-degree, shady morning breeze. My mind warred with wanting to be frustrated that I'd been rushed despite our ride not having arrived yet. But I was too preoccupied with the nerves that were now tightening and twisting in my chest.

Trey Turner.

Star running-back on the football team, the senior heartthrob—and my brother's best friend. Those two had been two peas in a pod since sophomore year when my family moved to San Francisco.

While Liam was the star quarterback of the team, Trey was the first-string running-back and, of course, best in the state of California. Both boys shared the responsibility of being co-captains of the team. And when Liam ran for and won student body president, Trey was his devoted vice president. Now, Trey and Liam would continue their rule together in college, since they both just signed to play for the D1 football team of Southern Desert University this fall.

Except, I didn't just know Trey Turner for being my brother's best friend. I knew him for the way my heart threatened to combust in his general vicinity.

"Oh, okay," I barely uttered before the honk of a black, topless Jeep flying up the road peeled through the morning air.

The vehicle pulled to a stop before us. The front doors missing from the hinges gave me an undisturbed view of Trey dressed in black pants and proudly wearing his football jersey. The scene was enough to shove my heart up into my throat.

"Hey, Triple Threat! Thanks again for the ride. I owe you one," Liam shouted over the stereo music as he easily slid into the front passenger seat.

"Anytime, but you do owe me." Trey grinned as he turned the volume of the speakers down enough for me to better hear the roaring of nervous energy in my head.

Neither boy acknowledged me as I quietly—not so gracefully—climbed into the back seat of the driver's side and buckled my belt.

"Name it," Liam said as the Jeep lurched forward, and we made our way to Harbor High.

Now, I knew my brother was a decently good-looking kid. He had tight, blonde curls like me that bounced over his forehead in the wind. A tanned, muscular physique from football and long days of surfing in the sun. Then sapphire blue eyes and a strong white smile.

But while my brother was handsome, his best friend was in a league of his own. I may have been a little biased, seeing as I was comparing him to my brother... But there was no exaggeration in saying that Trey Turner was a seriously blessed young man.

As the Jeep hurried down the road, the wind tousled Trey's light caramel brown hair, knocking soft waves into his forest green eyes. His eyes were framed by dark, long lashes any girl would sell her soul for. His smile was a weapon. Dimples flashed as if he knew just how lethal they were.

This boy would never understand the horrors of an ugly, awkward teen phase.

It took every bit of my very limited amount of "coolness" and self-respect not to drool at the rear-view mirror that gave me an unperturbed view of those green eyes.

That is, until…

"I need you to set me up with Tracey Carter. The cute cheerleader you said is in your physics class."

I suddenly found the black screen of my powered off phone very mesmerizing.

"Trey, no," Liam rejected bluntly, shaking his head of

honeycomb curls.

Betrayal etched itself into the lines of Trey's usually unblemished face. "And why the hell not?" he demanded.

His focus wasn't entirely on the road before us, which had me tugging on the seat belt across my chest, double-checking to make sure it was still doing its very vital job.

Liam's jersey twisted with him as he faced his best friend. "Trey and Tracey, for one, sounds so stupid together. And two, I was with Tracey over the weekend—if you catch my drift."

The dancing of my brother's brows caused the betrayal blanketing Trey's face to mold into something akin to disappointment and faint amusement.

"Of course you were," he huffed.

Liam chuckled, slapping his large, football-throwing hand on Trey's muscled shoulder. "What about that one girl that was doing my homework this last semester? Alyssa something?"

Trey side-eyed him. "You mean Olivia?"

Liam, the sweet boy, seemed to be using a lot of brain power before he finally responded, "Oh, yeah, Olivia. Why don't you hit her up? Bet you'd be making all her high school fantasies come true."

Trey scoffed, while I swallowed down the bile burning the back of my throat.

"Hey, May, are you alright back there?" Liam called back to me. My head was mushed into the back of Trey's seat as I wondered just how fatal it would be to throw myself out of a moving vehicle. Not at all doubting whether it would be worth it or not, though.

"Oh, hey, Maybelle. I didn't see you get in the car," Trey cheerfully greeted.

I responded to both boys by keeping my face pancaked against the back of the seat. Refusing to allow them to witness just how red my skin burned from the mere mention of my name on Trey Turner's tongue, I lifted one hand with a meager thumbs up. I considered if it would be more effective to casually open the back door and roll myself out or to leap out the open car roof.

Both options sounded worthy of the moment.

The boys accepted this response, and Liam led a discussion of how he "scored" the best this year with the girls. Then how much better college women would be. Plus a lot of other stuff I dissociated from to preserve the dwindling respect I had left for my twin brother.

Thankfully, it wasn't long before we pulled into the student parking lot. The band was outside, blasting the school anthem. An archway of balloons crowned the gymnasium double doors, and all the seniors filtered through.

Trey blasted his radio speakers as he sped into his assigned parking spot, a signal to all the students loitering in the lot that The Kings had arrived.

I wanted nothing to do with the approaching crowd of teens. So, in an effort to escape the car and the general area before we could be surrounded, I moved to grab my bag. Then I launched myself at the door handle.

Except, as I leapt for the door, it simultaneously flung open. Before I knew it or could save myself from the catastrophe, I went barrelling out of the lifted Jeep, free-falling to the asphalt. But instead of breaking my face on the street—I was caught in a couple of big, brawny arms.

"Christ, May, are you alright?" Trey asked, as his solid arms cinched in around my waist.

The raging curse storm of horrid language that threatened to spew from my mouth was just ridiculous. I worked to recover my balance, but the face-full of Trey *freaking* Turner's massive chest had me bumbling over myself.

I shifted a look back to the Jeep. My balance was offset by my stupid left foot that somehow trapped itself between the bottom sill and chair. I slowly twisted back to face him, thinking about how I often forgot how tall

Trey was until I randomly found myself in his arms.

Which…this would be a first.

I held two handfuls of his jersey on either side of his lower back. My skin was on fire. I knew every bit of my face scorched a deep red as I stared up at him through my lashes.

"My—my foot… It's stuck," I murmured. My biceps flexed under Trey's grip as he steadied me and peered over my shoulder to see that my foot was, indeed, stuck.

How? Why? What all-powerful being had it out for me today to put me in such a humiliating predicament?

Trey looked back at me, seeming a little surprised. But he quickly replaced the fleeting look with an easy smile and two irresistible dimples.

"I'm sorry. That was my fault. I wanted to be nice and grab your door, but I probably should've given you a heads up. Here, hold my hand. I'll get your foot."

I obeyed, holding to Trey's calloused hand while he smoothly slipped my foot out from the crevice between the back door sill and chair.

"There you go, Mayhem."

I reclaimed my balance and picked up my over-the-shoulder bag that had fallen to the road. Before my "fight or flight" could kick in and send me running, I paused, just for a moment. I quirked a curious brow at my handsome knight in shining football jersey.

"Mayhem?"

I witnessed a new side of Trey that morning, one I didn't know existed. One that blushed, one that looked a little unsure of himself.

He chuckled, recovering from the moment with a flawless, teasing smile pulling at his lips. It had my knees going weak.

Ignoring my previous doubts, I realised the universe was actually smiling on me today. Because Trey Turner leaned in close and spoke so low, it made my skin pebble with goosebumps.

"Mayhem, because you're kind of a mess, but a really cute mess." And then, as if he hadn't just all but destroyed me with that comment alone, he had the audacity to top it all off with a wink.

I was Jello. Melting Jello. Actually—more like juice. Seeping, dripping, sticky juice that was puddling and evaporating in the now bright California sun.

Say something witty, flirty. Be hot. Think sexy. Say thank you. For the love of God, at least smile… Nope. I spun on my heels and raced away; stone-faced.

I could never look him in the eyes again. I would need to move to Antarctica or bury myself in a six feet deep hole. Anything to never subject that boy to my awkwardness ever again.

"Maybelle!" Liam shouted over the crowd that now gathered around the two boys.

I heard him, but I refused to look back. He continued to holler after me, anyway. "Trey is taking us home after the rally, so meet back here!"

Perfect. Just perfect.

2

Slime And Snake Scales

Maybelle

The little voice in my head and soul was still screaming as I entered the gym, melding with the ridiculous cacophony of cheering from students that covered the bleachers.

I searched for a vacant seat to take refuge in. As I looked, Hannah Lacy was a beacon of hope as she stood above the crowd, signalling me to join her at the top of the right-side bleachers.

I strode to the steps and climbed up to the secluded corner, where I found Hannah sitting alone.

"Thanks, you're a lifesaver," I sighed. Hannah pushed her round glasses up the bridge of her nose as she gave me a soft smile. It was the only real greeting I could ever manage to extract from the shy girl.

Her attention retreated to the small book she had propped on her legs while I adjusted, placing my shoulder bag down between my knees. With my breathing calm and my cheeks no longer scalding, I peered over at the book she was devouring.

I couldn't contain my excitement as I tapped a finger on the edge of the book. "*Flipped?* That's my favorite book. Do you like it?"

Hannah eyed me from her peripheral. We were

usually content just using each other for companionship in crowded situations. Other than that, we weren't exactly friends in the general sense of the word. We never once hung out outside of campus walls—but we looked out for one another. I never liked that, but I also had never cared to change it until now.

I don't know if it had to do with the school year ending, my Trey-encounter-high or my social heart trying to break through my self-inflicted walls... But I felt it couldn't hurt leaving our time together with at least a small effort to be actual friends.

Hannah scrunched her nose and adjusted her glasses. A habit I noticed each time she engaged with something or someone other than her latest read. "Uh, it's alright, Bryce is kind of a jerk though."

I feigned astonishment. "What? — Well yeah, at first, but he's still cute."

Hannah stared back at me, unamused.

Feeling defeated, I surrendered instantly. "Keep reading. He gets better at the end."

She obeyed without another word or glance at me.

I loved my books, but only if they had romance, of course. *Flipped* by Wendelin Van Draanen was the official start of that obsession when I read the book in sixth grade. Now, a little older, I was into romances with a lot *spicier* tension.

The surrounding students all jumped to their feet, ripping me from my daydreaming of romance books. I stood on my bleacher seat, leaving Hannah below to her book to see what had everyone's undivided attention. The football team and cheerleaders galloped to the front and center of the gym, with Liam and Trey at the head of the herd.

Those on stage settled in as the students' lungs deflated from the sheer force of their screams, the crowd slowly sinking back into their seats.

I followed, taking my seat with the rest of the calming

audience. As a whole, the student body waited eagerly on the edge of their uncomfortable, bleacher seats while the president and his VP got their hands on a microphone.

The boys exchanged a glance I immediately recognized as an unspoken code between the two friends. One that radiated confidence and unity.

Trey, standing to the left, accepted the microphone first, a charming smile pressed up his lips. "Good morning, Harbor High!"

This greeting, alone, sent the fans back into a riot of enthusiasm. Trey and Liam joined forces. They took turns rattling off the agenda for not only the rest of the assembly today, but event specifics for the rest of graduation week. Today, we would be dismissed to go home after the rally. Tomorrow was class party day, in which each class would have an activity planned for the hour.

Wednesday was the official graduation ceremonial day.

Even just announcing a lame, not so extravagant schedule, Liam and Trey really knew how to work a crowd. They got the audience excited about boring things like Tuesday night's graduation rehearsal. They did well together, neither overpowering the other, both complimenting each other.

"Now for The Senior Last Dance," Trey yelled into the microphone. "Teachers and staff, we love you, but cover your ears because this is a senior only event!"

He handed the microphone off to Liam, who turned a dazzling smile on the students.

"After graduation, spend time with your families, and don't rush. Because we'll be meeting on Rodeo Beach at midnight, and we will be partying until the sun rises!" Liam punctuated his announcement by throwing an elated fist into the air, spurring the crowd into an upheaval of roaring applause.

The senior girls sitting directly in front of me were

already tittering about what they all planned to wear for the night out. The boys to my right boasted about the alcohol they planned to snatch from their dad's personal coolers and sneak to the beach.

And that there is the difference between men and women, ladies and gentlemen...

Trey and Liam proceeded with the rest of the rally program: a game of musical chairs made up of a few chosen faculty and students, followed by a dance routine put together by the cheer team. The cherry on top of the whole thing was the football team tackling their head coach, Coach Matthews, and slamming his face with a coconut cream pie.

Soon after that, to my delight, the rally was concluded, and everyone was excused to go home. I picked up my bag, said a quick goodbye to Hannah, then clomped down the bleachers, all while contemplating my plan of action for getting home unnoticed.

Option one: I could beat the boys to the Jeep and pretend to not exist in the back seat. Option two: I wait to see if they forgot about me entirely, allowing me to walk home alone. Thus, robbing me of the opportunity to humiliate myself in front of Trey again.

As I processed my options and concentrated on the steps down off the bleachers, I failed to notice the looming danger ahead. When I made it to the hardwood of the gym floor, a possessive, rough hand found its place at the small of my back.

Startled, but unfortunately, expectant of who I'd find, my gaze shot up to meet with the dark eyes of Clayton Thomas. The overpowering scent of too much aftershave singed my nose hairs as I gaped at the boy.

"Hey, Mason," Clayton said, smirking at my alarmed reaction.

My body instantaneously tensed and froze. I hated the reaction my body gave him. The paralyzing instincts that glued my joints still.

"Can I help you?" I tried to bite out. I glanced sideways at the surrounding crowd of students, but the gathering was too thick and noisy for anyone to notice my unmistakable discomfort.

Clayton Thomas. Your generic, not all too original bully. A boy who felt he could get away with anything because of his daddy's deep pockets. Pockets that offered up large sum donations to the school anytime Clayton found himself in a pickle with higher-ups.

The first time Clayton harassed me was behind the building at the end of junior year. I was scared, frozen then too, my only weapon being to glare at him with absolute disdain.

Thankfully, he didn't get past grabbing a handful of my rear before a group of prying eyes came around the corner, scaring him off. I never saw who witnessed the situation. Humiliated, I hightailed it out of there almost immediately after Clayton.

The jerk hadn't bothered me since then. He slid me an unwelcome wink here and there in the halls, making sure I knew he hadn't forgotten about me, but he hadn't been near as assertive or vocal. Which left me antsy and unnerved, wondering when he would strike next—until now.

His hand remained on my back with the delusional feeling of slime and snake scales against my skin. "I wanted to see if you'd be going to the bonfire after graduation. I'd love to see you there. Maybe we could hangout, and talk?"

He leaned in too close for comfort, but I didn't move, didn't push him away. I gripped the shoulder strap of my bag, knuckles white.

Clayton drew in closer, beginning to whisper something in my ear, but he halted abruptly. From the one hand still on my back, I could sense his body stiffen.

I peered up, tracking his gaze to—Trey. Clumped between a thick clutter of students, Trey's piercing green glare hit its mark. I'd never seen Trey look so intense.

The flexing hand on my back had me returning to Clayton. He had a fleeting look of fear, then frustration, before he slanted me a lazy grin that made me want to outright gag.

"See you around, Mason." Then he was gone, and with him left the ice that coated my joints. I spun back to where Trey had been, but he was engrossed in conversation again. Like nothing between the three of us had occurred.

My heart kick-started with the deep inhale of fresh, untainted air I sucked into my depleted lungs. Without wasting a second more, I opted for option one. I beat the large ensemble of students out to the parking lot and waited in the unlocked Jeep for Liam and Trey.

Almost forty-five minutes later, the boys dragged themselves free of the cheerleaders and joined me in the car. I kept my head down, refusing to acknowledge either boy, hoping to keep any and all attention off myself.

Except, as we started on the road home, I swear I could feel Trey's eyes on me. Like a sizzling awareness warming my skin. When we pulled up to the house, I exited the vehicle, this time, thank God, a lot more gracefully, and started up the driveway.

Before I could reach the front door, Liam finally brought me back into existence. "May, let mom know I went to the beach with Trey to surf. Thanks!"

I opened my mouth to reply, but the Jeep was already peeling down the road.

3

Stephanie Mason

Maybelle

My family's home was a humble spot. It had a cute red door with a white and black wood sign painted with *Mason* in bold letters atop the door frame.

I often thought it was a perfect sign to let anyone who might come lurking know exactly where we lived.

But my mom thought it was a darling decoration piece, so I didn't have the heart to voice my anxieties.

I passed the small family car in the driveway, noting my mom was home from work. Walking through the front door, I took in a deep breath of the sweetest aromas. Citrus, vanilla, and maybe a hint of cinnamon.

Stephanie Mason, my mom, loved having a scented candle lit in each room of our home. Most people would probably get a migraine living in this wonderland of fragrances, but not Mom. She was proud of her home, smelling so vibrant.

I entered, peering into the compact, front living space to find my mom in her favorite blue armchair. She was next to the window reading a self-help book, diligently annotating the page.

I had a lot in common with my mom. We looked alike, shared a lot of the same interests, but we were especially similar in our undying love for books. Except while my genius, therapist mother, read books on mental health and the meaning of life, I would forever be drawn to my books of romance and other worlds.

"Hey Lovebug, how was the rally this morning?" Mom asked, shutting the book and leaving her highlighter in between the pages.

"It was alright. Lots of screaming. Liam did great with his whole student-body-prez thing. Speaking of which, he wanted me to let you know that he and Trey went off to surf. I'm guessing he will be back later tonight." I dropped my bag on the floor and flopped onto the couch in front of my mom. I sprawled across the decorative pillows and cushions.

"Good to know. Wish my sweet boy had the forethought to come in and tell me so himself. But who am I but his dutiful mother, who awaits on his every whim," Mom said, punctuating the sarcasm of her statement with a wink. "Guess that just gives me more alone time with my favorite girl. So, what are *we* gonna do in the meantime?" she asked, her countenance always, ever so bright. "We could go get a treat, go for a beach walk, or—spice things up and go for a bike ride."

Smirking, I rolled from the couch to my feet. "I would love to walk the beach with you."

***

"How was work today?"

Mom and I strolled arm in arm in the glow of the afternoon sun, near the beach walk. There were hordes of people laying out, playing volleyball, biking, and running.

"It was amazing. We did an activity with the women called ice bathing today. It taught them how to breathe, overcome their fight, flight, or freeze responses, and they all did so well. I was so proud."

My mom was a very skilled and well-known licensed

Marriage and Family Therapist in the area. She specialized in Betrayal Trauma Healing for women. She held groups where women came together to learn how to live with their trauma and heal with a gained support system.

After everything she'd been through, my mom was a resilient powerhouse of a human being.

"Sounds cool. You'll have to teach me a bit about that," I said. Unbidden, my thoughts slithered back to my personal dilemma with freezing and the disgusting touch of Clayton's hand. A slight shiver ran down my whole body with the reminder.

Smiling, Mom pulled me closer as we continued our walk down the beach. "And how are you feeling about high school ending? It's insane that you're already here."

Nodding my head, I willed my train of thought not to be distracted by the incredible smell of churros being sold by a vendor we passed. "Yeah, crazy. I'm fine. I don't really know what I'm going to do with myself once I graduate, but I'll figure it out."

I sent out a few college applications because—well, everyone else was. A few colleges, including Southern Desert University, accepted me and Liam. SDU was my first choice in schools, but I didn't see a reason to rush into college if I didn't know what I wanted to do. Seemed like a waste of time and money not to have a plan or goal in mind.

A sharp tug on one of my stray curls had me whirling to find my mom trying and failing to be discreet as she pointed to a street corner. "Your team," she snickered.

This was one of our games, a favorite, especially in a crowded scene such as this. The game was only playable in a setting where we could easily watch copious amounts of people. As we studied our surroundings, we would point out only the most obscenely odd people, forcing our opponent to accept the individual as "their team". No one really ever won or lost the game. Well—whoever found the most absurd person usually got bragging rights, I guess.

Once, I pointed out a man making out with his chihuahua. That find had earned me a whole week of gloating, reminding my mom of the horrid scene.

I followed her pointed finger to a woman who stood waiting at an intersection. The woman was nearly two knuckles deep, digging up her nostril.

I grimaced and slanted my mother a look. "Your sixth sense for finding strange people is impressive."

She snorted, her gaze still eating up the sight. "Takes a weirdo to know a weirdo."

Mom tugged me along our path, picking up the conversation where we had left off. "I was going to say there's no rush. If you're not sure what you want to do yet, that's okay. You'll figure it out. I'm just so proud of you; I hope you know that. You amaze me."

My mother only stood about an inch shorter than me. Short enough to rest her head of blonde wavy hair onto my shoulder as we continued arm in arm.

"I know, Mom. I'm proud of you, too."

She kept her head on my shoulder as we approached a vacant bench just off the beach. Guiding me to the bench, she sat first, patting the spot for me to join. I did.

"You know," she started, her eyes looking out on the burning horizon. "Your dad would be proud of you too if he were here."

I glanced at her, a little surprised.

She didn't talk too much about dad. Not because it was a taboo topic. If I asked, she'd tell me anything I wanted to know, but it had been many years since my dad past. Almost sixteen years. Long enough that I had no recollection of the man.

My birth dad passed due to a rare form of cancer when Liam and I were only a couple of years old. From the few stories mom has told me of those days, it sounded like a time of pure bliss that was cut far too short.

"Why? I haven't done much," I mumbled, tearing my gaze away from my mother and out onto the people peppering the sand.

"May, why would you say that?"

Do I really have to answer that? That was the message I portrayed in the look I gave her. That earned me a reluctant chuckle.

She went quiet for a minute, watching the coast before she finally sighed. "Your father had the biggest heart. His love knew no bounds. He would've been proud of you just for getting out of bed every morning and going to school." Mom laced her fingers with mine, smiling. "He would have cheered you on when you were in sports. And he would've cheered you on when you dropped out to focus on school because he loved you."

Slumping in my seat, I relished in the way the breeze picked up, blowing salty mist at us. "You make him sound so perfect."

Mom sniffed at that. "He was far from perfect. He snored so loud the walls of our first apartment shook and he had the worst time management. I constantly had to tell him an event was at least two hours earlier than it really was." Giggling, she shook her head as she gave my hand a squeeze. "But he was perfect for me—in the way he loved me, needed me, listened to me, talked to me— befriended me…"

Trailing off, she looked down at her lap, licking her lips. "He was perfect in the way he loved his kids—he would've done anything to keep you and Liam happy and healthy." Straightening, she turned to face me, sea foam eyes bright. "I wish you could've grown up knowing a love like that."

Yeah, you and me both.

If only to know the love and acceptance of a good, generous, faithful father-figure and not—the opposite.

"I did," I said, instead. "I had you."

I could see the emotion welling up in my mother's eyes as she shook her head. "It's not the same."

4

Help

Maybelle

Tuesday and its own horrors came and went.

Liam and I, thank God, had our turn with the family car, and we drove ourselves to and from school. But we weren't spared from the corny games the teachers had lined out for us.

On a more positive note, Trey wasn't in any of my classes. So, I got through the day without anymore—moments—with him, embarrassing or otherwise.

Now, the sun was descending behind the horizon with a trail of blazing colors following its retreat. Tonight was the graduation rehearsal. Instead of staying at the school until the rehearsal started, Liam and I ran home to grab a snack. Now, we were back in the car, rumbling down the road.

My window was down, allowing the balmy air to tangle with my hair and kiss my face as we rushed by.

My brother and I usually spent car rides in silence. I didn't think we avoided conversations because we didn't like talking to each other. We just—didn't know how to talk to each other.

I think that skill evaded us a long time ago.

I also liked to believe Liam used the quiet moments

between us to think. Everything and everyone in his life was loud and chaotic. It made me happy to think that maybe he found peace in the safe, still moments between us. Like I did.

As I watched the world carry on outside my window, I couldn't help but discreetly study my twin from my peripheral.

Liam was beautiful, that much was for certain. He was beautiful in the way a mountain could be considered magnificent. He was solid. Vibrant with the colors of nature. Epic with sharp cliffs and tall, jagged rocks, but the thing about mountains is they're built over time. They're formed by the collision of tectonic plates. The buckling and folding of earth and stone.

So was Liam.

Life had molded, shattered, and rebuilt the boy sitting in the seat next to me. So much so, in the last few years, I felt like I hardly knew him. Liam and I had been close when we were kids. He was my hero, my best friend, but after we hit our teenage years, we grew apart.

Despite that fact, I looked up to him, even envied him for the way he took on life in stride. I aspired to be like him. To be a force like him. To remain put together, a leader and friend the way he seemed to always find so easy.

I needed to tell him that one of these days, just how much I truly admired him.

"You good, May?" Liam asked, breaking the silence.

Blinking, I nodded.

"You sure?"

"Yeah, why?"

His full attention was on the road, except for the few spare glances he directed at me. "You've been staring at me."

I ducked my head. "Sorry, didn't mean to."

Warily, he peered over at me again. "You sure there's not something on your mind?"

"Nope, I'm good," I said. "Anything on your mind?" I redirected.

Without hesitation, he shook his head. "Nope, I'm good."

And that was that.

When we parked, Liam didn't speak to me before jumping out of the car and racing up to the building. While he fell in step with a couple of his friends, I followed too far behind, to hear their conversation.

It wasn't long after I found my assigned spot for the rehearsal that I saw Liam and Trey walking up. They were in a fit of laughter over something—I bet—I didn't want to know.

Splitting ways, Liam took the seat next to mine. Instead of rushing for his designated spot, Trey stayed put. His hesitation to leave had me looking up to see that he stopped because he was watching me.

A little disbelieving of the moment, I glanced over my shoulder, sure he was eyeing someone or something behind me. Nope, no one was returning his focus and when I turned back, Trey was smirking and then he was waving. Slightly grinning, I returned his simple wave, and I almost died right there when his smile grew.

"Okay students, take your seats. Let's get started," our vice principal announced, which had Trey looking away and leaving to take his place.

The rehearsal was quick. Liam and I practiced crossing the stage with ease. As the last names were called, I leaned over to Liam and whispered, "I'm gonna go use the bathroom. Meet you in the hall?"

He nodded. "Sure."

I escaped the auditorium into the quiet, open hall. With everyone busy in the rehearsal, I had the girls' restroom all to myself. As I washed my hands, I barely noticed the squeaking hinges of the opening bathroom door. Until I twisted from the sinks to find myself, alone, standing face to face with Clayton Thomas.

Anxiety tangled itself through my ribcage and pulled taut on the noose around my heart as I watched Clayton grin.

"Hey, Mason."

I lurched for the door, but he was a wall, blocking my exit. "What's the rush?"

Trapped, I backed away from Clayton until the sinks were at my back, pinning me to the spot. his smile was oily as he stepped up into my space. "I was scared you left before we got the chance to talk more. Our conversation yesterday was cut too short."

Frozen to the spot, my body trembled as his smile widened with malicious delight.

Speak, Maybelle. Speak.

Instead, I bit down on my tongue. My mouth stopped listening to the begging of my brain. Clayton took another step toward me. His eyes darted to my feet. He snorted at the way they shuffled, trying to press farther into the immovable porcelain sink at my back.

"Come on, Mason. I won't bite," he said, holding a hand to me. He nearly closed the distance between us when he whispered, "At least, not hard."

I was going to be sick. With an inch of distance between us, the reek of that chemical-heavy aftershave burned my sinuses.

That smell.

I hated that smell. It was so, so close to the same invading scent that haunted each one of my many waking nightmares. The same one that had been present during some of the worst moments of my life. It was a smell I knew I would never forget, no matter how much time passed.

Lost to the terrors that smell shoved me back into, I hardly noticed the sound of the bathroom door opening until Clayton shuttered back from me.

"Occupied," he growled over his shoulder at the girl who peered at us through the cracked door. I recognized her immediately.

Hannah Lacy looked me right in my eyes. The eyes I knew were full of held back emotion, willing her, with all the unspoken pleas locked in my soul, for her to help me, but she didn't speak. Hannah pushed her round glasses up the bridge of her nose and walked out, leaving me alone to face my demon.

Twisting back to me, ignoring the way I inhaled sharply when his fingers grazed my neck, Clayton nabbed my long, curly braid off my shoulder. He held the braid up, breathing in a deep, embellished whiff.

"You smell sweet," he cooed, and I swallowed hard. Desperately trying to keep down the contents of my rolling stomach that threatened to crawl up and out of my throat. Dipping into my space closer, our noses nearly brushing, he smiled with all his teeth. "Makes me wonder how sweet you'd taste."

A whimper squirmed past my tight-lipped mouth. I refused to breathe, to allow his smell, his breath, his arrogance to invade my senses any further. Hopefully, if I held it in long enough, I'd at least pass out.

How pathetic.

I was pathetic.

"Maybelle?"

For once in my life, I believed in divine intervention. Watching my brother barge into the bathroom with Hannah Lacy on his heels, was the most seraphic scene I'd ever experienced.

"What the hell is going on here?" Liam barked and Clayton physically shrank back from me. Except that smile of his was an ailment still holding strong to his face.

"Ah, here comes brother. Nothing is going on. Me and Mason were just chatting."

Liam's usually light blue eyes were dark as he stared Clayton down. Then he was on the boy. Liam grabbed Clayton by the collar, holding him against the wall. They were almost pressed nose to nose as Liam asked, "What are you doing in the girls' bathroom with my sister?"

The tone of my brother's voice was deep, vicious. A type of anger I'd only ever witnessed from him once before.

The abrupt action had a startled squeak squeezing out of Hannah from her spot in the bathroom corner.

"Did you touch her?" Liam accused and Clayton laughed in his face.

"Don't be so dramatic. No, I didn't touch her. I didn't do anything, just ask her."

Both boys turned to me then. I had to hold the sink behind me in order to keep upright.

"What happened, May? Did he touch you?" Liam asked.

I was centuries old cobblestone, trembling and breaking down with the quaking earth. I couldn't make sound. I couldn't cry out; all I could do was shake my head and pray for the moment to end.

"See," Clayton snarked.

Liam didn't look at him. His eyes remained on me, silently pleading with me to say what I needed to, but I couldn't.

It shattered something deep in my heart to hear the long-irritated sigh leave Liam as he stepped away from Clayton. "Stay out of the girls' bathroom, you creep."

Clayton's grin was full of triumph as he slid me one last wink. "See you tomorrow, Mason." Then he slithered out.

Liam didn't look at me, and I wanted to burst into tears. Rather, Liam twisted to Hannah, who was still cowering in the corner. "Thank you for coming to get me, Lacy."

Hannah nodded, face a little flush as she stared up at my brother—awe-struck. But the reaction to my brother was brief as she turned her attention to me. "Are you alright, Maybelle?"

Honestly, I was a little surprised she asked, though

that girl was technically the only friend I had. Flustered, I nodded and said in an airy voice, "Yes. Thank you."

Smiling her farewell, Hannah pushed her glasses up her nose and exited the bathroom. Leaving me and Liam alone.

Still, Liam didn't look at me as he turned for the door and said back over his shoulder to me, "Come on, May. Let's go home."

I numbly followed Liam out to the car, keeping a respectable distance. The rehearsal had ended, and the hall was teeming with high schoolers. But my twin pushed through, not stopping when numerous students tried to get his attention.

He only stopped when his best friend threw an arm around his shoulders.

"Hey, where's the fire?" Trey asked with a chuckle.

Liam didn't answer, but he halted with his friend. The pause in our retreat allowed Trey to spot me only a few paces behind. With how his eyes widened at the sight of me, I figured I had failed to school my features into neutrality.

"Hey, is everything alright?" He pierced Liam with his questioning green eyes, but Liam was a lot better at playing pretend than I was.

The smile he sported was worthy of awards as he put a hand on his best friend's shoulder. "Everything's great. I just need to get May home. We still up for tonight?"

Trey studied my brother. Then his gaze fell on me again, but I looked away, not able to meet his eyes. I didn't glance back until I heard him say to my brother, "Of course, I'll see you tonight."

As soon as Liam resumed his pace, I raced up behind him, not stopping until we reached the vehicle. Once in the car, I anticipated we'd resume our same silence on the drive home. Just as we always did, despite the recent events—but I was wrong.

"What happened in there, May?"

I didn't look at Liam. I pitifully kept my eyes on my fidgeting and folding hands. "I don't know."

Leaving his hands on the wheel, Liam dropped his forehead to it. A round of heavy breathing passed before he looked back up at me. "I thought you were better, that you had stopped—freezing when we moved here. Aren't you in therapy?"

Why did it have to sound so small when he put it that way? It wasn't a nail-biting habit I hadn't kicked. It was a trauma response my body went into from years of terror. It wasn't just an easy fix. It was a lifetime of war between the body, mind and soul.

I am what they call one of the prey species. Like rats, mice or squirrels. When threatened, my body activates its freeze response. Freezing was how I survived the life I was dealt.

Hold still, don't breathe, keep quiet, obey.

That was the mantra that saved me from more hurt. The anthem that was on constant repeat when fear overpowered me. It was what kept me hidden when hunted. Now it was my prison. It was the shackles that bound me, offering me up as easy pickings to a cruel world.

I snorted, though nothing about this discussion was in the least bit amusing. "Therapy isn't a cure-all."

"I know that. I tried it, remember?" Liam reminded.

"For a week," I scoffed, unsure of why I felt the need to after he just saved me. I guess it was the only fight I had the courage to take part in. The only words I could control.

"I did therapy for over a year," he corrected, his tone still level.

Despite that, my tone was harsh, eager to be done with this night, this day, this life…

"Sorry, we can't all be as great as you."

"That's not what I'm saying, May," Liam tried to reason.

"Then what are you trying to say, Liam?"

He paused, and I knew the pause would carry. This conversation would stop here, because neither one of us was brave, nor knowledgeable enough to figure out where it could take us.

We didn't know how to talk then, and we certainly didn't know how to now.

Liam twisted from me, flicking his head up so his bouncy blonde curls would lift from his eyes. Without another word, he threw the keys into the ignition and took off down the road home.

The past clawed its way between us, suffocating the space. The past had a name—Richard. A man, a tyrant, trusted to take up the mantle of father but betrayed that sacred role. He was the sole reason we moved to San Francisco. The reason I struggled to find peace inside my brain and body. For years, Richard Amos may have been the one to hurt us, scar us... But the silence was our fault.

How ironic, us not being able to communicate. Despite the fact that we were the children of an accomplished therapist. You'd think we'd be able to talk about our feelings as easily as we breathed, but nope. We were still human, and our downfall was our inability to ask for help.

Liam didn't pull into the driveway when we made it home. Instead, he parked at the curb. I didn't need him to explain. He was leaving. Probably to go party, drink, and be with his friends. I couldn't judge him, though; we all had our forms of escape.

"Tell mom I'll be back later," he mumbled as I exited the car.

Before shutting the passenger door, I peered down at my brother. I wished I had the words. The knowledge of how best to mend the rift that had never been a real solid connection between the two of us.

"Are you going to be, okay?" I heard myself ask.

Liam looked up at me. For the first time in a long

time, I didn't see the happy, go-lucky boy who had all the friends and attention he wanted. I saw a scared, damaged boy, silently asking for help.

I opened my mouth, to say what, I didn't know, but Liam's mask was quick as it slid into place with a disingenuous smirk.

"I'm always okay, May."

I should've demanded honesty. I should've asked him what I could do for him, but I didn't. Instead, my smile was just as unfeeling as I nodded and shut the car door.

5

Tone Deaf and Dancing

Maybelle

I woke up to sunlight streaming through my bedroom window. It was Wednesday, the long-awaited graduation day. Seniors weren't expected at the school until this evening, but Liam, not to my surprise, but far from my delight, signed us both up to help with setup. Which meant we had to arrive at least an hour earlier than the rest of the student body.

I drowsily glanced over at my constant blue alarm clock. It was early. With so much spare time before I would need to get ready, and with the events of yesterday still weighing heavy on my heart, I decided to go for a run.

Running—not a favorite pass time for many, but for me, it was an escape. A little time of peace. A moment of pretend.

I rolled out of bed. Slipped on a pair of black leggings and a black sports bra. Over top, I pulled on a black sweater I left unzipped. Then I grabbed socks and a pair of black sneakers with white detailing. Obviously, I had a favorite color to work out in. I was reserved and pretty insecure, but I liked my stout body in dark workout clothes.

Standing before my vanity, I did what I could to tame my tangled nest of bedhead. I watered down my frizzy, ringlet curls with a spray bottle, then proceeded to French-braid them into two tight braids.

As I toiled with my hair, staring at myself in the mirror while I worked, I studied the reflection. My eyebrows were light, too light against the tan of my skin and barely cousins by similarity. My eyes were an undetermined mixed color of blue and green, and they were large. Almost bug-eyed if I looked at them too long. The number of freckles that burdened my nose and tops of my cheeks was unnatural.

It wasn't like I hated my face... I just—didn't get along with it. Eager to escape my self-abasement, I tore my gaze away from the mirror.

After brushing my teeth and slapping on a quick swipe of deodorant, I crept into the hallway, my wireless earbuds in hand. I warily paused, listening for the roaring snores that echoed from Liam's room two doors down from mine.

He slept like the dead most mornings after his parties. I could be screaming for my life right then and it wouldn't faze him, which was exactly what I wanted. I plugged my ear buds into my ear and blasted my music on high as I strolled to the kitchen, an extra hop to my step.

I was talented in some things, specifically in reading, writing, and sports, but singing was not one of those things. I was tone deaf, and I knew it, but it didn't stop me from belting my heart out to my favorite songs. Obviously, only when I was alone in the car or in the safe solitude of my home.

That morning was no exception. I spun to the coffeemaker, whipping myself up a quick cup while I sang to the beating music of *Stereo Hearts* by Gym Class Heroes. I slid through the kitchen, a bounce to each of my steps because when my need to squawk like a canary hit with the music, so did my need to "bust a move".

So, I danced—more like skipped and jumped around the kitchen off beat, while singing extremely off key. It was a true, unfiltered version of myself I wouldn't subject anyone to.

Spinning, I downed the rest of my warm coffee, then pulled an imaginary guitar out of thin air. I ripped out an amazing solo as I more or less squealed out the bridge to what was now *Livin' On A Prayer* by Bon Jovi screaming through my skull.

When the song and my impressive solo finally ended, the song faded into my ear buds. There was a quick pause of silence between songs filled only by my deep breathing. That pause of semi-silence allowed me to hear the quick and astonished, "Holy shit."

I stiffened. I knew that voice, and I knew the chuckle that followed that charming voice.

My eyes shifted forward to the sink. Maybe, if I moved fast enough, I could throw myself hard enough through the window sitting above the faucet. There wasn't much of a fall so I unfortunately wouldn't die, but the glass would be enough to send me to the hospital. That way, I wouldn't have to face the boy, who, no doubt, stared at my back like I was a psychopath.

"Christ, Mayhem. That was awesome."

That nickname.

I willed my now sweat-drenched hands to remove my ear buds that had moved onto another song and pivoted my body to face him.

His caramel hair was messy. His face was rugged with a lazy smile and the boy that stood on the opposite side of the kitchen from me was shirtless.

I'd seen Trey shirtless before at the beach and pool settings. But this moment was a whole new level of intimate as he watched me, fresh from sleep. The morning sun leaked through the windows. Casting his bronzed body in a fascinating combination of shadow and light contrasts.

Stunned, I knew my eyes were popping out of my skull, but at this point there was nothing I could do. I wasn't mentally prepared for this moment, so my body had a mind of its own as I ogled him shamelessly.

After a too long bout of silence, in which I continued to stare wide-eyed like an idiot, Trey smiled. He crossed his arms over his exceptional chest, and I finally collected my wits enough to clear my throat.

"Uh, what are you doing here?"

Smooth, Maybelle.

His grin widened. "I was with Liam last night. There was this party, and…I might've had a little too much to drink. So, uh, he drove us here in my Jeep and—" He brushed a hand through his messy waves of hair. "Guess he tucked me in on the couch." He shrugged, a hint of what might be shyness lacing his tone and movements.

Like Trey Turner could ever be embarrassed in front of me. Yeah, not a possibility.

My eyes darted to the couch that was a pile of blankets and cushions.

That was my new favorite couch.

"So, is everything alright?"

I turned back to the boy. The boy I still wasn't sure was real or a figment of my imagination. I tilted my head curiously. "Is what alright?"

"You seemed upset after the rehearsal yesterday and Liam was a little off last night. Everything okay between you two?"

Scatter-brained, I nodded aggressively, sputtering out the first excuse I could think of. "Totally fine. I just— started my period…so Liam offered to rush me home."

If only I were in the middle of oncoming traffic. I wouldn't hesitate before throwing myself in front of a bus. I waited for Trey to grimace, look a little disgusted at the mention of a menstrual cycle like most boys would. But Trey only nodded thoughtfully.

"Are you feeling well enough to go to the party tonight? I hear there's going to be karaoke." He gifted me a teasing smile that just about did me in.

I swallowed, collecting myself.

"I'm feeling better, but I honestly wasn't planning on it." I looked down, knowing I was being ridiculously awkward and curt, but I couldn't help it. Trey heard me sing. No—what he heard was more like shrieking. He saw me dancing. Playing the air guitar like, I was the lead guitarist, Angus Young, ripping out a world-altering solo. I gnawed on the inside of my cheek, refusing to look him in the eye.

From my peripheral, I could tell Trey was leaning over the kitchen counter that stood between us, resting his forearms on the flat space.

"Why not? This is *the* party, even bigger than prom."

I shrugged, unsure of what to do with myself. "I am not a huge fan of parties."

That was a lie.

I just wasn't a fan of making myself look like a loser by showing up alone. Which would absolutely happen because I was a friendless turd.

"Oh, come on, May. I get it if other parties, even prom, hadn't been worth your time, but you can't miss tonight. You'll regret it if you don't go."

The smile in his voice made me want to giggle—or barf. A lot of confusing and warring emotions were happening all at once in my muddled thoughts.

All because of him.

I was an obsessive psycho for this guy, and why?

Well, one, look at him!

He was jaw-dropping beautiful. And two, he was kind, personable, a friend to all. Trey had all the looks and a stunning side of personality to go with them.

And maybe—it was the way he looked at me the day we first met all those long months ago. The way he opened my car door for me, smiled so sweetly, and told me he thought I was pretty. I fell hard that hot summer day between our sophomore and junior years.

I was at the school, picking up Liam from a week-long football camp. I was wearing a lazy pair of soft jean shorts and a blue pajama tee. My hair was in a sleep-crazed knot on the top of my head, and that crazy, attractive boy had told me I was pretty.

It was a wild phenomenon I couldn't understand and refused to believe in, so I ducked my head and ran.

From that day on, I continued to run anytime he so much as looked at me, let alone tried to speak to me. Trey had only been trying to be nice to his new best friend's sister. Why else would he want to waste any of his energy on me?

I peered up from my hands that folded together as I recalled the long-ago, shoved away memories. "I don't know. We'll see how tonight goes."

His lips turned up into a winning smile. "That's not a no, I'll take it. So, where are you headed so early?"

"Just going for a quick run."

Trey's face lifted with the rise of his brows, and his head slightly tilted.

"Impressive. I hate cardio," he deadpanned the last part, and I couldn't stop the snort that escaped me. I was ready to follow through with my original plan of throwing myself through the window now.

My feet shifted away, ready to hightail it out the front door. But Trey looked at me in such a bold way that made me feel like I just gave him a challenge he was all too eager to accept. So, my feet slowly straightened back, remaining rooted in anticipation of what he might say next.

"What's so funny?" he asked as he leaned farther forward; green eyes narrowed in amusement.

Currently feeling more self-conscious than I'd ever been in my entire life, I fidgeted, trying to find a more comfortable position. I rested against the kitchen sink behind me. "It's funny that you hate cardio when you're the best senior running back in the state. Cardio is literally in the name."

He seemed to consider this and smirked. "Yes, well, I enjoy running after the ball, to open for a pass or to take it home for a touchdown, but to run for the sake of running. Not my idea of a good time."

I nodded, then deciding that sitting on the counter behind me would be a lot classier, I lifted myself up and sat myself next to the sink. While I maneuvered onto the counter, (immediately regretting the move when the top cupboards forced me to slouch forward, making me look anything but classy) Trey rounded the corner of the tabletop that had been between us.

Now, his back was to the counter as he folded his arms across his bare chest. Giving me a full view of him in grey sweatpants... I didn't know when I would wake up from this wet dream, but I prayed it wouldn't be soon.

"I understand," I choked out, trying to control my roaming gaze. "I used to play basketball. I hated running unless it was in a game, but after I quit, I realized I really liked the peace of mind that came with it."

He shook his head, bewildered. "You played sports? Why'd you quit?"

"I wanted to focus on school after we moved here." Another lie. I quit because at the time I could hardly find joy in waking each morning, let alone find joy in sports.

One of Trey's large hands lifted, rubbing the back of his neck as he said, "Interesting. How did I not know this about you?"

Smiling, I gave a quick, jerky shrug. "I have very few musical talents, obviously, but my three-point shot isn't bad, and I keep a level head in a tight game."

Eyes bright, he stared up at me, like he might be seeing me for the first time. "Wow, May, I do not know a lot about you. Do I?"

His viridescent eyes remained glued on me while he

adjusted his position until he stood directly in front of me. All he would have to do was take one step forward and my legs could wrap around his hips. My hands could tangle with those caramel curls and those lips…

My head slowly bobbed as I tore my eyes from his lips. "I—I don't make it very easy for people to get to know me."

"I can't argue with that." His head turned to the floor, brown hair toppling into his eyes as he peered up at me through dark, lowered lashes. A look that brought heat to my cheeks and belly.

His gaze was so intense, stripping. If he kept looking at me like that, he might see everything. He might see every faulty, charred part of my broken character and it was a reality I suddenly couldn't risk.

Trey Turner couldn't be let in. He couldn't see the very innate bits of my heart because if he did, he may never look at me like this again. He would never look at me like I was someone worth seeing.

I could feel my vulnerable, fragile self crawling back into its nervous shell of comfort as I kicked off the counter, away from him. "Well, I better get this run over with."

I tried to sidestep him, but as I moved, he was already there, grasping my fingers. He gave my hand a slight tug that halted my retreat and lured my eyes back to his.

Trey Turner had participated in a full conversation with me and now was purposefully touching me. This was officially the best day of my young life. I couldn't help but look back down at my short fingers entrapped in his large hands. I peered up at him, now having to tilt my head back to meet his gaze.

This moment, right here, was going to have at least three pages of my journal dedicated to explaining every minute detail.

He grinned down at me, dimples flashing.

"Thank you for the amazing concert this morning."

I grimaced and made to pull away, but he moved closer and held a little tighter to my fingers.

"And thank you for talking with me. I realize I have a lot more to learn about you."

He dropped my hand. But before I could try to take off again, he was grabbing for the zipper of my open sweater. He locked the zipper into the teeth and dragged it up to just over my chest.

His stare was heavy as he watched my body move with each breath. Flicking up, his green eyes locked with mine.

"And I plan to learn it all," he promised.

I entirely lacked the focus and confidence, really, to say anything cute or flirty back, so I did what I could manage. I smiled, no teeth, so as not to seem too eager, but big enough to show just how happy that comment had made me.

Trey smiled back as his hands finally left my sweater, allowing me to robotically walk out the kitchen. I stepped out the front door, toddled down the road to the neighborhood park.

That's where I sat my butt in the grass with a giddy grin plastered on my face and squealed like the smitten fool I was.

6

Trey Turner

I tiptoed through the Mason home, toward the bear-like snores echoing from my best friend's room. Peering past the door, I confirmed that Liam really was sleeping, despite his racket.

I didn't understand how the girls in this house got any rest with that kind of noise reverberating through the halls, but I was thankful for it at the moment. The noise was a signal that gave me the confidence to sneak down the hall toward the bedroom I'd only caught glimpses of through a slightly ajar door.

Natural light and a balmy breeze seeped in through her open window. I checked down the hall one more time before I pushed the door open and went inside.

Grinning, I stepped over a few pieces of clothing strewn across the floor. I padded up to her bed, the one I'd briefly seen her doing homework in or reading her books. Atop her nightstand was a picture frame. The picture was of Maybelle and her mom, embracing on the beach.

Maybelle Mason.

Her room wasn't what I pictured. I thought for sure the quiet girl would be tidier. More nit-picky. Instead, her bed was disheveled, and there were clothes littering the floor. Makeup cluttered a white-painted vanity on the far wall, but there was one area of her room that was pristine.

In the corner was a bookshelf. One layered in novels of every length, color, texture and width. Lowering to peer at the squat shelving, I confirmed my assumptions. The books were stacked in alphabetical order. I smirked, dragging my fingers along the spines of a few.

I liked knowing this about her. I liked knowing she was a little messy, except with her precious books. I liked knowing anything I could about her.

I was confident, borderline cocky. I could speak to any girl and not get flustered. But Maybelle *freaking* Mason was a whole other story. She terrified me. From the moment I first laid eyes on her, I'd been speechless.

The first time I saw Maybelle, she was picking Liam up from football camp and I all about drooled over my new best friend's twin sister.

My sixteen-year-old heart wanted nothing more than to hold her hand, kiss her, and take her to the movies. Now, my bit older heart wanted to do a few more mature things—but you get the picture.

I tried to talk to her when we first met, but she avoided me like the plague. I didn't take it too personally, though, because I soon realized that Maybelle thoroughly avoided *everyone*.

I thought she wasn't interested and couldn't care less that I existed. Probably wanting nothing to do with her twin brother's annoying best friend. I tried to move on with life. I focused on football and indulged in the occasional flings with other girls—mostly as a distraction from what I couldn't have. Unfortunately, no one sent my pulse rocketing or my stomach spinning the way my best friend's sister did.

As rejected as I felt by Maybelle racing away or shutting down when I was near, I had to consider it a blessing.

From day one of meeting Liam, he and I easily clicked. Before Liam, I didn't have friends.

I mostly kept to myself before the Masons had moved in. I focused solely on sports, my grades, and my mom. Those three things were enough to take over every spare moment I had, which left little room for friends and free time. When Liam came crashing through my life, I felt for the first time in a long time that I could just breathe. Like I wasn't so alone.

Maybelle, not liking me back, removed a potentially catastrophic hurtle from mine and Liam's friendship. Or, well, so I had thought… All that changed when she fell from my Jeep into my long-awaiting arms.

I got this kick of courage to try one more time to at least be a friend to her. Maybe get her to notice me as more than her brother's best friend before high school was done, and we all went our separate ways. I leapt from the vehicle to open her door like a gentleman because girls like that stuff.

Except, I didn't think to warn her. So, when the door swung open and she toppled out of the lifted vehicle, I panicked. I thought she'd be annoyed, making my efforts worthless. But fortunately for me, Maybelle wasn't annoyed—she was nervous.

I felt her tense in my arms. Her breathing quickened, and her heart rate rampaged. At that moment, I realized Maybelle Mason liked me because I made her every bit as flustered as she made me. This alone filled me with all the confidence to try harder for the girl I spent so long liking from afar.

Except, after the rally, when she ran back to the car and ignored me, I got stuck in my head again.

Did I read too much into her reaction? Maybe it was solely embarrassment and not nerves. Then I contemplated all the complications.

If it didn't go well with her, would it hurt my friendship with Liam? Would Liam even approve?

I stressed myself back into silence until this incredible morning. I was sound asleep on the Mason's couch, when I woke to Maybelle bouncing and singing through the kitchen. As I sat in awe, watching the quiet girl dance and squawk, all I could think was what a wonderful life it would be to wake up every morning to this version of Maybelle.

I'd always thought she was beautiful, but this morning I got to take her all in and I memorized her.

Her skin was a perfect, glowing bronze in the morning light that had flooded the kitchen. She had a twisted, mixed color of blue and green in her round eyes that were so goddamned enchanting when they were lit up by the sun. Maybelle didn't smile much, but I learned that, when she did, she smiled with her entire face. She had this nose that was paint-splattered with freckles that folded against each other when she scrunched her face.

I wanted her—needed her tone-deaf singing, her dancing, her shy smiles, her pouty, full lips, and oh god— that hair.

Maybelle didn't wear her hair down, but one day, I would see it. It was a personal goal of mine to get her in a position where she would have it down and I could tangle my fingers through the curls.

Our successful encounter was why I'd given into temptation and snuck into her room. I'd never been inside and after this morning, I was curious.

Everything about Maybelle intrigued me.

I pulled one book from the shelving. I flipped through the well-kept pages. A smile pulled from me as I learned that Maybelle liked books of other worlds, magic and romance. I mentally filed away the mental image of the cover, title and author for later use as I slid the book back into its place.

Turning from the bookcase, I swept one last look around the room, ready to leave before Liam or

Stephanie could catch me. But something grabbed my eye.

On Maybelle's left side nightstand, sat another book. I didn't think as I strolled around the bed, eager to know what fantastical world she was currently living in. Except, there wasn't a title on the cover.

It was a black, leather-bound book. Old and worn by the looks of it. Cautiously, I plucked it up, opening the cover trying to find a titlepage, but there wasn't one.

Instead, written in swooping cursive handwriting, I read:

Hi,
My name is Maybelle Mason.

Frantically, I slapped the book shut and dropped it back onto the table's surface. Obviously, this was a journal. I was already traipsing through her room like a creep. The least I could do was leave her journal, of all things, alone.

Except, I didn't turn around. I didn't leave the way I'd come in. No, I was still staring at that leather-bound book. Flexing my fingers, I tried to move, to look away, but again, I was curious. Too curious for my own good. I meant it when I told Maybelle I planned to learn about her. Everything about her. Fascination forced me forward and I reached for the book.

"Trey?"

"Shit." I flinched, shying behind Maybelle's bed.

Dead still, I crouched as I listened to Liam's footfalls down the hall and past Maybelle's closed bedroom door.

Rubbing a hand over my face, I sat baffled that those few written words were enough to distract me from the obvious silence that now swallowed the house.

Shaking my head, I spun for the door, creeping it open.

I could hear Liam bustling through the kitchen. I let myself out of the room, snicking the door closed behind me. I hoped to snake my way around the opposite side of the house, creating the illusion that I came from the bathroom. Turning, I took one long step, only to find myself face to face with Stephanie Mason.

Just my luck.

Stephanie's wide, sea foam green eyes bounced from Maybelle's bedroom door to me, then back to the door. I could see understanding leak into her features when Liam called my name again, and I still didn't answer.

I wasn't sure if I should run or beg for forgiveness as a knowing smile pulled up Stephanie's face. My knees buckled when she didn't speak and pressed her forefinger to her closed, upturned lips. Leaving me with a wink, she walked past me into the kitchen.

"Hey, mom," Liam said through a yawn. "Have you seen Trey? He stayed over last night, but I can't find him. And his Jeep is still out front."

I waited as an apprehensive sweat heated the back of my neck. But Stephanie continued to surprise me as she said, "I think I heard him in the bathroom. Just give him a minute. I bet he'll be out soon."

Swallowing, I sighed out the breath I was holding. Then I continued down the hall through the planned path around the house, unable to get my mind off that journal.

Dear Future Husband,

I wanted to tell you a little about why I wrote this book.

I'm not just a lovesick fourteen-year-old dreaming of my happily ever after. I won't lie and say that dreaming of a big wedding, finding true love and having lots of babies doesn't play a big part— but it isn't the main piece of it.

Let me explain.

I never knew my dad. My mom has a boyfriend, Richard, but I don't think I could ever call him "dad".

None of my grandparents are alive. My mom and dad were only children, so no uncles, aunts or cousins either. It's just us. Me, mom and Liam.

I realized, recently, the only other important man that will have a part to play in my life is you.

I may not know my dad, but that doesn't stop me from talking to him every day. I confide in him all the time, in my heart. I feel like I've gotten to know him in some weird way like that because I think he listens. Maybe even answers my questions or is there for me when I'm scared.

I feel like talking to you now, through the pages of this book, will help me know I've found you the day we meet, because I'll kind of already know you. It'll be like we've already had hundreds and thousands of conversations, making it easy for me to know I've found you.

You, this book, are my vault of secrets. My crutch when I feel weak. My protector when I feel scared. My balance when life is too turbulent and my anchor when I feel capsized by reality.

You are my everything and I know I'll have found you when I am your everything. When I am your vault, your crutch, your protector, your balance, and your anchor. When you are mine and I am yours, I will know you and I will love you with my whole heart and my whole soul.

Love,
Maybelle Mason

7

Invisible To Non-Existent

Maybelle

For over an hour that morning, I jogged continuous loops around my suburban neighborhood block. Waiting until Trey's Jeep was no longer parked out front of my family's home.

I didn't know what to make of the moment we had. All I knew was that I was high on the feeling. And would rather die of heat exhaustion from the exuberant amount of cardio I was doing than run into him again before I was emotionally ready.

As soon as the coast was clear, I bolted for my room, my adrenaline launching me at a neck-breaking speed.

I eagerly showered away all the anxious sweat from my body. I put on my fluffy pink bathrobe, then parked myself on my bed. Pen in hand, I was ready to document every detail of my encounter with Trey into the journal I snatched from the top of the bed-side table.

I wasn't a quiet girl who had nothing special to tell the world. I was quiet because I told my world everything through the words of a small leather-bound book.

Since I was in middle school, I recounted anything and everything into this little notebook. Every high and every low was detailed in the form of letters to someone

I hoped to one day meet. Like reading or running, it was an escape, an outlet. Except it was made with so much more hope for a future I could love, for a life I would not dread.

So, I sat for a while, writing out every look, touch, and smirk from Trey, with a girly grin tight on my lips.

***

We were a little behind for setup preparations. Liam had lost his other dress shoe, setting us back. Mom made a few "just like your father" comments but smiled as she dropped us off at the front of the fine arts building.

My hurried steps had my hair coiling onto my face and catching on my gloss. Overstimulated, I shuffled around the items in my arms so I could push the hair out of my eyes. Somehow, Mom had convinced me to wear my hair down. The curls were usually so crazed and ratty, but it was a special night, so I appeased her.

As we made our way inside, almost every single person we passed greeted Liam. While we strolled toward the entry doors to backstage, my twin was on cloud nine with all the recognition.

Not one soul acknowledged me. That was nothing new, but Liam and I rarely stayed together long in public. So, it was a little eye-opening to me, just how invisible I was next to my brother. I wasn't by any means jealous of the attention he got. Liam deserved to be seen. It was impossible for him to go unnoticed.

No, it definitely wasn't jealousy. For the first time in a while, I was just truly realizing how great of a job I did at making the world forget my very existence.

"Hey, Mason!"

Liam and I both answered the call as we looked ahead to see Noah Williams.

"Williams, how's it going, buddy?" Liam beamed at the boy as he pulled him into what qualified as the "bro hug".

Noah was Liam's pride and joy. He was a Junior and second-string quarter back on the team. At the beginning of the year, Liam had taken full responsibility to train the young football player, preparing him to take up his mantle once he left for college. Fortunately for Liam and the rest of Harbor High's football team, Noah Williams was a natural born athlete.

He was a handsome boy with deep brown eyes, beautiful dark skin, and cropped black curly hair with a genuine smile. I had seen and spoken to the boy a few times when I picked Liam up from practices. I liked him. He was always super kind, very respectful and…

"I don't think we've met. What's your name?"

Startled, I escaped my muddled thoughts to look down at Noah's outstretched hand. Desperate for help and maybe a mercy killing, I quickly glanced at Liam, who covered up a deprecating chuckle with his large hand.

If only I were a bug squished under a foot. That would be far less painful compared to this excruciating awkwardness.

Trying to spare Noah of the uneasiness I was currently drowning in, I pasted on a shy smile. But before I could fully accept Noah's hand and re-introduce myself, I was beat to the punch.

"That is *the* Maybelle Mason, Williams."

The three of us twisted to see Trey Turner lazily propped up on one shoulder against the wall. He was watching us with unabashed amusement. "You know her. It's impossible to forget a face as beautiful as hers."

A quick burst of heat rushed to my face from the compliment and a fiery stress rash inflamed up my neck and chest from embarrassment.

Cautiously, I peered back at Noah, whose unbothered countenance glowed with recognition. "That's right, Maybelle. You're Liam's twin sister. Sorry; it's been a minute since we last spoke. It's good to see you!" And while I was burning alive from my mortification, Noah spun back to Trey, already forgetting about me. "What's up, Turner?"

Noah stepped up to Trey and pulled him into another "bro hug".

Trey had on his white button up, black tie, and black pants. Same as Liam and all the other senior young men, but he wasn't yet wearing his navy-blue cap and gown. He left his tie undone, hanging on either side of his neck, and left the top three buttons of his shirt open.

Trey slapped the boy's back and when they parted, Noah looked at both Trey and Liam.

"I was surprised to learn that there are, in fact, brains behind those pretty faces. I mean, let me rephrase—none of us had any doubt the closeted nerd over here would finish top of his class," Williams said as he threw a playful elbow at Trey, who barely moved an inch to block the stunt.

Right. Just another vital brush stroke of the artwork that made up the sensational persona of Trey. He was borderline genius. A fact he had proven time and time again through prime grades and academic awards.

God obviously had favorites.

"But you, on the other hand," Williams said as he shoved at Liam's arm like a boy might do to get a rise out of an older brother. "You are the definition of a dumb blonde. You're just lucky you had a bunch of girls lining up the block to do your homework for you or you would've been hosed."

Liam must've known better than to try to plead his case. A sideways smirk tugged at his face as he turned away from the conversation.

A stunning, well-put-together, middle-aged woman strolled by in stilettos and a pencil skirt. Her cat-like eyes found Liam over sharp-framed sunglasses. Her eyebrows rose at him, but when he winked at her, she twiddled her long fingers at him.

Trey's chin dropped to his chest as his shoulders shook with obvious mirth. All the while Williams's awestruck expression blatantly admired the woman, she too sweetly smiled at Liam, continuing her long, overly swayed strut down the hall to the awaiting auditorium.

Gross. The things I would do to expunge that blip of memory from my head…

Entirely at odds with the disgust I was currently gagging on, Williams's eyes were bright with unrestrained idolization. Liam put a brotherly hand on his shoulder. "Not too bad for a dumb blonde, huh?"

Williams finally clicked close his gaping mouth to say, "I'm pretty positive that was one of our linemen's moms, you crazy motherfuc—"

"Hey, language," Liam chastised with an easy smile. He gestured to where I was still watching, listening, forgotten about until now. "There are young, impressionable minds present."

This earned Liam a glower from an unamused sibling and earned me a collective chuckle from all three boys.

"Alright, alright. The team is planning on sitting together to cheer you guys on, and I volunteered to save us a couple of rows. Good luck. I'm proud of you two idiots," Williams said before looking at me. "See you around, little Mason."

As Noah Williams departed from us, joined by a couple of other boys I knew from the football team, Liam pranced up to the wall where his best friend stood, leaving me to follow.

"Triple Threat! We did it! Next stop, SDU!" Liam cheered, swinging an arm around Trey's neck. He pulled his head down and tousled his caramel waves.

Trey shoved Liam off and grinned. "Can't believe I agreed to share an apartment with your sorry ass. I'm already sick of you."

Liam snickered. "Bull, you love me."

Trey chuckled, but instead of responding to Liam's

taunting like I expected him to, he turned his attention to me.

The assessment started at my toes. It meandered its way up my exposed, tanned legs. It lingered just under my collar bones, caressed my lips. Then widened at the golden curls that I rarely let loose like this.

Trey's emerald gaze intensified as he locked eyes with me. "You look incredible tonight, May."

I hadn't yet put on my navy-blue cap and gown; they were folded up in my arms with my silver handbag. A mistake I was now internally ridiculing myself for. I was struggling not to wrinkle the fabric I had locked up in my hold with anxiety and regret that I left myself so exposed to him.

I was in a forget-me-not blue, spaghetti strap dress, with a body-hugging skirt that halted just above the knees. My mom had bought it for me, hoping I would wear it to a school dance. Seeing as I didn't attend any dances, I felt the dress deserved to see the light of day for at least one special occasion.

"Thank you," I uttered and smiled lamely as I checked to see Liam's reaction to his best friend's obvious flirting. But he already moved on, talking to a group of senior girls I instantly recognized as part of the girls' basketball team. Realizing I was now utterly alone to face the boy that turned me into a bumbling idiot, I very slowly turned my attention back to Trey.

I did realize one thing after our fateful conversation from earlier this morning.

I liked when Trey looked at me—saw me.

It was scary thinking I might risk him seeing too much. Absolutely terrifying thinking I might reveal too many of the collected shards that made up the shattered bits of my damaged being. But I couldn't quite care at the moment. My chaotic thoughts and heart were in an orbit that revolved around Trey's all-seeing green eyes. And the feelings they fluttered to life in my usually numb spirit.

Instead of running, instead of shying away from his exhilarating words and piercing focus, I forced myself to speak. "You don't look so bad yourself."

Trey's dimples framed the wide grin he so graciously gifted me. "You're coming tonight, right? You're not staying home to read your books?" he asked, taking a step closer and my heart threatened to quit on me.

"Well, I can't miss karaoke, now, can I?" I teased, my confidence and voice wavering.

Trey's head tilted back with a laugh. "Nope, you really can't. The world needs to be blessed with a talent like yours."

Gosh, I was doing it. I was conversing and not entirely failing. Still feeling a tad unsure of myself, I bit the inside of my cheek, suppressing a scoff at Trey's comment. I let my eyes wander to find Liam readying for a group picture with the same team of girls from before.

"I won't hold you hostage in the corner. You better get over there or you'll miss out on the picture." I waved a hand to where my brother was now drawing up a larger crowd of students for a group photo.

Trey didn't follow my gesture. He stared at me, unperturbed, before reaching out and grasping one of my stray curls. His hand briefly brushed the exposed skin of my shoulder as he wound the golden tuft around his finger.

"You're never allowed to wear your hair up ever again," he said, just for me to hear.

My brows knitted together. "What—why?"

He shook his head and gently tugged on the curl intertwined with his fingers. The action made me rid us of more of the distance. I was nearly touching him now, with only my arms full of my cap, gown and small purse keeping the space.

What was he doing?

I barely existed to him before this week, so why was

he talking to me like this, looking at me like that, touching me? This had to be a game, a joke, maybe even a dare.

Had he found out I'd never been kissed? Did he like the challenge in that?

There had to be an ulterior motive because Trey Turner couldn't look at me, a ghost, like this and mean it. With that heart-breaking thought, I was eager to run, hide, crawl behind my safe, and usually impenetrable walls.

I didn't give him the chance to explain. Pitifully, I reached up and retrieved my curl from his fingers. "I better go help set up."

His brows furrowed at the excuse, and he moved like he would object or even pull me back. But Liam was a perfectly timed interruption.

"You ready to go help with the rest of setup, May? I think they want to start soon."

I nodded, returning the much-needed distance between me and Trey. I didn't turn back when Liam asked Trey, "You coming? I bet there isn't much left to put up."

Pause.

There was a pause, and it was enough to tempt me to sneak one peek back over my shoulder to see Trey's eyes were glued to me. Again, those green eyes saw too much. I had no doubt those eyes saw the puny shreds of my soul I so cautiously stuffed behind the walls of my stoned, beaten heart.

Then why look at me like that, like there was something other than a wretched apparition of a girl festering beneath my skin?

"Nah, you guys go ahead. I'll catch up with you after the ceremony." He returned to his spot, slouched against the wall. And I walked away feeling like his stare was tunnelling through my not so stable, self-erected walls.

Liam and I helped with the rest of the setup, not that there was much else to do like he had predicted.

Afterwards, we found our positions and within the hour, the ceremony commenced.

I pulled on my blue robe, already suffering from the itchiness of the fabric on my neck and shoulders. Liam helped me pin my cap onto the top of my curls. The speeches were brief. Which I, and probably many others in the audience, thoroughly appreciated. Soon after the speeches were given, the main faculty called out the graduating students' names in alphabetical order.

I quickly found myself just behind Liam, patiently waiting for his name and then mine to be announced over the speakers. I wasn't nervous or anxious as I anticipated my name over the loudspeaker.

Once upon a time, I'd been very comfortable in front of an audience. Performing the sport I loved under the pressure of cheering fans and booing opponents. This short trek across the stage would be a cakewalk by comparison. On the other hand, I had to push away the feelings of contrition that crawled up my throat as I recalled such moments.

Liam's name ricocheted through my skull over the nearby speakers and the crowd went nuts. My brother strutted across the stage. He proudly shook hands with the representing faculty and accepted his diploma.

But he didn't stop there. No, Liam would not be so basic. Topping off the strut, he stopped at the end of the stage and threw himself into a perfectly executed back flip.

The audience erupted into shouts, screams, and whistles. The boisterous excitement perfectly timed with the announcement of "Maybelle Mason". Allowing me to cross the platform, shake hands, accept my diploma and exit the stage past a bowing Liam before any cheers or claps could be meant for me.

Started out Harbor High invisible and ended entirely non-existent.

Again, a rush of memory hit me, but this time I

couldn't ignore the twinge of disappointment in myself. I thought back to when I was the captain of the basketball team, and a friend to all. The young, innocent girl with big dreams and a lot less baggage. I was different now and for the first time in a long time, the realization made me sick to my stomach.

Liam finally found his way back and dropped into the seat next to me.

"They called you? I didn't hear!"

I shrugged, letting him have his moment. "It's hard to hear up there. I barely heard it."

Liam accepted the excuse with a nod, then leaned into me and whisper-yelled above the cheering, "I'm real proud of us, May."

I twisted to peer up at my brother's smiling, sapphire eyes.

We may have struggled to talk about the important things with one another, but in the silences like this, there was so much said. In his look was the same relief and hope I'd seen from him the day we moved to San Francisco. He wore the same look he had on our first day of school and the day we filed the restraining order against Richard.

Each moment was one we didn't think we would survive to see. Days we thought would never come to pass because we had been stuck. Locked away and hurt. Not anymore. We were safe.

I just wished I could get my mind, heart and body to understand—to believe in that fact.

Smiling, I nudged my twin. "The back flip was cool." Liam beamed, draping an arm around the back of my seat as they continued to call names.

Trey's name was next in line to be called and Liam dipped over to say, "Trey said he would do a flip too." And that he did.

But while Liam sauntered swiftly, Trey swaggered gracefully. He shook the hand of each teacher as he mouthed "thank you". He paused with Principal Nobly, a short pudgy woman in her early sixties. He accepted his diploma from her. Instead of shaking her hand like the rest of the students, he grasped it and planted a smacking kiss to the tops of her age-worn knuckles. Then he winked before throwing himself into a quick cartwheel followed with a fluid back flip that he landed with ease.

Liam shot to his feet like a proud mother as he put all his pride for his best friend into his applause. "THAT'S MY BOY!" he hollered above the crowd.

The bromance was strong with these two. If they didn't inevitably marry each other, their future partners had better be ready for a lifetime of third wheeling.

Soon after, the ceremony concluded with us graduates tossing our caps into the air, the graduates and audience filtered out of the auditorium together. Friends and family met to exchange flowers and take pictures to look back on and remember this monumental night.

Liam and I walked out, side by side, to find our mom just outside in the hall. As soon as we were within reach, mom pulled us into a crushing hug. "Ah, I am so proud of you both! My graduates!" When she pulled away, she placed both of her hands on each of our cheeks. "I am so, so proud," she repeated, this time with a lot more emotion written in her words and face.

We both leaned into our mother's touch as tears lined her eyes. "Alright," Mom said, stepping back to fan her face with a flapping hand. "Let's get some pictures of you two. Do you have any friends you want to grab a picture with?"

Liam pulled me in with one arm to pose for the picture. I shook my head in answer to her question while Liam nodded. "Yeah, just a quick one with Trey and a few of the guys from the team."

Nodding, Mom held up a digital camera, prepped and ready to snap the picture. "Okay, say cheese!"

Liam obeyed as he grasped me in tight, plastering on

a cheesy grin while I hugged him back and smiled. The camera flashed. Before we could recover our eyesight from the light, two muscled arms wrapped around our shoulders.

"It's not a family picture without me."

I knew that voice, but I still peered back over my shoulder to be met with Trey's green eyes and dazzling dimples. I immediately whipped forward before awe could overcome me.

"Here, let me get out of your picture," I blurted, trying to twist out from under Trey's arm.

He removed his arm from my shoulder only to grab me by the back of the dress and gown, tugging me backward so I pressed firmly into his side.

He roped his arm through the back of my open gown, laying his arm in the space between the navy-blue robe and my thin, pale blue dress. His hand, now hidden, gripped the fabric of my dress at the opposite hip, pulling me taut against him.

The screaming of panic and excitement that roared in my head wasn't in English or made of any actual words. In my stress, I glanced over to see if Liam or my mom had witnessed the spectacle. Liam was oblivious as he exchanged a quick "hello" with a passing football parent. But Mom's face tilted to the floor as she hid what looked to be laughter.

Trey's cheek was a light pressure against my hair while his lips radiated a heat next to my ear. "You really need to stop running away from me, May," he said.

I stared up at him, absolutely baffled.

"Okay, you three, big smiles!" Mom announced before I could respond. My face must've disobeyed the melted putty I had for a brain, as I willed a smile to form, because my mom lowered the camera.

"Lovebug, smile for real please!"

I did everything I could not to target my lovely mother with a feral death glare.

Trey's fingers that gripped the fabric of my dress now traced up my waist and slowly stopped. I held my breath. Then they pressed into a sensitive area on my rib cage that sent me wriggling like a floppy fish.

A defiant smile pulled at my lips as I threw an elbow at his stomach. He didn't flinch from the blow, but he threw his head back with laughter as I continued to squirm from his tickling.

"Maybelle, you good? Just smile so we can take the picture," Liam lectured.

I glared up at Trey, who stared forward with a boyish grin teasing his lips. Reluctantly, I faced the camera and smiled as I watched my mom smirk behind the flash.

8

Take The Leap

Maybelle

It took a while, but once Liam finished taking pictures with his never-ending line of fans, we left the building. Mom, Liam and I piled into the car and headed to our favorite hole-in-the-wall restaurant to celebrate.

This specific family-owned restaurant was a preferred spot for us. It was the first place we stopped for food as a family of three during our long move to San Francisco.

It was owned by an older couple, Mr. and Mrs. Fernandez, but their son, Xavier, managed it. The older couple doted on us twins. They spoiled Liam and me like we were their own grandchildren with homemade gifts and treats.

But their son, Xavier, only had eyes for our mom. He was constantly giving her free sides of her favorite sopapillas. He'd wink at her from across the dining room, and gift her dinner special coupons, saying things like, "Maybe I could see you again this week? You'd get free food and company."

I always thought it was his way of asking our mom out discreetly. Coming across as politeness or flirting, depending on how mom saw it. Mom usually determined his efforts as platonic gestures. Even after years of them playing this will they or won't they game, Xavier still made moves while mom blushed, but always played it off as a friendship.

I expected tonight would be no different as Xavier strolled up to our table. He wasn't dressed in his usual work uniform but in a fitted black tee, and dark jeans. His hair was combed back, showing off the peppered white through his jet-black straight hair.

"How's it going, my favorite family?" he greeted, and I watched my mother beam.

"Xavier! We're good. Just celebrating. May and I graduated high school tonight," Liam boasted, leaning back in his ornately carved wooden chair.

Xavier brought his hands to his hair as he said, "Shut up. Feels like yesterday you kids were in here scared to death about starting your first day at a new school."

Liam snickered while Mom hummed in agreement. "They're growing up so darn fast, I can't keep up."

Xavier shuffled himself so he stood just behind Mom's chair as he placed a gentle hand on her shoulder. "It's crazy how fast they grow up. My Sofia just entered her bachelor's program for engineering. I still don't understand how she went from playing with dolls to being such an incredible woman in the blink of an eye," he said, as his thumb mindlessly swiped back and forth at Mom's bare shoulder.

I had to swallow the giggle that bubbled at the sight of my mom's deep blush.

Xavier was a proud, single dad of his daughter, Sofia. His wife, Sofia's mom, had passed over ten years ago. I eavesdropped on Xavier confiding in my mom about it during a slow dinner hour. The two bonded over being two single parents who lost the first loves of their lives to devastating circumstances.

I could only imagine how it must've felt for my mom, Xavier, and even Sofia to lose the people they loved so deeply and remember it all so vividly.

"Are you working tonight, Xavier, or are you headed out?" Liam asked, oblivious to the situation unfolding between Mom and Xavier.

Mom peered back up at Xavier, a small smile on her lips while he looked down at her, grinning. "My parents need help putting up a couple of new paintings they bought at an auction. I'm clocking out early tonight to go over and help them."

"Oh, but who's going to make me my Arnold Palmer? You always mix it so perfectly." Mom said, her smile taking over her entire face and crinkling at her sea foam-colored eyes.

Xavier snickered, then leaned in close to Mom's ear. "Don't worry, love, I already made it. Anna, the new hire, should bring it out with your food any minute now."

Again, her blush was undeniably red. Even Liam slid me a conspiratorial glance, now noticing the tension-heavy moment.

"I was thinking," Xavier said. Still snuggled up close to

Mom while Liam and I watched with glee-filled expressions. "Maybe tomorrow if you're not too busy with these crazy kids, you might want to go out with me? Possibly let me buy you a drink or two?"

This was the most forward he'd ever been with her. He was always so cautious—respectful. No matter how many times she turned him down to grab coffee or a quick lunch while us kids were at school.

I knew why Mom declined his offers. Before—with Richard—she had rushed into the relationship too fast, too easily and reaped the consequences.

We all had.

So, she played this thing between her and Xavier with so much wariness there was no room for anything to happen. Years passed since the nightmare had ended. Since we escaped safely and years of learning that Xavier was a good man.

I could see the denial cooking up on my mother's lips, so I answered before she could, "She'd love to! Liam and I will both be out, so it'll be perfect."

All eyes landed on me.

Liam slanted me a crooked stare because I never had plans out, especially with him. Xavier was most likely just shocked to hear me speak at all, let alone quip in the middle of their conversation.

Mom's attention on me was soft, grateful, because we both knew what my intervention meant. That I was okay, that I found a way over the past (at least in this aspect) and was giving her the permission to do the same.

She turned to Liam then, who nodded, giving his support as well.

Mom kept a thankful smile geared towards me and Liam as she said, "Well then, I guess I'm free. What time do you want to pick me up?"

Xavier's wide brown eyes glimmered as he said, "Does seven work for you?"

Mom finally turned her smile back up at him. "Perfect, it's a date."

Xavier kissed mom's cheek, winked at me and bid our family farewell before sauntering out of the restaurant.

We laughed through the rest of dinner, reminisced on the happy moments. Mom gushed over Liam, and his performance at graduation. Liam raved about his upcoming season as a college athlete. I watched my mom, the smile on her lips as she sipped on her perfectly mixed iced tea and lemonade.

***

Liam claimed shotgun in the car while I dutifully took the back seat.

"So, I will pick you both up in the morning?" Mom clarified as we set off in the car toward our final destination of the eventful day. Liam shook his head while he sipped on a to-go cup of soda from dinner.

Between slurps he said, "No, sleep in. You need to get all the beauty sleep to be ready for your big date tomorrow," he teased. "And Trey said he'd give us a ride home."

Mom side-eyed him. "And your friend won't be drinking tonight?"

He chuffed. "He promised his mom he wouldn't drink. That's why he offered to be the DD."

Mom nodded. "You wouldn't happen to make me the same promise, would ya?"

Liam didn't hesitate. "I love you, but no."

Stephanie Mason was what most would consider as the "cool mom". She wasn't naïve to the fact that there would be graduates, including her own, drinking at this party. Regardless of certain laws and her own advisement.

But the stance she liked to take was, "You're an adult, you can make your own choices. I'm not here to control you. But don't come crying to me when the consequences of your actions bite you in the butt."

"Okay, okay," Mom sighed. "Please don't hesitate to call me if plans change, though. I don't think my little mom heart will let me sleep in, let alone sleep at all while my babies are out all night."

During their conversation, I squirmed uncomfortably in the back seat. I couldn't deny the sinking feeling I got that something bad could happen tonight.

What if I ran into Clayton alone? What if I embarrassed myself in front of Trey again. Or what if I was walking down the beach all alone when a sink hole suddenly appeared, swallowing me whole? Nobody would witness the earth eating me. I would only be reported missing. And when they couldn't find me after a few hours of searching, everyone would forget I ever existed by the end of the week—if that.

"I think I'm going to stay home with you tonight,

Mom," I confessed.

She glanced at me in the rear-view mirror. "Excuse me? No, you have to go. It's graduation night."

Liam twisted in his seat to face me. "Why don't you want to come?"

I shrugged as nonchalantly as I could, feigning indifference. "I don't know. I don't have anyone to hang out with there. I'd have a lot more fun watching a movie at home with Mom or reading a book."

Liam shook his head, dishevelling his curly blonde hair. "You aren't skipping out tonight, and you won't be alone. I'll be with you." Missing my apparent scepticism of that vow, Liam continued, "You didn't go to prom. You can't bail on this too. You'll regret it."

I stared back at him; I couldn't argue because he had a point. I didn't go to prom, and I regretted it. Granted, nobody asked me to be their date for it, but I could've gone alone. Girls did that all the time. I could've too. I needed to stop letting my anxieties control my life. And how better to do that than attend a party I'd most likely end up looking stupid and lonely at?

"Fine. Fuck it," I said blandly.

Mom looked back at me, flabbergasted, while Liam roared with laughter.

Few minutes later, we pulled up to the dark beach lit only by the full moon and a bonfire surrounded by kids.

Liam jumped from the car, still dressed in his white button up, and black slacks. He left his tie behind on the passenger seat.

"Thanks, Mom! See you tomorrow!" He shut his door and, without a second thought, followed two girls to the party around the fire, abandoning his role as my companion a lot faster than I anticipated he would. I groaned as I dropped my head against my seat.

Mom twisted to face me, giving me a sympathetic smirk. "Come on, Lovebug. Be brave, be confident and have fun. Go find Trey. I bet he'd stay with you," she said in a motherly voice but followed it with a teasing wink.

I half-heartedly rolled my eyes but lost all the amusement as I fidgeted with my hands. "Please don't make me go out there, Mom."

Her smile was gentle as she unbuckled her belt to face where I sat in the back seat of the car. "What's going on?"

I shrugged, but that didn't deter her. "No, don't shut me out. Talk to me."

Heaving a deep sigh, I made myself look my mother in her pale green eyes. "I don't know. I just can't shake the feeling that something bad might happen tonight."

Nodding, she got a faraway look in her eyes. It was a look I'd seen many times from her. It was the look she had when she donned her therapist cap.

When she was here to comfort me, be my friend and greatest ally, it was obvious. The shift from consoling mother to therapist was transparent. She knew the difference and held the boundaries between the two roles until moments like this.

I didn't mind it.

I welcomed it. If I wanted, I could tell her I needed my mom to hold me and not the facts of a therapist to teach me. But I cherished the insight her mind was constantly racing with.

"You've experienced years of instability, years of chaos, and years of fear. Feeling anxious treading outside the lines of the safe zone you created for yourself is natural and it is terrifying." She reached into the back of the car to take my hand as she continued, "If anyone understands that more, it's me. I mean, you, my daughter, had to accept a date for me tonight because I was too scared to do it."

I eyed my mother then, seeing her in a whole new light. "You were scared? I thought… I thought you kept denying Xavier because of Liam and me. I—I'm so sorry;

I didn't mean to—"

She squeezed my hand. "Do not be sorry. Of course I'm scared. Richard—he hurt me enough that I've been terrified to trust anyone ever again, and it did have to do with you and Liam, too. I'm scared to fail you both again. I'm constantly wrestling with the fear that my choices will hurt my babies. And I'll have to just sit and watch, hating myself all over again."

She paused with that, letting her thumb caress the knuckles of my hand. "We're all scared. That's what trauma does. It shackles us. Constantly reminds us of what horrid things can happen if we put ourselves out there. It scares us away from opening our hearts up or making ourselves vulnerable in any way."

A single tear slipped down her cheek as she gave me a watery smile. "It's hard and may even seem impossible, but we have to live again, despite the fear, and it all starts with a leap."

She looked out the window at the crowd of graduates making their way to the center of the party. I followed her gaze, feeling that pit in my stomach hollow out as I pictured myself amidst the group.

When Mom's focus returned to me, it took on a light, teasing air. "And since you shoved me right out of my comfort zone earlier tonight, it's only fair I do the same for you. Get out there, make some memories. Give it a couple of hours. If it isn't going well, I will happily race right back here to get you."

My expression must've betrayed the unease I was tackling in my heart because she nearly fell into the back seat. She pulled me to her in a spine-crippling hug.

"You are Maybelle Mason, and you can do hard things," she whispered in my ear, and I hugged her back.

Kissing my mother's cheek, I pulled away. "I love you. I'll see you later."

Then I was *leaping*, exiting the car and making the terribly lonely walk down to the beach.

9

Mighty Dandy Right Hooks

I still wore my forget-me-not blue dress but replaced my graduation gown with my black zip-up to keep me warm against the cool ocean breeze. I wrapped my arms around myself as I stalked the outer shell of the social circle. Not in the least bit interested in inserting myself into the thick group.

Mom said take the leap. I took the damn leap, but throwing myself in the mess of bodies surrounding the fire was just suicide.

Instead, I bypassed the party to where the ocean met land. I stopped just outside of where the waves crested the sand, sitting myself on a dry patch. I slipped off my strappy sandals and dug my toes into the damp dirt. I loved the beach. I would've survived the night if I could've stayed right there. Unbothered to watch the waves and do all the people watching I wanted.

But that was, sadly, short-lived.

"Maybelle?"

I turned from the crashing waves to see a tall shadow of a boy. Deep eyes peered down at me, and his black hair absorbed the pale light of the moon.

"That's me," I confirmed.

He took a step closer. "Daniel, Daniel Aguilar? We

had math together."

I smiled up at him, recognizing Daniel for the quiet, ruggedly handsome boy who sat in the back of class. He drove a motorbike to school and smoked behind the buildings between classes. I shared my lunch with him once when I noticed he had nothing to eat. Other than that, we didn't really talk. Our acquaintance mainly consisted of shared glances when passing in the hallway and, apparently, math class.

"Right, of course. How are you?"

He stuffed his hands into his front, dark denim, pant pockets. "I'm good. You?"

"Been mighty dandy," I blurted, immediately berating myself.

What in the world, Maybelle? Mighty dandy?

Run while you still can, Daniel.

To my surprise, instead of cringing, Daniel smiled and chuckled before asking, "Can I join you?" He gestured to the area next to me.

"Oh, sure," I invited, as I patted the sand at my side.

Look at me, taking the leap.

Daniel sat with his knees up in front of him and placed two tatted arms on top of them, with a leather jacket clutched in one hand. Daniel was obviously the type of good-looking that screamed "bad boy".

He was tall, with black curly hair that hung loosely over his eyes. He had tattoos painted up his arms and a scruffy shadow along his strong jawline. I didn't know much about him, but he'd always been kind to me.

Liam didn't like him, which I never understood why. He mentioned something about Daniel and Liam's friend, Penny, not getting along—that Daniel had picked on her or something like that. Despite what Liam said, I had a hard time believing Daniel had a talkative bone in his body, let alone a rude one.

To further prove my point, the next moments were spent mute. Because who would've guessed the two quiet kids sitting alone would lead to a painfully awkward silence?

Frantically, I searched my brain for conversation topics, desperate to fill the stillness. "So, any post-graduation plans?"

Daniel shook his head. "No, not really."

He wasn't going to make this any easier on me.

I studied him from my peripheral, trying to see if he was as uncomfortable as I was. He seemed very content to watch the waves in the hushed moment.

More power to him because I couldn't stomach it.

I rose from the sand, holding my sandals by their straps in one hand. "It was, uh—good catching up. I'm gonna go find my brother. Have a good night, Daniel."

He nodded and gave me a twitch of a smile as I left him alone in his silence. I trudged up the beach toward the fire, searching for a new hiding spot, bitter I had to give up the perfect one. This was already becoming the longest night of my whole life and it'd only been a half hour since mom dropped us off.

Maybe I could steal a camp chair from the core of the party circle. Pull it to a far-off corner and read one of the books I downloaded onto my phone—*wow*.

I was a loser.

I glanced around for a familiar face, hoping to catch sight of Liam or even Trey at this point. They were nowhere to be seen in the dense crowd. Watching the party carry on and pulse to the music that blasted from a speaker, it all slowed as the feeling of isolation weighed heavy on my heart.

Moments like these, a compilation of the day's events and feelings, forced me to acknowledge that I still wasn't fixed. That after all the time, the therapy and healing, I still wasn't the girl I used to be. Maybe I had to accept that probably would never be me again.

Unbidden, tears pricked my eyes.

Screw taking the leap. I wanted to go home, lay in

bed, and read a book.

As I drew closer to the fire, I grabbed my phone from my sweater pocket, then pulled up my mom's contact.

I wasn't made for this. I tried, that's all that mattered, right? So, what if the source of my need to be home, to be alone was my anxieties, my brokenness and past? So, what if I was probably being weak, giving over control to my insecurities and heartache?

Maybe one day I could try to push myself more, try to put myself out there to make friends again, but today was not that day.

Just before I could press call and claim my shameful defeat, my phone was swiped from my fingers. The reek of alcohol, poor hygiene and a repugnant, chemical scent assaulted my senses.

Glancing up from my empty hands, I found a drunk Clayton Thomas had pilfered my phone. A sober Clayton was already a massive jerk, a wasted Clayton was not somebody I wanted to get to know.

"Who are you calling, Mason? Mommy?" Clayton slurred, looking at my phone. His dark eyes were bleary and bloodshot as he plopped the phone into his back pocket. I tensed as the attention of a dozen sets of eyes from the surrounding crowd landed on me.

"Yes. Please give me my phone back." My voice cracked against the sudden urge to cry or scream—maybe both. I held a handout to accept the phone, wishing that a sinkhole could, in fact, appear and swallow me whole now.

He rocked forward into my space. "Spend some time with me. I'll show you a good time."

A disgusted shiver vibrated through my body and, to make matters worse, my hands started trembling.

I really hated this guy… And that smell.

I wanted more than anything to scream at him. Kick him. Tell him to just…just… A lot of gross words came to mind that would make my mom faint to hear spewing from my mouth, but I stood silent. Even as his greasy hand snaked up and latched onto my elbow, pulling at me, I remained quiet while my mind raged.

My legs disobeyed my pleas to walk away, and my arms wouldn't pull themselves free from his grip. I wanted to fight. I wanted to run, but all I could do was freeze. My body took on a mind of its own. It shifted into survival mode. Recalling another set of unwelcome, violent hands on me and the blistering words that accompanied them.

The only control I had was in the glare of unadulterated loathing I levelled at Clayton. But he was too drunk to notice.

"Come on, let me take you for a ride." His eyes roamed my body. Then he pulled at me again. Harder this time, making me drop my sandals in the sand. "We could find some place dark and quiet," he sputtered against my ear.

I tried to search for help in the eyes of the people that watched the scene unfold. Conveniently, they all found themselves busy with other conversations. I never felt so invisible, yet so exposed, in all my life.

I pivoted, trying to find my brother. Except, when I found Liam, he was too preoccupied with shoving his tongue down the throat of a redhead girl to see my silent cries for help.

I was alone, utterly alone, and I had no one to blame but myself.

Clayton's grasp on my arm turned bruising as he slithered his other hand around the back of my neck, making me look at him. "Who are you looking for, Mason? It's just you and me here."

Tears drowned my eyes and fell off my freckled cheeks as his hot breath burned in my nose. I needed to speak. I needed to push him away. I needed to do something. I was a prisoner in my mind. So busy with pounding against the walls of my skull that I barely noticed Clayton released me until a right hook sent him sprawling into the dirt.

A chorus of gasps from everyone around joined Clayton's loud moans of pain. Like an answered prayer, Trey was there, his gentle hands cradling my face. His thumbs pushed my chin up as he inspected me.

"Are you okay, May?"

I managed a slow head bob, but I felt far from okay.

His thumbs swiped at the tears on my cheeks before he spun back to Clayton, who was groaning, face first in the sand.

In two strides, Trey crouched beside Clayton, shoving him onto his back. He gripped Clayton's face, his large hand muzzling the boy's jaw. Trey reached into Clayton's pocket, retrieving my phone before sliding it into his own pant pocket. Before releasing Clayton, Trey pulled at his face, speaking too softly for me to hear. But by the look of wide-eyed terror in Clayton's eyes, I felt a twinge of satisfaction and relief.

He pushed Clayton's head back to the ground before he stood and returned to me. He didn't stop walking when he reached me. He grasped my hand and whisked me away. He led me away from the crowd, the eyes, the noise, from Clayton, all of it.

Trey led me far enough down the beach that the music and chatter faded into a dull rumble behind us.

10

Broken Drunk

I was so relieved to leave the rowdy party behind that I hardly noticed Trey was holding my hand, fingers intertwined.

Key word: Hardly—I noticed.

We didn't speak as we trudged through the damp sand up the beach. But once we made it a significant distance, Trey halted and enveloped me in his arms.

I should've been a little taken aback by his sudden show of physical affection. But I was to overcome with the solace that flooded me as his grasp tightened to think too long on it. Instead, I impulsively wrapped my arms around his middle and held him back with equal fervor.

His heavy breathing was the only sound I could hear. Besides the rolling sea. One of his hands held to the back of my head, tangling with my curls. The other hand flattened in the middle of my back, hauling me into him.

Beginning to feel lightheaded, I released a deep breath that almost transitioned into a sob, but I quickly choked it down.

"I'm so sorry, May," he whispered, and I felt my own arms reactively cinch tighter around him.

Feeling like there was a high probability that I would break down in uncontrollable tears if I tried to look up at him, I nestled my nose against his chest.

"What do you have to be sorry about?" I asked, because, really, what did he have to be sorry about? Didn't he just do all the rescuing?

Trey laid his chin down on the top of my head. "I told you to come to this stupid party. I promise, I only got here about a half-hour ago. I started looking for you as soon as I got here. Of course, Liam didn't know where you were—" He paused and heaved a deep, frustrated huff. "Last thing I wanted was for you to be alone, least of all, harassed by that scumbag Clayton."

Hoping I wasn't about to unravel into a mess of tears and snot, I lifted my head from Trey's chest and chanced a look up at him. His jaw was clenched. In fact, his entire face was taut as he stared out towards the waves that crashed only feet away.

I didn't think as I lifted a hand and placed it on his cheek. My thumb swept back and forth like it could coax those beautiful dimples back into his face.

"Trey, what is this?" I whispered.

I didn't know why I asked, especially right then. Maybe part of it was to serve as a distraction from the Clayton situation.

But another weighty part of me needed to understand.

I needed him to answer the questions, doubts, and confusion I'd been contemplating all day. Trey needed to set me straight. Tell me it was all a façade. That he was only interested in looking out for his best friend's sister, and that I needed to get my head out of the clouds.

Or say what a very minuscule but vital part of me hoped.

He dragged himself away from the black of the ocean and focused on me. "What's what?"

Both of his hands were now on my hips, just under my sweater, holding to the fabric of my dress like at graduation.

He held to me so naturally, like his hands belonged on me and nowhere else. I dropped my hand from his cheek and held on to both of his sculpted arms just above the elbow. Filled with the need to mirror his fervent grasps.

"This, Trey. Us. Before this morning, we hadn't exchanged more than a few words in passing. Now you flirt, you touch me, and save me."

My heart was going to beat straight out of my chest. My brain was an anxious, chaotic mess of alarm bells sounding, pleading with me to run, to hide, to freeze. But I didn't. Instead, I took the leap.

"If this is a game for you, I'm not playing. I'm afraid my heart is too vulnerable with you for me to ever win," I admitted and surprised myself with my own fluent candor.

A flicker of self-pride sparked to life in my heart. Which was a very rare feeling I couldn't help but grapple onto, to carry me through this moment.

Trey's stare intensified, but his face softened at my confession. His hands that clenched in my dress tightened and tugged me closer. One of his hands left my thin dress to grasp around the back of my neck with his thumb caressing my cheek. He tilted his face down to me so his forehead could rest against mine as he whispered, "This is not a game, May."

I wanted to fall apart in this wonderful fever dream. There was no way that this was reality. The way he held me. The way his emerald gaze pierced my very soul. The way his lips parted. The way he smelled of spicy cinnamon. The way his head lowered to me; his breath minty sweet. The way he was about to gift me my first kiss, on a beach in the moonlight.

This could not be real.

But it was…

Because just as his breath mingled with mine. His other large hand now pulled and splayed across the small of my back. His lips briefly lightly met with mine, Trey halted.

"What the fuck?"

Huh, weird how the voice in my head sounds just like Liam.

Trey lifted his face from mine, peering over my shoulder. He filled in the confused silence with one word, "Liam."

I understood then.

I slowly turned from him to face my twin, who had a bottle in one hand, the redhead his tongue was assaulting earlier under his other and pain in his eyes. Like a knife were in his back and the blade kept twisting the longer he took in the scene before him.

The girl under his arm looked at me. Her intelligent eyes took in the scene, obviously trying to make sense of Liam's reaction.

Panicked, I glanced at Trey. He was staring at Liam, but he was holding onto the back of my sweater, still keeping me close, keeping me safe. My panic ebbed with that discovery. I let out a quiet, relieved sigh, thankful that it was too dark for anyone to notice the blush that now invaded my cheeks.

"What the hell is going on here?" Liam bit out.

My joints threatened to lock up in response to his anger, but I internally reminded myself that this was Liam. Liam wouldn't hurt me. He may be upset, but he would never hurt me.

"Nothing's going on, Liam. We're just enjoying our night, same as you," I answered, hoping to douse his rage with cool and collected responses.

He shook his head defiantly. "No, no, no, absolutely not." He removed his arm from around the redhead. His beer sloshed as he shoved his drink into her hands before he closed the distance between me and him. "It's time for you to go home, May."

Without warning, Liam sloppily grabbed my forearm and yanked for me to follow him. I was floored. So stunned, I didn't know how to function for a split second.

Liam had left me. He abandoned me after he promised to watch out for me. Now, he was angry I was with someone who had followed through with the promise he made. And he forcibly grabbed me—he laid his hands on me when he knew… He knew.

Against every nerve in my body trying to lock up against the aggression, I tore my arm free from his hold. "Get off of me, Liam!"

My demand held no sway as Liam instantly turned back and reached for me again. But Trey was a wall separating us.

"Liam, let's calm down and talk," Trey tried to coax as he extended a hand toward him, but my brother smacked it away.

"No, there is no way I'm leaving you alone on a dark beach with my sister."

Trey stopped, taking a step back toward me. "You know she's safe with me; I would never hurt her."

"Nope, you'll hook up with any girl that shows the least bit of interest. And my sister is not about to be added to that list as a high school finale or some shit like that."

Trey scoffed. "And what are you doing right now?" he accused, eyes darting to the forgotten girl still holding Liam's beer.

Before Liam could answer, the redhead shook her head and handed him his drink back. "Find me when you're done with the family drama." Without another word, she stomped off, back toward the fire, leaving the three of us alone.

Liam raked his hands through his hair and paced. Trey rubbed an exasperated palm over his face. I folded my sweaty fingers together, nervous from the tension. I was pretty sure that this was their first fight ever. These boys never fought over trivial things like sports, girls—

but now—they fought because of me.

I really could do nothing right.

Hoping to fix what I broke, I held to that barely lit up confidence that had spurred to life in me. I stepped out from behind Trey and closer to my twin. "Liam, I understand you're just trying to look out for me, but we're good. And I can look out for myself."

His attention shot to me. "Look out for yourself? Please, that's rich."

I felt that, and it hurt. My limbs trembled against the inevitable lock up, and my sliver of confidence nearly diminished. But while I fought this inner battle for control, Liam kept talking.

"You still can't get through one hard conversation without shutting down. After all this time. How do you plan to take care of yourself?"

The last bit of control I regained over myself snapped, but I refused to be silent while he criticized me. The scalding anger broiling in my blood powered my voice.

"How dare you."

Liam's brows rose in surprise, but I continued before he could respond.

"How dare you throw that in my face! I'm sorry I haven't recovered like you have, that I haven't bounced back from what we went through the way you have. I'm trying, Liam, I'm really trying, but you left me tonight. You left me after you promised to stay by me. I was fine, no thanks to you. While you were busy sucking faces with your high school finale, I had a little moment with Clayton Thomas."

The anger on Liam's face melted. He stared after me, stricken. "Did he touch you?"

I rolled my eyes because, of course, the all-perfect Liam wouldn't hear the part where I pointed out how he screwed up. He instead focused solely on who else there was to blame. "Yes, Liam. He tried to drag me off alone, but thanks to Trey, he didn't get very far."

He retreated a step and slanted a guilt-ridden look to Trey, who still stood with me. His mouth opened and closed, suggesting he wanted to argue something, but he dropped his shoulders.

"I know you'd never hurt her. You're nothing like Clayton. I was caught off guard by this. You never told—you never said anything about—" Liam's words stumbled, proving the number of drinks he consumed.

"She's my sister," he said, as if it could explain everything. Trey nodded in understanding. I huffed with annoyance.

That brought my brother's attention back to me. "I'm sorry, May."

Silently, I watched my twin, waiting for the shutdown. For us to follow our same patterns by stopping here, but he surprised me.

My brother took a step forward, dropping his beer bottle into the sand as he exposed the palms of his hands to me. "You're not the only one who's still hurting."

The air caught in my throat as Liam heaved a long breath.

"I'm not okay. I act like I am, like I don't need the therapy Mom has tried to get me back into. I pretend I don't wake up every night, scared that I'm in that house again. I act like I'm happy when I really feel like my life is a split second away from combusting. Like I'll blink and be back in that life where I had no power—where I had to survive the pain because I wasn't strong enough to fight back. Thinking I was alone and happy to be alone if it meant I could protect you from the shit I lived through every day. Not realizing you were going through your own hell all alone."

Liam didn't cry as he took another timid step forward. I didn't cry as he put his face in his hands and growled into his palms. Trey remained silent behind me as Liam looked up at me and smiled sadly.

"I am so broken, May, and I can't stand to face it. So instead of talking, I pretend I don't see it. I don't open up to Mom when she asks if I'm okay. And I don't cry when I remember what it was like to be helpless as someone took their sick desires out on me. I smile and I move on." He scrubbed a hand over his face, tears welling up in his blue eyes, his balance barely swaying. "I'm so sorry, May. You deserve a better brother than me. You deserve...so much more—" He didn't finish as he fell to his knees in the sand, sobbing.

I couldn't move. No longer because of my instinct to freeze, but from pure helplessness. This type of vulnerability was something I never witnessed from my brother, and I was lost. Terror of saying or doing the wrong thing paralyzed me.

"*...we have to live again, despite the fear, and it all starts with a leap.*"

No more thinking, no more fear—I leapt for my brother. I fell to my knees before him and I pulled him into my arms, letting him cry in my hold. Liam's sobs shook his whole body, and I clung to him with all my strength. Silent tears fell down my face. "Shh, Liam. I have you."

Twisting to peer over my shoulder, I looked up at Trey, who watched us, his green eyes glossy.

"What can I do?" he mouthed to me.

Remembering he had my phone, I asked, "Can you call my mom?"

Without a moment's hesitation, he nodded, stepping away as he pulled my phone from his pocket.

I continued to cradle Liam in my arms, even as his sobs slowed to heavy breathing. I basked in the moment of connection, of no longer feeling lonely in my pain, as much as I hated to see my brother hurt.

"May," Liam groaned.

"Yeah?"

"Can we go home?"

I let out a breathy laugh as I tightened my hold on my brother. "Mom is on her way."

Nodding, he shifted so his forehead rested on my shoulder, still sitting knee to knee with me.

"May."

"Yeah, Liam?"

He sniffled and then groaned obnoxiously. "You really got a thing for my best bud?"

Scoffing, I shook my head. "I'm not talking about this with you."

He shuddered in my hold as he nodded. "Yeah, I don't want to think about it either, but I need you to know he's great. Despite the crap, I said, he's good. I just—I'm broken and drunk. I'm a broken drunk," he sighed, and I cinched my arms around his middle.

"Oh god," he moaned. "Don't do that. I'll puke all over you."

Cautiously, I let go of my brother, moving my hands to his shoulders. I held him out, far enough for me to see him clearly. Smiling, I brushed a few curls from his forehead. "Puke on me and I'll kill you."

Eyes closed; Liam smirked. "I'd like to see you try."

"Liam," I whispered.

He squinted one sapphire eye open at me.

"I'm broken too," I admitted, a sad smile on my lips. "Maybe, from now on, we can try to talk more? Fix the broken pieces together?"

Closing his eyes again, he rocked back and forth on his knees like he was nodding with his whole body. "I'd like that."

"Hey, May." I turned to see Trey approaching, his expression riddled with guilt. "Sorry to interrupt, but your mom is almost here."

Nodding, I faced Liam, cupping his face in my hands. "Can you go wait up at the road for Mom? I'll meet you up there."

He snorted, as he pulled my hands from his face and

wobbled to his feet. "Yeah, yeah, just wait until I'm out of hearing distance before anything happens between the two of you."

My face turned tomato red. "Liam," I tried to scold, but he waved me off as he stepped up to his best friend.

He grabbed Trey by the back of the neck, bringing the boy to him. Their foreheads rested against each other as he said in a breathy voice, "I love ya. You're my brother." His other hand lifted to grip Trey's shoulder. "But I'm gonna kick your ass when I'm not seeing three of you. She's my sister, you sick bastard, and you didn't tell me."

Chuckling, Trey mirrored Liam's hold. "I'd expect nothing less. I'm sorry, Liam."

Liam pulled away, flapping a hand at Trey as he began trudging up the sand to the road. "I'll forgive you when I'm sober," he called back.

When I turned back to Trey, he was staring at me, stone-faced. He looked uncomfortable, almost as uncomfortable as I felt. Seeing him in the intimate quiet reminded me of our almost kiss… What would that kiss have meant? I now knew if I could have any superpower, it would be mind-reading, so I wouldn't be so confused by the boy in front of me.

Did Liam's frustrated, drunken rant have merit?

Was I just another name on a list, or did I mean something?

I shook my head with a mix of exasperation and confusion. Those were questions and thoughts for another day. For right now, there was one thing I hadn't said to the brave boy before me that I still owed him: "Thank you, Trey."

The corner of his mouth twitched up.

I braved on. "Thank you for looking out for me and making tonight very…memorable."

He laughed, shaking his head. "Yeah, very memorable." His tone and eye roll insinuated it would be memorable for all the wrong reasons. I almost agreed with him, but hesitated.

Tonight really wasn't the worst I ever experienced. It was, in truth, a very exhilarating night.

Tonight, Daniel was awkward, Clayton was horrible, and the Liam situation hadn't started out too great, but Trey… Trey was perfect. He rescued me, held me, made me feel seen. I lived tonight. I made memories, good and bad ones. That alone felt almost worth it. So, I shook my head.

"Tonight was memorable…unforgettable, in the best way possible."

Eyebrows raised; Trey let out a hearty chuckle. "Well, that might make you the easiest girl ever to impress."

Gradually, his features shifted to a serious expression as he moved closer. "I meant it earlier today when I said that I plan to get to know all of you, Maybelle. You're not a high school finale." He punctuated that with an irritated scoff. "You're so much more…you're—you're…" He paused, wetting his lips with the flick of his tongue. "You're endgame for me," he said this with so much finality and admission that my breath hitched.

What did endgame mean exactly? I didn't know, but how he said it, how he looked at me, made me quake with excitement to find out.

I smiled at him. Now lacking the ability to properly communicate or function, I left him with my smile. Then trotted through the sand to meet with my brother at the edge of the road where our mom soon parked.

I walked off that beach happy with hope dancing in my heart. I felt a change in my gut, a renewed elation for reality and what life had to offer me. I didn't like to be alone. I missed being a part of a team, a part of life.

Regret coiled in my chest, but I quickly quelled it. Life had dealt me a hand that made all of that impossible, but that didn't mean I had to keep to that path now.

I was safe, free to choose what I wanted, and I wanted

to go to college, make friends, date, go to a party or two. I wanted my life back. As I sat in the backseat of my mom's car, listening to Liam's drunken snores and the dull tone of the radio, I promised myself that I would choose myself.

"Did everything go alright tonight?" Mom whispered.

I smiled, looking at my brother, whose mouth was wide open as he slept. "I took the leap, Mom," I said softly from my place in the back seat.

She grinned at me through the rear-view mirror. "I'm proud of you, Lovebug."

As the car took a sharp corner, I felt something small slip against my hand. My journal, my prized possession. I forgot I brought it with me to graduation so I could finish writing about that morning with Trey.

I didn't hesitate before flipping to the next open page in the book. I scavenged my pen from the floor and then scribed not only the events of tonight but my promises to myself.

Making them tangible and real.

11

The Accident

Trey

I lingered on the dark span of the beach, far enough away from the party but close enough to watch as Maybelle and Liam shuffled into their mom's car and drive away. Once they were gone and the red of the taillights were far down the road, I exited the beach and climbed into my Jeep, having no desire to take part in the rest of the party.

I didn't put the keys into the ignition after sliding into my seat. Instead, I leaned my head back on the headrest and dwelled in the calm silence, thinking over the overwhelming events of the night.

After graduation, my mom and I went to dinner, then ran home so she could change into her scrubs for work. I volunteered to drop her off at the hospital for her shift. It made me late for the party to give my hardworking, nurse mother a ride to her night shift, but it was much needed time with her that I was more than happy to give.

I eventually showed up at the party and instantly searched for that beautiful head of curly gold. When my search was drawing up blank, I quickly found my best friend who I then wanted to throat punch. When Liam, the said best friend, told me he didn't know where the curly-haired, shy girl ran off to, I panicked.

I loved Liam like a brother, but damn it, he was an idiot sometimes. Maybelle wasn't helpless, but she wasn't fond of traipsing around large social gatherings all alone. That fact was obvious by all the plans she refused to attend and her very lacking number of friends.

After scouring the chaotic area around the bonfire a while longer, I finally found her, in the absolute last place I'd ever want to find any soft-spoken girl—with Dirtbag Thomas. I wanted to break my knuckles across something, preferably Clayton Thomas's face, as I remembered finding her alone with him.

I knew Clayton had harassed Maybelle before tonight.

My friends and I were behind the school building one day and witnessed Clayton with his grubby hands all over an unwilling blonde. My buddies hadn't recognized the girl before she ran off, but I knew those blonde curls anywhere.

After school, I found Clayton and pinned him against a wall in the locker room. I threatened to rip him apart if he ever went near Maybelle again.

As far as I saw, until the rally Monday, Clayton had heeded my threats by keeping his distance from her. At the rally I noticed him getting handsy, but I was stuck in the dense crowd, not able to get to Maybelle when she needed. So, when Clayton made eye contact with me, I made sure he knew that I saw him and that I hadn't forgotten the promises I made in that locker room.

Honestly, I didn't feel like Maybelle needed me to save her. She stood her ground and stared Clayton down like he was no more than dirt at both the rally and tonight. I was impressed, even awestruck, by her defiance.

She was stupid pretty.

When she strolled up to the ceremony building in that blue dress and those curls bouncing around her shoulders down to the shelf of that perfect ass… I had to lean against the wall for stability as I crossed my legs to hide the uncontrollable reaction happening in my pants.

I almost didn't speak as she and Liam passed me so I could stare without consequence. But I would've felt like a jerk if I didn't interfere on Maybelle's behalf during the awkward encounter with Williams.

I shifted in my seat as I remembered the rest of the night, specifically when I had Maybelle in my arms. The way her gorgeous eyes looked up at me and how she asked if this was a game. Admitting that, like me, her whole heart was on the line.

I tensed, thinking back to our almost kiss. The kiss I'd been fantasizing about for almost three years. Recalling the feel of her hauled up against me. Literally a breath away from finally pressing into her when the reminder of Liam's face, full of anger and betrayal, interrupted.

That sucked.

I was such a tool, letting my desperation and attraction for Maybelle fog my common sense. I should've talked to Liam about my feelings a long time ago. Liam was cool. He would've been completely fine with me liking his sister.

Tonight, Liam was caught by surprise, a little drunk, and finally had his arm around Penny Howell. The pretty redhead cheerleader he'd had his eyes set on all senior year. Liam and Penny had been best friends since Liam's first day at Harbor High. He was obsessed with her from the start, but she always kept him at arm's length when it came to being anything more than friends. She must've finally given into his begging tonight but finding me with his sister interrupted whatever they had planned.

God, I felt like an idiot.

I owed my brother an apology. And—I needed to talk to him about what his speech had been about. Liam never talked about what their lives had been like before their family moved here three years ago… But I couldn't get his voice out of my head.

"*I don't cry when I remember what it was like to be powerless. I smile and I move on...*"

I would need to call him tomorrow, after a day of sleeping off the alcohol and dramatic events of the night.

Checking the time on my phone, I saw how late it was, but it was only a few hours from when mom would need me to come pick her up. I wanted to sleep in my own bed, but I was too tired to drive home alone, and I was closer to the hospital from here, so I reclined my chair back and closed my eyes.

***

The chaotic ringing of my phone had me sitting up in my Jeep with a jerk. I glanced down at my phone to see my mom was calling. Instantly, I was filled with anxiety that I was late to pick her up, but the sun was barely turning the sky purple with morning and my clock proved that I still had a couple hours before her shift was done.

I answered the call curiously, "Hey Mom, what's up?"

There was hesitation on the other line. Thinking she couldn't hear me because of poor reception, I repeated, "Hey, Mom. Can you hear me alright?"

This time I was answered with a choked sob and sniffling.

"Mom, what's wrong?" I asked, panic gripping my gut as I waited. Hearing my mom cry always brought on a sense of urgency.

There was a deep breath fuzzing through the phone speaker before she finally said, "I'm alright, Hun. Where are you?"

Despite her answer, I could tell something was wrong, but I answered, "At the beach still. I fell asleep in my car."

She sniffed some more. "Okay, you didn't drink

during the party last night, did you?"

I shook my head without thinking, then responded aloud, "No, I didn't drink, I was just tired." I hesitated a beat before asking again, "What's wrong? What happened?"

Mom let out a relieved sigh, and her next words shattered my whole world.

"Your friend, Liam Mason and his family are here… There was an accident."

12

Dear Future Husband

Trey

I used to love hospitals.

Visiting my mom, the clean smell, the nurses bribing me with candy, but now it was a hellhole drenched in my heartache. The walls were colorless. It was eerily cold, and death polluted the air, making me sick.

Three weeks ago, I was at the beach when my mom called me to break the news that a drunk driver hit the Mason family, and they were brought to the hospital she worked the night shift at.

I didn't say goodbye to her before I hung up and raced to the hospital. When I entered the main doors, Mom was there, her eyes were rimmed with held back tears. I stumbled into her embrace as she led me away from prying eyes, informing me that Stephanie Mason had died on impact, and Liam…

Liam died on the operation table in the middle of emergency surgery only minutes before I arrived.

It was all a blur after that. I remembered collapsing to my knees, letting grief overtake me as my mom grappled me to her in a private hallway. I didn't cry, I couldn't, as my limbs shook, and stomach roiled. I could only free fall into an abyss of depressing mind numb.

Liam was gone. My best friend, my captain, my soon-to-be roommate, my brother was just…*gone.*

Overcome with emotion, I didn't listen or understand the next moments after I could stand from her grasp. Mom led me into a room where a girl slept hooked to tubes, wires, and machines.

Her beautiful, peaceful face was marred with cuts, blackening bruises and a line of stitches peeking past her hairline that swelled. Her damaged face was framed with those blonde curls coiling around her.

Mom and the other nurses that took care of the sleeping girl told me she suffered the least number of injuries, but the head trauma she received kept her asleep. The doctors believed she would wake up in the next day or two, but she didn't. She slept for a week, then she slept through the funeral, and she continued to sleep, showing no signs of waking up anytime soon.

Now, I spent all my spare time by her side, feeling hopeless, broken, but I refused to leave her all alone. I planned to spend every day of my summer there in the dingy hospital room until I had to move down to the dorms at college.

A stranger already replaced my best friend's place as my dormmate.

In the last few weeks, I started a routine: wake up whenever, eat at some point, stay with the sleeping girl, go home, maybe eat, and go to bed. Repeat.

When I came to visit her, I didn't sit in the chair that was always pulled up to the side of her bed. I couldn't bear to look at her tangled in tubes with her face still healing. So, I dragged the chair to the opposite side of the room and looked out the little square window that peered over the city and ocean.

I started that day the same way as I watched the world continue on through the small window while what felt like my world hibernated, stuck in a deep sleep I dreaded would last a lifetime.

But something was different about today. Maybe it was because I could see the swelling in her face had gone down significantly. The cuts were less harsh and the weight of loneliness a little too heavy.

Whatever it was, it had me sliding my chair back to Maybelle's side to watch her sleep, desperately hoping for those lashes to flutter, that perfect nose to scrunch, and those blue-green eyes that never could decide which color to be, to open and stare out at me. I continued to watch when the unbearable sob of defeat choked me.

If I could, I would take it back.

The flirting, the touching. I would never have encouraged Maybelle to go to that stupid party, because if she hadn't come, she might still be awake, and Liam would still be alive.

Liam would be packing and getting ready for college with me. Maybelle would be back to ignoring me, an alternative I would gladly replace with the current reality we'd been dealt. I wouldn't have been so dumb if I could do it over. I would've talked to Liam before wandering off with his sister. I would've been smarter, better.

For the first time since the accident, the back of my eyes ached, making my vision blur with tears. I scrubbed at my face with the back of my hand before any droplets could escape down my cheeks.

I looked back to Maybelle, acknowledging that unlike most patients, she wasn't surrounded with balloons, or get-well cards. She didn't have any family other than her mom and brother. So besides me, there was no one waiting for her to wake up.

Maybelle Mason was alone, and it was all my fault.

There was one item in her room that wasn't hospital equipment. It was that small, black, leather-bound journal I'd seen on her nightstand.

Now it rested on the side table next to her hospital bed. I noticed the book before but was too numb to care about investigating until now.

Leaning forward, I plucked the book up. I opened to page one.

Hi,

My name is Maybelle Mason. My mom named me Maybelle. She said it was a happy name that meant "lovable", so she calls me "Lovebug". Little bit of background knowledge is I am a twin, I am fourteen years old, my birthday is November 3rd. I am in middle school; I am a basketball player. My hobbies are sports, reading, and I love school.

I love to smile; it is my favorite thing to do because it helps me stay positive in the lowest times. My favorite color is green, and my greatest wish is for you to love me as much as I love you.

Love,
Maybelle Mason

I sat back in my chair, trying to understand the adorable letter I read. I knew this was a journal which made me respectfully close it. It was a breech in privacy for me to go reading something like this. I knew it when I found it in her room, and I knew it now. But I couldn't ignore the curiosity—a feeling other than pain and guilt that fluttered to life under my skin.

I wanted to know about who she spoke to when she wrote, "*My greatest wish is for you to love me as much as I love you*".

I gazed up at Maybelle.

God, I wanted to know her, all of her.

I mean… I promised her I would do just that, hadn't I? Yeah, this felt a bit like cheating, taking the easy road, but, in reality, nothing about this situation was easy.

What if she never woke up?

What if this was my only chance to get to know her?

I peered back down at the book, only hesitating a

moment before I opened to page two.

Dear Future Husband,
The reason I married you is because you respect me and encourage me to be the best me. You are my best friend. This journal is for you to know me, understand me more than anyone else ever could...

I paused and raked a hand through my hair.
Holy shit.
This was a book dedicated to the man she would one day marry. What kind of fourteen-year-old child thinks about that, talks like that? I really needed to put the book down now. It became so much more intimate, private, knowing that the journal was written for...for.... I stopped, a smile pulling at my lips as I stared at the book.
This journal was meant for me.
Leaning back in my seat, I tilted a bewildered laugh to the ceiling. I had officially lost it. What kind of bastard thinks something like that? Unconsciously, my fingers rubbed over the worn paper of the book filled with all the knowledge I was craving to ingest.
I didn't know Maybelle.
I wanted to know her but—peering down at the book again, I gnawed on the inside of my cheek. Perhaps it was the lack of sleep, the lack of hope in my life that slowly had me flipping to the next page, but I slanted Maybelle one last apologetic look, and I read on.

13

You Are Not Alone

Maybelle

Darkness. Tumbling, never-ending darkness.

A rhythmic pounding—each beat painful.

Everywhere ached, felt wrong.

The dark smelled clean, chemically sterile.

The air was chilled. There were sounds. Echoes, tittering, chattering, voices.

A dull glow punctured the blackness. There was a light past the void. Was there a way out? Was there a way to escape the engulfing emptiness?

No feelings besides the ache, the pounding, my person or being non-existent in the space. But that glow, that light, was starting to shove its way through, brighter and more piercing. It started to burn; it was too much. There was no way to call out. I was stuck, stuck, stuck in bright, helpless pain.

"Oh. My. God."

Thuds, thumps heavy and quick approached. A shadow above me dimmed the all-consuming light.

"Oh my God, turn those lights off and get me Chelsea Turner!"

The bright world stung—until it didn't.

Shapes, images, pictures focused and took root.

"Wakey, wakey, baby," the shadow spoke in a lilting

voice. Suddenly there was a warmth outside the fog, a solid embrace around a limb… My limb.

"My name is Betsy, baby. I'm gonna take care of you."

I willed my world to become clearer, fighting against the pain and forcing the world to intensify and centralize around me.

A beautiful round woman with plump cheeks, dark skin, and big eyes looked down at me. The woman, Betsy, pursed her mauve-colored lips as she held to that limb— my wrist—placing two fingers on the inside. "Good morning, Maybelle, or should I say good middle of the night."

A sharp noise had me jumping with a jerk, reminding me that every minuscule part of my being ached. Another woman strode up to me with tears streaming down her face.

She dropped into a chair next to my other side, opposite of Betsy. Both women were pretty, but neither looked like the other. The only similarities they had were in the clothes they wore. Both women wore the same color of seemingly comfortable light blue shirts and pants with a pair of sneakers.

"Maybelle, my name is Chelsea Turner. I'm Trey's mom." The woman, Chelsea, waited like I was supposed to know what any of that meant.

I squirmed with confusion. I was so lost, unsure of who these women were, who Trey was or better yet— what was a Maybelle?

Chelsea's misty eyes turned to Betsy with concern. "Has she spoken yet, Bets?"

Betsy shook her head and pursed her lips again. "I don't think the poor baby has gotten a chance to collect herself."

Chelsea reached for me, but I pulled away.

What was going on? Who were they? Where was I?

Oh god, my head hurt. I grimaced and put a hand to my head. I was aware of everything: my body, my limbs.

I could feel it all and it all throbbed with a dull hurt.

Chelsea adjusted on the chair next to me, briefly dragging my attention away from the pain.

"Sweetheart, can you tell me your name?"

I thought for a moment, my mind putty with no solid foundation for me to stand on. I tried to reply, but my dry mouth felt full of cotton.

Name. Name. Name. Did I have one?

Like an empty book of stale, vacant pages, my mind contained zilch on names. My tongue flicked out, licking my lips, but it all was all the consistency of sandpaper. I almost gave up, but the curiosity and the frustration to hear myself make sound won over.

"No." The sound was lower than I expected, but raspy and airy.

Chelsea's face fell. Betsy clicked her tongue like that answer was what she'd been waiting to hear before she left the room.

I was in a room. A dimly lit room that had little to it but blank walls, whirring machines, and a square, glass opening that showed off darkness and a sea of bright stars.

Chelsea's heaving sigh brought my focus back to the woman. "Your name is Maybelle," she informed as she gestured to me. "Do you remember your mom and brother? Liam and Stephanie?"

I slowly shook my head in response. I opened my mouth to try to ask questions, but the door to the room flung open and a man with dark hair, pale skin and peppered facial hair strode in with Betsy in tow.

"Hello, Maybelle," the tall man greeted as he approached my bedside. He was dressed head-to-toe but in navy-blue clothes similar to what Betsy and Chelsea wore, except he had donned a white coat that cloaked his shoulders and ran down to his mid-thigh.

"It is so good to see you awake. You had a very long nap. My name is Doctor Brown," he said as he put a hand to his chest.

I didn't reply or move, only evaluated. Doctor Brown—was such an interestingly accurate name for a man with rich brunette hair, dark scruff, and hooded chocolate eyes.

"I know you must be confused, maybe even frustrated. But we are going to help you understand everything and get you feeling better," he said softly, as if he were calming an animal that needed taming. He apparently did know a thing or two because I was seriously confused and extremely frustrated with the confusion.

My mind was reeling, racing, fleeing, returning, screaming for answers. I could recall nothing specific to my being, my identity, and it was terrifying—no, it was infuriating.

Doctor Brown's gloved hands lifted my arm and held two fingers to my wrist, same as Betsy did when I had first woken up. His grasp encapsulated more of my wrist than Betsy's touch had, but his was a lot more whispered on my skin.

"Nurse Turner," Doctor Brown addressed without turning to Chelsea, who sat up straight in response. "I need you to call your son off his hunt. I do believe he is going to have a tangle with security out there if he is not controlled."

Her eyes widened and, without another word, she was up and out the door.

Doctor Brown let out a huff of amusement before tilting my face up to look at him. He inspected my eyes by shining an unpleasant light into them that brought the ache in my head back with a vengeance.

"I hear you aren't remembering a whole lot, Miss Belle," he stated.

I squinted, studying the crinkled lines of the doctor's face, the firm set of his jaw and the thick, dark goatee laced with aged white.

Taking my silence as answer, he nodded and continued, "But you are responding and seem to be functioning very well. It would be hard to believe you just slept through an entire year."

A year? That's a long time.

Doctor Brown took a seat in the vacant chair that Chelsea had occupied. Betsy remained in the corner of the room, quietly watching, offering small reassuring smiles each time my gaze roamed to her.

"Do you remember your family?" he asked.

I shook my head, getting a slight twinge of knowing that fact should hurt…but nothing of merit came.

"Do you remember where you live?"

I shook my head.

"Do you know what two plus two is?" He quirked a bushy brow. I wanted to scoff, but I swallowed hard.

"Four," I rasped.

He simply nodded. "Do you remember the night you fell asleep?" He leaned forward now, observing me.

I paused. The only thing I could recall past the blankness of my mind was bright red and blue flashing, holding hands, blood—I stopped and shook my head aggressively.

Doctor Brown's head bobbed slowly. "That's not entirely unfortunate," he said, giving me a sad smile. He then rose from his chair. "I need to speak to a very upset and overprotective young man. I will be back shortly. In the meantime, Betsy will take care of you."

He swiftly left the room while Betsy replaced him in the seat next to me.

"You may have been through hell and back, baby, but you are lucky."

I slanted the lovely woman a curious look, silently asking what about any of this was lucky. Betsy gave me a full smirk, answering my silent inquiries.

"Because you got that boy out there who would do just about anything for you, meaning you're not alone."

14

My Mayhem

Trey

Two security guards stood between me and my girl. One short, and pudgy while the other was tall and skinny… How much more cliché could you get?

"I don't understand why you all are being so difficult! I have sat in that room almost every day for the last year. I should be with her when she wakes up," I announced, frustrated, at the floor of hospital staff, security guards and gathering onlookers who came to gape at the drama unfolding.

When I got the call from my mom saying Maybelle was waking up at around three in the morning, I leapt from my bed and rushed out the door to my Jeep. I managed to throw a black tee on but was out front, crawling into my car in only my boxers with my gym shorts in hand. It wasn't until I was stopped at a red light that I finally slipped the shorts on over my hips.

My Maybelle Mason was waking up.

The short, fatty officer approached me. I was itching to wipe the floor with the man, but before anything could really happen, my mom was a force between us both.

Chelsea Turner glared daggers at me, but I couldn't care. I had to get to my girl.

"Honey, I need you to calm down and take a seat,"

Mom said sternly.

"If she's awake, I need to be in there."

Mom nodded. "I called you because I know how much you care about her, but I also thought you could hold on to a thread of your common sense through this process. There are some things you need to know before you can see her. Doctor Brown is with her right now. He will be out here in a few minutes to update us on everything," she explained.

I sighed and dropped myself into a waiting chair along the wall, only a few feet from where Maybelle's room was.

The two security guards finally stalked away when they decided I was no longer a "threat" …assholes.

Mom joined me in the seat next to mine.

"Did you talk to her?" I asked, uncertainty marring my tone. I was nervous, scared for why they wouldn't let me just see her. Mom slowly nodded, staring blankly at the floor. I knew what I wanted, or needed, to ask, but I dreaded what the answer could be.

"Was—was she—could she…?"

Fortunately for me, my mom quickly caught on to what I was trying to choke out.

"She is fully aware and functioning really well."

I let out a deep breath that I'd been holding onto, relief flooding the pressure away in my chest. Mom put a comforting hand on my back. "Didn't you need to get back to school today for football training? You have a long drive ahead of you."

I shook my head. "I talked to Coach. He was understanding of the situation. He said I could have the rest of the week off."

Mom smiled. "Oh good, good."

Thankfully, we didn't have to wait too much longer until Doctor Nathaniel Brown was exiting Maybelle's room, approaching my mom and me.

"Heard you were causing quite a scene out here, Mr.

Turner."

I ignored the comment. "Can I see her now?"

He chuckled and sat in another chair next to me along the wall. "As soon as I am done explaining a few things, you are welcome to see her."

My leg started to bounce. "Alright, let's hear it then."

He leaned in toward me with his elbows propped on his knees. "Miss Belle seems to be doing very well. She is a little confused and annoyed with the brain fog, but she is listening and communicating adeptly."

"So, what *is* wrong with her?" I pushed. Not that anything could be wrong with my Maybelle. With how Doctor Brown was leading this discussion with vague good news and how my mom continued to stare at the floor, I could tell there was something wrong.

He adjusted before he said, "She is suffering from a type of Dissociative Amnesia. She is struggling to remember anything to do with her identity, her family and what happened the night of the accident."

That pressure in my chest was tight again, almost painful. "Is it permanent?" I dared to ask.

Doctor Brown shrugged. "Not usually, but it's too early to tell." He paused, peering over my shoulder at Maybelle's door, then returned to me. "When you walk in there, Mr. Turner, she will not know who you are."

My head bobbed up and down as I focused on a bulletin board across the hall.

Maybelle was awake. She didn't know who I was, but she was awake. In my shorts pocket, I could feel the imprint of a small journal that had been my constant companion, never leaving my person over the last year.

It would all be okay. It had to be okay.

"Okay, Doc. That all? I'd really like to see my girl now."

Doctor Brown snorted loudly, shaking his head. "Follow me, Romeo."

15

Am I Hot?

Maybelle

Betsy continued to fuss over me, checking "vital signs" and medical stuff like that I didn't understand. Doctor Brown had left the room about ten minutes ago to talk to a boy... What boy? Maybe the brother they mentioned?

I examined Nurse Betsy as she practically trotted around the room with too much excitement to each step.

"Wh-why are you so happy?" I croaked out.

Betsy pivoted to me; jaw dropped in dramatic surprise. "Well, look at you," she acknowledged. "I'm happy because that sweet boy, who's being barred out there, finally gets to see you after waiting by your side for almost a year."

I studied the woman while she tucked the blanket in at my feet. "Is he, my brother?"

She stopped her grinning. "No, baby, he's not your brother, but from what I've heard, Liam would've been by your side as well if he could have."

That wasn't cryptic at all.

I opened my mouth to snark out as much at the sweet-talking nurse, but the door opened, cutting me off. Once again, Doctor Brown walked through the doorway. "Hello again, Miss Belle. I'd like to introduce you to someone."

I gazed back, expressionless, showing no signs that I was the least bit interested, but he moved from the door, allowing me a full view of the young man that stood behind him.

The first thing about him that caught my attention was the brown, wavy hair containing hints of gold. Like chocolate ice cream with hot caramel sauce. My gaze melted down his face to the shadow of scruff along his jaw and upper lip, then back up to his dark, emerald eyes staring after me in wide anticipation.

He was waiting for my reaction. I instantly registered that everyone in the small room was waiting for my reaction. I felt like a zoo animal as they gawked at me in silence. Maybe sleep wasn't all that bad. The darkness of my mind didn't stare back at me all creepily.

Unable to handle the quiet and watchful eyes any longer, I slanted a pleading look to Betsy.

Betsy, in her corner, let out a hearty chuckle. "How about we exit for a few minutes and let these two get reacquainted?"

I scowled. That wasn't what I wanted at all, and the woman knew it as she shot me a wink before pivoting for the exit. She gestured for Doctor Brown and Chelsea to follow her out. Doctor Brown gave me a curt nod and smile before exiting while Chelsea grabbed the still nameless young man's hand. He returned the gesture, then she, too, walked out the door.

Whelp, it was quiet again.

This entire experience so far had all been overly dramatic and now exceptionally awkward. I felt exposed under this stranger's silent gaze, especially since I couldn't recall what I looked like. This boy was— pretty—very pretty, but for all I knew, I could have a snaggletooth, lop-sided face, and overgrown eyebrows that had absolutely no relation to one another.

I tried not to let the insecurity tighten with anxiety in

my stomach. If he was going to stare, then so would I. Tilting my chin down, eyebrows slightly raised, I peered at him through my lowered lashes.

I better be hot. This look could be intimidating, seductive even, if I were good looking, but if I was ugly—this probably looked horrifying.

He finally returned my stare with a challenging, quizzical look. "What?"

"He speaks," I mused roughly; my voice still terribly scratchy.

A low chuckle escaped him. "I'm sorry, it's just… It's been a long time waiting for you to wake up—I've missed you." His face softened with the admission.

"That's nice." I forced a smile. "And your name is?"

He joggled his head, shaking away the dazed fog from his eyes. "Right, sorry. It's Trey."

I gave him a pleased nod. "So…are we?" I wiggled a finger between the two of us. Trey picked up what I was laying down and gifted me another husky chuckle that warmed my achy limbs.

He hesitated for only a moment before he said, "No, I was best friends with your brother, Liam. We all went to school together."

"Interesting."

Again, lots of missing pieces to the information I was being given. Specifically, with the *was best friends*. I hummed with understanding, then gestured to the chair next to my bed.

"You can sit. I'm not a biter, just a napper."

A smile tugged at his mouth.

"I'm going to need you to be honest with me," I started, watching as Trey nodded and dropped into the seat next to me. "People have been beating around the bush all morning regarding my family and the killer knock to the head that put me to sleep. So, please, just be real with me. My brother—Liam, was it? He's dead, right? I'm guessing my mom is too?"

His face fell cold into a tight, stony expression. A muscle in his jaw jumped as he again nodded his response. I leaned my head into the pillow at my back, sighing with comprehension.

There was a tragedy. I waited for an ounce of pain, or sense of loss to hit me, but it never came. I guess it's hard to ache for someone you lost when you can't remember ever having them.

Trey watched me with that same pain-filled, stoic expression.

I smiled at him. "Thanks for being honest."

He gave me a sad up-tilt of his mouth. "Of course. Always."

"Okay, I need you to be honest with me again and I mean brutally honest, no lying," I said, intentionally cutting through the solemn tension that coated the air around us.

He adjusted in the seat, making me notice a black notebook he held tightly between his firm hands.

"Am I hot? Or should I continue to avoid the mirrors?"

This obviously caught him off guard. Trey's eyes widened, and then his head dropped between his shoulders as he shook with laughter. "Wow, you're not the Maybelle I knew."

"Is that a good thing or a bad thing?" I pushed.

He leaned in close, showing off a straight, white, teasing grin. "I haven't decided yet."

I shrugged coolly. "Well, am I hot or not? I'm on the edge of my seat here."

I wiggled in the bed, causing some of my blonde curls to fall forward. Trey's eyes darted to the stray locks that now draped over my chest, forcing me to freeze. He leaned in closer, slightly pressed into my bed as he took one of my curls and wound it around his finger.

I watched his hand lift and tangle with the tuft of hair, all while holding my breath and surveying the dark, heated, green depths of his eyes.

I didn't need him to answer me with words. I knew by the intensity in his eyes and the slight tremble of the curl in his hand.

I beamed at him before I whispered, "I'm drop-dead gorgeous, huh?"

16

Mayhem 2.0

She's awake, she's awake, she's awake.

Those words were on a loop in my mind from when I got that call from my mom to when I sat and talked to Doctor Brown.

She doesn't remember. She doesn't remember. She doesn't remember, had then droned on in my head until I stood in front of her.

I missed her, and that feeling almost had me falling to my knees in front of her when I entered that room. I wanted nothing more than for Maybelle to wake up so I could officially meet the girl from my journal.

In earlier years, I'd been interested—lured in by the beauty and sweetness of the girl that always remained out of reach. However, after that preview of her true nature in the last week before the accident and reading the precious journal that hadn't left my side once in the last year…

I was fucking infatuated.

I walked into that room with only one fear. That my Maybelle would be gone. I was scared the girl I'd gotten to know so intimately would be so far hidden behind her walls that there would be nothing I could do to get her back.

I clung to the hope that when she woke up, I would be able to persuade her out of hiding like I had before. Finally convince her to stay, but with no memories—I dreaded that part of her was lost.

I was thankfully mistaken.

She was just as beautiful as I remembered, and those damned blue-green eyes ripped the oxygen clean from my lungs, making it almost impossible to communicate. The girl in that hospital bed was the words in my journal personified.

I thought I couldn't get enough of her before, but now… I was in trouble.

Soon after Maybelle and I were done getting reacquainted, Mom came back into the room. She and I invited Maybelle to come home with us, stay with us for the night or however long she would like.

She agreed with a shrug.

While Dr. Brown wrapped up his final inspections, Mom ran to grab Maybelle some clothes from the house. As soon as she was back, she helped dress Maybelle in a pair of black sweats and one of her old blue tee shirts.

Per requirement of the hospital and the lack of muscle to keep her upright without assistance, we rolled Maybelle in a wheelchair out into the now sunbathed hospital parking lot.

For the next couple of weeks, Maybelle would require our help in moving around as she rebuilt the muscle and mobility in her limbs. A physical therapist would be visiting my mother's home four times a week for the following few weeks to exercise and strengthen Maybelle to get her back on her feet.

Once we wheeled her out to Mom's little Corolla, I bent down, wrapped an arm around Maybelle's waist, lifted and worked to lower her into the passenger seat. I noticed the pink blush of her cheeks, my skin mirroring hers and heating up the back of my neck.

Before she could fully be seated in the car, Maybelle tripped over her useless feet, but it only took me a handful of the waistband of her sweats at the hip to pull her flush against me and have her stabilized again.

Her hand on my shoulder tightened in reply.

I slid her a sidelong glance, expecting to see that sassy smirk I met in the hospital room, but her face was drawn, eyelids wavering. She was already exhausted.

My chest stiffened with apprehension. Once she was folded into her seat, Maybelle tried reaching over her shoulder for the seat belt, but I already had it, pulling and reaching over her to click it into place.

I crouched outside her door looking at both my mom, who now occupied the driver's seat, and Maybelle, who looked on the edge of falling back into a never-ending sleep.

"Are you alright, May? Are you comfortable?" I asked.

She eased her head up, and down, the slow movements betraying that she may be in pain. I looked at my mom, ready to argue that she should go back inside the hospital, but my mom knew me too well.

She wore a comforting smile and mouthed, "Breathe. Everything is alright."

I heaved a deep, slightly relieving breath. "Drive safe. I'll pick us up some breakfast and meet you both at home."

Mom nodded, still smiling, but Maybelle's head was already propped back against her headrest, her eyes screwed shut. I stood up and shut the door, concentrating on remembering how to breathe.

I arrived with the assortment of pastries from a bakery down the road for the three of us, but to my dismay, Maybelle was already sound asleep on the deep cushions of the living room couch.

Mom informed me that Maybelle had slept the entire car ride, woke up to walk with her up into the house until the sofa and was once again out like a light as soon as her head rested on the cushions.

I tried to ignore my screaming stress as Mom, and I ate a few of the baked goods I had picked up. Mom soon left me. She had worked that night and had to get at least some sleep in before she needed to get ready and head out for her next shift.

After she went to bed, I approached the sofa where Maybelle slept like the dead, not like she hadn't just slept for a whole goddamned year. I was so tempted to shake her awake, but I stopped myself. Instead, I sat in the armchair right next to her.

I reclined the chair back and was lulled to sleep, watching a few of her curls shudder from the small, even puffs of her breathing.

***

I started with a jolt, my eyes first darting to the girl who continued to sleep soundlessly on the couch, to the night dark windows, and finally my mother, who was coaxing me awake.

"Hey honey, you can keep sleeping. I just wanted to let you know I'm headed to work." She kissed my forehead. "Call me if you or Maybelle need anything."

Still groggy with sleep, I nodded, bleary-eyed. Then she was out the door. I sat up in the armchair, stretching my cramped body.

Peering over at the still slumbering girl, who looked like a dream as she slept on my couch. She was in my home and not in a hospital bed surrounded by blank walls and machines. I sighed a relieved breath.

The comfort of her in my world was fleeting because she was still sleeping, and watching her eyes closed and soft breaths continue to ruffle her curls made me nauseous. I felt trapped back in those first weeks of waiting by her side, face mangled, tubes and wires everywhere. My body viciously shuddered, driving me upward and to her side. I knelt beside the sofa Maybelle was curled atop of, on her side with her hands cuddled up under her chin.

I wasn't blind with stress enough to miss that she looked a lot more alive, sleeping like this than she ever had in the last year—which filled me with an ounce of relief—but it was not enough to stop me from placing a hand to her shoulder. I started by nudging her softly, but when she didn't stir, I pressed against her and rocked her shoulder back and forth.

"Maybelle?"

Her face tightened, scrunched, and her whole body went taut in reply. I paused my efforts and removed my hand from her.

A breathy "no" left her lips hitched with a whimper.

I lifted my other hand to the top of her head, stroking down her frizzy curls from her face. "You're okay, May, I'm here." We were face to face now, with me brushing her hair with my fingertips.

Another sad noise escaped her.

"Maybelle," I called with a bit more volume and force. Suddenly, her eyes fluttered open.

Blue-green perfection. I was so captured by those beautiful eyes that I failed to see her body move—until her knuckles were crunching up and into my nose.

"Oh, damn," I cursed, leaping away from the golden-haired ninja and sprawling across the floor onto my back. I held my face, vision blurry with trapped tears. In my watery sight, I could tell Maybelle was now sitting up, her shoulders encasing her neck as she cringed.

At least… I thought she was cringing until the woman started giggling. I peered up at her from the floor, hand still over my nose. I prayed it bled, so I didn't have to feel like too much of a wuss as a tear or two escaped to the tops of my cheeks.

"Sorry, is your nose alright?" she asked, her question

sandwiched between soft chuckles she was obviously trying and failing to hide.

I couldn't help but smile. "What's so funny?"

She shrugged, her full lips disappearing as she pinched them together. I dropped my inflamed nose, sat up from the floor and blinked away my watery vision.

"Oh, Mayhem," I hummed.

Her giggles stopped. An eyebrow quirked in query. "Mayhem?"

I shook my head, more laughter spilling from me in remembrance of one of my favourite moments. My mirth died off abruptly as I realized, only I could remember that moment.

That week no longer existed for her.

"Déjà vu," was my blunt response.

I stood from the floor and headed to the kitchen, ignoring her questioning looks. I woke her only to make sure she was okay, but now that she was awake, I didn't want her to fall back asleep just yet.

"Are you hungry?" I asked.

"Starving."

I opened the fridge door and called back to her, "There's cold pizza."

"Pepperoni?"

"Yes, ma'am."

"Perfect."

17

I Am Not Obsessed with You

Maybelle

Trey plated us both cold, pepperoni pizza slices, then joined me on the couch. I accepted my plate from him, graciously, and stuffed the first bite into my mouth.

I side-glanced the boy who sat with me on the couch, taking his own bite of pizza.

I had met him only just this morning. Yeah, sure, he supposedly knew me and my family—but as far as memory served, he was a complete stranger.

"You know what's weird?" I asked as I chewed.

"Hm?" he grunted with his mouth full, being a little more courteous than me by keeping his mouth closed.

I stared after him for a moment. As if sensing my scrutiny, he swallowed and paused before taking his next bite. His vibrant green eyes homed in on me. I nearly choked on my pizza and the awe coiling up in the back of my throat.

"I technically met you this morning. Now I'm eating your cold pizza and sleeping on your couch," I got out, holding his gaze.

Trey finally took another bite and gave me a closed-lip grin. "I know. It's pretty great."

With one last shared smile, we continued to eat our

delicious pizza in silence. I expected the quiet to make me want to run, but it wasn't stained with awkwardness.

We were just two acquaintances, one super kind and extremely pretty, while the other barely knew anything about anything and could only pray she didn't agree to stay with a serial killing mom and son duo.

It's fine, I'm fine. Anyway, where else could I go?

I apparently had no home, no immediate family. My best option was the nice people who claimed to know me. And if the gorgeous boy that is Trey Turner was a killer, so what, I could learn to see past his flaws.

I'm obviously joking, but in all transparency—he really is that hot.

The two of us finished our pizza, and Trey took the plates, rinsing them off in the kitchen sink.

"So, do I live on your couch now? Or do I have some extended family I can stay with? I don't really understand what happens now," I admitted.

Trey stopped rustling around in the kitchen. I turned a look back at him standing at the counter; eyes glazed over as he stared off into space. When his eyes finally jumped to mine, he smiled.

"Let me show you something." He approached the couch and stopped just before wrapping me up into him. "May I?"

I knew my cheeks were pink as I nodded and rose from the couch, now in his embrace, heavily leaning into him.

The most frustrating part about this whole day was my inability to walk on my own and the fact that everything in my body bugged me with an incessant, deep ache. All my body wanted to do was sleep, rest my cramping joints and stiff, almost non-existent muscles.

I had wanted to cry when we made it to Chelsea's car outside of the hospital this morning. Just from the little exertion to get up and get into the vehicle, I had a migraine that threatened to collapse me.

As of right now, if I was being completely honest with myself, I wasn't too far from experiencing that exact feeling, but I pasted on a brave face. I was far too curious about my surroundings and the boy whose warmth enveloped me to let my body's exhaustion take the wheel.

Trey shuffled me out of the main room down a warmly lit hallway.

"Is this when you chop me up and hide me in the basement?" I asked.

His expression didn't budge, but the corner of his mouth twitched. "We don't have a basement—there is an attic, though."

"Comforting,"

Leading with a wry smile, he guided me toward a doorway opening to a dark, unlit room. He held to me with one arm while reaching the other to flip the lights on.

The room was simple.

A small desk was up against one wall with a fun-sized twin bed against the opposite. The bed was quilted with a flowery pink bedspread, clouded with pillows and a plush periwinkle rug covered the center of the floor. There weren't a lot of decorations ornamenting the place. Except for a small bookcase full of volumes, next to the closet and three picture frames that hung above the bed.

I focused on the pictures, taking a step toward them. Trey moved with me until we were directly before them and the bed.

The farthest picture to the left was of two very similar-looking women; one older, one younger, embracing on a beach. The middle picture was of the same young girl from the first picture, except the older woman was replaced by a young boy with bright blue eyes and curly blonde hair. The two were dressed in navy-blue graduation caps and gowns. The last picture to the far right had the same two kids, dressed in the same getup, but standing between them was Trey. He also wore the graduation attire, looking a little brighter and younger than he did now.

I felt him watching me, just like he had when we first met, waiting for my reaction. I could guess who each of the individuals were, but I still asked, pointing to the middle frame at the young girl, "Is that me?"

"You still haven't looked in a mirror?"

I rolled my eyes. "One, I've been a little preoccupied today. Two, I can't exactly walk myself to a mirror. And three, you already said I was hot. What more do I need to see?"

Trey scoffed. "I didn't say that."

"Yes, you did, with your eyes," I mocked as I batted my lashes at him.

He grinned, but before he could quip back, I quickly added, pointing to the last picture of the three graduates, "And it looks like even then you couldn't keep your eyes off me."

His attention darted back to the picture, and I knew he saw exactly what I meant. The camera had captured the perfect moment—him smiling while totally ogling the blonde, curly-haired girl he held to his side.

He shook his head and heaved a deep sigh, feigning annoyance, before he forced me to turn back to the rest of the bedroom with him. "This is yours. My mom and I put it together just after your accident, in case you needed a place to stay when you woke up."

My eyes went wide, leaping to the bookcase of novels and then to the bed.

"This is all for me?"

His head bobbed in silent answer.

I gawked at the room as I moved backwards to sit onto the bed. Trey helped lower me, then sat himself next to me. The bed caved with his weight, dropping my light body completely flush against his side.

"It's yours if you want it. We wanted to make sure you knew you had a home to come home to," he breathed.

I placed a hand on my heart. "You know, I bet, even if I had my memories, this would still be the nicest thing that anyone has ever done for me." I twisted to him. "I honestly don't know what to say… Well, except thank you, of course, but that doesn't feel like enough."

He smiled down at me. "You being awake is thanks enough." His tone was hushed and before I could comment, he gestured to the closet. "It's full of my mom's old clothes she thought would fit you, so feel free to raid that for things to wear."

I looked down at my baggy sweats and tee. "I don't know. This style is kind of growing on me."

His gaze did a couple of lazy laps up and down my body before he abruptly rose from the bed. "You can use the bathroom directly across the hall. Oh, and here!" He strode to the desk and opened a drawer, pulling out a cell phone. My eyes again went wide as he handed me the device.

"You got me a phone?"

To my relief, Trey shook his head.

"It's yours, you—you had—um, misplaced it. I got it back and was holding onto it for you, but I forgot to give it back the last night I saw you. So, I held onto it, keeping it safe for until you woke up."

I stared at the phone. With how he stuttered around the explanation, I knew there were a few details he was leaving out, but I didn't ask for more. I instead raised my eyes to his. "It's cute and a little creepy how obsessed you are with me."

His brows furrowed. "I am not obsessed with you."

"Mhmm," I hummed. "Sure."

"I'm not," he said with more finality, but the little waver in his voice betrayed him.

I giggled. "You sat and watched me sleep for a year. Now, you've practically adopted me. That sounds a bit obsessive to me."

Dimples.

Trey had dimples that made a heart-stopping appearance as he waved off my teasing.

"I'm going to bed, if you need anything…" He hesitated, giving me a long once over. A coy grin pulled up his lips. "If you need anything, my bedroom is just down the hall."

He turned for the exit, taking one step out the door, instantly halting when I called his name.

"Trey."

"Yeah, May?"

"Thank you."

Again, dimples.

"Of course."

Dear love of my life,

Let me preface by saying you are my best friend and will always be my best friend. But before I get to have you, I have my mom. My mom is amazing. She's kind, she's beautiful, intelligent and someone I strive to be like every day.

My mom and I have been through thick and thin together. I remember nights when I was small of her singing me to sleep. I remember her reading me piles and piles of books during summer breaks.

But I especially remember the days she held me while I cried.

A slightly embarrassing but vital piece of information about me is that my mom still holds me and rocks me on her lap when I cry. Yes—even at sixteen years old, my mom lugs my body on top of her petite frame and rocks me while I cry.

I think she does it because when I was small, I used to hold her.

I remember, years after dad passed, and we moved in with Richard, Mom would crawl into my bed most nights, after I'd fallen asleep, and she would cry. I remember hooking my arms around her neck, holding as tight as I could. At the time, I hadn't understood why she cried… Now I do, and I wish I would have held her tighter.

But—yes, while you are my best friend and I will go to you, always, there may be times I still go to her, needing to be held by my mom and rocked while I cry.

Love,
Maybelle Mason

18

Your Mom Saved My Life

Maybelle

The next few days were a blur.

I was always sleeping, or how Chelsea liked to put it, always *recovering.*

I hated it.

The sluggish, hollow feeling of my body lacking the strength to even stand on my own two feet?

Absolutely horrible.

It had been eight days since I woke up. Eight days…and I was just as useless as when I had been in a coma. Except now, I was cognizant—fully aware of my stale existence.

The only time Chelsea encouraged, or more like, kindly forced me out of bed and into the land of the living was to be brutally tortured in my physical therapy sessions. It was cruel and unusual punishment, the stretches and exercises my body was being subjected to.

Annalise Jones, the sadistic tormentor that claimed to be a physical therapist, came to the Turner home the last three days to bend and push my body in ways I refused to believe were healthy.

"I promise, if we keep up with this, May, you'll be walking on your own in no time," Annalise promised in her chipper, southern accent as she pulled my joints into a new, excruciating position.

I had to keep my mouth closed when she said things like that, because I was all too tempted to scream at the woman each time. Despite that, I really liked her. She was a sweetheart, and what I appreciated most was how much she pushed me. Yeah, I may have wanted to maim her in the heat of a painful muscle extension, but I was starting to feel the progress.

I wasn't feeling strong by any means, but my body was starting to feel more solid, even reliable. Still, by the end of each of the sessions with Annalise, my body would ache with absolute exhaustion.

I got into a routine in which I would wake up at some embarrassingly late hour of the day. Eat what I could get down. Get through therapy without a scrap of my dignity left, eat again, shower, and sleep.

Each day was a poor regurgitation of the last.

Especially since Trey left back to school for football training at the beginning of the week. He had spent the first few days at the house, helping me settle in, but was gone by Sunday. Even when he was here, I didn't see much of him due to my "recovering". We hadn't spoken nearly as much as that first day, which I couldn't help but be a little disappointed about.

Trey said, before he left for school, that he would be back next weekend and would spend Friday night, Saturday and part of Sunday back home. But would have to be back at school before Monday.

Today, Thursday, I laid supine on my bed, staring up at the white, cloud-textured ceiling, mentally preparing myself for the torture session I had with Annalise in an hour. My gaze meandered and settled on the three picture frames hanging on the wall above my bed.

There was a shift in my chest, like a lightweight dumbbell had been placed there to rest, making it almost painful to breathe.

When I had first seen the pictures, I could only focus

on the facts, pointing out my face, and acknowledging the other unfamiliar faces of the people I couldn't remember. The photographs now only loomed over me as a reminder that I was a stranger in my own body. An outsider that had no real connection to the world around them.

It terrified me. I tried desperately, in the few hours I found myself awake and staring up at the ceiling, like I did now, to remember.

My brain was a massive library. Aisle after aisle, row after row of filing cabinets filled with memory files. I could spend hours scouring each of the drawers for the information I lacked. But each time, the files were empty—blank.

Two soft knocks clicked against the bedroom door.

"Come in," I answered.

Chelsea poked her head in, a wide smile splitting open her face. "Good to see you're awake," she said sweetly, but I cringed. It was a couple of hours after noon. Chelsea, being surprised to see me already awake, was proof of just how lazy I'd been.

"I know. I need to get up," I acknowledged sheepishly, but she stopped me from rising off the bed with a hand on my shoulder.

"You're good to rest until your session. I know it takes a lot out of you. Don't beat yourself up about it though, it will get easier."

I snorted. "I sure hope so. Annalise has been telling me the same thing."

Chelsea reached and brushed a ratted blonde curl from my forehead to behind my ear.

I adored Chelsea. Since I moved in with the Turners, she had continued to treat me with so much belonging, never making me feel like a burden or even a stranger, though I was.

"Can I join you?" she asked, gesturing to the bed space beside me.

I scooted over, allowing more room for her to sit comfortably beside me. She sat down on the edge, swiping her hands against her palm leaf, green dress pants, then adjusted the frilly collar of her flowery, white blouse with puffed sleeves that barely capped her petite, tan shoulders.

The pretty, professional, and girly clothing that she had worn the last eight days greatly differed from the clothing that now stocked my closet. It was all very basic, neutral colored clothing that leaned more toward comfort and casual. I was grateful for it. If I was wearing the blouse Chelsea wore now, I'd probably die. Made me feel claustrophobic just looking at the ruffles that brushed at her neck.

I, instead, wore a very light fabric, long sleeve white top, with a low, swooping neckline. The bottom of the shirt stopped just over my belly button, showing off an inch of my skin between the shirt and high-rise black yoga pants.

"Do you work tonight?" I asked as I remembered the light blue matching scrub set she had worn that first night we met. She'd been up with me every day, getting me to my therapy sessions and keeping me fed.

Had she also been going to work each night?

The blood vacated my veins, leaving me cold and uncomfortable with the thought.

Chelsea shook her head. "My boss gave me time off to help you these first few days, but I'm back to work Saturday night."

My lungs filled with relief.

She shifted, looking back at the wall, obviously admiring those three picture frames that stared holes into my soul.

"You know, I knew your mom," she said without looking away.

Curiosity and a bit of excitement shot through me, sitting me up straight. This was the first time someone brought up my mom. I heard so much regarding Liam from Trey and even the nurses when I woke up, but nothing specific about the blonde woman pictured next to me in that first photo. I turned to Chelsea, anxious and waiting.

"Trey didn't know I knew her." Her gaze finally slipped back to me, a sad half smile on her lips.

"Why?" I whispered, eager to know more.

In this moment, Chelsea wasn't expecting me to know. She wasn't waiting for my brain to be whole, but she was offering information that my mind craved to fill the blank files with.

"She was my therapist. Stephanie Mason was an amazing counselor that worked with women. Helped them heal, helped them overcome. I was one of those women."

She smoothed her pants again with her long feminine hands. She splayed her palms and fingers out across her lap, emotion flooding from her. Not in tears yet, but the heart, the story that lingered in her stiff movements.

"Trey's dad left me for another woman a couple of years before your family moved to San Francisco. I was a mess. I was so lonely and just trying to hold myself together for Trey. Most of the time, though, he sadly was the one taking care of me—I knew I needed help. Some ladies with sons on the football team at the high school talked about your mom being a therapist who specialized in helping women who suffered from betrayal trauma. That night I looked at her website and spontaneously signed myself up for one of her group sessions."

Chelsea let out a chuckle, turned and swiped at a stray tear that escaped down her cheek.

"I was so nervous. I was terrified there was a way I could mess up or that my hurt would be small compared to the experiences of the other women in the group—I don't know. I think I was more scared that nothing could help, that I was too broken. Stephanie Mason was the first one to talk to me when I arrived at my first meeting. Instead of introducing herself or even saying hello, she pulled me into a hug. I collapsed into her arms and just sobbed."

I soaked up every word, every chuckle and tear. My heart full, not for the loss and pain that Chelsea endured, of course, but for the love and emotion that spilled from her story.

"With one look, your mom knew I couldn't hold myself up alone for one more second, so she held me. One day a week, for months, your mother held me and the women of that group up until we started to hold each other up. Friendships and relationships blossomed to stabilize us in our own personal lives of turmoil. Then we got better at holding ourselves up. We relied on each other when needed, but we learned to be free and rely on our own strengths... Your mom saved my life, Maybelle."

Chelsea punctuated that last statement by reaching over and grasping my hand. "Trey knew I was in therapy, but I didn't tell him that the mom of his best friend was my therapist until those first weeks after the accident. I finally told him, and we realized we both had a shared interest in making sure you were taken care of. I hope you never feel alone in this. I can't imagine what you might be experiencing but know that this is your home now too. You may never get your memories back, but no matter if you do or you don't, you will forever have a place and people to call home. You understand me?"

I was crying. I couldn't recall when I started, but the tears poured from me. I hadn't realized just how much I needed to hear that. Even though I couldn't remember the family I'd been born into, the people I'd lost and the love that I once had for them—I was anxious and scared that I was alone, never to be completely accepted into a world I couldn't remember.

The only response I could give Chelsea was a nod as

I sniffled through the overwhelming tears. I didn't realize how much emotion I'd been holding in from the last week of events. The buildup of the confusion, the frustration, the loneliness, exhaustion, the inadequacy, and heartache from the last eight days finally came crashing down, and it felt so good to just sob, shamelessly blubber.

Chelsea's arm swooped around my shoulders, her hand pressed into the side of my hair, gently guiding my head until it laid on her shoulder as the sobs continued to come. Her fingers brushed through my tangled hair, hushing me calmly, holding me up.

Holding me up the way Stephanie Mason had once held her.

The way I imagined a mother would hold her daughter.

The way Stephanie might've held me.

That night I didn't fall asleep as soon as my head hit the pillow like every other night. I was awake, staring up at the ceiling again, my body energized with a whole new motivation. If I was going to be a part of this world around me—I needed to wake up, I needed to walk.

I stood myself up, leaning heavily against the bed. My limbs trembled from the soreness and excessive use from my earlier physical therapy session, but I hissed in a breath, and I made myself walk.

19

Bruises And Bookshelves

Trey

How is it that five days felt far longer than the last year ever had?

It was driving me crazy that I could only depend on my mom for small updates here and there on how physical therapy was hard for Maybelle but going well. And that she was asleep more than she was awake most days.

I needed to be there with her, not here.

I needed to help her through this, not at college.

I mean, it wasn't like I was just sitting here. Each of my days were full of work, football and preparing for the upcoming semester. My roommates and I recently helped move another guy into the apartment. I'd been finishing out a summer class I had TA'd for and I'd been spending a lot of time in the gym training and working through the anxiety of not being home.

But as much as I would love to drop everything and bail for home in the middle of the week back to the girl waiting there, I couldn't just throw the life I worked so hard for away.

The rest of the week, before I left back to school, had been devastating compared to that first day I had spent with her. That first day, Maybelle and I spoke, teased, had fun, but those last few days—she only had the energy to eat and sleep.

I felt stuck in a cruel limbo in which she was finally awake but wouldn't stay awake. It was killing me. Keeping me constantly on edge that she would just stop waking up.

All I knew was that I was thankful it was officially the weekend, which meant I could go home. Maybe while I was there, I could get Maybelle out of the house, take her to do something fun—keep her awake.

"Damn it, Bear!" a male voice hollered from the other room.

I was in my apartment, packing my weekend bag as fast as possible in order to get on the road. Past my door, I could hear the raging chaos of noises from the TV my roommates were playing video games on.

"Bear, I swear to god, man, if you let me down again…" The boisterous voice of Chad Larson ricocheted off the walls of our shared apartment.

I opened my bedroom door at the end of the hall, passing the other three bedrooms, and entered the compact living room. On the two-cushion couch, dead center of the room, sat Larson. Next to him, on the six-foot-long, massive bean bag, was Adam Steverson, better known by his friends and the team as Bear.

Larson was gnawing on the inside of his cheek, fingers clicking against the buttons of his remote while Bear sat stone-faced, like he would rather be doing anything else in the world.

Bear was the first to notice me and the bag in my hand. "Where are you headed?"

"Aye, pay attention!" Larson scolded.

Bear rolled his eyes.

I chuckled. "I'm headed home."

This had both Larson and Bear looking away from their game. "For the weekend?" Larson asked after pausing the game.

I nodded, dropping my bag on the kitchen counter so I could grab a couple of road trip snacks from the pantry. With two pop tart packs in hand, I turned back to face the guys who watched me like I might combust at any moment.

"What? Is there something on my face?" Keeping up with the theatrics, I brought my palm down the rough stubble on my chin, making a show of inspecting my hand for any removed debris.

Bear, in his deep tone, asked, "How's she doing?"

My whole first season at SDU, I left back home nearly every weekend, never joining the parties or celebrations. Getting home to sit by Maybelle's side, just in case she finally woke up. After a few months, Larson, being captain of the team, felt it was his responsibility to sit me down with Bear and ask if there was a problem. If there was a reason, I avoided them and the team every weekend.

We hadn't been roommates, or teammates for long before that, but it led to a friendship I needed more than they probably realized. It was the first time I ever opened up to anyone besides my mom about the beautiful sleeping girl I waited patiently for. The guys always tried after that to ask for updates on Maybelle each time I went home for the weekend.

"She's doing well. My mom said she's having a hard time with physical therapy and is still sleeping a lot, but she's doing good." I did what I could to sound hopeful, but by the skeptical look Bear gave me, I wasn't convincing.

"Speaking of your mom," Larson interrupted before Bear could ask more. "Tell her I miss her and that I'm still waiting for her to call me back."

Disturbed, I turned my attention to the blonde, six foot-two, football player. "You better be joking."

He resumed his game with Bear, the cacophony of noises erupting from the speakers again. "Man, my girl

Chelsea, is a MILF. I got her number last season so I could—" He put his remote controller down for the briefest moment to do air quotes. "*Check in on you*—as your Captain. But between you and me, I'm just trying to become your stepdaddy."

I nabbed a pillow that had fallen to the floor from the couch and chucked it at him, knocking the video game remote from his hands.

"Oh, shit, shit, shit. Bear, you better not fail me," Larson cursed as he scrambled to recover the controller.

Bear had a smug grin on his lips as he continued to play. I had grabbed my bag and pop tarts when Larson returned to the game with his remote.

"You—" Larson turned on Bear, whose grin was now a blatant smile. "Did you kill my guy?" Larson accused.

Bear shrugged, tossed his remote onto the couch and rose to approach me, leaving Larson muttering bitterly under his breath. I paused before walking out the front door as Bear slapped a large hand to my back.

"Are you doing alright?"

There were many reasons we called the big guy Bear. For one, the man was massive. He was easily the biggest and tallest on the team. He was our best lineman, a force of destruction that obliterated defensive lines and was an immovable wall of protection when it was his time to defend. But off the field, he was a teddy bear that talked about feelings when he got you alone.

I sighed. "I'm fine, man. Really, I just need to get home."

He gave me a half nod. "Well, when she's feeling well enough, you should bring her to visit. I bet we'd all like to meet the famous Maybelle."

I smiled at the thought of my girl meeting my brothers. "I'll definitely do that, hopefully in the next few weeks." I grasped Bear's hand. "I'll be back Sunday night."

He waved me off with a grunted goodbye and I was

out the door with Larson, calling after me, "Have a good weekend, son!"

***

"Mom, I'm home!"

"In here, love," Mom called from the kitchen.

The house was filled with the savory aroma of Mom's homemade lasagna, making my mouth instantly water.

Those pop tarts did nothing to satisfy my hunger on the long drive and my stomach ached for some actual food. I left my bag by the wall and sat at the small dining table that could seat four but was set for three. I scanned the room and the beginning of the hallway that led back to the bedrooms.

No sign of Maybelle, probably still sleeping, even though it was five o'clock in the evening.

Mom washed her hands after she finished chopping a head of lettuce for a salad she was working on. "How was your week, Hun?" She wiped her hands on a towel as she rounded the kitchen counter to hug and kiss me on the top of my head where I sat.

"It was good, long. A lot of practice and prepping for the upcoming semester," I answered as I stood to give her a proper hug.

"Remind me when your first game is again," Mom said into my chest before pulling away to get back to making dinner.

I followed her, stopping to wash my hands in the sink. "It's in three weeks, end of the month. And it's more a scrimmage to get people hyped up for the first official game and the start of the semester." I dried my hands, then went to work on preparing the other salad ingredients she had waiting on the counter to be mixed and dressed.

"That's right," Mom exhaled. "I don't know if I can make it to that one with my work schedule, but I'll be at the next one, I promise."

I waved her off. "Don't stress. It's just a scrimmage. Only students will be there—besides, you're no longer allowed to come to my games."

She put her kitchen tools down and faced me, brows knitted. "What? Why not?"

I snickered, "Because you're too pretty. A few of the guys are hoping they'll get a shot at becoming my stepdad this season."

Her eyes doubled in size.

"I'm teasing, but if you have Chad Larson's number, delete it immediately, please."

She giggled, nodded, and continued to chop up tomatoes. "Oh, I will, don't you worry. Also, a little off topic, but Betsy called, said something interesting happened at work last night."

"What happened?"

Mom didn't look at me as she continued to chop. "You know how Maybelle's story has been on the news?"

As much as I wished it wasn't, I had seen a few articles trending, talking about the "girl who lived".

Horrible Harry Potter reference.

Maybelle's unique story of surviving the accident that not only killed her family—but put her in a coma for a year—had hit the local news a day or two after she woke up. Thankfully, since she wasn't at her home, and no one knew who took her in. We hadn't been harassed by any curious drama seekers here at the house.

I nodded. Mom stopped her cutting and turned her focus on me as she said, "Well, apparently a man came in, pretty adamant about seeing her. He was dressed all spiffy, wearing some high-end clothing, so the staff suspected he was just some elite journalist seeking out the story. But he was so intent on seeing her that he wouldn't listen when they told him she wasn't there. Bets said they eventually had to get security involved. I guess it was a super inconvenient mess."

Straightening and pausing my work on the food, I asked, "Mom, is it safe for you to work there?"

She waved me down. "Of course. It all turned out perfectly fine. It was more bizarre than anything."

"They need to get better security there. Random people shouldn't be able to just walk in, demanding to see patients."

Snorting, Mom quirked a knowing look at me. "Oh yeah, Mister IDemandToSeeMyGirl?"

"That's not the same," I returned, unamused.

She only smiled down at the meal she prepared. A beat of quiet and chopping against a cutting board passed between us before I cleared my throat. "How is she?"

"She didn't have physical therapy today, so she's only left her room for a sandwich I made at around noon. Other than that, I haven't seen her." Without looking at my mom I could hear the sadness in her tone.

"Should I go check on her?"

She shrugged. "Might as well. Maybe she'll be hungry."

I immediately wiped my hands on a towel and headed down the hall, straight to Maybelle's room. I halted in front of her door, only allowing an instant of hesitation before I lightly knocked.

No response. *She must be asleep.*

I knocked again. No answer. I reached for the doorknob and opened the door. The bedroom door flung out at me, making me jump back as a blonde, hollering female rolled out into the hallway at my feet.

On the floor, on her back, was my Maybelle staring up at me wide-eyed with mirthful surprise.

"What the hell happened?" I demanded, crouching over her.

I swooped a hand under her neck and helped her sit up. She didn't seem injured, but she was hot to the touch, her cheeks red and her skin damp with sweat, like she just got done with a long jog.

Maybelle's astonishment turned beaming as she cackled. "Well, whatever happened to knocking? I was leaning up against the door when you opened it and sent me tumbling."

I wrapped an arm around her waist and hauled her up to her feet.

"I did knock," I defended.

She sniffed. "Not loud enough."

Pulling from my arms, she stood herself up against the wall behind her. She was standing by herself. I gave her a once over, noticing the white crew socks, black leggings that were painted to her legs, stopped at her ankles and the tight V-neck, long sleeve, blue-gray top that darkened in areas from perspiration. Her face was pink, and her long curls were pulled back into a high ponytail.

She looked so alive—and good… Really good.

I peered over her shoulder. Her room looked like a tornado had gone through it. Her cabinet of books had fallen to the ground, spilling out novels, and her bed was a disaster of sheets and pillows.

"What are you doing in there?"

Maybelle followed my gaze to see the destruction. She grimaced, then twisted back to face me. "Don't worry, I'll clean it all up."

I turned my attention back on her, my eyes catching onto a nasty bruise on her hip, peeking out under her shirt. I didn't think. I stepped forward, grabbing the hem of her top. Maybelle tried to retreat but was already sandwiched between me and the wall.

"Trey, wha—?" she gasped out, but I was already lifting her shirt so I could clearly inspect the angry purpling mark on her hip.

God, she would've had to hit her side stupid hard to get a bruise that dark.

My focus fell back on her face as I stood to my full height, the anxiety and fear in me mingling into something ugly. "That doesn't answer my question, Maybelle. What the hell are you doing in there?"

She was watching me quietly; her breathing heavy as she stared up at me. Her blue-green eyes moved down to look at the hand still holding her shirt up and my thumb that now subconsciously swiped back and forth across the dark mark. When her eyes returned, they narrowed. Her hand slipped up between us, pressing against my chest until I was backing away, dropping her shirt.

She shrugged, while a sarcastic grin tightened across her pale face. "I'm practicing."

"Practicing what, gymnastics?" My hands trembled, wanting to grab for her again. I forgot to check her head and make sure she didn't hit it in her fall.

She quirked a brow at my irritated tone, her smile falling. "It's good to see you too, Trey."

Shit…

She sighed, turning in past the doorway. "Tell Chelsea I'll be out for dinner in a few minutes." And she shut the door in my face.

It was about ten minutes later when Maybelle emerged from her room. She had changed out of her sweat-drenched clothing into black sweats and a forest green, crop top, tank that made her eyes appear more viridescent. Her hair had been taken out of the tight ponytail and braided to the side, falling over the front of her shoulder with stray curls springing out to frame her face.

She was practically walking on her own, given the wall was doing a lot of the work to hold her slight frame up. I rushed to my feet when she limped out of the hallway, moving to her side and extending my arm to her.

She kept her eyes trained forward and reluctantly accepted my outstretched hand for the last few steps between the wall and the table.

She must be tired, her attention and hold on me being so weak.

I was quickly corrected when Maybelle saw mom. She glowed brightly with an enthusiastic smile. "Chelsea, hey! Sorry I haven't seen much of you today."

I pulled out the chair for Maybelle, eyeing her as she sat, still not acknowledging me. Feeling a little uneasy and, honestly, like an idiot, I cautiously took my place at the table between her and my mom

Mom's eyes danced between us; brows pulled together. "It's okay. I know you've been tired. Your body is still recovering."

She offered Maybelle a scoop of salad. Maybelle held her plate up to accept it as she shook her head back and forth. "Oh, I wasn't sleeping."

Mom and I both stopped dishing up our plates. I itched to ask her what she'd been doing if not sleeping, but that previously hadn't gone so well. So I waited for my mom to ask, "What were you doing all day if not sleeping?"

Maybelle scooped herself up some lasagna. "I've been practicing my exercises and stretches that Annalise taught me and making myself walk. I did take one spill over my bookshelf, which gave me a pretty cool looking bruise on my hip, but other than that, I'm really getting the hang of this whole walking thing."

I wanted to burst. What was she doing pushing herself so hard to the point she was falling and hurting herself?

"That's amazing, Maybelle."

I whipped my head toward my mom, whose face split open with a proud smile. She turned that smile to me expectantly. "Don't you think so, Trey?"

In what world could she think this was a good idea?

Maybelle turned to face me, a small, smug grin pulling at her lips, waiting for my response. I straightened in my seat, feeling like I just fell into a trap. Both women watched, waiting. Mom's smile soon faltered while Maybelle's grew more complacent in my silence.

"I honestly think you should have someone with you if you're going to be pushing yourself like that," I answered.

Maybelle propped her head on a hand. "Interesting. Well, if you'd been around to see me walk more, you'd know I have come a long way in such a short amount of time and do just fine on my own."

I sniffed. "Yeah, tell that to your bookshelf."

"That happened in the middle of the night when I first tried to walk on my own. I didn't fall over the rest of the night or at all today."

I sucked in a breath, putting together the details of her argument.

Mom stiffened next to me, obviously realizing my same concern when she asked, "May, honey, were you up all night and all day?"

Maybelle retreated a bit, folding her hands on her lap. "I'm not tired."

But she was. I could see it in the dark smudges under her eyes and her drooping lids.

"You're definitely tired," I volleyed, finding myself trying to poke the bear.

She shot me a glare, placing a hand on the table. "I am not."

Her nose scrunched, and her eyes turned to slits with defiance. It was really—really hot. I couldn't hold back the taunting smile that now gripped my own features.

Mom leaned over the table, intervening by placing a hand over Maybelle's now balled fist. "It's okay to be tired, May. It's normal. We all need rest."

Maybelle's face softened when she faced my mom. "I lost an entire year of my life to sleeping—I need to stay awake. I can't sleep for one more second. At least, until I can walk better. I need to—live—but I can't do that if I'm constantly sleeping and filled with the anxiety that I'll stop waking up."

She stared at her lap, refusing to meet our eyes. I

understood. She was just as scared to sleep as I was watching her sleep. Maybelle slowly stood from the table holding her dinner plate. "Thank you for dinner. If you don't mind, I'm going to eat in my room. Have a good night."

Standing tall on trembling legs, Maybelle successfully staggered to the wall and slid down the hall to her bedroom.

My attention wandered back to my mom, who studied me like a hard equation.

"What?"

Her face turned up as she put a hand to my forearm. "My sweet, overprotective son." She shook her head. "I know it's scary because you care about her, but she isn't made of glass. She isn't fragile, but her heart is right now. She needs you to believe in her more than you fear for her."

I slumped because she was right, but she wasn't done.

Mom squeezed my arm once more. "It's no longer your job to fix and bandage up all the problems. I know you were put in that position growing up, but Maybelle Mason is leaps and bounds more independent than I ever was. She is not going to shatter, but she might burn out if you smother her."

She said this so simply. Like the topic of my roles in being her protector and fixer at a young age after dad bailed was a common topic of discussion.

It wasn't.

But again, my mom had a point. She and Maybelle were very different, but that didn't mean Maybelle didn't need someone looking out for her too. It just meant I needed to adjust my approach.

20

Stay

That cold pizza my first night might've been delicious, but this lasagna was a whole other level of exquisite goodness.

I sat on my bed, devouring my dinner, wishing I could go outside my room to thank Chelsea for the best meal I could remember having. Except my pride would not allow it, which was childish, but I didn't care.

I was just so angry… But more than anything, I was frustrated at myself for looking forward to seeing Trey. I was excited to show him how well I was walking, to talking with him, to hearing how his week had been.

And, ugh, I hated to admit it, but I was exhausted.

I rose off my bed and placed my finished plate on the desk against the other wall. My legs still shook under my weight, but I didn't need to hold on to anything to cover the short length of my room now, which was progress.

At this rate, I bet I could walk the length of the house with no help by next week. My pride at the thought dwindled as I scrutinized the fallen bookcase, felt the soreness in my bruised hip and remembered Trey's concern, his fear—his lack of faith in me.

Forget him, I thought.

I was doing great, and that's all that mattered. There

were bound to be a few bumps and scrapes here and there along the way. But what I couldn't get out of my head was the feel of his hand caressing my hip and him pressing me into the wall.

Trying to distract myself from the thought, I knelt before the case and scattered books. I lifted the empty shelving and began filling it with the novels. A few of the books were beautiful, decorated with sparkling details and leather-bound.

One book was open on the floor. Plucking it up, I skimmed the first pages.

Pride and Prejudice by Jane Austen.

What felt like minutes soon turned into hours.

I had plopped myself on the floor, with my back against the wall, and was about halfway through the beautiful, infuriating, confusing story of Mr. Darcy and Elizabeth Bennet when a loud knock on my bedroom door made me jump.

"Come in," I called, my voice shaking with surprise.

My door opened to reveal Trey, still as handsome as ever, which made me fume. He couldn't act the way he had and be that pretty—it wasn't fair.

"Hey, sorry to bother you. I saw your light was still on and wanted to check in. Make sure you're alright."

I looked at the digital alarm clock on my desk. It was already past midnight. "I didn't realize how late it was." I looked back at Trey, who studied me in the doorway. "What're you still doing up?"

When he first got back from school, he'd been wearing a royal blue shirt with his school's name painted across the back. He wore jeans and sneakers, but now he was in black shorts and a gray t-shirt that clung to his built upper body in all the right ways.

I was shamelessly—murderously—gawking at him as he stepped further into my room.

"I couldn't sleep after how dinner went," he admitted, his head bowing as he looked at me through lowered lashes.

Nodding, I used the wall to get to my feet, my joints stiff from sitting on the floor for so long.

Trey met me at the bed and offered his hand to help lower me to the mattress. I accepted his help but paused before settling onto the pink quilted spread. I looked up at him, still astonished by his height compared to mine, as I stood level to his broad chest.

"How about you sit with me, and we catch up?" I offered as a truce and gestured to the bed.

He accepted with a smile, and we both fell into the pillows. The two of us sat shoulder to shoulder. I grabbed a pillow from my side and hugged it on my lap while Trey folded his arms over his front.

"May, I owe you an apology," he started.

I scooted sideways so I could better face him as he spoke because, yes, he did owe me an apology.

"I let my fear overwhelm me today. I'm happy to see you walking and doing well—you have no idea. But I let my fear of you getting hurt cloud that, and I'm sorry."

I placed a forgiving hand on his knee, giving him a gentle grin. "Damn right you should be sorry. Do you know how excited I was to show you how far I've come?" I playfully swatted at his muscled shoulder, feigning anger as I folded my arms and turned away from him.

He snickered behind me, and I felt the mattress move as he adjusted. "What do I have to do to make it up to you, May?" He was much closer now; his breathing tickled the back of my neck.

My breath hitched as I forced myself to keep my chin high and give a half shrug. "I don't know, handsome. I fear this might be the end of our friendship."

I felt his fingers at my sides, his mouth pressed up close to my ear. "I'm afraid that just won't work for me."

Before I could respond, Trey had me hauled up in his lap, attacking the sensitive areas of my sides, making me squeal. I writhed and squirmed in his hold, screeching and laughing uncontrollably.

He pinned my arms down with one of his hands, then slapped the other hand over my mouth as he hushed me through his own laughter. "Hush, May. Mom's asleep and has work tomorrow. You'll wake her if you keep squawking like that."

I slipped one of my hands out of his grasp and pulled my mouth free of the muzzle. "Stop the torture and I'll stop my screaming," I whisper-shouted up at him.

His deep laugh reverberated through me. "I'll stop as soon as you say you forgive me and that we're still friends." He leaned into me, still holding me up on his lap.

"Hmm I don't know…" I hummed but his evil fingers dug into me again, sending me wriggling. "Okay, okay, okay, I forgive you!"

Trey didn't fully press back into me, but his fingertips teasingly danced at my hips.

"And?" he drawled.

I shook my head. "And we're best friends. Now get your hands off me, you sadist." Sitting up, I rolled back onto the bed, leaving my legs draped across his lap. Trey vibrated with amusement as he rested his hands on my knees.

"You know," I started, catching my breath. "You and my physical therapist would get along well."

He dropped his head back against the wall, slanting me a look. "Yeah? Why do you say that?"

"You both find too much enjoyment in torturing me."

"Hmm, yeah, you should definitely introduce us."

This—this was the Trey I'd been looking forward to talking to and hanging out with. The friend who ate pizza with me and knew how to joke. I heaved a deep, content sigh.

"So, how was your week?" I asked, hoping to keep

him here with me longer, keep him talking—keep myself awake.

His hands kneaded into my knees, relieving the achy tension in my joints. "It was good, busy. We're getting ready for classes and the season to start in the next few weeks." He straightened as he put more pressure into his massaging.

I couldn't help it; I groaned. "That feels so good."

Letting my eyes fall close, I rested back on my pillows. He continued on, making the aches in my taut limbs mold to his magic hands.

"I should go. Let you get some sleep."

My eyes shot open, and I latched onto his arm before he could stand from the bed. "I'm not sleeping, please, don't leave yet."

Stupid, I felt so stupid for my begging, but I was too scared to care about how pathetic I might've looked. His brows furrowed as he held the hand, I grabbed him with.

"What's wrong?"

I couldn't meet his eyes. "I'm just—I don't want to sleep yet," I said, as my eyes grew heavier. He didn't reply right away, studying me as I kept my attention on the floor.

"May, it's okay to sleep. We all need it. And from what you said at dinner, it sounds like you've been up for almost forty hours straight. You really need to sleep."

His thumb brushed back and forth across my knuckles as he spoke. I couldn't argue with him. I knew he was right by the way I struggled to hold my eyes open and yawned every two seconds.

"If you want," Trey continued. "I could stay with you, sleep on the floor, and make sure you're okay."

I peered up at him, meeting his gaze.

I nodded. "I would like that, and could you wake me up when you wake up? No matter how early—please." I refused to sleep away any more of my days, especially the few days I got with him.

He squeezed my hand. "Of course, I promise."

So, we set him up with a blanket and a few of the extra pillows from my bed on the plush, periwinkle rug next to me.

Just before sleep finally took me, I twisted in the dark, making eye contact with eyes of green that were lit up by the soft light of the moon pooling in through my bedroom window.

They darted across my face, like he was sketching my features with his gaze. Then his hand lifted, reaching up so his fingers could brush along my jaw as he pulled a few curls off my cheek.

"Good night, May."

As my heavy eyes finally slid shut, the last thing in my sight was the boy asleep on my bedroom floor. Just like how we spent the last year, with Trey by my side, making sure I didn't feel alone even as I slept.

Having him there, knowing I wasn't by myself and the assurance that I would wake up with the start of the day like everyone else, I swiftly drifted away receiving a full night's rest—well earned.

Dear best friend,

Something you should know about me is I love books.

No, I don't just love books. I need books. If I am being totally and completely honest with myself, books are my gateway drug.

Do I know what a gateway drug is? No, not really.

Books are the gateway to different worlds and stories that I am thoroughly addicted escaping to every spare chance I get. That sounds like a gateway drug to me.

Anyway, enough about drugs.

All I'm trying to say is that I love books because they are my escape.

I love my mom. I love my brother. With all my heart…but this life is difficult. I probably sound so stupid when I say that.

I am only fifteen years old.

What would I know about the difficulties life has to offer?

I probably don't, but I can't deny that there are days, weeks, even months, I spend wishing I could be in a magical new world. A world where I am the main heroine, a character written with the courage to fight back, created to win against the powerful hand of evil and the heart to reach a helping hand out to those in need.

"There are no happy endings in real life."

That's what Richard always tells me when he sees me reading my books. He says I shouldn't spend so much time in fake worlds, reading about happily ever after's that will never be real. That I should spend more time accepting reality and life for what it really is.

I can't help but think that he might be right.

The lives I've lived through in the books I read are epic, beautiful, full of love, magic and enchanting endings… Then I wake up, and reality drowns me under its melancholy weight, reminding me that I am not powerful, I am not the epic heroine, and I am not written to win.

I think that is another reason I write to you.

You are an escape. A life... A happily ever after I earnestly pray for every day. One that I find myself running to in my dreams. With you, books wouldn't have to be a getaway from my heavy existence, but a joy in a beautiful life I share and cherish with the one I love.

I melt into the pages of this journal, eager for the day I can melt into you. One day. One day I won't want to escape my life. One day, maybe, I'll want to live it.

Love,
Maybelle Mason

21

Check Mate

Maybelle

I was on a beach, and I was running. My joints didn't buckle, my muscles didn't give out, and my heart raced with the beat of each stride.

I was alive.

I sprinted, ready to continue my chase with no end in sight until my path forked. Two roads laid before me. I glanced to the right, curious about the emptiness it offered. Something inside me, something forgotten, reached toward it.

Ignoring the internal pull, I turned to the left. The road was long, built with dips and turns, but not too far down; near the middle, there stood a man. I couldn't make out his features. He seemed more ghost than man, an illusion waving to me.

As I stood between both paths, I had a sinking feeling that I was forgetting something. Something—or someone. Stepping forward, I decided on my path, but as I moved, my legs collapsed, and I fell.

***

Morning sun struck through my window, setting my small bedroom alight. It made those messy caramel waves and green eyes glow as he knelt against the bed and brushed the sleep-crazed curls from my face.

"Morning, Mayhem."

Trey had followed through with his promise.

I blinked the world around me into focus. My attention fell down his torso… He was shirtless.

Where did his shirt go—actually, I didn't quite care.

I reached toward him and placed a hand against his cheek. "You, my friend, are so pretty; it hurts."

His head rocked back as he guffawed. "Excuse me?" he chopped out through his raspy, sleepy chuckles.

Half of my face beamed at him, while the other half remained plastered into my pillows.

"You heard me."

I gave his cheek a quick pat, then curled back in on myself. He was still crouched next to my bed, eye level with me, watching me with a smile tugging at his lips.

"So," I started as I yawned, sat up and stretched my arms up into the air. "That do we have planned today?"

Still watching me with that slight smirk, Trey shrugged. "I have a couple of ideas. I have a date at noon. After that, I'm all yours," he said as he draped his upper body across the bed next to me.

A date… Cool, cool—perfect timing because around noon I was going to be throwing myself off the Golden Gate Bridge. Yeah, we barely knew each other—or I barely knew him—but come on. A date? What was he doing going on dates with other girls during the little time I had with him?

To mask whatever was happening in my head and the tightness in my chest, I went with what I knew best: childish teasing and fake confidence.

"Oh, a date, hmm? Is she cute?" I waggled my brows down at the muscled, tanned boy that had the audacity to lay himself across my bed like he owned it.

Well—I guess he did.

Trey quirked a brow. "Yeah, she's way cute. Known

her forever. I think you'd like her." He rolled up onto the bed, his back against the wall, his arm lazily propped behind my back against the pillows.

"Well, you have fun with that," I said as I scrambled away, putting distance between me and what I wished was breakfast.

My legs felt strong under me today, even after all the work I put them through the last couple of days. I wobbled but successfully made it to my door and opened it.

"Thank you for keeping me company last night, but I better get dressed and ready for the day." I forced an overly wide grin as I held the door open and gestured for him to leave.

Trey stared, a sly smile now teasing his enticing lips. This defiance was a large contrast from the paranoid boy that treated me like a fragile, glass doll last night and I liked it.

"I mean, unless you're wanting to stay for the show?" I said, folding my arms across my chest. "I don't think your date would quite appreciate it, but I don't mind the company."

His face burned bright red.

Check mate.

He stood from the bed in all his shirtless glory. I would've shamelessly swooned if not for my bitter pride. He strolled confidently up to me, but I refused to retreat. Stopping only inches from me, he dipped his head in close.

"You're right," he said in a hushed tone that had me instinctively and stupidly leaning toward him. "She wouldn't appreciate that."

And I was left alone, on the threshold of my bedroom door. He sauntered away while I held my breath, worried that if I exhaled, it'd be a loud curse that escaped my mouth.

I skipped breakfast to avoid Trey and the odd jealousy

that now racked me. Instead, I entered the bathroom, showered, and washed my matted curls.

Wrapped in a luxurious, fluffy white towel, I exited the shower, my wet hair falling down my shoulders and back, past my butt.

Turning to face the mirror, I took another towel and scrunched it in my sopping curls. Over the last week or so, I did what I could to avoid the mirror, never taking time to study the reflection in front of me. That first day I looked in the mirror, I was genuinely scared of what I saw.

The being before me was pale, frail, and stale looking. Like the life had been sucked clean from me, down to the bones. Now the figure that stared back smiled, cheeks pink, hair bouncy, body filling out in certain previously caved in areas. I felt pretty and finally could recognize bits and pieces of the girl pictured in those three frames above my bed.

I was awake. I was *alive*.

I dressed myself in a simple, cotton, heather-gray, capped sleeve shirt, and straight leg whitewash jeans. After getting dressed, I tossed my mass of drenched curls around, trying to decide what to do with them. A minute of contemplating passed before I left it alone to dry freely.

Exiting the bathroom, steam rolling out with me, I found Trey leaning against the door frame. His eyes went wide as they fell on the damp curls that coiled around me.

"What?" I asked, resting against the opposite side of the frame.

He wore a plain black shirt that hung tight to his chest and shoulders with well-fitting dark jeans. His brown hair was wet, like he too just got done with a shower.

Trey pulled his gaze from my hair, giving me a full once over before landing right back on my curls. His hand lifted to grab a long lock of my hair, twirling the strands around his finger as he held them up between us.

"This," he started, "is my favorite thing in the whole world."

I slanted him a curious look. "My hair?"

He nodded, not breaking eye contact.

Chelsea came around the corner of the hall, then, wearing a darling modest, light blue sundress, her hair in loose waves and a cream-colored purse on her arm.

Smiling, she stopped in front of us. "Oh, hey you two!"

I smiled broadly while Trey slowly untangled his finger from my hair.

"Hi, Chelsea," I said as I felt him then continue to pull and play with the curls dangling against my back.

Her grin only grew as she tucked her hair behind her ear. "Trey, are you ready for our date? We need to leave in the next twenty minutes if we want to make it to our regular place by noon."

I spun back to Trey, whose smirk was smug as he slid me a wink. "Told you she was cute."

Trey one, Maybelle zero.

He turned back to his mom. "Yeah, Mom. I'm ready for our date." He brushed by me, breezed a quick kiss to the side of Chelsea's head and continued on to his room; that was only a couple doors down from mine.

"Sorry Maybelle, I forgot to ask you, are you comfortable spending a couple of hours alone? Trey and I always try to fit in a quick lunch date when he's in town, but we won't if that makes you uncomfortable." She bridged the distance by placing a hand on my upper arm.

"Of course," I replied. "Don't stress about me. I started a book last night that I've been wanting to finish. You two have fun."

"Okay, thank you, and I put my number in your phone in case you need anything. Do not hesitate to call."

Not long later, Chelsea and Trey left on their mother-son date, leaving me to my own devices.

For the first time since waking up, I was alone. No one was in the next room, no one to hear if I called out. I shook away the eerie feeling the silence brought. I retreated to my room, retrieved the book I started. Instead of staying in my room, I ventured into the backyard.

The yard was quaint, with beautiful plush grass, but what caught my eye was in the far corner between two trees. A net hammock hung up, ready and waiting for me and my book.

***

"Mayhem," a baritone voice called out a couple of hours later, pulling me from my story.

"Hi," I answered, my nose still between the pages of my book. I hadn't realized Trey's quick approach until he was in front of me and plucking the novel from my hands. I tried to snatch it back, but he halted me with one held up finger.

"You can read later. Right now, we're leaving," he said as he grasped one of my hands and pulled me to my feet.

The last couple of days of pushing my physical limits were catching up with me. Instead of letting him go and walking on my own, I looped my arm in his and held to his massive arm as we walked the stretch of the yard.

"Where are we going?" I asked, with my eyes focused on the ground in front of me.

"I was thinking ice cream, but the rest is a surprise."

He helped me up into his black Jeep that was parked out on the road and buckled me in before hopping into the driver's seat. He threw the car in drive, and we were on the road.

As we drove, I plastered my face to the window, watching the passing roads, buildings, and people. I knew I'd been a member of the world that bustled past the glass, but I couldn't recall any specific memories, moments, or personal experiences—which drove me absolutely insane.

It was the feeling of remembering the tune of a song, but no matter what you did, you couldn't recall the name or specific lyrics. Or when you remember someone's face, but their name just sits on the tip of your tongue and never leaves spoken. The incessant lack of recollection only dries your tongue out and makes your head hurt with frustration.

Instead of punishing myself by trying to remember, I watched the road and the passing world, fascinated, soaking it all in. Trey didn't speak, only drummed his fingers to the beat of *Look After You* by The Fray humming from his radio. But out of the corner of my eye, I caught glimpses of him watching me, a smile pressed to his lips.

We soon pulled into a drive-thru, up to a massive menu with about a thousand different variations of burgers, custards, and ice cream cones. Trey ordered, paid, and I graciously accepted my treat as he pulled the vehicle into a parking spot.

"How was your date?" I asked, sucking on my red plastic spoon. Trey bought us both chocolate custard cups with hot caramel drizzled on top.

It was fabulous.

He licked at the ice cream that smeared across his upper lip. "It was good. It's always nice getting to sit and talk with my mom."

Trey Turner really was a sweet boy, inside and out. I didn't know if it had something to do with his obvious appreciation for his mom, but I went quiet, realizing just how easy it was to be enthralled with this boy in the short time I knew him—or remembered knowing him.

I placed my finished custard in the cup holder before leaning my back against the door to face him. "So, we were friends before, correct?"

He eyed me, taking a bite of his custard before nodding.

"What was that like?"

He turned his body to me, head tilting curiously. "What was what like?" he asked, discarding the rest of his custard into my finished one.

"Our friendship," I answered. "Were we always like this?" I flapped a finger, indicating the unseen connection between us.

He stared at me thoughtfully for a moment before putting the car into drive. "Put your seat belt on."

I folded my arms over myself, refusing to let him avoid my questions. Trey didn't argue. He only put the vehicle back into park, extended over me with ease, grabbed the belt, and quickly locked it into place over me.

Before retreating to his seat, he flicked my nose. I snorted, giving him a playful shove back to his side of the Jeep.

Smirking, he drove out of the parking lot, back onto the main road. "Uh, our relationship was—" He hesitated, rolling over his words before he continued, "Let's just say our friendship was blossoming before your accident."

I watched him intently, my knuckles pressed to my lips as I studied him and worked over his words in my head. "What does that mean?" I finally asked, not able to figure out his implications.

Trey let out a strained sigh as the vehicle rolled to a stop at a busy intersection. With the red glow of the traffic light reaching in through the windshield, painting the tension between us a deeper shade of want, he turned his eyes to me. He held my gaze in a way that hummed with quiet fascination. That one long look was enough to tell me there was something intimate Trey was hiding with knowing delight.

I sat up and leaned an elbow on the middle console.

"You had a big fat crush on me, huh?" I asked,

wagging my brows. He snorted, like he'd instantly deny the claim, but he, instead, didn't confirm nor deny my accusation. He only turned his focus back to the traffic lights that were now green, a shy smile playing across his lips.

I grinned to myself, sidling back to my side of the vehicle.

We soon stopped in front of a small house with a sign across the front door that spelt, *Mason*. Immediately, I whipped my head to Trey, who was already out and walking to my side of the car. He opened my door and gestured for me to get out. I stared at him, trying to catch up with whatever was going on.

Noticing my hesitation, he stood himself beside me, his body pressing into the open vehicle. One hand pleasantly rested atop my knee, the other on my upper arm. I watched him, glimpsing back and forth between the front door and those happy, deep green eyes.

"What are we doing, Trey?"

"This is the surprise."

He dug into his back pocket and pulled out a set of keys, dangling them in front of me.

"Liam gave me keys to the house. He was always forgetting stuff that he needed me to grab for him. Or sometimes after parties he'd be so wasted, I had to sneak him into bed without your mom seeing. So, he gave me keys to come and go as I pleased," he said this with a sad smile pulling at his lips, no doubt recalling such memories.

Memories with my brother. My family.

For the first time, I envied him for the memories he could remember and be sad about.

I envied his recollection and claim to the house that laid before me. I never ached to remember what could hurt me. The people, the lost life. Here was the one place I was born to belong in, and I couldn't remember it. He could see and feel for this place more than I could, and it made me feel so…misplaced.

I turned my attention ahead, fighting back the sudden rush of emotion that threatened to drown me.

I couldn't go in there. I didn't belong there.

Trey brought my knee out past him, turning me until I faced him and the house fully while he fit himself between my legs. I sat slightly above him due to the massive wheels and lift of the Jeep.

He cupped my face in both of his calloused hands as he surveyed me. "You don't have to go in if you don't want to. But I have a few things I wanted to grab for you in there. You're welcome to wait out here if that would make you more comfortable."

I stared back at the house.

What was I so scared of?

That I might remember? Yeah, maybe.

That Trey was hoping this would jog my memory and I would only let him down? Yeah, that wasn't a fun thought.

That while those three picture frames above my bed stared holes into my soul—going into that home, my forgotten world, might feel like enduring a pointless chase for a reality I couldn't reclaim as my own… But unless I took a chance, I wouldn't know anything for sure.

I sucked in a deep breath. "I'll go in if you hold my hand the whole time," I whispered, my grin perking up.

Trey's face split into a wide smile. "Of course."

22

Gulps And MILFs

Maybelle

The drive back from the Mason home was quiet.

The setting sun was now only a soft orange glow in the West, making way for the stars and moon to be seen over the city lights. I held tightly with one arm to a small backpack Trey had found in that house and stuffed full of random items I hadn't yet seen.

While he went into the small home, down a hallway where I lost sight of him, I remained in the front room where a couch and an armchair near a window stood. Atop the cushion of the armchair was a dust-ridden, self-help book. The same copy I remembered seeing Chelsea read before dinner some nights.

Inside, the home was dark. It had a lovely citrus and cinnamon aroma about it, like someone recently burned a candle or doused the walls and cushions in perfume.

The home wasn't messy, just from the looks of the first room I stayed in, but it was mucky. Cobwebs hung from the ceiling. Tables and chairs were coated in a thin layer of dust. Despite the lack of cleaning, the house was definitely, at some point, a home, a safe place for a family of three.

I thought I would be overwhelmed with emotion upon entering the house, but I was indifferent, unfamiliar to my surroundings. I didn't care for it—which was a relief.

I held to my conversation with Chelsea from the other day. It helped me enter the home without panic. The knowledge that even if this place could never feel like home for me, I did, in fact, belong somewhere.

I had a home. I had my people.

So, I wasn't racked with guilt or burdened by curiosity to investigate the bones of my forgotten past. I only waited patiently for Trey to gather the things he wanted.

The ride back home, Trey held my other hand, his thumb swiping back and forth across my knuckles. We didn't talk, only sat in tranquil silence until we were home, standing in front of my bedroom door.

I handed the backpack to him, but he gently pushed it back toward me. "I got that for you. You don't have to go through it yet, but I think you'll appreciate the items inside."

I pulled the pack against my chest. "Thank you for tonight, Trey."

We were in the hallway, but my bedroom door was open to the window on the far wall that allowed the pale glow of the moon to paint across Trey's face.

He revealed a slanted grin before his hand was up, his fingers brushing a couple of curls out of my face. I ducked my head to hide my giddy smile and the obvious butterflies fluttering in my gut.

His hand moved from my hair to cup my cheek. I watched him patiently, my stomach aching with anticipation as I studied his every move. His focus was on my lips.

"I guess we should tell Chelsea we're home. I bet she's wondering where we are." The statement had leapt from my mouth, unbidden. My nerves were exploding with the need to ramble—to distract.

Trey's soft, crooked grin turned wide and smug as he inched closer to me. "Mom is at work. I texted her we made it home."

"Oh, so, she's not here?" I asked, voice cracking.

He shook his head, his other hand now curving over my hip. "Nope, it's just you and me here, May."

Gulp. Yes, I gulped.

"Are you headed back to school tomorrow?" I really could not control myself, but Trey didn't seem fazed as his face neared mine.

"Yes, around noon."

He was whispering now, and his breath was warm on my skin. His hand on my cheek now tangled up in my hair at the nape of my neck, keeping me close.

An inch. That was the only space between our open mouths now. I wanted to kiss him, to tangle up against him. To feel him feeling me and we were so, so close. I closed my eyes, clung to the bag in my arms, and tilted my mouth ever so slightly up to him.

The inch of space disappeared as skin met skin… Only, it wasn't lips on lips. He kissed the corner of my mouth—mostly my cheek.

I opened my eyes, and he was staring at me with the biggest, maliciously teasing smirk on his face.

"Mayhem… I think you might be obsessed with me."

My mouth gaped as he laughed. I scoffed, trying to take a step back, but his hold on me didn't falter.

"Well—It's not like it's a secret," I barked out, through my now rapid breaths. "I've been very vocal about how attractive I find you."

Staring up at him, I halfheartedly pulled against his grasp. Trey brought me back against him and buried his face into my neck as amusement shook him. His upturned lips pressed into the bare skin beneath my ear as he said, "God, you're addicting."

His lips trailed up my neck, lighting my senses on fire. I was melting, losing my hold on the bag in my hands and my grasp on reality.

"For the record," he whispered as he nipped at my

ear. "You are the only thing that occupies my thoughts." His feather light kisses trailed from my ear, across my jaw and up my chin, making my head roll back.

"You were right that first night," he spoke so sensually low, his voice hummed against my skin. "I was obsessed with you then, but I am entirely consumed by you now."

His mouth collapsed against mine, and this time he did not miss. No, Trey knew exactly where to go as his kiss overtook me. The hand in my hair gripped and begged for more while his other hand left my hip, plucked the backpack from my arms, and tossed it around me, into my open bedroom.

The spike of feeling and emotions that flooded my system with each new touch and sweep of his tongue against my lips made me quake.

I thought I was awake before, finally started real life when I made the choice to walk on my own, but that was nothing compared to the fiery warmth coursing through my veins.

Trey's heart raced against my chest as both his considerable hands cupped my face. His thumbs stroked my cheeks as he broke the kiss. I didn't open my eyes, hoping to remain in the blissful moment with only the sound of our heavy breathing filling the space between us.

"May," he prayed into the air. I opened my eyes and met Trey's smiling forest green gaze. "I've been wanting to do that for a really long time." He pressed himself against me for one last chaste kiss on my lips before pulling away to place a peck on my brow.

"Goodnight, May."

Then he was gone, his body heat and presence stolen from me as he strolled down the hall to his bedroom. But before leaving the hall into his room, he slid me one last look.

I was still standing in the same spot, like an idiot. I

gawked after him, lacking the brainpower to function after such a magical moment. I stabilized myself against my door frame, straightening my posture.

His smile grew.

Still unable to use my words, I hit him with a mock salute, followed by a quick wave as I nearly stumbled into my bedroom. Once I shut my door and leaned up against the other side. I inhaled, filling my lungs with a full needed breath.

I fell asleep that night with a smile on my lips as I replayed those words Trey said to me and the patterns he kissed up my neck.

He left the next morning just before noon, but not before grabbing my phone and putting his number in my contacts. He told me he would text me every day and that he planned to be back home by Saturday morning.

The rest of Sunday passed. Chelsea and I ended the day by eating dinner and watching a romcom together. I didn't hear from Trey that night, but Chelsea got a text from him saying he made it back to school safely.

Monday came with another torturous session of physical therapy with Annalise. I couldn't deny the pride that swelled in my chest when Annalise was absolutely dumbfounded by the progress I made in the little time we had apart.

That pride was quickly crushed by the end of our session, though. I was sore and utterly weak at the conclusion of it, sending me off to bed for the night pretty early. Still no word from Trey. But Tuesday morning I woke to see one missed call and three unread messages from a contact under the name, *Boyfriend*.

Two of the messages sent the night prior read:

Boyfriend: Hey! Sorry I've been MIA the last couple of days, how are you?

Boyfriend: I realize it's late and you're probably asleep. I'll text you tomorrow! Sleep well, May.

The last unread message was sent that morning only minutes before I woke up.

Boyfriend: Good morning, Mayhem.

Thankfully, I was alone in the privacy of my room because I smiled like an idiot while typing out my reply.

Maybelle: Good morning…boyfriend?

Boyfriend: That's me.

Maybelle: Brandon?

Boyfriend: Who the hell is Brandon?

Maybelle: I'm sorry, Tanner, baby.

Boyfriend: You're not funny.

I snorted as I typed.

Maybelle: Oh, come on. I had to tease you for the "boyfriend" stunt.

Boyfriend: I was just trying to make my intentions clear.

Maybelle: One kiss and you're smitten?

Boyfriend: I was smitten long before that first kiss, May.

Wow, this boy…swoon.

I needed a minute to catch my breath and figure out a decent reply, so I rolled out of my bed, limbs a little flimsy, to dress myself in some jean shorts and a cornflower blue tank before I flopped back onto the bed.

I laid on my stomach, legs kicking up behind me as I opened my phone back up to a new message.

Boyfriend: What are your plans for today?

Maybelle: Maybe some reading this morning, therapy this afternoon and a romcom marathon with Chelsea later tonight.

Boyfriend: I bet my mom is loving having a movie buddy.

> **Maybelle**: I know I appreciate the company. It's been fun. Are you up to anything half as exciting?

> **Boyfriend**: My plans aren't nearly as fun as cuddling up with you for a movie. I have practice, training and then a few guys from the team are coming over for pizza tonight.

I paused, lost for words because, yes, while I loved the last couple of movie nights with Chelsea—I was, I hated to admit it, jealous.

I wanted friends to eat pizza and hangout with, but I only had two friends in the world and one of them was rarely around. That was my next thing I needed to conquer once I could walk without stumbling. Get outside and expand my circle.

Maybe I'd even get a job, go to school, join a club. The options were endless. I'd find something. I just needed to walk, to become more independent.

I would, I had to.

> **Maybelle**: I need to get going. Can we talk more later?

> **Boyfriend**: Can I call you before bed?

> **Maybelle**: It's a date.

My time with Annalise came and went, leaving me feeling brutally abused. I showered off the pained sweat and dressed in PJs, a teal tank top, and black shorts.

Before leaving my room, I glimpsed the backpack Trey had packed from the Mason home—my old home—still lying on the floor from where he tossed it in the middle of our kiss.

Later. I would deal with the bag full of mystery items later.

Chelsea and I only got through one movie later that night before she was dead asleep on the couch. I draped a blanket over her, turned the TV off, then retreated to my room to find one missed call from Trey.

I smiled as my phone pinged with a message.

> **Boyfriend**: May? Are you awake?

I dialed up his number. The phone only rang twice before he answered.

"May! How are you, gorgeous?"

I giggled. "Doing alright, handsome. How are you?"

"Better now," he said with a sudden ruckus of voices blustering out in the background on his side of the phone.

"Is your party still going on?" I asked, smirking at what I made out to be a voice calling Trey's name repeatedly. Like a needy child begging for attention.

He grunted. Whatever he said was muffled but

sounded a lot like scolding. "No, it's just my roommates. I went into my room, but they heard me on the phone and came to investigate. They thought it was my, and I quote, *super-hot mom*. I swear—"

I snickered. "I don't blame them. Chelsea is a MILF."

He groaned over the line while another voice called out, "See! Maybelle gets me."

"Get out of here, Larson. And May, don't encourage him, please." Multiple sources of laughter echoed to me, joining my own.

Suddenly, an uproar of Trey yelling and the other voices bellowing ricocheted through the speaker. Loud enough that I had to remove the phone from my ear until another unfamiliar voice addressed me.

"Maybelle?"

"Yes?"

"This is Bear. You're coming to the scrimmage next Friday, right?"

All the background noises went silent, even Trey. I hesitated, not exactly sure what to say. I knew what I wanted to say, but I didn't quite know what to say.

"Uh, hi, Bear," I said, the other line still expectantly quiet, "I mean I'd love to but—"

"She said yes!" the voice belonging to Larson whooped out, sending the rest of them back into their chaos of hooting and hollering.

Oh shoot.

Trey's distinguishable laughter was back at the front. "Hey, May, these guys aren't going away anytime soon. Can I call you again tomorrow?"

I smiled to myself. "Of course. Goodnight, Trey."

"Goodnight, Mayhem."

Guess I'd be getting out there and making friends a lot sooner than I anticipated—which meant I needed to be walking ASAP.

23

That Book Belongs to Me

Trey

It was late Thursday night. I should've been exhausted, especially since practice ended about an hour ago and it was well past my bedtime, but I was wide awake.

Soon, I'd be Face Timing my Maybelle.

We texted whenever I had free time. We had that one call the guys interrupted, but that was the only contact we'd had over the last few days. Tonight, we were calling because I finally convinced her to open the backpack I packed for her that night in the Mason home. But she only agreed to it if I opened it with her.

I changed myself into a pair of comfortable black gym shorts and a faded, gray, dry-fit tee I knew did my body justice. I had to dress to impress for my girl. I'd taken notice that when I wore clothing that painted to my sculpted build, Miss Maybelle had a hard time keeping her eyes off me. That was the goal of all this, to make this girl want me. To make her long for me almost as much as I longed for her.

It blew my mind just how easy it was for us—now that she couldn't remember. I wanted her to remember, of course, for the sake of remembering her family.

But I also selfishly loved that she couldn't remember

her life, the things that made her quiet, and the nightmares that made her muscles and joints lock up.

I suddenly felt a little sick with the heavy knowledge and secrets I alone held.

I got up into my bed, trying to focus and remind myself that I would be seeing her face. Laying my back against the headboard of my bed, I pulled out my phone, feeling it vibrate. Maybelle's name scrolled across the top of the screen.

She was calling ten minutes early.

I smiled as I answered the call. Maybelle and her massive mane of messy curls filled the small screen, stealing the breath from my lungs. She was wearing a black sports bra with an open, gray zip-up across her shoulders. The look would have been simple, maybe lazy on anyone else, but on Maybelle…

Jesus, this girl was a type of beautiful that had me believing angels did walk among us, and I was lucky enough to be a personal witness of one.

"Hey, how was therapy?" I asked, trying and failing to get my focus off the little of her body that was showing and back on her face.

She beamed. "Better. It still kicked my butt, but I don't feel half as exhausted as I usually do. And I can walk across the house without using the wall. Given— I'm slow, but at least I can do it on my own."

Her toothy grin was contagious. I smiled proudly back at her. "I'm proud of you, May. You're doing extremely well in such a short amount of time. I'm impressed."

She tipped an imaginary hat to me.

I chuckled, sitting myself up higher on the bed. "Alright, are you ready to open the bag?" I asked, a thrill expanding in my chest.

I wasn't hopeful the things I got for her would suddenly fix her memories. I was content with allowing her to heal and remember with time. But I felt a few of the items could connect her to herself, to her family and the things she loved.

As I watched her, I felt the exposed emptiness in my back pocket. The space that was once filled by a little, black journal I held tightly to over the last year.

Maybelle's smile wavered a split second before she recovered and bobbed her head up and down.

"Yeah, let me grab that."

She put the phone down, facing me toward the ceiling. Then she was back, propping me up on the bed so I could see her while she sat on the other side of the mattress, hands busy with the backpack. She was biting into the inside of her cheek, staring off to the side, like she was mentally running away.

"May."

Her eyes slowly panned back to the phone.

"You don't have to do this, you know? The last thing I want is for you to be uncomfortable."

My stomach tightened with the anxiety that she would back out, but I meant it. I would never pressure her if she wasn't ready.

"I want to look at it. I'm curious to know what you packed, but I'm nervous…" She paused for a moment, eyes darting away then back. "I'm nervous you're expecting me to remember, and I'll disappoint you when I don't." She squeezed the bag tighter to her chest, like a lifeline as she waited for my response and my heart cracked at the sight.

"May, I'm not expecting this to be some kind of cure. I just wanted to get you some things I thought might help you learn about who you are, where you come from."

Her grip on the bag loosened, and I felt like I could breathe a little easier.

"Promise?" she asked as her mouth quirked to the side.

"Promise."

"Fine," she breathed. "I'm ready."

Unzipping the bag, Maybelle went in for the first item, which was a white novel with a little upside-down chick on the front. "*Flipped?*" she asked, opening the book cover to read the author's name. "*Flipped* by Wendelin Van Draanen."

My smile grew wide as I watched her study the book. "Yeah, that one was your favorite," I explained, remembering how I'd seen her read and re-read the short novel through the years.

She smiled at the book before putting it off to the side. "I'll start it tonight."

The next item she removed was a small pair of wireless ear buds. "Oh, these will be nice. I've been wanting to listen to more music."

"I bet. You're a music and singing prodigy."

Maybelle dropped the earbuds and her jaw. "No way. For real?"

I nodded back fervently.

"Hmm," she hummed. "How cool. I'll have to give that a try. Maybe I'll serenade you soon." She gifted me a sideways smirk, and it took everything in me not to burst at the seams with laughter.

"Okay, last thing," she announced, and I tensed, knowing exactly what was sitting at the bottom of that bag. She tugged out that small, black, leather-bound notebook. The journal that was full of the sweetest words, gentlest thoughts, aggressive goals, dark nightmares, and beautifully written dreams. She opened to the first page of the book, her eyes skimming the words scribbled across it.

That same page I read at her bedside a year ago.

A small gasp escaped her. "Is this mine? This whole thing?" Her hand covered her mouth as she continued to study the first few pages.

"Yeah, you've been recording your life since middle school. I thought it would be a good thing if you're ever curious or have questions about your past. You can ask the person who was there for all of it. You."

I was sweating, hoping she would cherish that little, bound book of pages like I did. The book that got me through the last year in one piece.

"Wow," Maybelle whispered as she flipped to the next page. Her soft, stunned look suddenly turned astounded. "Oh, my—I dedicated this whole thing to my future husband," she said, eyes still searching. A beat of silence passed before she gingerly placed the book on her lap. "This is a lot. Thank you, Trey. For all of this."

I sighed with relief. "I'm so glad you like it. I hope you can—" Maybelle cut me off with a targeted stare that made me snap my mouth shut.

She held up my journal, accusatory eyes still tracking me. "Now, Mr. Turner, how did you know this was my journal and that it dates back to middle school?"

Shit. I didn't think that one through.

I didn't think that through at all.

"Uh." I fumbled for words. I could totally fib… Bend the truth, spare my pride and her opinion of me this round.

"I read it."

Nope, guess the strategy was all honesty tonight.

Maybelle's eyes widened. "Trey Turner," she gasped. "You are so obsessed with me. It might be creepy if you weren't so cute about it." Her laughter howled over the phone.

I couldn't argue with that. I was so obsessed with her that it probably should be considered a little stalker-like. But I had all the best intentions, which had to count for something.

Right?

"I cannot believe you read my journal. The journal I wrote for my husband," she hiccupped through her belly laughs.

I stared after her, intensely watching the way her smile revealed the ghost of a hidden dimple on the right side of her mouth.

When Maybelle smiled, it wasn't just with her lips, but with her whole being. Her eyes, her face, her body exuded a light I wanted to immerse myself in every time she deemed me worthy of witnessing it.

The Maybelle I knew before the accident hardly revealed a smile of this caliber to me. Life hadn't given her the chance to experience the tender joy of smiling so bright and it had me craving to pull her close. To hold on to her. To shield her from every evil and never let her go, so nothing in this world could take that light from her—or me, ever again.

"Oh, Mayhem. You and I both know that book belongs to me. I'm just letting you borrow it."

Her face contorted, silently asking me where I found the audacity to claim such a thing.

Yeah, that popped out a little presumptuous, I'll admit it, but that book was *mine*.

I just needed to be patient for the day she knew it, too.

***

Friday night finally rolled around. I was supposed to leave early Saturday morning for home, but I couldn't wait. I got to my apartment from training, showered, dressed in sweats and a long sleeve tee. My packed bag was in hand as I made my way out, hair still damp, before the small party of people gathered in my living room stopped me.

Larson and Bear had a couple of girls sitting with them on the beanbag and couch. A kid from the team named Sam was holding one girl hostage in conversation. She looked bored to tears. I almost felt bad for her, but the poor, awkward kid needed the practice socializing. The girl would be fine to listen to his ramblings a little while longer.

Two people sat at the kitchen countertop. The guy turned in his stool, seeing me approach with my bags. "Hey, Turner. How are you, man?"

I smiled at my old friend. "Hey, Williams."

Noah Williams took up the position of first-string quarterback and captain of our high school football team during my first season of college ball. He quickly became the number one high school quarterback in the state of California.

There was a line of colleges begging to put him on their teams, but Williams followed in the footsteps of the guy who took such care to teach and befriend him at a young age.

He even wore Liam's old number—number three.

Now Williams, Larson, Bear and I were all roommates. It was comforting to have someone here with me from home. Someone who knew and loved Liam a fraction of what I did.

"Trey! Oh my god, how are you?" That voice put my whole body on edge.

Juliette Miller was a lean brunette on the cheerleading team. She was a conventionally attractive girl that was tall, with soft features—she was nice. Really nice, but the last conversation we had left a sour taste in my mouth.

Juliette was a year older than me. This was her third year with the cheer team and her uncle was my defensive coach. She was well-known and well-liked by everyone I knew.

Just before this last summer started, she asked me out.

I obviously said no. I was spoken for by a girl in a coma—who didn't know it yet. Avoiding the part that made me sound like I crazed stalker, I explained to Juliette I couldn't go out with her because I was already in a relationship.

"Oh, I didn't know you were seeing someone… Does she go here?" she had asked.

I shook my head. "*No, she's from my hometown, but I go home to see her every weekend.*"

Nodding, she smiled at me, but it wasn't a happy or understanding expression. "*You know my uncle is your coach, right?*"

Her question had stunned me. I sat, eyeing her for a moment, unsure of how to respond.

"*Uh, yeah,*" I finally uttered.

She only pursed her lips before saying, "*Good, just checking.*"

We hadn't spoken since.

I put a hand on Williams's shoulder, then nodded my acknowledgment to Juliette, who sat on the stool next to him. "I'm headed out. I'll see you Monday," I said to my friend before I swung my bag over my shoulder and stepped toward the front door.

"Alright, man, drive safe and have a good weekend home," Williams called back.

I was out the door and headed toward the stairs for the parking lot when the echo of light footsteps came clicking up behind me.

"Trey."

Turning, I startled as Juliette wrapped herself around my neck. My arms remained stiff at my sides while she muffled her words against my shoulder. "I hate to see you go. We have so many fun things planned for this weekend. I was hoping we could catch up."

I swallowed hard, unsure of what to say. "Yeah, wish I could, but I have plans with my girl. I'll see you around next week."

Pulling from the embrace, I tried to turn back down the hall, but Juliette grabbed my hand. "You know, I'm starting to think this mystery girl isn't real. If you didn't want to go on a date with me, Trey, you could've just said so. I'm a tough girl. I can handle rejection."

"Juliette," I sighed. "I can assure you she is very real. And you're great. I'm just not on the market."

She watched our hands as I pulled mine away. She smirked, then turned bright eyes up to me. "Well… when things change you know where to find me."

She spun, striding back to the apartment.

"Things won't change," I called, feeling the need to clarify.

When Juliette reached the door, she turned a big smile on me before saying, "It's okay, Turner. I can be patient."

***

The drive home was long, longer feeling than usual after that.

I just wanted to see my girl and get some sleep. When I pulled up, it was close to two in the morning. I shot off a text to Mom, letting her know I made it, then beelined it for Maybelle's room. Like I expected, she was fast asleep and looking so goddamned beautiful I wanted to weep with relief.

I reverently dropped my bag against the wall next to her desk. I slid the door closed, then quietly knelt beside her bed. I just wanted to see her and then I'd get to my room.

At least, that's what I told myself.

Maybelle was on her back, curls billowing all around her head and across her face. I silently sucked in a breath as I brushed a few stray hairs off her cheeks.

I was caught in the Twilight zone. As I gently let my fingers trace the patterns of freckles painted across her face and the bridge of her nose, I couldn't help but wish I could sit here forever, watching her sleep. She was enchanting, beyond breathtaking.

The moonlight glimpsing through the window was just enough to light up her hair, the skin of her throat and those plump, kissable lips.

I needed to stop staring like a freak and get to my room. I placed a light kiss on Maybelle's cheek, then readied to stand when a small hand wrapped around my wrist.

"Trey?"

Now that voice—that voice sang to me. Just hearing her speak unraveled the tightness in my chest. It warmed my skin and relaxed the tension in my shoulders.

I pivoted to see her eyes were still shut, but her hand clung to me.

"Hey, May. Sorry to wake you. I just pulled in," I whispered as I knelt back down, resting my elbows on the mattress pressed into her soft side.

A tired smile pulled at her lips while her eyes remained closed. "I'm glad you're home."

"Me too," I said, my voice low as I placed a kiss to the knuckles of the hand that still hadn't let go of me.

She rolled onto her side, fully facing me before her eyes fluttered open. "Stay with me? Wake me up when you get up?" she whispered, partly into her pillow. I placed a light peck on her nose, which she scrunched in response.

"Of course."

I salvaged a pillow and blanket, then fell asleep on her rug, watching the moonlight dance across her face and curls, touching her in a way I wished I could.

A couple of hours later, I woke to a gentle tug on my arm and light whispering. I blinked my eyes open to find Maybelle leaning down from her bed, pulling at my arm. It was still dark, but the purpling light of dawn was ghosting her bedroom with its presence.

My vision finally cleared, and I was cognizant enough to register what she was saying.

"Come here," she whispered, tugging me up toward the bed. I obeyed without a second thought.

She scooted forward, making room for me to climb in the bed behind her. I wrapped her body up in my arms, feeling warm, and at home.

She nestled into me like I was her home too.

How far we'd come from avoiding one another in high school, too nervous to make a move in fear of rejection. From me sitting by her side as she slept a year away, to now holding desperately to one another, cuddling in her bed, in my home.

I planted a kiss in the curls I couldn't stop obsessing over before pulling my Maybelle tighter into my chest.

Life was good. Life was so, so good.

Dear friend,

It's a bad day today.

Richard ran out last night. Mom thinks he left because of her so she's been in her room crying all morning. I want to tell her it's not her fault. I want to tell her the truth. To tell her it's my fault… but I can't—I don't know how.

I don't know where Liam is.

I think he stayed the night with a friend.

But I'm in pain.

I can't wrap my head around what happened.

I was left alone with Richard last night. Mom started school and was gone at a study group. Richard was drinking, but that's nothing new. He always drinks when Mom is gone.

When he drinks, he gets loud, says hurtful things but… last night. It wasn't just his words that hurt me. There are purpling marks imprinted on my skin. Fingerprints where he grabbed me, a dull hurt where one of his metal rings cracked against my skull.

I don't understand what caused it, but when it started, all I could do was freeze. I didn't struggle, I didn't move. I let him scream.

When it was over, when my vision blurred with tears, Richard apologized. He said he didn't know what came over him. He said he was angry and that he never should've done that.

Then he left me, still curled up on my bedroom floor.

I should be with Mom, see if she's alright, but I can't get myself to leave my room. Partly because I'm scared that Richard will show back up and because I don't want Mom to see me like this. She has enough on her plate. She doesn't need me adding myself to it.

I hate seeing her in pain. I don't know all the ins and outs of her and Richard's relationship, but I can tell she isn't happy. I don't understand why she stays with him.

Granted, I've never asked.

Part of me wonders if that's just how relationships are—

Painful.

I don't remember what Mom's marriage was like with my dad, but by the way she smiles when I ask her about him, and that she kept his name, "Mason", I imagine she was happy with him. At least happier than she is with Richard.

You know… I don't think I want to get married.

Seems a little redundant for me to write that to you, of all people, but I don't have anyone else to talk to about it.

I don't want to get married because I don't think I have the ability to trust anymore. I think the capacity to be vulnerable is another thing I've been stripped of in the last years. Along with my pride, my courage and my smile. I'm so scared of being taken advantage of. I'm terrified of being hurt emotionally and physically. I'm scared out of my mind, and I think it's a fear that has plagued me a lot longer than I'm willing to admit or that I was ever able to truly understand until now.

I think that terror I feel when thinking about being married to another individual is one of the biggest reasons I started this book… It was so I could get used to the idea of being so close to someone that they know all my fears. They know all the ways to hurt me but choose not to.

I'm scared that I might not meet you in this life because of my fear to open myself up to you, or anyone else, for that matter. But I think I'm more terrified to continue the rest of my life the way it's been so far.

I am a rug that is constantly trampled over. A punching bag that takes the hits. A useless thing that is ignored or mistreated.

I won't do it.

I can't.

I don't think I can survive a lifetime of this.

There is so much I don't know, so much about life I don't understand, and so much that I fear.

That isn't a life I want to live.

A life where I am imprisoned in my skin. An existence where I am barred from connection and interaction, all because one individual proved to me the dark depths humankind can reach. That man has stolen so much from me, but I refuse to allow him to confiscate my faith.

So, for you, for me… I will hope.

I will hope for a life where I meet a boy who is gentle. A boy who grows to be a man. A man who will see me, who knows me inside and out.

A man who knows every way he can break me, but, instead, helps build me.

I will hope for a me that is vulnerable. A me that is accepting. A me that can breathe without tears and a me that can learn to trust again.

Hope.

That is what you, my beautiful book of written words, are to me. You are my hope, bound by ink and faith. You are the hope I hold to, the hope I carry in my battered heart for a better, more peaceful life.

Love,
Maybelle Mason

24

The Plot Thickens

Maybelle

The weekend with Trey home was needed. I almost shed a tear when he had to leave me again for school.

Saturday morning, I woke up in his arms. His soft breathing puffed through my hair.

It was a beautifully surreal moment making me want, for the first time, to stay in bed. I could've stayed snuggled up in his massive arms, happy and warm for the rest of the weekend.

Later that morning, Trey and Chelsea did a quick brunch date while I stayed home, reading the book Trey got for me. After their date, they came home to grab me for a day at the beach.

We spent our time reading and sunbathing, which was heaven on earth for me. The cherry on top: Trey was a shirtless, sculpted masterpiece I got to admire through sneaky glances over the pages of my book. He laid himself out on a towel in front of me, a tanned muscular feast I got to sit and devour with my eyes.

He, unfortunately, didn't sleep in my room that night. He fell asleep on the couch during a movie we'd been watching, after Chelsea left for work.

I wanted to cuddle up against his hard body, but I

wasn't eager to break my back trying to squeeze onto the small, stiff cushions. So, I went to bed, but not before draping a blanket over him and planting an innocent kiss on his cheek.

Sunday morning, I woke to sunlight forcing its way through my shutters. Thrilled to rise with the sun all on my own, I got up, put on a comfortable pair of what Chelsea called *mom jeans* and a swoop neck, long sleeve, black top before walking out to the living room to see Trey.

He was still sleeping on the couch, which made me puff with pride because this was the first time I was awake before him. The best part: I didn't feel exhausted being up this early. I was well-rested, and my body felt energized for the new day.

I tip-toed into the kitchen, searched in the fridge for eggs, butter, and bacon. Then I got to work. Within a half hour I had breakfast cooked for two. Perfect timing because my handsome breakfast date rose from his sleep, caramel waves a pretty mess on his head.

"Good morning, sleeping beauty. I made you breakfast," I announced, beaming as I set the table.

"Wow, you didn't have to do this," he said, peering at the food I plated, stretching his arms above his head.

I filled him a glass of orange juice, then gestured for him to sit. "Hush, sit down and let me treat you."

He sat down at the spot I had made out for him. I tried stepping away from his side of the table, but he was already pulling me back to him by the waistband of my pants. He tugged until I fell backwards onto his lap. My legs draped over one side, as his arms immediately caged me.

Smiling, I laced my arms around his neck.

This was the place I wanted to spend the rest of my quickly fading time with him. Right here on his lap, in his arms, was my new home.

"Seriously, May. Thank you. This all looks delicious."

I scoffed. "Well, don't thank me until you try it first. It might be gross."

My gaze cautiously landed back on the food in front of us. Trey chuckled. I hadn't realized he moved one of his arms from around me until his fingers pinched my chin, turning my attention back to him.

His sensual green eyes flicked back and forth between my eyes and my lips.

He pulled my face into his, our lips meeting in a soft, inviting kiss. I could feel the fingers around my waist tangle to the denim loops of my pants, while his hand on my chin traced down my throat. His fingertips danced across the exposed skin of my neck and swooped back around to cup my nape.

Every one of his touches was so methodically placed and timed with the exploration of his tongue in my mouth.

Trey brought me in tighter, deepening the kiss for a brief second that teased and stole the breath from my lungs. He slowly pulled back, gliding his tongue across the seam of my now slightly swollen lips. When he broke the kiss, both of us lightly panting, he licked his lips and his smirking eyes met mine.

"You are delicious," he whispered and placed another kiss to the hollow of my throat.

Wow.

Forget eggs and bacon. Breakfast was right here and now that I'd gotten a couple tastes, I was eager to take a bite—but I couldn't, not yet. There was a little warning bell going off, some place deep in my subconscious, warning me, pulling me back with a message I felt in my bones.

Slow was good. Slow was safe.

It still took every ounce of my depleting self-restraint to stand from his lap and sit myself on the opposite side of the table. And by the look of his smug smile, he knew it.

"Your first game is this Friday, right?"

I stuffed a large bite of eggs into my mouth, noting that Trey's intense gaze was still glued on my every move.

After a couple of beats, he finally answered, "Yeah, what about it?" He took a chunk out of one of his bacon pieces.

I swallowed. "Is it okay if I go? I was serious when I said I wanted to go, but I also don't want to be a bother."

I absolutely wanted to be a bother, but it was up to Trey and Chelsea to chauffeur me around.

He nodded as he finished up his bite. "Of course, I already talked to my mom about it. She's going to drive you out after your last therapy session on Thursday. You'll stay with me at my place Thursday and Friday night, then we'll drive back here together on Saturday."

Excitement bubbled in my belly; I was going to college for the weekend. Not just college, a football game, maybe a party or two. I tried to stifle my level of overwhelming exhilaration by pinching my lips together, but who was I kidding? I could hide nothing from the boy who watched me like it was his job to.

Trey smiled back. "You excited?"

I nodded, plopping another bite of eggs into my mouth.

"Good, I'm excited for you to meet my friends."

I was looking forward to that too.

The front door opening and closing had us twisting in our seats to see Chelsea entering the house.

"Hey mom," Trey greeted at the same time I called out, "Morning, Chelsea."

Even after a full night shift, Chelsea was stunning with her brown hair up in a tight pony and her eyes bright with her smile.

"Hey, kids."

She entered the kitchen, placing her purse on the counter as she targeted Trey with a look. "You remember Mrs. Jacobs?"

Nodding, he shoved another bite into his mouth. "The neighbor three doors down?"

"Yes," she answered as she filled a cup of water from the fridge. "I thought she and her husband were visiting their son in Arizona for the next few months, but I think he came to visit them instead. I keep seeing the same man, about my age, hanging out in their driveway."

"Oh," Trey grunted around a mouthful of food as he shot me a look. "That's interesting, Mom. If you want, I can go down and check on them?"

She shook her head. "No, no. I don't want to bother their family time. I just thought it was strange. I also think I need some sleep. I'm always paranoid over the weirdest things when I'm tired."

With that, Chelsea came up to Trey, placing a kiss in his curls. "I am going to bed, have a wonderful week and drive safe, please."

"I will, Mom."

Around midday, Trey left back for school and this time, both me and Chelsea got a text when he made it back safely.

***

"Chickadee, I am so proud of you. It's only your third week of PT and you are killing it. By next month, I bet you'll be running laps," Annalise pronounced, elated, as we finished the session.

Dripping with sweat, I was feeling like a twisted pretzel.

I wiped my damp forehead with the back of my sleeve, then took a swig of water before responding, "Thanks, Anna. It's all thanks to you and your lack of empathy for my weak, sleepy bones. I'll have you know, there were days that I thought for sure you were going to break me in two."

Her snorting laughter echoed through the Turner

home as she packed up her equipment.

"Well, I couldn't just let you sit around, being a lazy bag of bones, sleeping your life away now, could I?"

She gathered the remainder of her things, then placed them in a pile near the front door before she turned back to me, hands on her hips. The humor was gone from her mouth but still playing in her big brown eyes.

"What?" I asked, suddenly feeling like I did something wrong.

Annalise approached a few steps, an accusatory finger pointing at me. "What have you been doing to get so good in a short amount of time? You couldn't have gotten this good in just the little time I have to work with you, so, spill. What's the secret?"

My mouth went a little dry, but I took a quick, inconspicuous glance around the room, down the hall and in the kitchen to make sure Chelsea was out of earshot.

"I've been going on walks. Not a big deal."

The southern belle quirked a brow at me, urging me to continue.

I heaved a long-irritated sigh. "I've been walking the neighborhood at night after Chelsea goes to bed or to work. It's really not a big deal, though. I've been walking great."

She didn't look convinced.

Instead, she grabbed my hand and sat with me on the small sofa against the wall.

"I noticed you wincing a bit more than usual today."

I grimaced, remembering the spill I took the other night when I couldn't catch my footing in time after tripping over a curb. My knees were all scuffed up and joints a little sore, but how was I going to get better if I didn't push myself?

"I'm fine. I tripped over a curb. That's all."

Annalise shook her head, intensity filling her movements and eyes. "No, no, sis. That's not okay.

You're healing, you're growing. You cannot do this alone, especially out on the streets of San Francisco at night. Do you have any self-preservation instincts? What if you fell and hit your head? You're not in the most peak condition to come out on top of an injury like that." She paused, took a deep breath. "You are incredible for pushing yourself so hard. I'm seriously impressed. But there is a difference between pushing your limits and just being stupidly reckless."

I looked away. I wanted to throw my hands in the air and yell, but she didn't deserve that.

"I won't spend another second confined to a bed or house because I can't function on my own, Anna."

"I'm not expecting you to but give yourself time. If you don't, you'll end up doing something else that's gonna take away all that progress you've worked so hard for, or worse. Take away the ability to ever do things on your own ever again."

She rose from the cushions, slinging her bags of equipment over her shoulder. "Just be careful. I'll see you tomorrow."

She left me alone, huffing and puffing. She didn't understand. She had no comprehension of what this was like for me.

Nobody did.

I wasn't going to sit by anymore, letting life run past me while I slept. I wanted to live, and that is what I would do.

I stood from the couch. I needed to change and get washed up but when I entered my bedroom to grab a change of clothes, I immediately halted at the sight of the small, black journal sitting on my desk. It had been left untouched since the night I pulled it from that bag of items Trey collected for me.

I plucked up the book and laid myself out across my mattress, opening to a random page near the end.

Dear Future Husband,

Exciting news, I'm graduating from high school in a few months. It will be nice to get out of here, start anew. I created a facade for myself here at Harbor High that I don't entirely enjoy. I'm quiet, I'm lonely… I'm like a ghost that just sort of floats around, contributing nothing to the world around it.

Given, I did it to myself, but when we first showed up in San Francisco, I was happy to be a ghost. Just dust that fell through the cracks going unnoticed. With everything that happened before, I was happy to be invisible, but I miss what I used to be.

I miss sports. I miss people. I miss life. I don't know how I will ever be able to change, though. I think I'm stuck no matter how much I wish that wasn't true. I think my life is completely altered by the past and there is nothing I can do to change it.

Theatrics and my dramatic, depressing thoughts aside, I did start applying for a few colleges. There aren't any specific schools I want to attend, or anything I specifically want to learn, but I applied. I was accepted by a few of my chosen. One of them being Liam's school. Check the back of the book!

Love,
Maybelle Mason

Now seriously disappointed and depressed, I opened to the back of the book to find a few letters. A couple of them were from schools I didn't recognize, but one I did.

An acceptance letter to SDU—Trey's school.

Hmm… And the plot thickens.

I turned back to the sad page I just read.

Was I really like that?

Deep down, was I prone to giving up, always and forever, a ghost—alone?

I slammed the book closed. That may have been how the old me functioned, but not now.

I refused to allow it. Forget Annalise and forget just walking. I was going to run. I was going to sprint.

25

Little Mason

Maybelle

I was on my way to college, and I was vibrating with excitement. I was going to be staying somewhere else other than my small room, which made me want to weep with joy.

Don't get me wrong, I loved my space and couldn't be more thankful for Chelsea and Trey's generosity in giving it to me—but I needed out.

I finished the book Trey got me on Tuesday and may have shed a tear or two with how darling it was.

Pre-coma me had great taste in literature I learned.

After finishing *Flipped*, I decided it would remain my favorite book post-coma.

The rest of the week, I had nothing to do except read more of the journal. I started from the beginning, instead of jumping around randomly, and I truly got hooked on my writing and stories.

Judging by the entries at the start of the book I wasn't always so doom and gloom. I once was happy, hopeful even. I wondered what happened… I guessed I would learn the more I read.

It was intriguing, reading my biography of experiences I couldn't remember. It felt foreign, maybe like a prank someone was pulling on me until I read statements that resonated with me so deeply it could only be my words.

I read a lot about my mom and our relationship. My mom and I had been close. My brother, Liam, and I—not so much. Despite that, I could feel the love and admiration I had for my twin brother leaking through the pages with each written word.

I read about my time in sports, hobbies I had, and skill sets I didn't know I possessed. There were entries I talked about my thoughts on books and current events of the world. There were more than a couple passages of a fifteen-year-old Maybelle breaking down the philosophical messages of Mary Shelley's *Frankenstein*.

Honestly, I was an odd child. So odd it was almost adorable—in a way. As I continued to read, I started falling in love with not only the child I'd been, but also the idea of this ominous future husband.

This innocent child that wrote so fervently on the pages, fell in love with someone who listened, understood, loved, protected, and valued her on a level that she already mirrored.

A love story that was writing itself before the main characters entered the scene.

It was inspiring.

This little girl—well, me—had fallen in love with a man she never met but knew without a doubt that she would know him when she found him. Because she took the time to get to know him—and maybe herself—through the pages of a blank book.

I wondered if she ever met him. If I knew him before I forgot. How devastating if that girl found her forever pen pal only to lose him to my broken memory.

My eagerness to learn more had me packing the journal with me for the weekend in case I got more time to read.

"How was your last therapy session today?" Chelsea asked as she pulled up the ramp onto the freeway.

I cringed.

Unfortunately, me and Annalise didn't make up from that conversation Monday until the very last second. We were all business the last three sessions, except for the hug I pulled her into just before she walked out the door.

It was quick, but it healed that little tear between us before our relationship as doctor and patient ended. I got her number before she left. We planned to meet up for coffee in a couple weeks as a check-in and I was already really looking forward to it.

My first friend outside of the Turners.

"It was good, but as much as I love Annalise, I'm happy it's done," I admitted as I watched the world speed by my window.

Chelsea giggled. "Yes, it'll be nice not having to watch your poor body get stretched apart like a rubber band four days a week."

I smiled. Chelsea was there for almost all of my sessions, supporting and cheering me on the entire time. Even after I could get myself up and ready on my own for therapy, she was still there. A quiet companion during some of the worst pain I could remember feeling.

I was lucky to have a Chelsea Turner in my life.

"Sorry I'm ditching you this weekend." I brushed a few of my frizzy curls from my face. "We'll have to catch up on our romcoms next week."

Chelsea put her hand on my knee, giving it a gentle squeeze. "Oh, don't you dare be sorry, sweetheart. We'll catch up on our movies, but I want you to have the best time this weekend. Besides, I won't be home either." She punctuated with a wink.

"Oh, okay. What kind of mischief are you getting up to?"

She smoothly lifted and lowered her petite shoulders.

"I have a date." A coy smile pulled at her red tinted lips.

I nudged the woman playfully. "You hottie. Of course

you do. Who's the lucky guy?"

"It's a secret, and this stays between you and me. I'll tell Trey when he's home this weekend." Chelsea tried to shoot me a serious look, but shy humor still lingered.

"I swear, it's our little secret."

A few hours passed, and I was hopping out of the car in front of an apartment building. The sun had set, making it hard to make out all the surrounding details, but the building was attractive enough through the barely lit night.

Even in the limited light, like a moth to a flame, I found Trey leaning up against a wall. His arms were folded as he waited.

He sat up from the wall strolling to me and the car, a pleased smirk on his face. As he approached, I thought he might hug me, but he dipped last second, pulling my bag away to sling it over his shoulder. Then he placed a delicate kiss on my cheek, leaving me breathless.

"Hey, Mom. Thanks for driving her here," he said, bending down into the open passenger door.

"Of course. I hope you guys have the best time," she said.

"Are you sure you're okay making that drive back right now? We can make room for you here tonight."

Chelsea waved him off. "I work night shift. I'm used to functioning on little sleep. I'll be fine. You two get inside and tell Chad I said hi."

He shook his head. "I won't be doing that, but okay. Drive safe. Let me know when you make it back."

"I will—I love you both."

I went rigid. That one was new.

That one phrase sparked a couple of raw emotions to the surface. Emotions I didn't know how to name or address.

"Love you too, Mom," Trey said before shutting the car door and looping his arm around my waist, leading me to his apartment.

Chelsea loved me. I was loved.

Gosh, I had to stop thinking about it or I was going to cry like an idiot right here and that wasn't what this weekend was for. This weekend was for fun, making friends, and being with Trey.

Trey gripped my hip tight against him. "You're quiet. Is something wrong?"

I shook my head, hoping to break free of my scattering thoughts. It didn't work.

"Yeah, sorry. That was a long drive and I'm a little tired." I swung my arm around his back and returned his hold. "But I'm happy to see you."

"I'm happy to see you too. I'm having a hard time believing you're really here. It all feels a little unreal. Anyway, I should warn you. My roommates are all waiting in the living room. They've been looking forward to meeting you."

We went up a few flights of stairs that left me only entirely breathless, but I wasn't crawling by the end, which I considered a win.

Not too far down the hall, after I took a moment to catch my breath, we reached a door. Trey opened it with a key. Through the opened door was a small lit up kitchen and just past that, three young men sat waiting.

Two were on a small couch, practically sitting on each other's laps due to the sofa being too tiny compared to their massive builds. The other man was sprawled out across a large, plush beanbag.

The first man to approach me was tall, leaner than the other men with black curly, cropped hair, and deep brown skin. His smile was wide—familiar.

"Hey, little Mason." He towered over me, pulling me into his rib cage for a bone-crushing embrace.

I tried to peek over at Trey, silently pleading for help, but he was passing us to put my bag on the kitchen counter. When the boy holding me tight, cutting off the circulation, finally pushed back to look at me, silver lined his big brown eyes.

I could only stare awkwardly. Obviously, he knew me, but I didn't have a clue to who he was.

"I'm sorry. Remind me your name," I tried to say gently, but I recognized the flash hurt in his eyes.

"Right, no memories. I guess I deserve that for the last time we saw each other." He chuckled weakly.

Yeah, I wouldn't know because I didn't know when that last time was.

"Sorry." He cleared his throat, taking a long step back from me. "I'm Noah Williams. I knew your brother—Liam. He was like an older brother to me." He licked his lips, before smiling. "It's-uh-good to have you here."

The silence blanketing the air draped heavy over my shoulders as I smiled back. "Happy to be here," I managed to say before twisting to the two unnamed men watching us.

"Alright, which one of you is Larson?"

The tall, incredibly pretty, Disney prince looking blonde before me cautiously pointed to himself.

"Chelsea says hi."

The quiet carried for only a beat before Larson smirked.

"Of course she does."

Then he turned on Trey. "You were supposed to let me know when they pulled up so I could go out and see my girl."

Trey scoffed, but I spoke before he could retort. "And you must be, Bear?" I guessed, taking a step toward the broad and—well—bear-like man.

His shaggy hair and eyes were dark. Thick black hair nearly covered every square inch of visible light skin, and a groomed beard grew along his jaw.

A smile peeked through his facial hair as he bobbed his head up and down. I closed the distance, wrapping my arms around his wide form.

"It's good to meet you," I muffled into his chest.

He immediately returned the embrace, completely cocooning me in a—Bear trap.

"Alright, alright. It's late," Trey butted in, draping his arm over my shoulder. "We all have to get to bed. It'll be a long day tomorrow, so goodnight. See you boys in the morning."

He started leading me down a hallway, but Larson grabbed my arm, pulling me out from under Trey.

"Uh, no. She just got here," he said, my back against his front as his hands cradled my biceps.

Bear grunted what sounded like an agreement while Williams took a step toward me and Larson. "Yeah, what's that about, Turner? You talk about this girl nonstop, then when she gets here, you monopolize all the time? We deserve some Maybelle time too."

Trey stared at his friends, jaw slack with a hint of a smile. "It's late. What do you plan on doing with her?"

Larson, the big friendly giant, leaned his head forward so when I tilted my head back and looked up, we were making eye contact. "Have you ever played Call of Duty?" he asked.

"Nope, but I'm a fast learner."

His grip on my arms flexed. "Okay, Maybelle's on my team."

Bear took a place on the beanbag, remote in hand, while Larson and I sank into the small couch, fitting a lot better than two of the boys sitting on it. Williams sprawled out on the floor on his stomach while Trey pulled up a stool from the kitchen counter. Within minutes, we were all hollering. Larson was trying to instruct me on the functions of the remote while simultaneously yelling at Bear and Williams to do better.

A few times we had to pause the game so Williams and Larson could bicker a bit before resuming. Bear kept to himself, quietly massacring us all repeatedly.

I was terrible at it but enjoyed every second. The weekend was already off to a great start.

We got away with about two hours of video games before Trey pulled the remote from my hands. He tugged me off the couch, toward the bedroom at the end of the hallway, and told the rest of the guys to go to bed.

The final straw was probably Larson and I squabbling over who dropped the ball on who. All while Bear was snoring on the beanbag, and Williams chipped in to support me, if only to piss Larson off more.

"Okay, you take the bed. I'm all set up on the ground," Trey said as he shut his bedroom door behind us.

His room was simple, sleek. His bed was all black covers, pillows with a folded gray blanket at the end of the mattress. To the right side was a black dresser next to a door leading to a private bathroom. To the left was a closet and a frame on the wall of what I guessed was his old jersey, probably from high school. Next to his bed, a nightstand stood with a lamp and a small picture frame atop it.

I walked to it, picking up the picture to see it was the same one on my wall at home. The picture of me, Liam, and Trey on our graduation night.

"You're welcome to change if you need. You can use the bathroom. I'm exhausted so I'm going to crash on my little spot, but if you need anything I'll be right here," he said as he made his way to the left side of the bed, where a pillow and blanket sat on the floor.

I met him there, grabbing his arm, and stopping him from laying out on the makeshift sleeping spot.

"Please, I won't sleep tonight if you're on the ground while I'm in your bed." I pushed him toward the mattress, but he was immovable.

"What's wrong? We do this at home."

I tried to push harder, but he didn't so much as sway.

Dropping my hands to my sides, I looked up at him. "Are you really arguing with me about sleeping in the same bed right now?"

His eyes went wide for a second before a smile overtook him and he lowered himself onto the cloud-like mattress.

"No, ma'am," he conceded, his hands lacing up my hips, pulling me forward until I nestled perfectly between his legs.

"Good," I tried to sass, but it came out all breathy.

Trey's hands splayed out against my sides, flexing before he latched on, pulling me up and over himself with minimal effort. He laid me out beside him on the bed.

We were on our sides, facing one another in the dark. Close enough to feel the other's breaths.

"I really like your friends," I whispered.

His hand lifted, fingertips tickling across my cheek before falling and finding a home intertwined in my fingers.

"Good, they really like you, too."

My eyes were heavy, and the feel of Trey's hand in mine, plus the closeness of his body easily lulled me to sleep. As I drifted, I could've sworn he spoke to me and I might've answered, but I was too far gone to recall those exchanged words.

Instead, I was dreaming.

Dreaming of running, sprinting in the sand. The sea air was combing through my curls. The waves were crashing with the beat of my heart, and I was running down a path.

A path that felt like running home.

***

I woke up early that morning.

Since I didn't get to walk last night, I decided I would have to wake up at the crack of dawn to get in the exercise and go unnoticed by Trey.

I was out the door, shoes on with the sun only just

turning the sky a pale blue. The air had a chill, and the hustle and bustle of the world was quiet, barely waking for the new day. I walked nearby streets, across a couple local parks and through the apartment complex.

It was the longest I'd gone yet, and I was hardly winded.

This weekend just seemed to get better and better.

Then a risky idea lit a light bulb above my head.

Annalise's southern accent drifted in, to warn me against it, but I was already pushing the common sense away. I stood on a sidewalk, a parking lot away from Trey's apartment. The walkway was flat enough.

So, I tried to run. I tried to sprint—two steps in and I was eating concrete.

I fell so hard—I lay there in the middle of the sidewalk for a few minutes, despite the passersby that paused their morning stroll to ask if I was alright.

Fortunately, nothing broke, but my already scuffed up knees were looking a little gnarly. I didn't dare peek at my elbow when I saw blood smeared the sidewalk. Instead, I trembled to my feet and limped myself back to Trey's apartment.

I ever so quietly slid the door open, snuck in and closed it. I readied myself to turn and tiptoe back to Trey's room, but a muffled laugh stopped me dead in my tracks.

"Morning, little Mason."

I turned slowly to see Noah sitting at the kitchen counter, eating a pop tart.

"Hi," I huffed.

He took another careless bite of his pop tart. "Where have you been sneaking off to?"

I stood straight, tying my arms behind my back to hide my elbow. "I was just getting some fresh air."

He made a show of inspecting his pop tart before slanting me a skeptical look. "And your elbow?"

I lifted my uninjured elbow, checking out the skin in

front of him before quirking a curious brow. "What about it?"

Standing from his seat at the counter, Williams finished his pop tart, nabbed a towel from the kitchen counter and wet it under the faucet.

"Come here," he ordered, ringing out the cloth in the sink. I obeyed. When I approached him, he took hold of my arm and cleaned my aching joint.

"You going to tell me the truth now?" he asked; his eyes trained on my nasty scrape.

I sighed, hating having to admit defeat. "I was walking, and I tried to run. Made it two steps before I face-planted."

He snorted, and I swatted his shoulder. "Can you please keep this between us? I don't need Trey being more overprotective around me this weekend."

His dark eyes met mine, holding for only a moment before he went back to work. "I'll keep quiet about your fall if you keep quiet about seeing me eat his pop tarts."

I grinned then hissed when he wiped at a particularly sensitive spot.

He left my side to reach up into a high cupboard where he pulled out a first aid kit. He recovered a bandage and placed it on my elbow. "Alright, good as new."

"Thank you, Noah."

I turned to retreat down the hall, back to Trey's room but Williams cleared his throat.

"You know, I get it; Trey's protectiveness can be a little smothering at times but cut him some slack. It's how he cares for the people he loves and it's nice knowing someone cares."

26

Wrong Time, Wrong Mayhem

Maybelle

I successfully snuck back into Trey's room without being discovered. The athlete was exactly where I left him, draped over the massive, fluffy bed.

After allowing myself a moment to gawk, I retrieved my outfit I planned for the game today and crept into Trey's private bathroom to shower.

The bathroom was cramped, but fresh, white, and clean. The towels he had were big, plush and an elegant black. He even had an air freshener plugged into the wall that was scented with a spicy note I didn't know the name for.

After my shower, I wrapped myself in a towel. I was applying the makeup Chelsea bought me earlier in the week. There was a peachy gloss for my lips, a pink blush and mascara. Chelsea told me I wasn't allowed to use foundation because my skin was too good, and my freckles were too cute to cover up.

I finished applying my blush and mascara but was in the middle of painting my lips glossy when there was a soft rap on the door.

I set down the gloss, tightened the towel around my body, but let the towel wrapped in my hair topple out onto the floor just before I opened the door.

Before me stood a sleepy Trey, who must've just woken up by the look of his half-mast eyes, messy hair, and the imprint of the pillows on his face.

A lazy smile spread first, then his emerald eyes almost fell out of his face as he skimmed my body up, down, and back up again.

He cleared his throat and stood straighter against the door frame. "Wow, uh, yeah, just wow."

I glanced down at myself, then back at him. "Wow, what?"

He gave me a conspiratorial look that told me I should know, but I didn't. I was in a towel. My hair was a wet mess. What was wow about tha—ah.

I was *only* in a towel. Practically naked.

How I brushed over that fact before opening the door, I would never know. My skin was now hot and probably super pink, but I held my ground and gave Trey my prettiest smile.

"Oh, this old thing?" I said in a proper voice as I made to curtsy in the towel like a dress. Except, when I pulled it up at the corner, I nearly flashed him my lady bits and my cheeks turned a deep strawberry color.

I risked a look at Trey, who was watching me with amusement. His eyes doing things to me I wished he would do with his hands.

"Um," I started, needing to ease the tightening tension between us. "Do you need the bathroom? I'm almost done."

He scrubbed a hand over his face and jaw like he was desperately trying to wake himself from a trance. "Nope, just wanted to check in on you. You hungry? Bear is making breakfast; I can tell him to cook you something."

I swallowed, bobbing my head up and down, flirting with the idea of asking him what he was thinking. Or even better, just accidentally letting my towel fall from my hands, see how he handled that.

"Yes, thank you," I said instead, smiling like a little devil with the ideas twirling around in my head.

He narrowed his eyes. His hand took up a spot on the door frame above my head as he leaned in delightfully close. "What's going on in that pretty head of yours, May?"

I held his eyes with mine, not letting my smile waver as I shrugged. "Just thinking about how you might react if my towel just…slipped." I popped my lips with the pronunciation and his eyes went ablaze.

That was my answer. He'd react in the best, most sensational way.

Trey bent down into my space, lips brushing by my ear. "Why don't you and see what happens?"

Didn't have to tell me twice.

I was ready to let the cloth fall, to kiss him with no barriers. Just skin on glorious skin. My fingers twitched and taunted with the temptation when a loud fist pounded on the bedroom door.

I jumped back, hands painfully latching to my towel.

"Turner, Maybelle. Bear has breakfast ready. Get your asses out here," Larson bellowed from the other side of the door.

"Go to hell, Chad," Trey growled back, and I couldn't help giggling.

Larson replied with a curious, "Okay?" And a couple of mumbled remarks we couldn't hear as his loud retreating footsteps echoed down the hall.

Trey faced me again. His features were tight as he put both hands on either side of the door frame and took full inventory of me still standing under him, trembling from the rush.

"Where were we?" he asked, and I smirked.

"I was about to get dressed and you're expected for breakfast."

His brows furrowed with obvious disappointment, lips rolling together. "Right."

We remained like that for a beat. Like we could soak up every detail of the tension-filled moment as we both gave each other one last once over.

Me, with an overly sweet smile, shut the door and Trey, with a hand raking through his messy hair, left the room.

About a half hour later, my hair was a dry, frizzy mane that curled down past my hips.

I needed a haircut.

I walked up to the bathroom mirror to inspect my outfit in the reflection. I brought jean shorts for my outfit, not thinking about my already scuffed up knees and how they were super red and angry looking now. I considered wearing a pair of leggings instead, but it was too hot, and it would drag down the top I wore special for Trey.

I cleaned up my knees best I could, came up with a story about them being rug burns from falling in physical therapy. Then I headed out the door to the kitchen, which smelt like what I imagined the word *home* to smell like. A warm, buttery, cinnamon, vanilla and citrus combination that wrapped its comforting embrace around your senses and welcomed you in to stay.

Trey was sitting at the counter with Larson, while Bear was in a black apron whipping up pancakes with his back to me. When I exited the hallway, Larson was the first to notice and, by his growing smirk, I'd done well with my outfit choice.

Bear turned to face me, giving me the perfect view of the scrawl across the front of the apron that read, *Mr. Good Looking is cooking*. He grinned, one hand holding a pan of pancakes while the other held a spatula.

"Good morning. I love the team pride you got going on."

At Bear's acknowledgment of me, Trey finally turned to see me, and his reaction was everything I'd hoped for. His eyes were wide. A muscle in his jaw ticked while his merciless gaze roamed up my exposed legs to the SDU football jersey Chelsea had fished out of his closet at home for me. It was his first season jersey that had his name printed across the back and his number thirty-three.

I spun to show off the name and number on the back, ecstatic with Trey's focus on my every move.

"You guys like it?"

Larson and Bear both peered over at Trey, who was still silent, shamelessly gawking at me.

Larson cleared his throat. "I think you look hot."

Trey turned with predatory slowness to glower at Larson, who smiled smugly.

"Thank you, Chad." I beamed as I pranced into the kitchen to join Bear. He'd made the fluffiest pancakes I'd ever seen. Joined by caramel syrup and chopped up strawberries with homemade whipped cream.

I went to stick a finger in the whipped cream for a quick taste, but Bear was already there, giving me a solid booty bump that sent me stumbling a couple of steps.

"Get out of my kitchen," he growled through his beard-covered smile.

I chuckled, sucking my finger clean of the dollop of cream I successfully pilfered. I obeyed the chef, leaving his part of the kitchen to sit next to Trey, who was still mutely watching me.

I took the seat, then leaned over and whispered, "Your staring is getting a little creepy now."

He snorted and dropped his face in his hands, muttering something I didn't catch but still managed to make me smile.

After breakfast, the guys spent the rest of their morning packing their things, getting dressed and in the zone for the scrimmage. During which, I lay across Trey's bed reading through my journal while also admiring Trey in his jersey and jeans as he packed and prepared his things.

The scrimmage wasn't until tonight, but before there would be a tailgate party held out in the parking lot. It was planned with ample time for the players to hangout before they would need to head in with the coach to prep.

A few hours later, we all packed up. Trey, me, and Williams in Trey's Jeep while Larson and Bear rode in Bear's Ford Raptor. The football stadium was a less than a ten-minute drive from the apartment and the parking lot was packed to the brim with vehicles, tents, cookers, and people partying.

I thought that seeing this many people together in one place might be overwhelming, but nope. I was made for this. People, events, friends, excitement—I was made for college.

Trey parked the car while Williams hopped out of the back seat to open my door. As I jumped out, he adjusted my sleeve that had ridden up my arm, covering up my bandaged elbow. He shot me a quick wink before throwing his arm over my shoulders, walking with me and Trey into the crowd.

"Hey, Turner. Is Penny coming?" Williams asked over me to Trey, who trailed close by.

"She told me she'd be here, but she's bringing a date."

"No way," Williams called back. "Is it serious?"

We meandered past a loud group of drunk frat boys before Trey said, "Yeah, sorry to break it to you, man. She sounded pretty head over heels for this guy."

His hand wrapped around mine, pulling me out from under Williams's grasp into his own. All while keeping pace through the gatherings of students eating barbecue, drinking and speakers blasting music.

"Damnit, don't tell me that." Williams dropped his hands with a slap against his sides.

Trey chuckled, hugging onto me tighter.

I glanced sideways at him. "Who's Penny?"

He pressed his head into my hair, lips breathing past my ear. "I'll introduce you to her tonight. I think you'll like her."

At the edge of the tailgate party, a massive horde of football players and cheerleaders sat together. Music blared from a few freestanding speakers, and some players, including Bear, were cooking hotdogs and burgers on portable grills.

As we entered the party of blue and gold, a few football players stampeded over to us. They tore Trey from me and Williams from his sulking into a herd of men, leaving me to admire the spectacle from the outside.

The conglomerate of men that unified in tackling, hugging, and fist bumping one another with massive smiles and roaring greetings was a sight to behold.

"Maybelle?" a lilting voice called me from behind.

I pivoted to see fiery, long, red hair, a bright smile, and lots of freckles. Before I could reply or confirm that I was Maybelle, the red hair and freckles had me pulled into a tight, spine-crippling embrace.

I couldn't return the hug before she pulled away, still beaming with a familiar smile. "You probably don't remember me! I was friends with your brother. My name is Penny Howell!" And again, I was pulled in for another squeeze that cleared the air from my chest.

A little flustered, I stumbled for a response as I broke myself free from her cinching arms. "H-hi. Uh, it's good to meet you." I had to shout in order to be heard over the football men, music, and if Penny couldn't hear me, she didn't show it. Her smile was unwavering.

"Hey, Penn!"

Williams left the football fold to sweep the girl off her feet, spinning her around and placing her back to the ground with a smacking kiss on her cheek.

That wide smile of hers twitched.

"Hi, Noah. I'm excited to watch you boys kick some booty this season!" Penny punctuated the statement with a very playful, very friend-worthy pat on the shoulder.

Williams, to his credit, caught on.

He stepped back and resorted to hugging me to his side.

Geez, these people are touchy.

"Did you re-introduce yourself to Maybelle here?" he asked.

Penny nodded. "Yes. I didn't think she'd remember me from—uh… graduation night." Suddenly the atmosphere between the three of us was thick, and I felt suffocated by it.

"Yeah, don't take me not remembering you personally. I don't remember much from that night—or any night before that," I chopped out through a forced grin.

Penny's attention whipped to me. "No way."

I lifted and dropped my chin. "Yup." I brought my finger to my temple, giving it a quick tap. "The doctor said it's amnesia."

Sadness passed over her still somewhat stable smile. "So, you don't remember Liam?"

"Nope," I replied, and probably too quickly with how Williams flinched, and Penny's smile disintegrated.

I cleared my throat, searching for a way out of the conversation I just brutally murdered with the dull butter knife that was my wit. "Where's Trey, Noah?"

Williams took a second to react before pointing past me to where I had spotted Bear grilling. "He's over by the grills. Want me to walk you over there?"

I screamed "*No*" in my head but thankfully had the self-control to give him a respectable headshake. I walked myself over to the big, burly, bear of a man who flipped burgers like it was his calling in life.

"Hey Bear."

"Hey, you. Enjoying the party?" he asked as he flipped a patty.

"It's alright. Do you know where Trey is?"

He twisted. "He's being held hostage over there." He

pointed with the spatula to a truck that Trey leaned against and next to him, tracing her fingers along his bicep, was a pretty, brunette cheerleader.

It was a strange feeling that burrowed and made a home for itself in the pit of my stomach. A feeling I couldn't name, but a feeling I refused to let grow.

Strutting with all the confidence I didn't feel, I approached Trey and the cheerleader. When he noticed me, he didn't look guilty or shy away. He smiled at me like he was seeing me after a long time apart.

That feeling in my stomach became a little less weighty.

I parked myself on his side, facing the other girl. "Hey, handsome. Who's this?"

His smile faltered as he shot a fast glimpse to the girl who stepped up closer to him. His mouth opened and closed for words, but the brunette beat him to it. "Oh my god, you're actually real."

I pinched my lips together, unsure of how I was supposed to respond to that. She didn't give me a chance to before she said, "I'm Juliette. Trey's friend."

I slanted Trey a look. He was already grinning at me. Reaching down, he laced his fingers with mine. He brought my hand to his mouth and placed a kiss to my wrist. All while keeping his eyes locked with mine.

Juliette's attention followed the touch before returning to Trey with a forced smile. "I'll see you after the game." She got up on her tiptoes, her chest pressing into his shoulder as she whispered, "Score a touchdown for me." She winked at him and strutted off.

I needed a shower after that encounter—actually—after all the encounters tonight.

"Who's she?" I asked again, eyes still on her retreating form.

Trey's face quirked sideways at me. "Are you jealous, Mayhem?"

Oh, honey. Wrong time, wrong Mayhem.

"No." I pulled my hand from his and folded my arms across my front. "Not jealous. Just confused."

His brows furrowed. "Confused about what?"

He turned so only his shoulder leaned against the truck, facing me fully. It was difficult to stay focused with him all pretty in his jersey like this, which just seemed to bother me more.

"Don't play dumb with me, Turner. I'm not in the mood."

I pasted my back against the truck, my focus forward, with Trey in my peripheral.

"May, Juliette means nothing to me. I promise."

When I didn't respond, he lifted from the side of the truck to stand in front of me. I turned my gaze toward my feet, but he caught my chin between his forefinger and thumb, forcing me to meet his eyes.

"I promise," he said again.

I didn't trust myself to open my mouth and say the right things, so I only managed a sorry half nod.

"Come here," he said, bringing me against him. I obeyed, allowing myself to be engulfed in his warm embrace.

"Maybelle!"

Trey didn't let go of me as he peered back over his shoulder to see Penny trotting up to where we stood.

"Hey, sorry to interrupt you two, but you boys need to get going and us girls need to get some good seats," she said as she tossed a red lock of hair over her shoulder.

Trey pulled back from me to give Penny a hug.

"Good to see you Penn. Take care of my Maybelle for me, please." He winked at me, then joined the parade of blue and gold football players on their way to the locker rooms while Penny led me into the stadium to what she called "the best seats in the house". Right down the middle of the bleachers and directly behind the boys standing on the sidelines.

Penny talked through the whole first half of the game,

telling me all about her good friend Daniel, whom I would have the privilege of meeting near the third quarter. She spoke about how she did cheer but quit recently. How she didn't know what to do with her education and touched on her rocky relationship with her mom.

I listened, bobbing my head now and then to show I was listening. Then I had the worst thought cross my mind as I heard everything Penny had to say.

In one conversation, I knew more about Penelope Elizabeth Howell than I knew about Trey Turner—or myself, for that matter.

After halftime, she leaned over to me. "Are you thinking about coming to school here?"

I tied my fluff of curls into a knot on the top of my head. "I don't know if I can. I got accepted before the accident, but I don't know where I would live or how I would make it work."

I winced as I watched Bear lay waste to a small lineman that was poorly paired against him on the line.

"Girl, live with me."

I got whiplash from how fast my head spun to look and make sure I wasn't being punked, but there, Penny sat, that big smile plastered to her lips.

She must've seen the disbelief etched into my face, because she said, "I'm serious. We have two other girls in the apartment that keep to themselves, but we have an opening in my room. You could totally live with me. I could even get you a job with me at the coffee shop I manage. Come on, it would be perfect!"

Again, the plot thickens.

"I appreciate that. Maybe I could get your number? Keep in touch about it?" I asked, suddenly overwhelmed with the possibilities.

Penny was gleaming as she pulled her phone out.

We exchanged numbers, and the night suddenly seemed so much better.

"Monedita," a deep voice called out over the rampage of the crowd. It was Penny's turn for a bit of whiplash as she twisted to the very tall, very dark, very, very handsome boy strapped in a leather jacket and black denim.

Penny leapt from her spot, right into his arms.

She broke the hug and gestured to me. "Daniel, this is Maybelle."

Daniel's black eyes pierced me with a look I couldn't identify. There was sadness, there was happiness, and there was a lot of familiarity. This boy knew me. I stood, holding a hand to him, but he ignored it as he pulled me into his tight hold.

"It's good to see you, Maybelle," he said into my ear, and I easily held him back.

The scrimmage ended with the buzzer ringing through the field. Done with the stiff bleachers, I jumped to my feet. My new friends weren't as eager to move. Daniel was holding Penny's thigh while she clasped firmly to his arm, her head resting on his shoulder.

"I'm going to go find Trey and congratulate him. I'll text you, Penny. It was good to meet you, Daniel!"

They waved me off, and I ran onto the field with the rest of the students, weaving through the crowd. I first found Larson, who had two girls under his arms. I skimmed by Bear, who was speaking to what looked like might be his grandparents.

After a long bout of searching, I finally found Williams, but no Trey.

"Hey, little Mason," he called. "Follow me. I'll help you find Turner."

I followed him down the field, holding to the hem of his sweaty jersey so we wouldn't get split up. When we broke through the crowd to the outskirts of the field, Williams and I both halted.

The sight before me had that unknown feeling coiling up in my gut again, festering into a dreadful heaviness as

I watched my Trey kiss Juliette for all to see.

27

Game On

The tailgate party was a mess.

Not at all what I imagined Maybelle's first outing to be. After being ripped from Maybelle, Juliette had cornered me. She kept me isolated by bringing up topics and questions about the upcoming football banquet. Reminding me that I would need a date and other stuff I didn't care to pay attention to. I only focused on finding Maybelle in the crowd and when I saw her stomping up to me and the cheerleader, I almost fell to my knees before her.

Once the cheerleader bailed, I could see the interaction had affected Maybelle more than she was letting on. I wanted to hold her, comfort her, tell her there was nothing to worry about. But all too soon, I was pulled away again with the team and she to the bleachers.

The scrimmage was a success.

Bear destroyed our opponent's defensive line. Larson was a commanding voice that worked well with the quarterback. Even Williams got to take to the field for the first time this season as second string QB, proving to the coaches, the team and the rest of the school that he was far from a failed investment.

Liam would be proud.

The game ended, and friends, families and coaches rushed the field. I stalked about the flood of bodies, looking for Maybelle. I said "hi" and acknowledged the families of my brothers as they approached me, but I kept it brief.

I needed my girl. I needed to get her home, spend some much-needed time with her, and fix this *confusion* she had. Oh, I'd fix it alright. I planned to show her just how not confusing my feelings for her were.

My head was on a swivel as I made my way to the outside of the crowd. Hoping to get a better visual of the entire mass of people.

"Trey!"

In answer, I turned around to see a flash of a blue and gold cheer uniform before arms noosed around my neck and my face was being devoured.

My body tensed, and my lips were stationary as my brain tried to catch up with the assault. I latched onto the hips of my assailant, grabbing, pushing, fighting the urge to chuck her like a rag doll.

When she finally released my face from the steel trap, lips smeared in red lipstick, Juliette's angular face filled my vision. The rest of the cheer team circled us, shaking their pompoms.

All the surrounding noises were a blurb of ruckus. The only distinct sound I could make out was the shouting of my name.

"Trey!" Juliette called over the tittering and cheering of the pompom girls around us. "Be my date to the football banquet!"

The proposal sounded a lot more like a command than an invitation, and I knew she intended for it to come off that way. The cheerleaders stopped shaking their sparkly pompoms, and the audience went eerily quiet.

So many eyes were on me.

I couldn't make out any familiar faces in the surrounding crowd.

I was stuck.

At a loss, I managed to bob my head up and then down. Juliette's freakishly long arms tied around my neck once again as she reached for another kiss on the lips. This time I was prepared and dodged with the turn of my head, letting her land one on my lower cheek.

Before pulling away, she spoke low enough that only I could hear her above the crowd, "Sorry, but I'm not *that* patient."

She grinned, shot a wink at someone over her shoulder and bounced her way to the other girls without another word to me. As they trotted away, more of the faces in the gathering around me came into focus.

Maybelle's face was hard, eyes misty, as she held to Williams's arm like he was an anchor keeping her stable in the tsunami of emotions that were taking over her bright features.

She couldn't have seen the whole thing... She couldn't have seen Juliette kissing me. I glanced at Williams and by the worry lines in his face—I knew they saw everything.

Too fast... I couldn't catch up with the mess unraveling before my eyes. It was too fast.

I made to approach her, to slow her down. I just needed one second. One second to explain, to fix, to ease her worries, and erase those doubts. I just needed a moment. I needed it all to slow down.

I managed a few steps toward her before she turned her back on me, walking away on wobbly legs. I kicked up my speed, getting myself between her and her escape.

"May, please, just pause one second. Let me explain—" The look on her face destroyed me. She peered up at me through tear-filled eyes, face flushed.

I did this.

God, this night was falling apart right through my fingertips, and I was helpless in salvaging it. I lifted a hand to her face, but she jerked away.

"I'm getting a ride home with Bear. I'll see you at the apartment," she said, avoiding my gaze.

No, no, no, she needed to stay. We needed to talk. I needed to take care of her.

I stepped toward her, and she immediately backed away. "Trey, please," she implored, a small whimper escaping through her harsh tone. I wanted to die right there.

I stapled myself to the ground, against every fiber in my being begging me to hold her, to not let her leave me.

Instead, I saw Bear approaching. I faced my brother and nodded for him to join us. "Can you get her home?"

To ask made me sick, but if this is what she wanted— I'd do it. I'd give Maybelle anything she wanted. Even if what she wanted was less of me.

Bear nodded without hesitation or questions asked. He slung a burly arm over Maybelle's shoulders, leading her off and away from me.

A hand landed on my shoulder, and I turned to look at Williams. "You got a little something right there," he said as he raised a hand to his own lips. He placed his forefinger there, tapping, then to his cheek as he wiped his thumb across his jawline.

I followed his lead and swiped the back of my hand across my lips to find cherry red lipstick staining my knuckles. "Oh fuc—did Maybelle see?"

He didn't need to answer me. I knew, but it still gutted me when he nodded before giving one last sorry pat on the back.

Williams also ditched me for a ride with Bear, leaving me alone in my Jeep. I sat staring at the steering wheel, baffled by the last half hour of a hailstorm I was just thrown through.

Right now, all I knew was I needed to get to her. I needed to talk to her, to plead my case.

I put my car in drive and sped my way home.

When I entered the apartment, there was a quiet,

hollow feeling. The guys were all in their post-game lounge wear. Larson and Williams were at the kitchen counter. Bear was lying out on his beanbag.

I stalked in and dropped my bags on the kitchen floor. "Where is she?"

I turned for the hall, but Williams was up from his stool and there with a hand on my arm. "She needs some time alone. Give her a minute. Sit down and tell us what happened."

Hesitating, my eyes darted from the hall and to my friend. I knew he was right, but it still took every ounce of self-restraint to follow him to the couch.

Bear sat up, resting his elbows on his knees while Williams and I sat on the minuscule sofa. Larson listened from his place at the kitchen counter.

I put my face in my hands, letting out a defeated groan. "If any of you laugh, I'll kill you."

The three men shared looks as I cleared my throat. "I honestly don't know what happened. All I know is that cheerleader practically assaulted me. I was looking for Maybelle and then all I could see, and feel was Juliette. She was like a muzzle I couldn't get to release my face. And while my mind was going a mile a minute trying to deal with what was happening and everyone watching, I agreed to be her date to the football banquet."

"Well, just tell her you change your mind," Larson offered.

Williams shook his head. "He can't do that."

Sighing, Larson folded his hands together. "And why the hell not?"

Williams looked at me, like I would know what he was talking about, but I was just as clueless. "Juliette is Coach's niece," he said, as if that was explanation enough.

When Larson and I both continued to stare back at him, he slanted a pleading look at Bear.

With a resolute breath, Bear said, "One of our

defensive linemen was benched tonight because he rejected a date with Juliette." He paused, letting that sink in. "He has a girlfriend." His dark eyes focused on me then as he asked, "Are you okay?"

I shook my head, more out of frustration than answer. "I'm fine. This—Juliette—none of it's important. Maybelle is my priority. I need to make sure she's okay."

Williams shifted in his seat. "I'm gonna be honest and not sugar coat anything because I love ya. But without knowing everything you just said that scene looked pretty bad. Give her some space. She was pretty upset. She didn't talk the entire way home and locked herself in your room as soon as we got back."

I dropped my face in my hands again, muffling my loud, discouraged groaning.

I needed to at least try.

I stood from the couch. "Pray for me, boys. I'm going in."

I was already down the hall when Larson called out from behind me, "God speed, brother."

I reached my bedroom door and knocked. Nothing. I clicked my knuckles across the door a few more times, and finally heard a soft, "Come in."

It was cold, but I was sweating profusely.

I nudged the door open to see Maybelle sitting on the edge of my bed. Her hair was damp from the shower. She was dressed in a fitted white tee and black yoga pants.

She didn't look at me as I entered. I let the door shut behind me, but instead of approaching her, I leaned my back against the closed door.

"May. Can we talk?"

She sat up straight, twisting to meet my gaze with a smile that didn't reach her eyes.

"Sure," she answered, her tone chipper, which terrified me more than if she were standing in the corner of my room with a knife. She patted the mattress next to her, inviting me to join. I cautiously approached, settling myself next to her on the bed.

She sat herself sideways, facing me fully. "What would you like to talk about?" she asked.

I dragged my hands across my pants. "I wanted to explain what happened tonight. Juliette, she—"

Maybelle cut me off with an eager flap of her hand. "Oh, Trey, please, you don't have to explain," she said earnestly.

Drawing back, I scowled. Of course I needed to explain.

I opened my mouth to try again, but she stopped me. "There's nothing to explain because you don't owe me anything. We kissed a couple of times. That's it. It's not like we're officially together or anything," she said this so carelessly. Like my world wasn't falling apart with every word coming out of her mouth.

A couple of kisses and that was it? Is that really all she thought we were? Had I fumbled? Had I not made myself obvious?

"No, May. We're a lot more than a couple of kisses," I insisted, but she was already shaking her head.

"We barely know each other. For crying out loud, I don't even know your middle name." She turned her head, squeezing her eyes shut before saying, "I just think we need to start over. Get to know each other, and just be friends."

I was losing her; she was running away to hide behind her walls, and I couldn't keep up. Maybelle had spent years dreaming of running away. I knew those dreams. I knew what she desperately tried to escape from—and right now—she was escaping me.

She fidgeted with her hands on her lap and whispered, "I just—we don't know each other, Trey. We're more strangers than we are friends."

I could feel the knife she stabbed through my heart, making the wound bigger, spilling with all the hope I had gripped to the last year watching her sleep.

"That's not true." I reached for her hands, but she pulled them away.

"Yes, it is, Trey. We've barely gotten to know one another since I woke up with you living here. And you said, word for word, that our friendship before the accident had only been blossoming."

"No, you don't understand," I shoved out. "We—I've been waiting for this, for us." My voice was hiccuping like a prepubescent teen, but I couldn't help it.

I'd been so patient, so hopeful, so ready to have my chance with the girl from the journal… The girl I'd fallen for through words—and it was all shattering right in front of me.

"No, I don't think you understand. It's not the same for me because I don't remember waiting. You're beautiful, god, you're amazing from what I've seen in the last few weeks. But that's all it's been for me. A few weeks."

"Maybelle, please—please just—" I began, but she stood from the bed, pivoting on her heel to face me.

"I don't think you're getting how tonight went for me, Trey, so allow me to put it plainly. I met your friends alone while you were off chatting with some cheerleader. I then sat with your friend and learned more about her in an hour than I've learned about you since living in your home.

"And do you know how stupid I felt wearing your football jersey like a smitten girl, while I watched you and said cheerleader kiss for the entire stadium to see? I was humiliated but realized that I have no right to be jealous or confused because we aren't dating. And as of right now, you and your mom are all I have in the world. I can't lose you both if things ever went really wrong between us."

She sucked in a deep breath and took a step toward me. "We can't do this—I can't do this anymore. I-I just don't know you."

And that there was the kicker. I finally had her. The wait was supposed to be over. The woman I was beyond in love with was awake and alive right in front of me and she didn't know who I was. While I was cursed and blessed to know every intimate detail of her.

I was the joke, and this was the punchline...

Maybelle heaved a long sigh before she walked towards the door. "I'll let you have your room. I'm going to sleep out on the couch."

Closing my eyes, I took a second to gather myself before standing. "No, you're not." I nabbed a pillow and the extra blanket, tucking them under my arm. "I'll take the couch; you sleep in here. Be ready to head back home in the morning."

Ignoring the ache in my body to pull her close, I left before she could get her mouth to open to argue.

When I slugged back into the living room, the guys were still in their spots and waiting. Bear gave me a forlorn smile. Williams stared aghast at the bedding under my arm while Larson turned away to hide his laughter in the crook of his elbow.

I dropped my stuff on the puny couch, already feeling the crick in my neck and back.

"I'm using your shower, Larson and I'm borrowing a change of clothes," I said as I made my way to the first bedroom on the right. Larson was shouting, but I didn't hear nor cared to hear as I shut and locked the door behind me.

***

I woke before the sun tinted the sky a grayish blue. My body felt as if it had been trampled and beaten in the night.

That little couch would've been uncomfortable for Maybelle's tiny body to sleep on. So, my massive, over six-foot, football body didn't stand a chance and, to make matters worse, I had a migraine that threatened to cripple me.

I sat up from the couch, stretching out my achy body as I thought back to last night.

Maybelle's "friend" agreement was crap, and she knew it. I could move slowly if that was what she needed. I could be patient. I waited by her bed for an entire year. I could be her friend, let her learn what I already knew.

That she and I were endgame.

I brushed my hands over my face groaning with exhaustion. We had to be okay. We would be okay.

But what she said about losing me and Mom came rocketing back. Maybelle was scared. She was scared to ruin things so badly she would lose the only family she had.

Could I really push that line of her anxieties?

The slight creak of hinges cut through my thoughts as the front door crept open and… Maybelle snuck in. She let the door click closed before she turned around to see she wasn't alone.

She jumped when she at last saw me sitting up on the couch. "Geez, I really need to get better at that," she huffed through a startled breath.

I couldn't help the smile she always seemed to pull from me. Even if she did practically smother my heart with a pillow last night.

"What were you doing outside?" I asked as I stood to my full height.

She stared back at me, her lips pinching together as she folded her hands behind her back. "Uh, I was just on a walk."

I quirked a curious look at her, and she avoided my gaze. I took a step forward and her round eyes met mine. My grin tipped at the sight of her still reacting to my every move.

"Mayhem, I'm your friend. You can tell me where you

were sneaking off to this morning." I couldn't help the twinge sarcasm in my tone.

She squirmed under my scrutiny. Her hand lifted to tuck a lock of hair behind her ear, and that's when I saw red.

I was upon her in one long stride.

Maybelle backed up flush against the door. "Trey—"

I pulled her hand out from behind her back and up for me to see. Small rocks and dirt poked from the crevices of her shredded palm.

I held tight to the hand I was already inspecting as I reached with my other hand around her back to pull free the other palm that was also torn.

"What happened?" My question came out as more of a command. Instead of shrinking from my tone, Maybelle scrunched her freckled nose up at me.

"Nothing, I tripped. That's all," she said and tried to pull her hands away, but my grip on her didn't waver. I lifted her arms and her sleeve fell back, revealing a bandage on her elbow.

My focus darted to the wound, and she heaved an annoyed breath. I shifted my hold to her forearm, allowing me the mobility to turn her still pressed against the door.

Barely a day-old, nasty scrape was sitting under the bandage, tainting her perfect skin. I remembered then the sight of her scuffed-up knees from yesterday. I had meant to ask about them but seeing her in my jersey distracted me.

I pressed Maybelle's back against the door again, barring her in with my hands planted to the wood surface. "May, sweetheart, I need you to start explaining and no lying, please."

She remained bold as she licked her lips, gaze locked with mine. "I was practicing," she said plainly, but her brows rose in challenge. And just like that, I was back in that first week, terrified of my fragile Maybelle, breaking, or falling asleep. Seeing the tumbled bookcase and that angry, purple bruise on her skin.

I dropped my head against the door, my forehead just above her shoulder. This girl was going to be the death of me. I sucked in a few deep breaths before I pulled back enough to look her in the eyes.

"So, you were out there on the streets, alone, practicing walking by yourself, before the sun was up? Correct?"

She nodded coolly.

"Have you been doing this back at the house or just here?" I asked, my hackles rising with each breath.

"I go out every night to walk after Chelsea goes to work or bed. I've been fine though," she puffed through her rapid breathing.

I chuckled harshly as I grabbed her hand and showed it to her, palm up. "Maybelle, this is not fine."

She tore her hand away and pushed from the door, bringing us almost nose to nose. "I'm not made of glass, Trey. I want to walk. I want to run. I want to do things on my own. A few scrapes and bruises are inevitable. Get used to it."

For a long moment, we stared one another down. The space between us was mere centimeters. Our breathing was quick and short, and our heart rates thrummed between us.

As pissed as I was with the infuriating, reckless woman in front of me, I wanted to kill the remaining distance between us. I wanted to press myself into her, lace my fingers in her hair and hold her against the door as I kissed her.

But I wouldn't.

I wouldn't push past this; I would respect the boundaries she set.

I could win her back in other ways. Show her that there was no way for her to ruin or lose anything with me, that she was stuck with me whether she liked it or not because we belonged together—Hold that thought.

Maybelle's hands curled into my shirt. She wasn't pulling me close—not yet—but I could see the war. The desire and restraint battle within her.

She wanted me.

Oh, I wanted to give in. To fall into her silent pleads, but an idea crashed like lightning against my skull.

This. This was how I would get her back.

I wouldn't get her back playing friends or letting her sideline me. No. I was going to make this feisty, stubborn girl see me. See us. I didn't need to win her back because she was already mine.

I pushed forward, leaving no doubt that I too would give into temptation. Maybelle fell for the bait, closing her eyes, tilting herself up, inviting me to kiss her. That's where I halted.

"This whole friend thing isn't sounding so fun now, is it?" I whispered.

Her eyes opened wide just in time to see me wink and push off the door, leaving her still pressed into the immovable surface.

You want to be friends, Mayhem?
Fine. Game on.

28

Big News

A week had passed since that long, awkward ride back home to Chelsea. I almost kissed the ground when Trey and I arrived home, freeing myself of the painfully quiet vehicle. Trey seemed unbothered by the tension that made me bite my right thumbnail down to a nasty nub.

Trey and Chelsea went out to dinner that Saturday, early evening, for their mother-son date, and I was beyond thankful for it.

I didn't see Trey again before he left back to school. He took off early that Sunday morning.

He didn't text or call me that week. I'd be lying if I said I didn't miss him, but if I learned anything from my weekend at college, this was how it had to be, or I would risk everything.

Not only was my stupid, vulnerable heart on the line, but acknowledging that I hardly knew Trey caused a lot of unrealized insecurities to tunnel through my chest.

The main one being that the Turners were the only individuals in the world offering to care for me, to give me a place to come home to, support me and be a family for me.

If things went bad between me and Trey—I could

lose the only people I had in the world.

And Chelsea—Chelsea loved me.

Would she still love me if her son and I crashed and burned? I liked to think I knew them well enough. That the Turners would never abandon me. But there was a deep-rooted fear inside me, needling me with the idea that I was being too trusting.

Anyway, this week was far too busy to think about Trey.

Fat lie, but that's beside the point.

I'd been cooking up a plan, finalized all the details Thursday but was waiting to announce my news until Trey was home to hear them in person.

I was giddy with excitement as I slipped on a fitted, spring leaf green, capped sleeve tee with whitewash jeans in the bathroom.

Today was a good day, and I knew it would only get better because I did the impossible this morning.

I ran.

Granted, it was more like a bouncy, fast walk that was a spectacle to witness and left my joints screaming. But it was enough, and I didn't fall. Next up, sprinting, and tonight was the first step to getting there.

I paused, making eye contact with myself in the bathroom mirror, giving my image one last once over before exiting.

New, more apparent freckles smattered across the bridge of my nose and tops of my round, rosy cheeks. My hips were fuller and the green top I wore made my eyes favor a sea foam color. My arms looked powerful under the fabric. My honey gold curls coiled around me as I combed my fingers in the roots and fluffed to add volume.

My hair was now my favorite feature of myself. Earlier in the week, Chelsea took me to get it cut. The hairdresser shortened the curls from past my butt to my mid back. The length was still elegant and long, but the coils sprung with so much more excitement at the loss of the extra dead weight.

I no longer looked plagued by remnants of exhaustion or appeared stale with the lack of life.

I was pretty.

Jumping at the sound of the front door opening and closing, I overheard Trey and his mom greeting one another in the kitchen.

It was time.

I left the bathroom. The house was filled with the amazing aroma of a new pasta recipe Chelsea was trying out and I already knew by the taste of the air that it was going to be life-altering delicious.

When I entered the kitchen, I found Trey straining the boiled pasta noodles with his mom. The universe must hate me because he somehow got prettier in the last week.

His muscled arms bulged against the fabric of a plain white tee. His wavy hair fell a tad longer, and messier across his brows. The shadow along his jaw line was thicker with scruff.

Focus Maybelle, focus.

Chelsea and Trey were speaking low, recapping his week of training and preparing for classes to start next week.

My hands were trembling. I was going to explode my secret all over the place. I sucked in a deep breath and held it in as I made my way to set the table.

I was so enthralled with my big news and how I would present it, I briefly forgot how tensely uncomfortable things might still be between me and Trey until I reached for the utensils in a drawer to his left.

Simultaneously, he reached for a serving spoon, causing our hands to make contact. I instantly halted, but Trey was smooth as he let that light touch continue to slip up my wrist, gliding it across my forearm and off my elbow. Sending a ruckus of shivers through my bones while he took a step back, giving me a good view of his smirk.

"Hello, friend."

The greeting should've been upbeat. Something I imagined Penny would've called out to me in that high-pitched chipper voice of hers, but Trey's husky baritone made it sound so unbearably, frustratingly sensual.

Like something I'd want him to whisper into my ear as he pinned me against a wall, creating a physical storm between us that would drown—no—annihilate the term "friend". Leaving no chance for a platonic survival—*Pause, delete, delete, delete.*

Not the type of thoughts to be having for a guy who kissed another girl in front of me or whom I just recently banished into the friend zone. Nope, I needed to pull my mind out of the pleasurable, very dirty gutter and focus.

No matter how fun and enticing that gutter may seem.

Trey Turner was off limits. End of story.

I relaxed and slanted him my own mocking smirk as I gave him a light, friendly pat on the beefy shoulder.

"Hey, buddy," I chirped back, and his face fell into a grimace.

Smiling, I grabbed the dinner utensils I previously attempted to retrieve, setting forks and spoons on the three place mats at the small dining table.

I didn't listen to Trey and his mom as they continued to catch up. Instead, I pulled out my vibrating phone to see a couple new messages pop up across the top of the screen.

Penny: Girl. I am literally quaking.

Penny: Please tell me you told them.

I bit my lip to hide the glee that threatened to give me away too soon.

> **Maybelle**: Sitting down with them right now. Call you after.

Penny's super friendly peppy-ness had startled at the football scrimmage. But I grew fond of it through the night and more attached as we continued to talk in the following days.

"Who are you texting, Maybelle? Is it Penny?" Chelsea asked as she approached with the pot of pasta straight off the stove.

I told Chelsea about Penny when she asked how my weekend out of town had been. She was thrilled. She even joined me on a facetime call with Penny the other night to introduce herself.

Dropping my phone into my back pocket, I nodded. "Yeah, she wanted to call me later."

I ignored Trey's curious gaze. I wondered if it surprised him to hear I wasn't entirely friendless without him.

Chelsea's demeanor was sunshine as she took a seat at the table. "I'm so glad you made a friend. Especially with Penny Howell. I met her mom once. Bit of a stern lady. A little difficult to talk to, but Penny has always been so sweet."

I sank into my chair, draping my napkin across my lap. Perhaps this was the perfect moment? No sense in waiting until after the meal if we were already on the topic.

"I'm glad you feel that way, Chelsea," I started, my

heart suddenly crawling up my throat. "Because she asked me to move in with her and I said yes."

The emotional shift in the room was so abrupt, I regretted not planning out my presentation of the big news more. Chelsea's expression fell with wary concern while Trey's brows furrowed.

"Penny lives in the dorms as a student. You can't just move in," he said, breaking the silence.

His immediate assumption that I didn't know that or hadn't thought that far ahead was almost insulting. To the point I wanted to snark back with a sassy comment or two, but I bit my tongue.

"I understand. That's why I enrolled at SDU. I guess I had applied and was accepted before the accident. I actually found my acceptance letter in that bag you got for me." I smiled while the crease between Trey's brows deepened. "At the scrimmage, when I met Penny, she said they needed another roommate. So, I called the school on Monday. They're allowing me to start this semester since I had a pretty good excuse for missing those first semesters. I start next week with everyone else."

I looked at Chelsea. I already knew that Trey wouldn't be totally on board for this right away. He would want me to be kept safe at home.

So right now, Chelsea's opinion and approval mattered more than anything. She had helped and pushed me so much. If she didn't think I was ready for this, I would listen.

Her considering eyes studied me. "Will you live close to Trey?"

I nodded. "I'm pretty sure it's less than a five-minute walk from his place." I turned to Trey, but he didn't confirm, deny, or show any signs he was listening to the conversation. His focus drifted to a random spot on the far wall.

I twisted back to Chelsea. The worry lines in her face

had softened a fraction, but her lips still held tight in consideration. She squirmed in her chair before letting out a deep breath.

"Just one more thing," she said. "You'll still come back home to visit, right? Because I'm not changing that room. It belongs to you, and I'd love to see you in there reading your books on weekends when you're not busy and continue our romcom marathons together."

I choked back the sudden emotion that threatened to launch me into a full-blown sob. Chelsea had a gift in saying things that made me stupid emotional.

It was embarrassing.

"Of course," I tried to say in a normal tone, but the words escaped in a sputtered whisper.

Her uncertainty immediately broke into a bright grin. "How exciting," she exclaimed. "This is such fun news. I'm so proud of you. And now I have two college kids to brag to my friends about."

She gestured for my plate. I handed it to her, and she dished a beautiful helping of the pasta. She then reached for Trey's plate, dishing him up as well.

"It'll be nice to have you driving home together for the weekend instead of Trey making that drive alone," she said as she returned him his dinner plate.

I peered back at Trey, who was still watching me. His dark-framed green eyes slipped down to my hands that sat folded on my lap. The old, healing scrapes on my palms burned with the attention.

He never should've caught me sneaking back into the apartment that morning. It was humiliating enough that I had eaten asphalt in front of a sweet old couple on their morning walk.

I tucked my hands under my legs.

The rest of dinner was spent with me explaining the job I had lined up working with Penny. Then Chelsea and I planned a shopping trip to get room decor, clothes, and other necessities I would need in my new apartment.

My heart was full to bursting as she and I schemed together.

Trey excused himself early from the table to shower while Chelsea and I made our way to the couch to watch a romcom she picked.

She didn't stay long enough to finish the movie though. she had to change into her scrubs and leave for her shift at the hospital. Once she was gone, I retreated to my room and pulled my phone out. The phone only rang once before Penny picked up.

"Excuse me, where've you been? It was cruel making me wait for an update this long."

"I'm sorry, Penn—But I have good news."

Before I could explain the good news, she squealed a pitch that made my ear drums ring.

"Oh, my gosh, Belles! I'm so excited! This is going to be the best semester yet. Mark my words!"

She was practically screaming over the line, and I couldn't help the giggling thrill that bubbled from me.

I had no doubt of that promise.

Knuckles rapping against my bedroom door cut our conversation short. Seeing as the football player and I were the only one's home, I heaved a tight breath before I bid Penny goodnight.

"Come in," I said, and Trey entered my room.

"You still on the phone?" he asked.

"I was talking to Penny, but we're done."

He ran a hand through his shower-damp curls, standing at the foot of my bed. His eyes remained forward while a muscle in his jaw ticked.

"Are you doing alright there, buddy?" I asked, but he didn't look at me. Instead, he grabbed the journal from my desk and sat on my bed. He flipped opened the book to a random page near the end, skimming his gaze over the written words.

"Have you read it all?" he asked.

I sat up, tucking my legs underneath me and reclined

my back against the wall with the three picture frames above me.

"No. I left off on an entry from late middle school about a summer camp trip that went awry."

He lit up and in one movement, flipped open the journal to the exact page of said entry.

"That's one of my favorites. I would pay money to see little Mayhem get so annoyed with a camp counselor she graffitied a cabin wall with a Sharpie. I can't believe the counselor punished you by making you scrub the wall with your toothbrush. That's just too damn funny."

His hair bounced with his laughter as he pointed to a specific place on the page. "And I quote," he started, "*I scrubbed that wall for almost two hours. I don't understand why Counselor Katy, aka, the wicked witch of the west, has such a problem with me. But it was my responsibility to warn future campers that had the unfortunate luck to have her for a counselor with my artwork.*"

His grin was wide when he looked at me.

"I'm surprised you didn't get sent home for drawing a giant depiction of her as a witch, riding a broomstick across that wall."

He turned to another spot in the book.

I shrugged. "She must've been a witch of a woman. How else did they know my drawing was about her? I didn't say anything in there about labeling the artwork. Or I'm just that good of an artist."

Trey snickered without looking at me. "You might have a point with her being a witch but do our eyes a favor and leave art alone."

I scoffed. "Please, I can't be that bad."

He slid me a look. "We had art class Junior year together. Even your stick figures are abominations."

His eyes fell back on the book. I scooted closer to him, reading the passage over his shoulder.

Dear Future Husband,

I've made it to high school!
I thought I'd try out for the volleyball team. Don't get me wrong, basketball is my sport, but I thought I would take a hit at volleyball since they had an opening, and I didn't have anything going on until the winter season when basketball starts.
So here I am.
Tomorrow is our first game of the season, but it's out of town. Seven hours out of town, to be precise, and to make matters worse…
The school is making us share a bus with the football players!
I know, regular girls would be flipping out to be hanging out with the football players all day, but me, well…
It just means I have to be in the same enclosed space as my brother, his loud teammates, and all the guys I really like aren't on the football team.
They're all the nerdy, sweet boys.
The football players are so full of themselves, and they are going to be very stinky on the way home after the games. I am cringing just thinking about it. Well, wish me luck, I have to get to bed, goodnight!

Love,
Maybelle Mason

Trey snorted while I grimaced as I finished reading the last line of the passage. Little Maybelle was trying a little too hard for the *I'm not like other girls* façade with that one.

"I'm trying not to take offense to how fourteen-year-old Maybelle felt about my kind, but it was pretty ruthless."

Refusing to let on that, I agreed with him full-heartedly, I rested back, my shoulder brushing his. "Fourteen-year-old me was a smart girl. Football boys are loud, trouble and *very* stinky."

He glared. "Take that back."

"Can't," I said, crossing my arms over my chest, not missing the mischievous glint in his eyes.

He set the book off to the side, and I tensed with anticipation.

"Tell me, May." He turned toward me, his broad chest taking up my view. His sweet, minty breath clouded my common sense. "Do the sweet, nerdy boys still do it for you?"

His tease was stupid and childish, but I still swallowed hard, losing all sense of self-preservation as I held his stare.

"Absolutely," I croaked, the lie coming out as unsteady as I felt.

He shrugged, his grin skeptical as he pulled away, leaving me feeling cold with his absence. "You keep telling yourself that, sweetheart." He opened the book back up and was reading through another page when I finally gained my composure.

"Trey," I began, but he didn't look at me. "Are we good?"

His head cocked sideways. "Why? Whatever do you mean?"

"Don't play dumb, Turner. I mean since last week. We haven't talked, and I wanted to make sure we're good."

He reverently closed the journal and put it back in its place on the desk before turning to me. "If we're going to talk about this, then I need to say a few things with no interruptions. Can you do that for me?"

I rolled my eyes but proceeded to nod and wait for him to continue. Satisfied, Trey straightened, locking eyes with me. "First off, my middle name is Tory."

A strangled quiet fell between us, held together only by my tightly pressed lips, but I couldn't contain it long.

I erupted with jeering laughter. "Excuse me?"

He rolled his eyes. "Yeah, yeah. Laugh all you want."

And that I did, shamelessly.

"Trey Tory Turner," I said, testing the sound. "Yikes."

He playfully shoved at me. "Now you know why that wasn't the first piece of personal information I divulged to you."

Yeah, I understood the hesitation.

He got a faraway look in his eye before he continued. "It's an old name. Mom said it was the name of a great uncle that served in some war. I didn't care to remember the specifics because I was too busy feeling betrayed when she signed me up for my first high school football season using my full name."

I slapped a hand over my mouth. "She didn't."

He tilted his head to me, brown waves falling over his green eyes. "Oh, she did. My team got real kick out of it." He chuckled, shaking his head. "They wouldn't let me live down the shame—until Liam…" his voice trailed off as he faced forward. "Your brother gave me the nickname, Triple Threat. Said that even if my name was the cruelest joke he ever heard a parent play on their kid, it didn't mean it had to be something I had to be ashamed of."

"That's sweet," I sputtered out lamely, a little lost in his eyes. "That's what you needed to tell me without interruption?"

"No, but out of all the things you had to yell at me about last week, not knowing my middle name seemed to mean a lot to you."

My lips pinched together again, holding in each of the racing thoughts of my mind. He didn't let me stew for long though.

"What I need you to hear me say, without interruption is that what you saw last week between me and Juliette was nothing. It was actually a fucking crime, but that's beside the point. If I had the choice, May, I never would've kissed her."

He paused, letting that last part sink in while I bit

down on my questions. "I also think the friend thing you want between us is bull and I have no doubt that you know it too, but I'm willing to play along, for now. You want to be friends? You want to get to know each other more? Fine, but I'm not going to pretend my feelings for you aren't more than friendship."

I went utterly still as Trey inhaled a deep breath and exhaled. "I once told you that this, us, was end game for me and I meant it. I want you, May. I've been waiting for you to be ready. I waited in high school. I waited through your coma, and now I'm willing to wait until you're ready to accept it or remember that you want me too."

I had no words for the admission he just sacrificed before me. The silence that spilled between us was my only ally and I held to it as I gathered my thoughts.

One thought did itch at the forefront of my doubts and as much as I wished I could ignore it, I couldn't.

"Can I ask you something?"

He nodded and I heaved a breath. "Are you going to that football banquet thing with Juliette?"

The silence engulfed us once again, except this time it was stifling. Trey's eyes widened then closed as his head bowed.

That's what I thought.

I did want him, and I had no doubt he wanted me too, but I was a clueless cannon ball that just blew up his reality. And I was planning on integrating myself into more of his life when I moved.

I wanted to get to know him more, create a real foundation for a friendship I could depend on, despite the memory loss. But more than anything, I wanted to learn more about myself, apart from my forgotten past. Without the fear of losing my only support system as I did so.

Trey offered a much-needed subject change as he reached for my hand, tracing the lines of my still healing palm. "I do have one request for when you move out there."

"And that is?" I asked, wary of the way he studied the fading scrapes and bruises in my skin.

"No more walking or trying to run by yourself."

I snorted and tried to pull my hand away, but he didn't let go.

"Calm down. I'm not asking you to stop. I'm just asking that you stop going out alone. I will walk with you every day. Morning, night, rain or shine I'll be there. Just, please, don't go out alone anymore."

"Hmm," I hummed. "That's a very friendly offer."

He shrugged. "What can I say, I watch out for my friends." The tension in the room dissipated as I laced my fingers with his.

"Fine. Deal."

29

Moving Day

I can't do it, Penn. I'm not strong enough."

"You got this, Belles; I believe in you."

"Your faith is misplaced; I am a weak, weak woman."

"Just look away." Penny supplied.

I continued to gawk. "Easier said than done."

Larson sauntered up to where Penny and I stood in the far corner of our shared apartment.

"Couldn't help but notice you two ladies staring. What's caught your atten—oh, Maybelle, you naughty girl."

He followed my stare to the sweaty, shirtless, tanned, pack of abs on Trey as he carried a box into the living room.

"You're one to talk, Chad. I heard you begging Bear to take his shirt off earlier," I said, as I slanted a smirk at him.

He wasn't fazed. "I can appreciate my boys looking like chiseled gods without it being weird, May. You can't, and your ogling is teetering on the point of scandalous." I scoffed, but Larson wasn't finished. "Besides, I harass Bear because it's fun. See how he's the only man here who has left his shirt on in this sweltering heat? Poor boy is shy, and his scowl is so funny under all that fur."

As if on cue, Bear faced us, his bushy brows and beard downturned in what I guessed was a frown.

Trey, Noah, Chad, and Bear came over that morning to help me move my things into my new apartment room I now shared with Penny. It was mid-September. While it should've been a nice day, a heat wave hit. So, we were moving boxes, my bed and whatever supplies Chelsea packed me, in ninety-degree heat.

Larson was the first to lose his top, showing off light skin molded into a canvas of lean muscle. Williams was next and gorgeous, with brown skin taut against athletic strength.

But as pretty as the other half-naked men were, I couldn't tear my eyes away from Trey. I was lost in my wonderland of muscle daydream when—

"Careful there, May, or I'll have to charge extra for the view."

My mouth snapped shut, and Trey's crooked smile revealed a dimple.

I tipped my nose up at him. "Oh, did you think I was looking at you? I was actually looking at Williams."

"Do not bring me into it, Mason," Williams huffed over a stack of boxes in his arms.

Trey turned his smile on him. "I can't blame her. You are looking extra fine today."

Noah dropped the boxes inside mine and Penny's room as he swiped the sweat off his brow. Then he smooched the air in Trey's direction, partnered with a wink.

"You boys are too funny," Penny gushed as she unloaded a box in the kitchen.

Feeling a little useless, seeing as I wasn't exactly strong enough to carry much of anything yet... I put myself to work on unloading the boxes of clothing into my closet.

With a box in hand, Williams followed me into the

bedroom.

"How does it feel to officially be at college, little Mason?" he asked, setting the box on my bed, and opening it with a box cutter.

"Surreal," I sighed.

"It's fun to have you here. Not to sound sappy but having you here with us—like—heals a part of my soul." His mouth clicked shut.

I turned to look at the shirtless mountain of a football player. He pinched his lips tight, like he too couldn't believe he said something so corny.

"Huh?" I finally asked.

He rolled his eyes. "I'm not Bear. Talking about feelings isn't my strong suit. I was just trying—I don't know what I was trying to say."

"No, don't give up now! It was just getting good," I pressed.

He heaved a long, annoyed breath. Obviously pained to keep trying to explain himself. "Liam was my hero. He was there for me when I had no one, even though I was younger. I knew I would follow him after high school into college. It was supposed to be us three here. Trey, Liam, and me. Now that you're here, it just feels…right, I guess. Complete."

He covered his face with one of his enormous hands.

Sobered by the serious tension of his words, I said, "Thank you, Noah. I'm happy I'm here too."

I placed my hand on his forearm, giving it a quick, coaxing squeeze. A comfortable silence carried, but the sound of a motorcycle engine rolling in shattered it.

Williams's head fell back as he groaned.

Daniel Aguilar had arrived.

I smiled. "Daniel is really nice. You should try getting to know him." Though I had only spoken to the quiet boy twice.

The first time was at the game, when Penny introduced us. The second was when Penny and I Face

Timed one night so she could help me apply for financial aid. He was on the phone with her and even then, he only said, "Hi," and a final, "Bye," to me as we hung up the call.

Despite that, I recognized what Daniel didn't say with his words, he made up for with his actions. While Penny spoke, he always kept constant contact with her. Like a protective hand on her leg, or an arm around her shoulders.

Williams side-eyed me. "I know he's nice, Maybelle. That's the problem. He's my competition. I can't like the guy."

"Well, have you tried talking to Penny about how you feel?" I asked.

He nodded. "I tried after the scrimmage. It didn't go very well. I guess there isn't really a competition. She's pretty smitten with that guy."

I felt bad I couldn't encourage my friend to keep trying. While Williams was great and would treat Penny with all the love and respect she deserved... Anyone with a pair of eyes could see she and Daniel were it.

"Chin up, you're great and I know you'll find someone just as great."

His fallen face didn't change, but he nodded standing from the bed. "So, what's the deal with you and Turner?" he asked, and my accusatory eyes narrowed at him.

"Nice subject change."

He shrugged and waited for a response.

"There's no deal. We're friends and that's all," I said, busying myself by hanging my shirts up in the closet.

"Friends?" Williams barked. "I doubt that will last long."

I paused mid-fold of a shirt and shot him an annoyed look, but he wasn't looking at me. I followed his gaze to Trey's football jersey that poked out from under a few other shirts.

Well, crap. I definitely forgot to give that back... Or

may have just forgot to hide it a little better. Either way, Noah Williams caught me red-handed for a second time.

A nervous giggle escaped me. "Weird. How'd that get there?" I leaned across the clothing, plucked up the jersey, and tossed it under my bed.

Williams shook his head at me as I returned to hanging up my clothes. "You're a weirdo."

When I didn't answer, but my deep red blush was enough proof of how I felt, he spoke again, "Are you playing friends because of what we saw between him and Juliette?" He approached, leaning a broad shoulder against the wall next to me.

"That and you all forget that I'm new here." I bit out, my embarrassment feeding into my tone with more harshness than I meant. "You guys may know me, but I don't know you. I barely know myself and I have a lot to learn before anything can happen between Trey and I again."

He continued to stare at the side of my face, crossing his arms over his bare chest. "Okay, you have a point," he conceded. "But the funny thing is, none of us really know you either."

I paused and looked up at him. "What do you mean?"

"We all knew Liam, but you and I, I think, only spoke twice before the accident. I believe you met Penny once and Trey was close with your family. But I don't think you guys talked much until that last week leading up to the accident."

I bit the inside of my cheek, considering this before I said, "Well, kudos to you guys because I never would've guessed. I thought for sure we'd all been at least friends before. Considering how welcoming everyone has been."

"You were super quiet. Hard to get to know or even talk to kind of quiet. Before, it made no sense to me that you and Liam were siblings, let alone twins. Except for the same hair and all that, of course. But now—" He paused, looking like he might be stumbling over his emotions. "I meant what I said earlier. It really is like having Liam back. You're easy to be friends with like he was. The only difference is, you're a lot more enjoyable to look at."

A surprised laugh erupted from my throat at the sudden shift in the mood. "That's good, I guess."

Williams's brilliant white smile was verging on heartbreakingly gorgeous as he chuckled.

"You know, random thought, but what if you and I went to this football banquet thing together?"

His eyes tapered skeptically at me.

"Don't look at me like that. We'd go as friends. I just thought better go together for a fun time instead of sulking over what we don't have right now," I explained, gesturing with my head out to the living room.

From where we stood, we could see Penny embracing Daniel and Trey unpacking boxes with Bear.

Williams appeared to be considering the offer for a moment but shook his head. "No. I can't do that to my boy."

I snorted. "Your boy is taking a hot cheerleader to said banquet. Trust me, he'll be fine."

"You know he doesn't want to go with her, right?" He adjusted himself so his back leaned flush against the wall.

"Then why is he going with her?"

"Juliette, unfortunately, is our defensive coach's niece. When Coach found out they were going together, he made a massive deal about it. Then he practically threatened bench time if Turner were to do anything to upset her. He's taking her out of obligation. And—let's be real—he's too good of a guy to flirt with the possibility disrespecting her or Coach. Even though, he has every right to after the shit she pulled that night after the scrimmage."

He put a hand on my shoulder. "Let me talk to him. A friend date to the banquet would be great, but I want to make sure he would be cool with it first."

I nodded. "Okay, just let me know."

Suddenly, a fully dressed Larson popped his head in past the door, a wide smile splitting his face in two.

"Hey, boxes are unloaded, and I'm starving. You're buying me lunch, May. Let's go." And he was gone, down the hall, trying to put Bear in a headlock who was entirely unmoved by the effort.

Williams sat up from the wall, putting a large, bare arm around my shoulders. "Don't worry. It's on me."

Dear future husband,

I've been in therapy with my mom and Liam since the move to San Francisco. The therapist we've been seeing is having me do an exercise. One that requires me to tell someone I trust my story…

Besides Mom and Liam, you're the only one I have. But it's time I've told you the whole story. The story I've struggled to find the words for until now.

Dad died when Liam and I were too young to remember, leaving Mom completely alone. As a young, single mother of two, twin babies, she hastily threw herself into a new relationship, barely knowing the man.

Richard Amos had been with our mother for years. We lived with him, and he helped raise us, but that man never earned a spot as our father.

Richard was a man made from money and a spoiled life. He was always clean shaven, dressed in neatly pressed attire and hair combed back. But we didn't know Richard for the way the world saw him. We knew him for his frenzied anger, his unforgiving words and vengeful actions.

Mom told me in earlier years, he'd been good. She even loved him at one point. I can't remember any of the good, no matter how hard I try. I only remember the bad.

I guess that's what trauma does. It's the wine-red stain, soiling the white silk of life, tainting enough of the surface to leave you questioning what color the cloth originally was.

We each experienced our own personal layers of hell through the years and the three of us did it quietly. I still don't understand if it was out of shame or us trying to protect one another.

Either way, we isolated ourselves.

I watched Mom deteriorate in that relationship. While Richard may have started out as someone she loved, he manipulated and abandoned her for the bed of many others. After everything, Mom explained she endured the relationship out of necessity. Staying there to give Liam and I a roof over our heads while she went through school.

I think that was part of it, but I think a larger part of her also hoped he would stop. That he would choose her.

A wish I knew she regretted after the night it all changed.

Richard was always vindictive and aggressive with his words when Mom wasn't looking. But when she started school and was gone for hours at a time, that was when the abuse escalated.

That night, Mom was gone at a study group for school. Liam was out with friends, leaving me home alone with Richard.

The times Mom was gone, I usually hid in my room, mentally running away to whatever book I was reading or writing in this book to you. I remained quiet, praying to whatever listened that I went unnoticed by the predator stalking outside my bedroom door.

But my prayers went unanswered.

My bedroom door splintered open as Richard forced his way in. I was frozen stiff on my bed, clutching to you—this book—as he stumbled toward me.

He was already yelling at me when he reached my bed and I was already somewhere far, far away. In my mind's eye, I was on a beach. When his hand grasped my ankle and yanked at me, I imagined the tide cascading over me and pulling me into its deep embrace.

When his smell swarmed me, I held my breath, letting the waves swallow me. I held tightly to the scene in my head. Running away, just as I always did when his violent hands gripped and pulled my skin. I desperately listened to the fictitious sound of water lapping and not the vicious words he tore at my soul with.

But when the back of his hand caught my cheek, I tumbled back into reality. A reality where I was alone, blinking past the stars in my vision to see him standing over me.

I knew better than to plead my case, because no matter how innocent I was, I would still be punished. Instead, my body locked up, and I held still.

Hold still. Keep quiet. Obey.

Richard's arm was up as he prepared to hit me again. I didn't run to the beach in my head this time. I tilted my eyes to this journal, crumpled pages splayed out on carpet where it fell.

I'm done dreaming. *It was the one thought I had, the one I accepted as I closed my eyes.*

Except Richard's hit never landed. He was yelling when I opened my eyes. Not at me, but at Liam. My brother was in the doorway of my room, blue eyes wide as he looked at me and then Richard on top of me.

Liam didn't speak; he didn't blink as he strode to Richard. In one hit, Richard was on his back. In two hits, Liam had Richard on the run.

After that night, the police were involved, an investigation ensued, papers were filed, but Richard Amos was never found.

Refusing to believe he's gone for good or keep us anywhere he can reach us, with a new understanding of the full truth, Mom packed us up and we ran. For a brief time, fleeing our life is what finally brought us all together, turning us into this unstoppable unit, to escape that man and the pain he caused us.

But the unity didn't last long.

Today was our last therapy session all together. Liam dropped out.

I understood why. During the session, he admitted to what life with Richard had been like for him. It wasn't like what Mom, and I went through. His was different. Richard didn't just hit him, but he found him at night, climbed in his bed and abused him in secret.

Liam said that he never had the courage to stand up to Richard, not until he saw him with me. And it shattered something inside me to hear him say it…because I think if I'd known what he was going through, I too would've been brave enough to finally speak, to fight.

We are both strong for each other but not for ourselves.

He isn't the only one who's pulling away.

Since the move, Mom and Liam have taken off with their newfound freedom, creating beautiful, successful lives for themselves. They're making friends and building communities, while I keep falling back down in that fathomless pit of self-loathing and shame.

I closed up again, refusing to taint their happiness with my own darkness. I keep it all in.

I accepted a fate that night. I made a choice.

A choice that haunts me.

I feel like I'm fading. Like I'm outside of my body. A ghost coasting through my very long, very dreary existence.

Hope.

It's a strange concept. One that you embodied for me for so long. Not a hope for someone to want me, or a hope that I'm worthy of love.

You were the hope that I could love and live without chains. That I could give my heart freely without fear. You were a dream on a sandy beach. A path I took without hesitation.

I'm hesitating now. My faith is falling short. Breathing has become a chore. Waking up is a battle and living is the war.

I'm lost and I'm not sure I know the way anymore. I'm scared he won. I fear that I lost the one thing I wouldn't let him, or the past take and I'm not so sure where that leaves me.

Maybelle Mason

30

I Want to Live

Trey

It was too early for this, but I was up and waiting outside Maybelle's door at the ass crack of dawn to walk with her.

Since she moved here, we'd been meeting up in the early hours of the morning. School had started back up. So, after our walks, I ran to strength training with the team. Then I had classes and ended my days off with football practice.

Only two weeks and some days into the semester, and I felt like I could hardly keep up. As exhausted as I was, though, I wouldn't give up these early walks with Maybelle.

They were the highlight of my day.

I hadn't lied to her when I promised I would walk with her every day, no matter what. Morning, night, rain or shine, I would be there… For as long as I breathed, Maybelle Mason would never walk alone again.

She emerged from her apartment, snicking the door shut. Her golden curls were fluffed haphazardly from a long night of sleep. She wore a white sweater tied low on her hips. It hung over attractive blue leggings that paired with her matching sports bra.

She spun from the door, eyes shimmering azure, with

a bright grin taking up her entire face.

"Am I going to be spending the rest of my life waiting on you, May?" I felt my smirk mirror hers as I watched her freckled nose scrunch up at me. It took every ounce of my limited control not to grab her and kiss every damned freckle on her face.

"I couldn't find my other shoe."

Naturally, I peered down to see she wasn't saying she had struggled to find her shoe but later found it and was now ready. No, Maybelle couldn't find her shoe, so she now wore two different sneakers on each foot.

"You realize you could've worn the sneakers you had the matching pair for?" I asked, the timbre of my voice wavering on a chuckle.

She shrugged. "The thought crossed my mind, but not until after both shoes were already on my feet." She brushed by me, her steps bouncy. "Come on, Turner. We're burning daylight!"

"There isn't any daylight to burn yet," I grumbled under my breath, glancing at the stale blue of the waking sky.

Of course, Maybelle Mason was a morning person.

It would've surprised me if she wasn't.

It only took me a few long strides until I was by her side, and we started on our regular, roundabout path. One that took across campus, through neighboring apartment buildings and right back here.

"How are classes going?" I asked.

She was biting the inside of her cheek as she focused on walking fast. She took cautious steps that wouldn't bother her knee.

Couple mornings prior, she stumbled at the end of our walk trying to climb the stairs to her apartment. She bruised her knee. Maybelle didn't leave her fallen spot on the stairs for at least ten minutes. She stayed put, fuming with frustration at the lack of control she had over her tired limbs.

I hadn't said anything. I only joined her on the steps, allowing her to rest her head against my shoulder while I wrapped her up in my arms.

I still thought she was pushing her body too hard, but with each morning walk, I started to understand why she did it.

Maybelle was the embodiment of what it meant to live and not just survive. Even after the mess of losing her family, losing her memories, and her coma she wouldn't sit still. She refused to let one day pass her by without progress, accomplishment and memories made.

Maybelle wanted to wake up, so she did.

Maybelle wanted to walk, and she did.

Maybelle wanted to run... And I guess you could call whatever the hurried, super jerky walk she did, "running." Now, Maybelle wanted to sprint, make friends, go to college, create a name for herself and she would... She already was.

"What in the world even is algebra?" she finally griped in answer to my question I almost forgot about. "I don't know if I'm dumb or what, but I'm screwed."

"Have you tried finding a tutor or a study group?" I asked, as we slowed our pace.

"Yeah, I met up with some other students after class and I couldn't follow a thing they said. They could've been speaking a foreign, dead language and I wouldn't have known the difference."

"Do you want help? Like a private tutor?" I asked, hiding the smirk that teased my mouth.

She didn't notice.

Her eyes remained tracked on the path ahead.

"If you know someone, send them my way. I'll take all the help I can get."

Now my smile was on full display.

"Okay, I can fit you in on Sunday mornings. We can meet before each of your exams to make sure you are ready for them," I planned while Maybelle side-eyed me.

"Thanks, but no."

"And why not?"

"Because."

"Mayhem."

"Turner?"

I sighed, irritated with the laughter bubbling at the back of my throat. "You're being complicated for no reason."

She walked faster. "I'm not trying to be annoying; I don't want you to help me because I know how busy you already are."

I was honestly surprised. Surprised that she wasn't saying no to be stubborn but thoughtful of my loaded schedule. Not that Maybelle wasn't usually thoughtful. Since deciding to be just friends, she made it a mission to make it impossible for me to take care of her. Like if she were to agree to any of my offers of help, she'd let me in too close.

"I know Sundays are your only day off. I don't want to take up the little time you have. I appreciate the offer, though." She began to skip-walk which was what I determined to be her attempt at a run.

I widened my walking strides to keep up.

"Maybelle."

I knew that would get her attention; I rarely used her first name. The name was too cute, too adorable to call the infuriating woman I found so unbearably attractive. And calling her Mayhem always brought a gleam to her eyes that challenged me in the best sort of ways.

She stopped her trot. She quit moving all together, facing me fully and gave me her undivided attention.

I would need to use that strategy more often, apparently.

"As your friend, I would want nothing more than to spend my free time with you. Especially if it will help you pass your class," I vowed, the platonic word tasting bitter on my tongue.

She stared up at me with considering eyes.

"Are you sure?" she asked.

My god, yes, woman.

I'd spend every waking moment with you if you'd let me.

"Yes, May."

***

"I got it!"

The apartment door tore open. I couldn't help the slight disappointment I felt when it was Penny smiling on the other side of the door.

"Oh, Trey. Hey, what's up?" she asked, blatantly taking in my disheveled appearance.

I'd been at the gym, working myself into a frenzy. Maybelle had only been in my world for a couple of weeks. She was barely a few minutes' drive away, and it was killing me. I was trying to give her space, respect her friend boundaries, but tonight I surrendered to what I wanted.

Just this morning I'd been with her for our walk, but it wasn't enough. I needed more. I needed all of it, all of her.

Earlier I was antsy. I wanted to call her, ask her how her day was. See if she wanted to move up the tutoring we scheduled for Sundays to today. But I controlled the urges and instead threw myself into strength training at the gym.

That hadn't lasted long. Before I knew it, I ditched my equipment in the middle of a set, threw my stuff into my car and sped straight to her. Still dressed in my sweat-drenched shirt and shorts.

"Hey, Penn," I breathed, still winded. "Is May here?"

Her smile turned smug as she opened the door for me. "Come on in, Loverboy."

I followed her into the apartment to the room she and Maybelle now shared. She knocked twice on the door before entering. "Hey, hope you're decent. You have company."

Following Penny into the room—hoping the exact opposite—I was pleased to see Maybelle wasn't indecent in the terms of modesty. But she was in the sense that she was caught wearing something truly delicious.

"Huh—" Penny huffed as she glided about. "I'm surprised to see you reading something other than one of your dirty little romances."

Locking eyes with me over the pages of the journal she was reading, Maybelle's face burned a fiery red.

"Wow, Penn. Thanks for the heads up," she drawled as she closed the journal. Then she stood from the bed in nothing but the tiniest shorts I'd ever seen and—my football jersey.

The jersey had looked good on her the day of the scrimmage, but now, it was a whole new kind of attractive. Her fluffy blonde curls fell over the front and her tiny cotton shorts showed off her tan, strong legs.

Shrugging, Penny flung herself out on Maybelle's bed with a satisfied grin. "Oh, I'm sorry, Belles. Hey, Trey, do you think you could get her more jerseys, or at least a few shirts with your name and number on them? Belles wears this one to bed every night and I'm afraid she'll wear it out in no time."

Maybelle looked about ready to maim the sweet redhead. I stepped between a furious Maybelle and her scheming friend, acting as a willing shield.

"Absolutely," I said, which had Maybelle's eyes flicking up to me. "I'll give you my last name any way you like."

She didn't speak, but her nose scrunched, and her eyes rolled as she took a long step back from me. She perched on the edge of Penny's bed that lined the left wall and I followed, taking the seat beside her.

"Oh, my gosh, you two are just the cutest," Penny crooned, sprawling herself out across Maybelle's sheets.

"Our Belles here really is such a stunner, isn't she, Trey?"

"She really is," I answered, ignoring the way Maybelle glared at the side of my face.

Sitting up from the bed, Penny pinned me with a wide-eyed, blue-gray stare. "Has Maybelle told you about her admirer?"

"Penn," Maybelle groaned in warning.

"Shh, Belles. Trey should know who his competition is."

Shaking her head, Maybelle stood from the bed, giving me the sweetest view of those damn shorts. "I'm going to take a shower."

Before she could take one more step toward the exit, I had her hand in mine. She fought for only a second before following my tugging until she was back at my side on the bed.

"Tell me all about this competition," I encouraged Penny as I leaned back. Reaching behind Maybelle, I played with the coiling curls falling down her back.

She grumbled a few colorful words under her breath as she slouched against my touch. Penny's smile doubled in size.

"Okay, okay, so at the coffee shop Belles and I work at, there was this guy on her second day that came in and ordered from her. I'll say this, he's older, but he's handsome. He's got gorgeous blonde hair and dresses all fancy. Like in pressed slacks and stuff. But that's beside the point. He tips Maybelle every time he comes in, just for taking his order!"

She paused, slanting Maybelle a smile. "But the craziest part is that ever since that first day, he's been at the coffee shop every single day. The days Maybelle isn't there, he grabs his coffee and leaves. But the days she's in, he takes a seat at one table in the far corner of the shop and just watches her."

Furrowing my brows, I looked to Maybelle, who seemed totally unbothered by this. I turned back to

Penny and asked, "What's his name?"

Maybelle peered up at me, confusion in the lines between her brows while Penny chirped, "Rick, I think. That's what we write on his orders. Right, Belles?"

She didn't look at Penny. Her eyes were on me. I twisted, meeting her blue-green stare with my own.

"Why do you want to know his name?"

I shrugged. "So, I know I have the right guy when I come into your work to teach the prick it's not polite to stare."

"Please," she scoffed, breaking our eye contact. "You'll do no such thing. He hasn't done anything wrong and I'm not so sure it's me he's staring at. I've caught him eyeing Penny on more than one occasion."

"I don't care who he's staring at, May," I said, nudging her with my shoulder. "I'll still kick his ass."

Penny giggled and checked her pinging phone before launching up from the bed. "Oh Trey, you're such a dreamboat. Take care of my bestie, will ya? I gotta go. Daniel's here to pick me up. I'll see you both later."

With a blown kiss, she left the room and shut the door. Leaving Maybelle and me alone, still sitting side by side on Penny's bed.

"You stink," Maybelle muttered. "Did you come straight from the gym?"

Before I could answer, she was on her feet, headed for the closet. Again, giving me a fantastic view of her in those shorts.

"I—I was—Yes, I was at the gym." Desperately trying to refocus I asked, "What's got you in a sour mood?"

She turned to hit me with a look. "I'm not in a sour mood."

Smirking, I gestured to the general area above her head. "Yeah, tell that to the dark cloud you got hovering over you."

She rolled her eyes, but they didn't return to me. They

fell heavily on the journal resting on her mattress.

Peeling my eyes from her beautiful legs to the book, she watched like it might grow fangs and eat her, I stood to grab it. She turned away then and her rummaging in the closet had me halting where I stood.

"What're you doing?"

She didn't look back at me as she continued to sift through hangers and clothes. "Looking for a different shirt."

"What? Why?" I barked, sounding a lot more frantic than I meant to.

She looked at me over one shoulder before returning to the closet. "Because I want to wear something less— irritating."

"Rude."

"What was tha—" she started to ask but was cut short with the surprise of me pulling at her by the back of my shirt.

"Trey," she growled.

"Mayhem," I mockingly growled back.

Puffing out a breath of surrender, she stopped rebelling and joined me on her bed.

The twin bed was propped in the far, right, back corner of the room. Allowing me to rest on the pillows and rear wall while she sat perpendicular to me. Her legs draped over mine, with her back against the side wall.

"What are you doing here, Turner? Didn't I just see you this morning?"

I grabbed my book from the comforter. "Yeah, but I missed you."

As she squirmed for a comfortable position, I opened the book to an entry she wrote about her and Liam learning to drive. She'd gotten the hang of it fairly easily and passed her test on the first try. Liam, on the other hand, ran over every single cone and had to retake the test three times before he finally passed.

God, I missed that guy.

"What are you reading?"

I couldn't see her face over the pages as I flipped to a passage closer to the beginning of the book. "I read the entry about you and Liam getting your licenses."

Snorting, Maybelle moved her legs from off me and settled next to me. Resting her back along the wall, giving her a better view of the scrawled-on pages. "That was a funny one... You've read the whole thing, right?"

I looked away from the book to Maybelle. She wasn't looking at me, but her hands were fidgeting together on her lap as she stared forward.

I nodded.

"Can you tell me what I was like before the accident?"

I'll admit, I didn't know what to say. I wasn't expecting her to ask that. So, I said the first thing that came to my mind, "Quiet—I think you preferred books over people. But while I and many others had mistaken it for shyness, I think it was heaviness."

I didn't think that exactly made sense, but Maybelle nodded again, seeming to understand.

I knew where this was going, and it hollowed my gut out as those perfect blue-green eyes found mine. "So, you know what happened to her—I mean—me and Liam?"

I did, and it was devastating to think about. To think my best friend and this beautiful girl had gone through so much and no one knew—*none of us knew.*

Maybelle was always reserved, off in her own world. We just thought she preferred the solitude. But Liam... There was no guessing of the hell he had endured in his life because he was always good, always "happy".

I felt sick the day I got to the sections of the book that Maybelle admitted to the cruelty they survived.

The sick feeling surfaced more from a desperate place of helplessness. I could only read and relive those horrible moments with an innocent little Maybelle. Unable to fix or do anything about it because it was already done. I was powerless, clutching to the book the way I wanted to hold her in a time where she felt utterly alone.

"Yeah, May, I know," I whispered.

She sighed, dropping her head to my shoulder. "Is it bad that I don't know how to feel about it?"

"What do you mean?"

Her shoulders nudged up and down in a lazy attempt at a shrug. "I don't know. It's depressing and infuriating. I'm angry at that man for what he did to those children—for what he did to me, but I'm also angry with myself."

Twisting, I turned to look down at her. She lifted her head with my movement.

We were close. So close I realized I had let the book settle on my lap and rested one hand on the bare expanse of her thigh.

Careful, Turner.

Not the time, nor the place.

Slipping my hand down to a more appropriate place on her knee, I looked her in the eyes. I was desperately trying not to ruin this moment between us. She was finally opening up, which was something she hadn't done since the Juliette fiasco.

I refused to lose the moment, especially to a topic as serious as this.

"Why are you angry with yourself?"

Maybelle's exterior was numb as she dropped her gaze from mine to the book on my lap.

"She gave up. She fell apart. She stopped trying to live a happy life—*I* stopped trying to live. And while I don't understand my own..." She shook her head incredulously. "*Trauma*—I can't help but think that deep down I'm weak. That maybe I'm meant to quit."

Her eyes returned to mine.

She watched me, and I took the moment to watch her right back. Then I reached for the book.

"May I?" I asked and Maybelle nodded. "While you

slept, this book was the only thing I had. The only thing that gave me hope. Hope that I would one day get to know the girl in the writing. I read it every day. Took it with me everywhere. I practically memorized the whole thing."

I opened the book to the very last page and handed it back to her. "Out of everything, this entry was my favorite. I read it every time I was feeling too alone."

Maybelle looked from me to the book and swallowed hard as she read the first lines.

Dear Future Husband,

I want to live.

I just had the craziest roller coaster of a night ever. I went to a party, by myself! Not by choice, but that's beside the point. I pushed through it alone. It sucked at first, little awkward at times, scary at others, but Trey Turner was perfect. I think my little infatuation with my brother's best friend just became a serious crush. But we can talk more about that another time.

Right now, I want to tell you that I'm done just existing through each day, barely scraping by quietly. I am done being the ghost.

I want to live.

I want to make memories, good and bad ones. If tonight has taught me anything it's that I can be happy even through the bad times. I could focus on what went wrong for me tonight, and regret coming, but I won't!

I experienced adrenaline, excitement, courage, fear and I feel triumphant. I can overcome my body's reactions to fear. I can overcome my anxieties. I can beat the past and I will.

Like Mom told me earlier tonight, all it takes is a leap and I think I'm ready. I am ready to dive headfirst back into life. To wrestle back my happiness, my freedom and my hope. To live the way I want.

The past hurts, but I'm not going to fear the future because the past sucked. I'm going to live a great life knowing that I survived the past. And if I can make it through that, then I can get through it all. I know it will take time, but today, I feel the change.

I am ready to smile again. I am going to create memories, make friends, go on dates, go to school, learn something I love, and I am going to be great. <u>Because you and I deserve a Maybelle that strives to be great.</u>

I love you,
Maybelle Mason

When Maybelle finished reading, I cleared my throat. Her watery eyes blinked up at mine.

"You wrote that the night of the accident. You wanted to change, you wanted to beat the past, and I think you did. I think you woke up from your coma ready to start over. To make the most of your life despite the tragedy. You could've used every excuse to hide from the world and fall apart, but you didn't. You woke up, and you ran, May."

The numb indifference that had been present from the moment I showed up tonight melted from those wide eyes. She looked at me the same way she had that night on the beach and the night we shared our first kiss.

She stared up at me with so much vulnerability, openness, and acceptance. There were no walls when Maybelle looked at me like this. There were no locked doors barring me from her. It was all open, inviting, and I wanted to rush in.

Let her lock the door behind me and never leave.

"The Maybelle then and the Maybelle now aren't quitters," I said. "I think you just needed time, time to find yourself again," I whispered, noticing that when she nodded, her lips nearly brushed mine.

Don't run. Let me in. Let me stay.

My eyes closed and I almost let my desperate thoughts out between us. I was damn near ready to beg, but Maybelle's hand on my shoulder stopped me short.

When I opened my eyes, her eyes were closed. She

didn't open them as she rested her forehead against mine.

"You just liked that entry because I talked about having a crush on you, huh?"

With our heads still pressed together, we both laughed under our breaths. I didn't answer her as both of her hands came up to cup my face, her eyes remaining closed.

"Thank you," she whispered. Then she broke my heart as her eyes opened, and I was shut back out. "It's getting late."

Drowning would've felt better than the way my lungs and idiotic heart constricted.

I nodded. "Yeah, I'll go."

Maybelle lifted one of her hands from my face to brush at the hair that fell over my brow. "I'll see you tomorrow for our walk?"

"Of course."

A smile graced her full lips, but it didn't meet her eyes as she said, "Good night, Trey."

Depleted of my will to live, I slipped off the bed, but stopped when I reached her bedroom door. Every instinct was kicking at me to go back. To kneel before her and plead with the girl that owned every part of me to keep me. To let me keep her. As I looked back at Maybelle, who watched me back, my commitment to her was reinforced.

She was everything to me. The girl who watched me with those big, beautiful eyes and a closed off heart. One day she would let me in and would let me stay, because she was mine and I was hers. She was my vault, my crutch, my protector, my balance, and my anchor.

Maybelle Mason was my hope.

"Goodnight, Mayhem." And I walked away.

31

Magnet, Heart, Chaos

Trey

In my first year of college, I didn't go to any college parties. The only parties I could've attended were on the weekends. I spent almost every spare moment of my weekends on either extra football training or by Maybelle's side.

So, when Larson barged into the apartment this afternoon saying all the boys were going to a frat party together, I was less than enthusiastic.

I immediately told him, "No" and fled back to my bedroom. I would've happily remained that way if Bear hadn't come into my room asking about my feelings.

That conversation alone had me nearly begging Larson to get me to that party.

The four of us climbed into Bear's truck. It was Friday night, one of our last free Friday nights before the season was in full swing. Next week would be our first game, meaning my mom would be in town for the weekend.

I missed going home most weekends to visit her, but with my schedule, I couldn't make it back as much. Usually, I'd feel guilty over the idea of my mom spending so much time alone, but she recently admitted she was seeing someone.

She refused to tell me any other details but by the way

she brightened on the Face Time call and freaking giggled... I knew she was happy, which, in turn, made me happy. My mom deserved the world. Every bit of happiness the universe had to offer, she deserved it. It at least owed her that much after all the crap she'd dealt with.

All too soon, Bear's truck pulled up to a frat house. A thousand cars surrounded the place. Music blared from the open windows. Couples stood together in the shadows of the front lawn and a few crowds of students socialized along the porch.

Bear pulled his keys from the ignition as Larson spun in the passenger seat to look back at Noah and me.

"Okay gentlemen, as your captain, I'll remind you to not drink too much. Don't stay out too late and don't be stupid. We have early practice tomorrow morning. Now as your roommate and friend, get shit faced. Bear is DD and send all the hot brunettes my way." Without another word, he was out of the truck, strutting up the small steps of the porch into the house.

Bear grumbled as he rolled out of his seat with Noah and I in tow as we approached the chaotic mess of people.

An unexpected weight of memory hit me as I entered the throng. The last house party I attended Liam had been by my side. Back then, I didn't stalk in behind my teammates, dreading the crowds and boisterous music. I had swaggered in by my best friend, confidently joining the party, ready and excited for a night of stupid fun.

What I would give to be back in that moment right now. To see my best bud flirting with a random girl in a corner. Watch him dance with no rhythm at the core of the party or dominate in a quick game of beer pong.

"You want a drink?" Williams asked me over the blaring music.

I nodded, even though my stomach ached. I needed a drink or two if I was going to make it through tonight.

We left Bear to a couple other guys who stopped him and meandered through the groupings of people to the kitchen. There were stacks of cups and a variety of beverages lined up along the countertop.

Williams snatched us a couple of beers from a cooler on the tiled floor. We both cracked them open and scanned the crowd as we sipped.

I couldn't help it as I fell back into the past, imagining Liam here. He wouldn't have been nursing one beer in quiet seclusion. That guy would've downed a couple of drinks before arriving, prepped and ready for a good time. He would be in the dead center of the pulsating jumble of students, howling with amusement. A magnet that attracted anyone and everyone in for a good time.

Liam was the heart, the chaos, the center of it all.

I got whiplash from my double take of golden coils of silk hair in the center of the dancing bodies.

At first, I had the fleeting thought that it was my imagination conjuring up Liam. I tumbled back into reality as I recognized my Maybelle at the center of the dance floor.

My eyes fell out of my face as I watched the once shy, and only-reads-books-Maybelle, jump around with Penny laughing beside her. Like Liam, Maybelle had no rhythm. She bounced up and down, not even to the beat, but she was, no doubt, loving every second.

I couldn't help the sense of déjà vu I felt as I watched her. Noticing the way everyone nearby admired her, pressing in closer.

She was a magnet, the heart, the chaos, the center of it all.

I chuckled at the thought of Liam standing beside me, watching his sister now. I imagined his jaw hitting the floor before he joined her. Happy to see his sister finally enjoying herself for once.

Williams nudged me with an elbow, knocking me out of my daydreaming.

"I'm gonna head out back to join a game of ping-pong or whatever they got out there. You comin'?"

I shook my head, gesturing to the center of the floor.

He followed, then turned back to me with a knowing smirk. "Go get her," he said, patting me on the shoulder as he stepped away.

He only made it a few steps before a short, dirty blonde-haired girl with glasses stopped him. She smiled before pulling him away from the crowds and he happily followed.

I knew I needed to approach Maybelle and not continue to stare like a creep, but she was just so mesmerizing... That is, until I realized she wasn't just laughing and dancing with Penny—but with someone else.

My mouth went dry as I recognized Sam Cameron pressing himself against her.

Sam was an awkward freshman that warmed the bench this season. Bear had recently befriended and invited him over now and then. So, I'd seen his lack of skills in speaking to other women. Except, there he was, laughing, dancing, with his hands on Maybelle's hips.

My heartbeat pulsed at the base of my neck. My stomach churned as I watched her face Sam and hook her arms around his neck, swaying her hips.

I was going to be sick.

I took a step forward. Ready to put an end to whatever was happening, but a large hand landing on my back stopped me.

"Trey, how are you doing, man?" asked Austin Lunt, starting point guard for the SDU basketball team.

My eyes danced back and forth. I took a strong swig of my beer and turned fully to Austin. I tried concentrating on the man in front of me and not on the love of my life dancing with Sam Cameron, of all people.

"Hey—man—I'm good. How are things with you?" I accepted his outstretched hand.

"All is well. Never thought I'd see you at one of these, though. What finally got you out tonight?"

Austin and I met in a study group last year. We hit it off with our same interest in sports, Call of Duty and pizza. We'd hung out a few nights for studying. But those always turned into nights of video games and delivered pizza.

He invited me to a load of parties, but I turned him down each time with no real excuse. He probably thought I was some social wreck and left me alone about it after a while.

"My roommates dragged me here," I said over the music. I peered back over to the dance floor; my blood going cold when I didn't find Maybelle there.

I put a hand on Austin's shoulder. "Sorry, I gotta go."

I moved past him, scanning the crowd, searching for gold curls. I didn't find blonde, but I did find red hair, a tall man in leather beside her. I strode through the mess, pushing people aside until I was in front of Penny and Daniel.

"Where is she?"

32

Why Him?

Maybelle

Sam Cameron.

Maybe it was the way he blushed when I teased him. The way he tried to make small talk about politics. Or the way he was one of the biggest dorks I'd ever met but was well-equipped with lean muscle and a handsome face.

Whatever it was, I'd taken a liking to him.

Sam and I met the first day of classes. He approached me after a lecture. He introduced himself, then launched into a ramble about the current foreign conflicts of the world.

I didn't understand what he was saying, but I said something sarcastic like, "Wow. You really know your stuff."

He lit up, not recognizing the mockery in my compliment.

Since then, we'd had two coffee dates.

After the first date, I came home to Penny and our other two roommates, Abigail, Madelyn, loitering in the living room. All awaiting to hear how my first college date went.

When I told them my date was with Sam, Penny and Madelyn grimaced.

Abigail had never met him. So, she had no opinions to share, but Madelyn and Penny were adamant that Sam Cameron was the most painfully awkward boy they'd ever encountered.

I understood. Sam was uncomfortable, but I learned that when I slid him an actual compliment, a flirtatious touch or glance here and there, he became a whole new person. His ramblings weren't as long or random and his darling, bashful smile teetered toward a confident smirk.

The party tonight was for Penny and me to have a girls' night out but shifted when we ran into Sam. Penny instantly and happily called Daniel, asking him to come keep her company while I followed Sam out onto the dance floor.

Tonight, there was no sign of his shy awkwardness. His grin was adorable. His shaggy, dirty blonde hair was combed back, showing off his brilliant hazel eyes, and an olive-toned face. His sculpted body was dressed tightly in a light teal tee and jeans, hugging his legs.

Sam was almost proud as he pulled me through the crowd. As we danced, his large hands latched onto my hips, swaying in sync with me even though I was far from in beat with the music. I tied my arms around his neck, pulling myself against him.

I had to look up to meet his eyes because, *wow*. He was tall.

Not as tall as Trey, though.

Nope, I was just going to shove that thought deep, deep down. As much as I hated to admit it, even to myself... There was a minuscule—sort of large amount of me—that invested in Sam because he was a distraction.

Terrible, I know.

My self-control with Trey Turner was pitiful. The other night when he'd come over to my apartment, we read my journal. We talked about the nightmares of my forgotten past, and I'd been so close to giving in. To giving into temptation and kissing him on my bed.

I mean, how could I not?

He had been so… I didn't have the words to describe how good that boy had been at that moment and, well, every other moment. I was so angry reading through my book and a little horrified by the forgotten life I had "lived". But Trey opened my eyes to the girl I was—the girl I am.

Sam gripped my hips, pulling me back into the present as he leaned in against my ear. "Want to go somewhere quiet?"

I pulled back, a sugary smile splitting my lips. "Lead the way."

After Penny found Daniel, Sam led me up the stairs of the frat house. I didn't have to guess his intentions as I spied the many couples in the loft.

A rush of apprehension moved through me as he walked us into a dark room. He flipped on the lights, revealing an office or meeting room. Only a desk and a bookshelf lined the wall, while a few boxes of what I guessed were storage towered in a corner.

He slid the door shut behind him and deflated with a deep sigh. "Sorry. I needed to hear myself think for a minute." He combed a hand through his sweat damp hair, a blush taking over his neck and face. "And I wanted to talk to you."

My mouth pulled tight, smiling at his shy admission. I sat myself on the edge of the desk. The effort made my shorts hike up, and my feet dangle off the ground.

"You look nice tonight."

His blush faded into the handsome grin the way I knew it would. "Thank you. Uh, are you having fun tonight?" he asked, leaning his back against the door behind him.

"For my first party, I'm not disappointed yet."

He beamed. "Good."

I watched as he fidgeted with the hem of his shirt, his

nervousness obvious from my side of the room. "What's on your mind?"

He looked at me, surprise taking over his features.

He must not know how loud his body language was. He took a deep breath before finally saying, "I wanted to ask you something."

I nodded for him to continue, and he licked his lips. "There's this banquet thing for my football team coming up. It's held on the Saturday after the first football game. It acts as a fundraiser, team bonding experience. The cheer and rally teams will be there. Faculty too. Families are invited. There will be dancing, and I hear they serve a lot of this yummy cream puff—"

"Sam," I interrupted his long-winded explanation.

His mouth clicked shut as he watched and waited.

This was perfect. I'd been waiting for Noah to get back to me about our date to the banquet as friends. Except it soon became clear he wouldn't dare ask Trey for his blessing. He felt it was too much of a violation of *Bro Code*, so I'd given up on the idea.

But now—

"I would love to go with you," I answered.

"But I didn't ask."

I giggled. "Were you not going to ask me to be your date?"

"No, I was," he corrected earnestly.

I smiled at him. "Well, you have your answer."

He approached the desk and wrapped me into a tight embrace. He stepped between my legs, burying his face into my neck.

"Thank you," he mumbled into my shoulder. Which I would've found endearing if not for the way his hold caught my arm between our bodies.

Sam eased back enough so my arm could escape, but he continued to hold me against him as he still stood between my legs. His face was so flushed red I could almost feel the heat of his blush radiating from him.

"Maybelle, could I—may I—kiss you?"

I tensed at the odd thought this might be his first kiss. I batted away the intrusive idea and placed my hands on his chest. Then I entwined my fingers into the cotton of his shirt.

"Yes," I said, pulling him to me.

Sam's kiss wasn't hasty, it was slow. It wasn't hungry. It was tentative. His kiss wasn't overwhelming, but sweet and simple. One of his trembling hands lifted to cup my cheek while the other rested against the desk underneath me. Our kiss followed a gentle rhythm, like a lullaby.

It was soothing, and it was precious… But that was it.

I tried to scoot into him, mold my limbs against his. I searched with my body for a connection, a spark, a jolt—anything. I came up empty-handed, even as his tongue prodded my mouth open for more.

That's when the office door crashed open, making me yelp while Sam leapt a solid five feet away.

I couldn't believe my eyes as Trey stormed into the room, past Sam and up to my perch on the desk. He stopped before me, replacing Sam in the spot between my legs.

His green eyes were ablaze.

"Mayhem, sweetheart, it's past your bedtime," he grated out through gritted teeth.

He wouldn't dare. Oh, but he would.

His large arm snaked around my waist, lifting me off the desk and to my feet. I planted myself on the spot and glowered up at him. I opened my mouth to speak, but he cut me off.

"You can yell at me on the way home, love. Now, move."

He had my hand in his, tugging me out the door, leaving poor Sam behind.

In less than a minute, Trey had us downstairs, out the front door and amongst the parked vehicles. I recognized

Bear's truck immediately. We hiked around it, putting the vehicle between us and the still very vociferous party.

I finally ripped my hand from his. "What the hell, Trey?"

He didn't heed me any attention. His phone was out and against his ear.

"Trey!"

He put a finger up for me to wait. I nearly lost it. I wanted to snatch his phone and chuck it into a brick wall, or better yet, his head.

"Bear, you busy? —Want to do me a favor and take Maybelle home? —I appreciate you."

He hung up the phone.

I was growing thoroughly impatient. I fisted my hands at my side, staring daggers into the side of Trey's face until he finally turned to me.

"Sam? Really?"

"Are you going to tell me what that was all about, or just be a jerk?"

A muscle in his jaw feathered as he raked a hand through his caramel hair and pivoted away from me.

"Trey," I demanded.

He spun back. "Why him?"

The unspoken question in his face made me stumble. "W-what?"

"Why him?" Trey repeated. *And not me?*

"He's sweet."

"Sweet?" he scoffed.

"What's wrong with sweet?" I shot back.

The green in his eyes shone through the dark. "I know you, May. You don't want just sweet. You like a challenge," as he said this, he took a step toward me.

"You want confidence," he said with another stride that made my entire body tremble.

Another long step. Only inches laid between us, and I refused to back down.

"You want someone who will listen. Who will hold

you. Someone who can keep up." He pressed in so close I couldn't help but fall back into the truck door.

I didn't take my eyes from his as I whispered, "He kissed me."

He shuddered. "I know. I saw."

He placed his hands against the car, by either side of my face.

"It was nice," I said, biting my bottom lip. His mouth tilted up to show off a dimple.

"Nice?" he snarked. "How romantic. That's how I'd describe a spring day. Not a good kiss, but to each his own."

"You're being rude," I said, crossing my arms over my chest. Like the added barrier between our bodies could soothe my beating heart.

Trey chuckled, the laughter sounding more forced than amused. Taking a step back, he looked me up and down, his gaze falling heavily on my lips.

"And how would you describe our kiss?"

Mind-melting, devastating, addictive... My lips remained sealed. I refused to speak, knowing I'd say something damning if I did.

His grin widened. "That's what I thought."

"I didn't say anything."

"You didn't have to," was all he said before Bear came around the corner, serving as a welcome interruption.

His focus darted between us. "Hey, May, I'm here to take you home."

I blushed, realizing I was pressed into the truck while Trey stood about a yard away from me. "Please, don't feel you have to leave early because of me."

"No, I should be thanking you for the escape. There was a drunk girl in there asking if she could try braiding my beard." Despite the tension, my smile twitched up as Bear stroked his beard protectively.

"Okay. Maybe we can grab some food on the way

back? I'm starving." I was leaving, and not because Trey insisted. But because I was exhausted and so done with the mess of a night.

"Absolutely," he said. "Text me when the other guys are done, and I'll be back to pick you up," he directed at Trey as he stepped into the driver's seat while I had to jump into the passenger seat.

I reached for my door, but Trey was there holding it open, a smirk playing on his lips.

"Goodnight, Mayhem. Also, we're tutoring tomorrow morning after our walk. Don't be late." And before I could even exhale my rebuttal, the door clapped shut.

"I hate him," I grumbled, slumping into my seat.

Bear's eyes shifted to me, remaining more focused on the road as we rolled down the street.

"You okay?" he asked, and I failed to notice his paw-like hand move until it was wrapping around my little hand. "You wanna talk about it?"

I really loved this mushy, gushy, full of feelings teddy bear.

"I'm good. I just need to eat and get to bed."

I smiled and Bear gave my hand one more squeeze before returning his to the steering wheel. I peered out the window, thinking about Trey as much as I wished I wasn't. Then I thought about Sam, probably still alone up in that room. I needed to call him and apologize, but not tonight. I was done with drama and boys tonight.

Except my imagination didn't get the memo, as images of me and Trey kissing filled my mind. My kiss with Sam had been—for lack of a better term—cute. Sam was cute. He was an adorable guy I could see myself love getting to know...as a friend, but Trey had a point as much as I despised admitting it.

Trey's kiss was more than nice.

Trey's kiss stirred up feelings I would never imagine using to describe a relationship between friends.

33

Pretend

Maybelle

I wanted to be late. I so badly wanted to go against Trey's reminder to not be tardy to our walk and tutoring session. Just out of spite, but there I was. Up and sneaking out of my apartment to find a grinning Trey waiting outside my door.

"Jerk," was my only remark as I brushed past him to the stairs and our regular walking path, barely lit by the dim morning.

Trey swiftly caught up, keeping pace right next to me, just as he always did. "Still bitter about last night, then?"

Snorting, I shot him a withering look, but still that grin shined on. "Can we not talk and get this over with?" I pleaded, and Trey—to my surprise and maybe dismay—nodded and strolled on.

Oh. Somehow, I felt like that completely backfired on me.

No. I wanted this, the quiet. For Trey to let me be.

I wanted this.

The trek felt extremely long with the still tension of last night's events hanging heavy between us.

Fine. I could admit to myself…

I liked when Trey fought me—for me.

Fought to talk to me, tease me, spend time with me,

and enrage me in the most exhilarating ways. The fact that he wasn't this morning, after what happened last night, had my heart in the pits of my stomach.

It shouldn't.

We continued on, still silent.

What I appreciated about me and Trey was the silence between us wasn't smothering. It was relieving. Even amidst the leftover uncomfortable stress from the conversation the night prior. I could just be in the company of his quiet presence. Let my mind whir with thoughts or go still with content. It was a freeing sense I only had the pleasure of feeling with him.

I felt a little more clearheaded as we neared the end of the walk. I peered over at him, ready to talk about last night, but he looked—well, he looked like crap.

Correction—it wasn't possible for Trey to ever truly look bad, but with the way his eyes drooped, his skin paled with a twinge of green—

"Are you okay?"

He dragged his eyes to me. Licking his lips with a hard swallow, he nodded, once. When we reached my apartment door, he huffed, "See you in a bit."

I wanted to stop him. Argue that maybe we should postpone today's tutoring and get some obviously needed rest, but Trey was hustling. So instead of hollering down the hall at him and risk aggravating my neighbors, I went inside to shower.

About a half hour later, I was walking to Trey's apartment.

I loved my solo walks. Almost as much as I loved the walks with Trey, but there was something about the walk alone that had me checking over my shoulder. I didn't know why, I just felt—watched. Even on my short treks to Trey's apartment from mine, I never quite felt alone, and it was an unnerving thought.

Ignoring my very paranoid feelings, I made my way into the football den. At the kitchen table sat Larson and

Williams playing… Monopoly.

"Ah, pay up, Williams. That would be my property you landed on," Larson said, holding his palm out to accept his payment owed.

"I'm so done with this game. This shit is rigged," Williams griped but proceeded to pay up.

The door snapped shut behind me, alerting the two boys to my arrival.

"Hey, May, you want in? We could start over so you can join," Larson offered, but Williams stood from his stool.

"You two have fun. I'm out."

I approached the counter, peering over their board. "Thanks, but maybe some other time. I'm here for tutoring."

Williams stretched out his long wingspan as he spoke through a taut yawn, "That's right. It's Sunday, huh?"

I nodded.

"Turner should be chilling in his room if you want to head on back there—or you could ditch the loser and hang out with us. The choice is yours, but there's an obvious right answer." Larson's sideways smile revealed one carefree dimple as he winked.

I patted him on the shoulder before spinning for the hall. "Thanks, but no thanks. My math grade is in need of too much help for me to skip even one tutoring sesh."

I made the descent towards Trey's room, with Larson's half-hearted "boos" rolling down after me. When I reached the room, the door was slightly ajar. I couldn't help but sneak a peek through the crack.

I could spy half the dresser along the right-side wall and most of the bed that was snug in the middle of the room, but no Trey. Then I noticed his bathroom door. It was closed but light scraped out from underneath.

I slipped inside the room, letting the door click shut with my entrance.

Trey had to be in the bathroom because his room

held no trace of him. Except his shoes and shirt he'd worn that morning were in a pile next to his dresser.

I dropped the backpack I had slung over one shoulder full of class supplies onto the bed.

"Trey?" I called out, more to let him know I was there than in search of him.

I heard rustling in the bathroom and then a labored groan. "Yeah?"

Curiously, I tiptoed up to the door. "It's me—Are you still up for tutoring?"

"Oh—uh, yeah. Sorry, I lost track of the time. Just give me a minute, please."

Perfect, because there was something I'd been dying to do since the first time I saw his room. Some snooping.

I checked out the closet on the left side wall first.

Lots of dark colored athletic clothes, of course. A couple hoodies and jeans, but what caught my attention most was a slick, black suit, white button up and black tie. The ensemble sparked too many tantalizing imaginations of a dapper Trey picking me up for a magical date to the opera or the ballet.

That's enough, Maybelle.

Everything was hung up neatly, and his shoes were organized in a line on the floor. Each pair matched up and positioned together.

He seemed to have everything planned. Every innate part of his life efficiently placed in constructed structure. Trey thrived on order. A fact I was well aware of since I first met him. But what had me smiling was that I knew I was anything but order. I was a chaotic mess and yet, Trey and I seemed to work so well together...

Moving on.

There wasn't a lot of storage space in the room, but there was one last place I hadn't pillaged yet. My eyes fell onto the short nightstand sitting beside the bed. I knelt before it. As my fingertips skimmed the brass knob of the drawer, a gut-wrenching heave sounded from Trey's bathroom.

Startled, I shot to my feet, forgetting about the unsearched dresser entirely as I pushed my ear to the door. "Trey? Are you alright? What was that?"

A moment passed and then another hurl tore open the quiet air on the other side. I didn't wait for his response; I opened the door.

He was kneeling in front of the toilet, forearms propped on the bowl as he retched.

Oh, no... The roiling in my stomach forced me back for a moment to inhale the fresh air of his room before returning to the bathroom.

I would not pity puke; I would not pity puke.

I crouched next to Trey. He was shirtless. Sill in his black athletic shorts from earlier and trembling with a line of saliva trailing from his mouth to the bowl of the toilet. ——

"Trey..."

I brushed a hand against his scalding forehead. Waves of brown hair fell in heaps over his bloodshot eyes.

He straightened, wiping his mouth with the back of his hand as he inhaled an unsteady breath. "Sorry, May. Just give me a minute. I can be ready soon."

I scoffed. "Absolutely not."

I left his room and entered the primary space where Williams and Larson had returned to their game.

"Where's your barf bowl?" I asked and, as I suspected, I didn't need to explain myself. Williams pointed to a cupboard door. I opened it to find one large, stale, pea green plastic bowl.

The family barf bowl, *everyone has one.*

I snatched it and hastily returned to find Trey right where I left him. I fell back to my crouch beside him. "You got more in you, or can you stand?"

He looked at me then, red irritation in the whites of his eyes enhanced the vibrancy of the green. "May, I promise I'll be fine. Please, go sit on my bed for a minute.

I'm already feeling a little better. We can go over your homework and anything—"

I stopped him by placing a soothing hand on his cheek.

He leaned into my touch, his eyes fluttering closed.

What I would give to touch him like this all the time…

Stop it.

I stole my hand away, making him look at me again. "Let me take care of you, for once."

Trey watched me, exhaustion drooping his face.

He opened his mouth, and I shut down his case before he could exhale. "Trey. Please. Let me do this."

Finally, he slumped, which I considered as his surrender.

"Thank you. Now, let's get you into the shower and get control of that temperature."

He stood with me when I beckoned and followed me to the shower. When he shucked his shorts down his legs, I left the room, ignoring the pang of curiosity begging me to look.

While he showered, I tidied the bed, readying it with a cluster of pillows. After which, I pulled out a pair of black sweatpants and an over-sized, old school pride tee from his dresser drawers. I took the ensemble of clothes, including the underwear I snatched from the top drawer, and folded them into a neat stack.

"Trey?" I called with a few knocks against the ajar door.

He grunted.

I pushed the door open a fraction more, keeping my eyes on my toes. "I have some clothes for you to change into. Can I put them on the counter for you?"

"Yes. Please."

Tentatively, I stepped in, placing the stack of loungewear onto the bathroom sink counter. I strained to keep my eyes glued to the ground, even as the shower shut off.

"I'll just leave them right here," I said, eyes still downturned. I nearly facepalmed myself because—*duh*—I literally just told him I was going to leave them there.

When the shower curtains screeched across the bar holding them aloft, the temptation to glance up, just once, was too strong. I needed to walk away, let the poor boy dress without me peeping in on him like a perv.

I spun on my heels to find a half-naked Trey standing there in a towel, looking half dead.

The horny cloud in my brain cleared as I stepped up to him with his clothes.

"Put these on and we'll get you in bed."

He nodded, causing droplets of water to drip off the soaked curls of his hair. When I held the clothing out to him, his large hands enveloped mine.

My eyes shot to his.

"Thank you," he let out on a sigh.

I gave him a lame smile. "Get dressed, Turner."

When he later exited the bathroom in only the sweats, I shot an accusatory look at him.

Even ill, his smile was—invigorating.

"I'm overheating. I promise I'm not trying to seduce you… I mean, unless you want me to."

I was impressed I had the willpower to roll my eyes and look elsewhere.

Gosh, what was wrong with me? Poor boy was sick as a dog, and I couldn't help but want to get a quick peek of him naked in the shower or think of how he'd react if I just casually jumped his bones.

Ever since our stupid conversation outside that stupid party about our stupid kiss, I'd been a pathetic mess of want. Unable to get the images of our kiss and Trey's hands on my body out of my mind.

I faced his bed, doing my best to ignore the chaos in my head and heart as I turned down the covers for him. "Lay down. I'll get you some water."

As Trey stepped toward the bed and I to the door, he stopped me with a hand on my arm.

"Mayhem," he whispered.

I faced him with a step closer. "Trey?"

He swallowed hard. "I appreciate your help, but please, I'll be okay. You should go. I don't want to get you sick."

I took another step toward him, and he stepped back. "Trey."

That smile.

"Maybelle?"

"Please stop trying to take this away from me."

That smile fell, and confusion replaced it. "Taking what from you?"

This time, he didn't back away when I neared him. "My chance to take care of you. You've done so much for me. More than I deserve. Please, for once, allow me to be there for you. It can't be compared to the kindness you've shown me, but at least it's something."

His eyes softened; his lips pinched tight as his head bobbed. He got into the bed, and I retrieved a water for him.

His skin no longer looked sickly, but it was flushed and on fire. I retreated to the bathroom, soaking a small washcloth in cool water and ringing out the excess. I placed the chilled cloth on his forehead and his eyes blinked open at me.

Those eyes.

They studied me, like he was memorizing me.

They followed the shape of my lips, the shifting of my throat, the rise and fall of my breathing. Then the way the mattress caved in as I perched on the edge.

He shouldn't be looking at me like that.

I can't want him to look at me like that.

"So, about last night." It was the first subject that came to mind and the best way I knew how to get him to stop looking at me like that.

It worked.

Trey's focus went vacant as he forced a jeering grin. "What about it?"

"You can't do that."

He eyed me. "You're going to have to be more specific than that, love."

I rolled the term of endearment off my shoulders. "The whole possessive alpha dog crap. You interrupted—a moment—between Sam and I, then dragged me out to the cars and sent me home like a child. You can't do things like that."

I expected him to bicker with me more, tease, but he didn't. His head slumped to the side of his pillow, away from me.

"How is Samuel today? Not too shaken up, I hope." A sly smile tugged at the corner of his mouth with his question, but he still didn't look at me.

"Fine, I think," I said, and I immediately regretted it.

His head jerked back, green eyes narrowing. "You think?"

My lips pulled into a tight line. *Shit.*

"May, have you not reached out to the poor boy since last night?"

I fumbled, stumbled, and bumbled for the right words, but what could I say? No, I hadn't checked in on Sam… Or replied to his last texts he sent me the night prior and this morning. But that part, I would not admit to Trey.

"I've been busy."

It was a sorry excuse. I knew it and by the look he leveled at me under the damp cloth still pasted to his head. He knew it too.

"How long have you been feeling sick?" I asked, hoping he could follow the subject change. I was a fool.

"Since last night. I thought the nausea was from seeing you and Sam together, but I guess not."

If looks could kill.

"Okay, okay, I'm done," he yielded. "How's work been? Is that creep still bothering you?"

I shook my head and sighed. "Rick hasn't bothered me; Penny was exaggerating the story to get a rise out of you. He stares at Penny far more than he stares at me," I tried to reason, but with how Trey's eyes widened, I knew it didn't help.

"He shouldn't be staring at you at all."

"What's wrong with a little harmless staring?"

His brows knitting together had me biting back a giggle. He didn't respond right away; he more just watched me like I deeply offended him.

"What?" I poked him in the broad, bare chest. "Let me guess. You're the only one who's allowed to stare at me?"

"Exactly."

Scoffing, I adjusted, and his resting arm nudged against my thigh. I recognized then that I had drifted farther onto the bed, always lured in by his magnetism.

I needed to get away, put distance between us before I did something truly crazy.

"I should let you get some rest," I said. I scooted off the edge of the mattress but stopped when his fingers hooked through the belt loops of my pants.

"Don't—stay, please."

And there went all my willpower, right out the damn window. I was weightless, hovering as I followed the pull of Trey's fingers back onto the bed, deeper into his space.

I really was a weak, weak woman.

Before I knew it, I was lying next to him, sinking into him. His arm wrapped around my back, and my cheek pressed into the skin of his chest.

He was so warm, and not because of the fever. Trey always radiated a heat that I wanted to bathe in. Just a moment, I could bask in this feeling of him for just a few more moments.

His hand on my back floated up into my hair. His

fingers combed through the ends of my curls, down the line of my spine. A riot of goosebumps erupted along my skin with the delicate touches of his firm hands.

"Maybelle." His whispered prayer of my name smelled sweet, minty.

My eyes were growing heavy as I answered, "Yes, Trey?"

His hand continued to toy with the ends of my hair as he inhaled deeply. "Have you gotten to the part in your journal where you talk about what your perfect day would look like?"

I smiled, letting my hand draw patterns across his chest. "*My perfect day would be a day in the sun with you by my side. I don't care what we are doing, where we are. As long as the sunshine is on my face, and you are holding my hand,*" I recited from my recent memory of the passage.

He sniffed a laugh. "Yeah."

He took one curl, winding it around a finger as he pressed his cheek and chin into the top of my head. "You know, you actually sound in love when you write to him," he noted, his words breathing through the golden frizz on the top of my head. "Do you think it's possible that you really fell in love with someone you've never met?"

I only needed to ponder his words for a breath before I nodded against his chest. "Yes."

I could believe it was possible to fall in love with someone I'd never met, because—if I was being honest with myself—I was falling for someone I couldn't remember.

The hand in my hair fell still against my back again, then cinched me up into him. "May, can you stay with me, please?"

"I am."

His head rolled side to side. "No, I mean—*stay* with me, for the night."

I lifted my head then to find viridescent eyes. He had removed the wet cloth. I couldn't differentiate between my scalding skin and what could've been his fever. He needed a hospital if that heat was his fever.

"For the night?" I asked, breathless.

Trey's hand came up, cupping my cheek.

"Or however long you'll give me, but if you're going to stay—let me pretend you chose me. Pretend that last night didn't happen. Let me hold you and pretend that I never have to let you go. Pretend with me that nothing and no one else exists. Let me pretend you choose this: us. You can go back to reality tomorrow, May, but please, stay with me. Let me hold you and let me pretend you're mine."

My heart tripped, skipped, and ripped through its cage, desperately reaching out to him.

"Please," he mouthed, and I knew he would not ask again. It wasn't a choice; I already knew my answer.

I slid up, closer. We were sharing the same air, giving, and breathing each other's inhales and exhales.

I could do this, give him this.

Give us this. Let it just be us.

Resume reality—tomorrow.

I leaned into the hand, caressing my cheek. The moments were eternities dragging on and the hope that gleamed in his gaze melted away.

"I'm yours."

My words glided out on a soft wind, levitating between us. Then I didn't think I caved into him. Trey hauled me completely on top of him, tangled me into him and his sheets. Feeling his skin, I could tell his fever had broken. But my fiery nerves were blazing, burning, thrumming.

I was his. Just for tonight. Pretend.

We were pretending. *Pretending.*

We didn't leave the room, the bed. We didn't eat. I curled up on him, held to him like I could absorb him into my soul. Trey sprawled out on me, playing with my curls.

I was his, and he was mine.

Pretend. Pretend. Pretend.

That silence, our silence. That peaceful, encompassing silence was with us through the hours. It was with us in the pillows, the bedding, dancing across our skin.

I was his, and he was mine.

And when tomorrow came and I left, I couldn't stop pretending.

Dear Future Husband,

Whenever my feelings are at a bit of a low, I turn to you my book of empty pages. When life is good, I feel good, independent, and solid. But when I'm low, I am embarrassed, stressed. And the only one who won't necessarily judge me or has the energy to listen and understand me is you, this book…

That's sad, right? Totally and completely pitiful.

Times like these, I feel so alone, and I feel like all I have is this book. A book of only my own thoughts and feelings to accompany me in my grief and I can't help but scoff at how pathetic that is.

I am so alone that all I have in the world is an empty book.

All I do is cry.

All I do is mourn my life.

All I do is wish I had more than blank pages bound by leather to hold me as I weep on the floor of my bedroom. Utterly and completely alone.

Can you hold me?

When you find me, when you have me, can you hold me and never let go? When you—my book of listening pages, are made real—can you tuck me in your arms and keep me safe from this crippling loneliness? This solitude I am slowly growing more and more accustomed to.

Can you hide me away from this scary world and pretend with me that it is just you and me? Pretend with me that nothing else exists. That you and I were made to hold one another, be with one another, safe and together.

I long for the days that I have you. I long for the days that it won't just be my writing I have, but your thoughts and words. I long for the day I won't crave the smear of ink on my fingers but the feel of your skin against mine.

I yearn for the days that I won't just cherish the silent, freeing moments between me and ready paper. But the quiet moments we share between sweet kisses.

I am eager for the days I am not smiling at my own thoughts relayed on these pages, but hearing you laugh or seeing you smile.

One day. One day you won't just be a book, but you will be mine and I won't have to pretend that I'm not alone because one day I won't be.

Love,
Maybelle Mason

34

Team Turner

Maybelle

Chelsea, Penny, and I prowled through rows upon rows of dress racks, pawing at the glittering gowns. I hadn't realized how extravagant this whole football banquet ordeal was until I finally remembered to tell Penny I was attending as Sam's date.

Without a response, Penny had scrambled to my closet, searching for what, I had no clue.

In twenty minutes, she had each piece of clothing stripped from my closet. It had all been strewn about our room when she announced we would be going shopping.

I didn't understand why I would need a new dress. But even Chelsea, who arrived earlier that Friday morning, insisted a dress shopping trip was in order. So, the three of us piled into Chelsea's car and sped straight for the mall.

I tried on over thirty dresses, in colors of pink, lilac, red, green and colors I didn't know the names of. Chelsea and Penny had dismissed each one. Sending me hiking my skirts back to the dressing rooms to try on the next gown.

"Don't stress, Bells. We'll find you the perfect dress for tomorrow," Penny called from outside the dressing room.

I didn't answer right away because I was holding my breath, trying to squeeze into a skintight, black, strapless dress bedecked in rhinestones. I feared that one full exhale would have each stitch in the hem snapping.

"I don't think I'm the stressed one here, Penn," I puffed through a strained, tightly held breath, but Penny wasn't near the dressing room anymore by the sound of it.

I could hear her voice across the store squealing with excitement, "Chelsea, you angel, yes! This one is perfect!"

Her tittering steps approached just as I finally got the black dress to fully glove my body. I opened the door to her standing there with the biggest, cheesiest grin on her pale, freckled face.

"You're hot," she said, giving me a quick, appreciative once over. "But take that off. This is the one," she announced, pushing a new dress into my arms.

"Well, grab me some scissors because I'm not getting this thing off without tearing it. Or dislocating a joint," I speculated, gesturing to the black fabric tightening and pulling at my curves.

Penny twirled away from me to Chelsea, who perched on a small sofa in the common room each dressing stall opened up to.

"All hands on deck, Chels!" she hollered, and Chelsea needed no more instruction. She was up and all three of us went to work on the dress.

"Okay, I'll take top, you take bottom," Penny instructed Chelsea as we stuffed ourselves into the small stall, clearly oblivious to the ulterior meaning behind her comment.

I slid my bestie a sidelong, suggestive glance.

She scoffed. "You've been spending way too much time with Chad Larson. Get your head out of the gutter and relax your muscles. This is going to be a tight fit," she said, studying the small space we had to work with.

This time, even Chelsea snickered like a preteen boy with me at the unintentional innuendo.

Penny rolled her eyes. "Alright ladies, on my mark, get set—Pull!"

After a few minutes of wheezing laughter, shouts of "suck in" and a butt-load of humiliation for me, we finally peeled me free of the stupid dress.

Now, I exited the dressing stall in the most beautiful article of clothing I'd ever seen. And by the look of Chelsea and Penny's stunned, slack-jawed demeanors, they felt the same.

Penny covered her growing, giddy grin with both hands, kicking her feet on the ground. Chelsea put a hand over her heart, tears lining her eyes.

The dress was formfitting from my torso to my thighs, with string straps and a skirt that snaked the floor as I walked. The fabric was silky soft and shimmered in the light. But it was smooth, no rhinestones or glitter need be applied. The neckline dipped, a flattering fit to my small chest. The bodice fell open in the back, reconnecting to hug my waist and follow the hourglass shape of my hips.

The dress was decadent, absolutely stunning. The color, though, was breathtaking. A light, pale forget-me-not blue that made my eyes sparkle like the sea.

I spun to face Chelsea and Penny, who both stared in awe. "It's perfect!" Penny squealed. Chelsea only nodded with a watery smile.

"You think Sam will like it?" I asked and as I expected but refused to acknowledge, both Penny's and Chelsea's faces fell.

"Oh—uh, yeah. Sam will love it," Penny said.

***

Penny, Daniel, Chelsea, and I filed into our seats as the boys entered the stadium. The football team was a wave of excitement and determination as they ran across the field. The crowd went wild, erupting into a chaos that made my ears ring.

I scanned the team, noting how Bear stood taller than the rest. Larson was the one hyping the team up, each down. Williams hung his arm over another teammate.

I knew I should've been searching for Sam's number nine, but my eyes fell on the Turner, number thirty-three jersey. And that is where my attention remained for the duration of the game.

"I'm so proud of them," Chelsea said as she and I stood from our seats, the last ten seconds of the clock running out.

Daniel and Penny had left during halftime, leaving Chelsea and me alone to scream and cheer at the nail-biting last quarter. Our boys had pulled through with a last second touchdown.

"They killed it," I agreed.

We both walked down to the field, entering with the other few permitted family members of the players.

Almost instantly, my eyes met with Trey's smiling green ones as he approached. I was so busy staring I missed the incoming football player until I was tackled from the side.

Noah Williams lifted me into the air.

"Did you see that game, little Mason?! We wrecked them!" he howled, spinning with me slung over his padded shoulder like a sack of potatoes.

I was tempted to tease him. Point out that if not for that last-minute touchdown, scored by Trey, they would've been the wrecked ones. I thought better of it.

Let him boast, they won, they deserved it.

"Yes, very good. Now put me down before I throw up." He ignored me, swinging me around with a gripping arm around the backs of my legs.

"Bring it in, my guy!" he shouted.

Confused, I thought Williams was talking to me. I realized, as I was slung forward and sandwiched between two sweaty men, that he actually addressed Trey. Now they both smothered me between them in a group hug. With Williams at my back, I looked up to face Trey, who pushed himself against me.

He was smirking, and I was blushing.

Pretend. Pretend. Pretend.

"Oh, my gosh! You three stay right there. This deserves a picture!" Chelsea exclaimed, fumbling with her purse.

Trey pressed against me even tighter, and I glared up at him in response.

His chuckle vibrated through my chest as he leaned in, breathing a whisper into my ear, "Don't act like you don't like it, May. Me pressed against you. Just like that night."

I tried for only a moment to gather myself, but I didn't have the wherewithal to reply. We hadn't talked about that night once in the last week. I thought we were going to do exactly as Trey offered—pretend.

That we would put on the false front that those long hours alone in his bed hadn't been the best, most beautiful moments that had occurred between us. That the one fake night of being together hadn't completely toppled my defenses.

Nothing truly physical happened between us. Nothing past the soft exploration of his fingertips up my arms. His face nuzzled into my neck as I held him, or his gentle breathing dancing through my hair as he slept.

No, nothing physical past the desperate need to hold to one another and never let go. Now... I couldn't say the same thing for us emotionally. I may not have touched Trey's skin past the waistband of his pants, and he may not have explored my body past the neckline of my shirt, but our hearts...

They were a tangle of feelings. A writhing jumble of emotions. Stroking, taking, giving, exploding, and creating in the most obscene and sentimental way two souls could intertwine.

I thought I got away unscathed and my defiance to remain anything but his was still intact.

Spoiler: It wasn't.

Truth was… My heart was still hauled up in that bed, that night, twisted in the sheets and in his arms.

Thankfully, I didn't have to reply because Williams's arm, that was wrapped around my middle, released to jab Trey in the stomach.

"That's enough. You can't whisper cringey shit in her ear like that while we're all pressed together like this," he chided.

"Noah, smile, hun! And Maybelle, wrap your arms around Trey," Chelsea directed, bringing each of our attentions back to her and the camera. Williams and I reluctantly obeyed, while Trey smiled proudly for the picture.

Chelsea and I walked with the boys back toward the locker rooms to shower and dress. Trey and Chelsea planned to go out for their mother, son date as soon as he was ready. So, I was looking for my roommate, Madelyn, who said she'd give me a ride home after the game.

Trey and Williams left us girls for the showers while I glanced at the edge of the stands. I scanned the faces for Madelyn, missing the man in front of me until I was stumbling into his awaiting arms.

Frazzled, I glimpsed up to see Sam smiling down at me. Fortunately for me, he wasn't sweaty like the other guys, because he sat sidelines the entire game, but I wasn't complaining.

"You came."

He beamed down at me, his arms around me, hugging tight. I hated the fact that Larson's voice was in my head, spitting off a string of inappropriate jokes using that one line. I really had been spending way too much time with him.

"Oh, uh, yeah, had to support my team."

My arms were still uncomfortably stiff by my sides, so I quickly brought them up around his waist. He pulled me even closer, encouraged by my reciprocation of his affectionate touch.

"It means the world to see you here," he said so dreamily I was surprised he didn't break out into song like a Disney movie prince.

"What can I say? I love sports."

Geez, awkwardness must be contagious because I was catching whatever this poor boy had. I was stilted, tongue-tied, and desperate to leave.

I peered behind Sam, seeing Chelsea watching—and visibly cringing.

God, this was humiliating. I tried to create distance by pulling his hands from my waist, but Sam's unexpected kiss caught me completely off guard.

I stilled completely.

I wished I had wings. Wings that could fly me up, up, up into the flames of the sun, burning this whole encounter off my skin. Chelsea, bless her soul, cleared her throat, making Sam startle and break from the kiss.

"Hi, you must be Sam. I'm Chelsea," she said as she held her hand out to him. He released me, demurely facing her and accepting her hand.

"Yes. You're—aren't you—it's nice to meet you," he stuttered, but Chelsea only smiled kindly.

"It's nice to meet you too," she said.

I could see the gears turning in her head, looking for an excuse for us to get out of the situation. Except the oddest, most bizarre thing came out of Sam's mouth.

"You're Trey's mom, right? How do you know my girlfriend Maybelle?"

*His wha*t?

I could hear Chelsea answering him, but I couldn't focus on what she said. Maybe my amnesia got worse, and I didn't remember the conversation where I agreed to be his girlfriend? No. We'd seen each other only once earlier in the week to make sure all was well after the drama of the party. The girlfriend topic was never brought up.

Not so much as hinted at.

I would've remembered a conversation like that, and I wouldn't have agreed—because I wasn't *his*.

I opened my mouth. What I would've said, I didn't know, but Sam beat me to the punch, planting a kiss on my cheek.

"I'll see you tomorrow, babe. Good to meet you, Ms. Turner." And he was gone, prancing off into the locker rooms.

I was stunned. Chelsea was stunned. We both stared at one another, slack-jawed while the crowd moved around us.

Chelsea was the first to speak, stepping up next to me. "So, when were you going to tell me you were dating someone?" Her tone wasn't serious, her gentle voice edged on teasing, but I still felt like my heart was in my stomach.

"If I'd known I was in a relationship, you would've been the first to know," I grumbled, dropping my face into my hands.

She tittered and pulled me into her comforting embrace. "Oh, the joys of boys and dating."

We stayed wrapped up in one another as I regained my stability. Chelsea—always my rock.

She brushed at my hair, combing at my frizzy curls.

"So, why him?" she asked.

I stiffened, feeling like I was reliving that night outside the party with Trey. The obvious hurt in his eyes as he asked me the same thing. I didn't have an answer this time. I sighed into Chelsea's embrace.

"I don't know. He's nice. He was there, I guess, and he was new. A relationship I created myself. Not someone from my forgotten past or a random person befriending me, just out of loyalty to Liam. A boy who was interested in me for me."

Someone safe. I thought to myself. Someone who I could ruin things with and not lose everything.

I slumped with the admission and Chelsea squeezed tighter.

"I get it, but sweetheart, no one here is friends with you solely because of Liam or your mom. That may be what brought us all together at first, but we all love you for you. You created these relationships yourself. No one else did that for you."

She pulled back, inspecting my face as she tucked a few rebellious curls behind my ear.

"And a few of us, me included, love you more than most," she said, a meaningful glint in her eye that I wasn't expecting. She continued, "I'm proud of you, and I want you to keep making friends. If Sam is something you want to continue to explore, I will support you full-heartedly. But excuse my boldness when I say, I have and will always be Team Turner." Chelsea punctuated her statement with a wink that had me on the verge of panic.

I stepped back, wide-eyed.

"Oh, Chelsea, Trey and I are just friends," I rushed out, my palms clammy, knees trembling.

Her smile was full of genuine love as she shook her head, her focus landing on something over my shoulder. "Sweetie, friends don't look at each other like that."

I followed her gaze to Trey, who had a small crowd surrounding him. Each individual stared up at him, laughing and congratulating him on a good game, but his attention wasn't on them. It was on me.

His mouth curved into a smile. His eyes were soft but unyielding and when he saw me looking, he slowly lifted one hand to wave at me.

It was one of the cutest things I'd seen him do. It made my belly erupt into a flutter of feelings I couldn't name.

Chelsea moved to my side, hooking an arm around me as she said, "Just know, no matter what happens, you're my girl. Whether that means you come home to me with Trey or another man, you'll always be my girl."

***

I laid in bed that night, staring up at the ceiling, mulling over Chelsea's words.

Could I, do it? Be with Trey Turner?

Stop pretending and just be?

My stomach clenched, and my body shook with anticipation. My previous fear of losing the Turners if things were to go badly between us held no weight.

But I still didn't know him. What if I got hurt?

Well, didn't I know him?

Trey was good, he was kind, patient. He took care of his people and even after everything, he continued to take care of me. Yeah, I didn't know every detail about him, but he knew me, every piece of me, and he valued all the pieces. Even the broken parts I still didn't fully remember or understand.

What I did know—without a lick of doubt—was that I couldn't stop thinking about him. Trey was the magnet I was drawn to. My heart longed for him, my skin craved him and I lo—liked him.

Maybe. Maybe Trey and I could be it. The whole thing was still incredibly intimidating, of course, but the idea of me and Trey together was no longer a definite no but a maybe.

A possibility.

I wrapped myself up in my blankets, feeling like for the first time in weeks I could hope.

Hope for a future where Trey and I won out in the end.

35

On My Knees

Trey

Earlier that Saturday morning, the walk with Maybelle had been quiet. Too quiet.

I tried to talk to her. Desperate to start up any conversation, but she only gave me one-word answers. Even to questions that required a lot more than one-word explanations.

She didn't look sad or upset. She just seemed preoccupied. I swear I could see the gears shifting in her brain, hard at work. I wanted to ask her what was going on, help her with whatever was on her mind, but I knew Maybelle. She wouldn't spill her secret thoughts unless she wanted to. Candor was now one of her key personality traits and one of my favorite things about her.

She would talk to me. She just needed to work through her internal clutter first. So, I let her be, knowing that when she was ready, she'd tell me everything.

Now, I was in my black suit and black tie, matching my brothers for the football banquet. We decided to carpool. Williams and I, together with our dates in my Jeep. Bear, whoever he was taking and Sam, of all people, with my Maybelle, were riding together.

Larson had taken off early since he was giving a speech. He wanted to be there before the rest of the crowd.

"So, Samuel, I hear you and our little Mason have been seeing a lot of one another lately." Williams sprawled out on the couch next to Sam. Sam sat dressed in his black suit, black tie, hair combed back with enough gel to last the apocalypse and a Coke can from our fridge in his hand.

He'd been at the apartment for the last hour, dressed and ready to go. Bear invited him over early to hangout—figures. But the man sat in the same spot, quiet, clutching the soda can for dear life while his focus darted to me.

I couldn't help but puff my chest out a bit. I had scared the poor kid shitless that night when I interrupted his kiss with Maybelle. Apparently, he hadn't fully recovered from it. Which was honestly unfortunate because I didn't hate Sam as a person. I thought he was an idiot that had no game, but we were teammates—brothers.

I just couldn't wrap my jealous head around why Maybelle would kiss him *and* go to the banquet with him.

And that's exactly what this was, *jealousy*.

Maybelle and I finally had our chance. After all the waiting and uncertainty, we finally had a chance but she friend zoned me. Now, I had to sit back and watch as my girl kissed and went to the banquet with another man, and it hurt.

Stay with me and let me pretend you're mine.

That day, that night, those year-long hours in my bed were on constant repeat in my mind.

I'm yours. That statement alone kept me from being suffocated by the envious, strangling thoughts and the self-torture of watching Maybelle with anyone but me.

She'd been mine, and I was always hers.

Sam's eyes flinched to me at the question before he straightened. "Yes, we have."

Williams nodded. "That's sweet, man. Maybelle is an awesome girl. I know any of us here would do just about anything for her." He eyed Sam, leaning forward.

I couldn't help but grin.

Sam took a long swig of his Coke. Then announced like a proud asshole who thinks he's won something, "Yeah, she's my girlfriend."

And I guess he had. Sam fucking Cameron had won it all if he got to call Maybelle Mason his.

I'm yours… Pretend.

Every muscle in my body pulled so tight it felt like they might tear under the skin while Williams choked on air and doubled over in a coughing fit.

"Your girlfriend?" I asked, the hard skepticism obvious in my voice.

Sam only nodded boldly, oblivious.

Is this why she'd been so quiet this morning? Did she not know how to break the news to me?

Pretend. Pretend. Pretend.

Out of the corner of my eye, I noticed Bear creeping out from the hall. His eyes were heavy on me with a sorrowful-ridden expression before peering at Sam.

"When did this happen, Sam?"

Sam, seeming a lot more confident with the big lineman part of the conversation, rolled back into the sofa. He slurped at the can of Coke before saying, "Last week. We became officially official at the party when I asked her to be my date for tonight. She also came to the game to support me last night."

I was going to break him in half. All previous guilt at not liking my teammate was drop-kicked out the window. What was this scrawny, awkward as hell kid doing getting with my girl? My Maybelle!

I'm yours.

A knock on our apartment door interrupted before I could demand more answers. Williams, still recovering from his coughing fit, cleared his throat, then answered the door.

"Speak of the gorgeous devil."

He glided aside, allowing a perplexed, giggling Maybelle to float over the threshold. My heart stopped dead in my chest.

It was graduation night again, Maybelle in a tight powder blue dress. A bonfire in the distance, the waves crashing behind us and my arms cradling around her for the first time.

The dress she wore now was an identical shade of blue. It made her eyes favor a devastating azure, but this dress was far more elaborate and mature. The front delved into a deeper V neckline and fell past her knees to an elegant length that brushed the floor. A slit carved up the side of her thigh, revealing up to the hip. And the woman who wore the dress was not the same girl from that long ago night.

Her curls fell in heaps along her bare, bronzed back, framing her face like they had. Except tonight she didn't hide behind a sweater, or a collection of things scrunched up in her arms. Maybelle Mason strutted in on white, heeled shoes, wearing her exposed, sun-kissed skin proudly.

Oxygen escaped me as her alluring blue eyes landed on me. A sensual smile tugged at the corners of her glossy, blush pink lips.

"Hi," she said, approaching me—only me.

Not her so-called boyfriend, not Bear, not Williams, but me. And the way she looked at me screamed anything but friend.

I'm yours. I'm yours. I'm yours.

I opened my mouth. I wanted to tell her she was beautiful, no angelic, breathtaking, unreal... I wanted to say so many things but couldn't get my damned mouth to move.

"Maybelle."

Sam appeared at my side and my mouth snapped shut.

Right... Boyfriend.

But Maybelle's eyes remained on me. Like she couldn't be bothered to spare a glance toward the idiot who claimed her as his.

"Your shoe is undone," he said pointedly, cutting through the trance. She finally tore her eyes from me, kicking a foot out to examine the loose strap of her heel.

"Lookie there," she huffed, a trace of embarrassment hiding in her annoyed tone. She bent down, but I was already there, down on one knee.

"I've got it," I said, my voice taking on a gravelly note.

I internally scolded myself for being such a fool for a girl taken by another guy. Except my self-chastisement fell apart when Maybelle steadied herself using my shoulders. The slit in her dress fell open as she raised her leg for me and revealed too much—no—not enough.

I glimpsed up to find her smirking blue-green eyes on me. I couldn't help but grin back, letting my fingers brush along the smooth skin of her ankle.

Christ, her legs shimmered in the dull apartment lighting. Like she put glitter in a vanilla scented lotion. It made her appear that much more ethereal, untouchable.

But there I was, on my knees, touching her.

"Thank you, Trey," her voice lowered too as her fingers dug harder in the tops of my shoulders.

I tried to drag out my work of the loosened strap. There was only so much stalling I could do before it got uncomfortable for everyone, and I was brutally taunting that line.

Finishing with the strap, I collared the base of her ankle with one hand, lowering her foot back to the ground. I let my touch slowly slip up her calf as I risked one last, full inhale of her sweet, vanilla scent.

Then I rose, coming face to face with Maybelle. She opened her mouth like she might say something, but Sam Cameron was there, lacking the necessary social skills to see he was interrupting a great moment.

"You look beautiful tonight, babe."

Maybelle's glossy mouth clicked shut.

That was the reality gut punch I needed to remember myself and where I was. I turned away, leaving Sam and Maybelle alone.

I shot a quick look at Williams as I grabbed my keys. "You ready?"

He was crouched in the pantry stuffing one of my pop tarts in his mouth. I couldn't care right now, I just needed out of there.

He nodded, concentrating on chewing his food before swallowing and saying goodbye to Maybelle and Sam. I didn't bother. I was already too far down the hall to hear her say goodbye.

36

Hearsay And Breakups

The banquet was beautiful.

It was held in an event center. Large tables and chairs scattered about the place. At the front was a stage where the head coach and other important members of the team gave speeches. They expressed their appreciations, reminders about the fundraiser and goals to make this the best season yet.

Larson, as the captain of the team, got up to speak. He'd been so nervous about his speech. To my surprise, He showed up, out of the blue, earlier that day at my apartment asking for help.

After running through the speech with me a few times, and some words of encouragement from me, Larson felt ready. Who would've thought the smooth, sweet-talking Larson would be nervous about anything?

Now, we ate the dinner provided of grilled chicken, filet salmon, roasted vegetables, salads and yummy cream puffs. Sam and I hadn't spoken much. Not because he wasn't talking. No, Sam wouldn't shut up about some current political dispute happening on the opposite side of the world.

The problem was, I didn't have the motivation to return his same energy tonight. I was still bitter about the whole girlfriend fiasco. I planned to confront him about it. Not until after the banquet, though, so he could focus on enjoying his time with his team.

Another thing that had me biting my tongue in silence was sitting across the table from me. She clutched Trey's arm like one would a pool noodle in the middle of a turbulent sea.

My Trey.

Juliette was a whole new kind of irritating tonight and my head pounded because of it. Especially since Trey wasn't doing anything to deter her. It was almost like he welcomed her incessant touches and never-ending interruptions. Which had my blood broiling.

One small saving grace was that I was at a table seating people I mostly knew. While Sam was to my right, Bear was sitting to my left, a quiet, comforting presence. To Bear's left sat a girl who rivaled Penny in fun, outspoken, excited behavior. She was short, had bobbed chestnut brown hair, deep brown eyes and a darling round face.

Her name was Gracie, and I adored her.

Bear's date had the attention of everyone at the table. She told hilarious jokes and stories that almost had me shooting my water out of my nose.

Williams was also at the table, across from me, next to Trey. His date was a beautiful girl with dirty-blonde hair, round glasses perched on her nose that she adjusted each time she was addressed. I hadn't yet caught her name, but with the way she and Noah shared stolen looks and shy smiles, I already loved her.

"No way!" Williams shouted across the table, bringing me back to the conversation at hand. "You're telling me you actually lived in Egypt?" I followed his line of sight to see his question was directed at Gracie, who beamed.

"I swear it's true," she insisted. She opened her mouth to explain more but Sam interrupted by clearing his throat.

"You know Egypt was ruled by a monarchy until 1953, but was officially recognized as the Republic of Egypt until 1958, when—"

"Nobody cares, Sam," Juliette snipped in over Sam's already uncomfortable interruption.

Sam shrank. More like melted away in his spot while everyone else looked ready to scurry under the table. I honestly wouldn't be too far behind them.

Against instinct, I twisted in my seat to face Sam as I put a hand on his shoulder. "I care, Sam. You can tell me all about Egypt, but first I'm very curious to hear what brought Gracie and her family there."

I let my hand sweep reassurance across his back, and he sat up straighter with my support.

The tension at the table loosened as Gracie smiled. "My dad's a skilled cardiologist and took up a position there for a few years," she explained.

I nodded, making vile eye contact with Juliette.

Williams helped pick up the conversation where they left off. He turned to Bear, adoration on his face. "How did a quiet guy like you find such a cool girl?"

I leaned over, detaching myself from the silent war happening between me and Juliette. I wanted a good view of Bear's upturned features, framed by his now combed and well-trimmed facial hair.

He slanted Gracie a sidelong glance that had her giggling. "She asked if she could try braiding my beard at a party."

Williams almost spit out the drink he was chugging. "Come again?" he asked through choked breaths.

My eyes jumped to Trey's. His intentional smirk told me he remembered that night, too.

Hadn't that only been a week ago?

Gracie was laughing uncontrollably at Williams's

reaction while Bear smiled. His shaking shoulders were the only testament of his mirth.

Bear and Gracie. They were together. A week wasn't long enough to know every bit and piece of a person, and yet here they were—together.

And by the way, Bear's large arm was slung over the back of Gracie's chair, the way she smiled longingly up at him, or the way his hand found hers under the table... They weren't playing friends or being cautious of what they didn't know yet.

They were just together.

At the thought, I realized I hadn't looked away from Trey and he was still staring at me.

The eye contact had drawn on far longer than what could be considered a platonic glance between two friends. Now it was nearing a point of seeing inside. Peering through the very depths of who we were, and I was under no inclination to turn away.

I wanted to see everything those green eyes offered. I wanted to know every good and charred part of this man's soul. I would—I had to. And I wanted him to see me.

All of me.

I didn't look away, and neither did Trey.

"So, Marybelle," Juliette's voice broke in, shattering the trance. But my eyes remained on Trey's. I refused to let her pilfer this moment fully. Or allow my gaze to follow the pattern her finger drew along his bicep. "How did you meet everyone here?"

I tore my eyes from Trey, mourning the lost connection as I looked at Juliette through lowered lashes.

"It's Maybelle," I corrected, filling my tight-lipped smile with all the sour sweetness I could bear. "Trey, Noah, and I went to high school together. Then I lived with Trey and his mom for a few weeks before I got settled here."

She didn't deserve the whole sob story. So that was

where I stopped, but by the sneer in her eyes, that wasn't where she planned to stop.

"Really?" she exclaimed. "You lucky girl. I'd give anything to sleep in the same house as Trey," she drawled as her finger trailed up his shoulder.

I felt a twinge of satisfaction at the way he bristled with the exploring touch.

"I bet you would," I quipped, coolly grabbing my cup of water and taking a sip.

Williams cut in then. Trying to steer the conversation away from me, which I appreciated. Something about football or what not. I didn't listen.

I retained eye contact with the girl across the table as I lifted a fork full of salad to my lips. Juliette followed my movements. A feline smile grew on her red painted lips.

"Is it true that you started a year late because you were in a coma, practically brain dead?" Her voice was slicing. Loud enough to obliterate any further conversation.

The whole table shut down, but all eyes rested on me. My brows furrowed as I looked at Trey. He watched me intensely, jaw ticking. I returned my focus to Juliette, whose face was too smug.

I put my fork down with the salad still clinging to the prongs and folded my hands in front of me. "Coma, yes. Brain dead, obviously not. Just a bit of memory loss," I said, letting a slight smile play at my lips.

In my peripheral, I couldn't help but notice Williams's date put a hand to her mouth. Her eyes were wide with disbelief.

"Wow, what a conversation starter," Juliette mused, her tone drenched in sarcasm. "And didn't your family die? Pretty sure I heard in the news it was a car accident, drunk driver, I believe."

Wow, real classy, this one.

"Juliette—" Trey started, but I cut him off.

"God, you really should come with a warning label," I sighed as I took the napkin I had splayed out on my lap and thrusted it onto the table. "Thank you, Juliette. We can always count on you to molest the fun out of everything. Especially our poor football boys, from what *I* hear."

Thankfully, my voice was steady, bemused even. But a hurricane of emotions roiled under my skin and only got worse when Juliette's smile widened. She got the rise she wanted out of me. My stomach clenched as I caught sight of judgmental glances from members of neighboring tables.

They glared at me with disgust. Probably having only heard the part of the conversation that would damn me and not the cheerleader princess.

I turned to my date. Sam's eyes were wide, but he didn't speak. *Of course, now he shuts up.*

Really sick of tonight and not caring to change the narrative where I looked like the bad guy, I twisted back to Juliette. I was ready to bark out something truly despicable, but I was stopped by Bear, who towered over the table.

He was focused on Juliette and only Juliette.

"Enough," his one-word command was gruff and had Juliette shrinking back. "I think it's a good time for us all to take to the dance floor."

I hadn't noticed the crowd that gathered in the open area of the event center, nor the music that rose in volume. Lights dimmed, and couples waltzed out to the floor hand in hand.

Bear extended a hand to Gracie, who accepted his gesture with a smile and followed him out to the floor.

I was ready to hightail it. I liked dancing, but the last thing I wanted to do was head out there with Sam. Listen to him ramble while Trey and Juliette swayed together for me to watch.

"Maybelle."

My attention tore from the cluster of dancing couples up to Trey, who stood up from the table and waited. His hand was outstretched to me.

"Dance with me."

The confusion on Juliette's face was priceless. I almost took my phone out to capture the memorable moment.

Instead, I slid a quick glance to Sam. I expected him to look sad, maybe, but the sweet boy hadn't noticed the conversation shift. He was safely off in another world called YouTube, watching an informative video on the camels of Egypt.

Unwilling to waste one more second, I stood, rounding the table to accept Trey's hand. "Let's go."

"Trey!" Juliette whined at our retreating backs, but he paid her zero attention.

He led me out to the floor, our steps quick as he spun me back to him and placed his hands on my hips. My hands laced around his neck in response, and we swayed to the beat along with the rest of the couples.

He leaned into me, his lips brushing past my ear. "You look incredible tonight, May."

My anxieties were instantly forgotten. I blushed. No, I burned red hot as Trey pulled back from me and smiled a smile that threatened to melt me completely.

I stood up on my tiptoes then, letting my lips brush his ear. My belly celebrated when he shuddered at the touch. "You don't look so bad yourself."

He laughed then; his eyes gleaming.

"What so funny?" I asked.

He shook his head, his shoulders still moving with the choppiness of his mirth. "I don't know why I ever told you that you weren't the Maybelle I knew when you first woke up. You've always been the same. I just didn't see it before."

I quirked a curious brow at him. "Is that a good thing?" I asked, mimicking the exchange we'd had in that hospital room only moments after we met.

So much had changed since then.

I changed so much since then.

Trey was gentle as he pressed me into his chest. "Yes."

His gaze trailed back to the table. I didn't follow his attention. I knew where he looked as he sighed. "I'm sorry for what she said to you."

I didn't respond right away. I let my focus fall on some random balloon floating on the opposite side of the building. Yeah, that sucked, but Juliette's remarks regarding me weren't the thought that pin-pricked my mind. I focused back on Trey before I let a question out that I'd been contemplating.

"Why aren't you dancing with her? What about your coach?"

His arms tied around my waist. "What about him?"

"Won't he get upset with you if she tattles?"

His green eyes remained on me and only me. "I don't care anymore."

I should've kept my mouth shut, been happy with the current alteration in situations. I should've enjoyed the night with him, holding me so tight to his body, but that wasn't who I was.

My brows furrowed.

"Huh," I grunted. "Punctual as always, Turner."

Williams interrupted Trey's response by bumping shoulders with him. He and his date swayed obnoxiously back and forth, nudging into couples with each of their movements.

Trey's smile for Williams melted into confusion when he returned to me. "What does that mean?"

"I just mean that your timing on choosing when to care or not is seriously impeccable."

We went silent then. His eyes were intense as they searched mine, but both our hands fell. We didn't dance. We stood in the center of the jumbling bodies, only holding one another's gazes.

"May, I'm sorry," he said first. "I didn't mean for this

all to happen. I was trying to make the best situation work with what I'd been dealt."

"With what you'd been dealt? What does that mean?" I asked, unable to control the hiccup in my tone.

Was I that much of a burden, a sack of unbearable weight placed on his shoulders he felt he had to struggle with? A problem he had to work on solving.

His eyes widened, understanding where he'd taken me with that comment. "Maybelle, no—" he started, but I was already shaking my head.

"Pretend," I scoffed out bitterly and the word had him going completely stiff. "That's all it ever was, right? All it was ever going to be?"

His entire body was visibly taut under the fabric of his suit and tie as he stared holes through me. "That's all you seem to be willing to give me," he finally uttered out at a volume only I could hear above the music.

I took a step back from him, like the blow of his words was something I could evade.

Trey closed the distance again with a step forward. "Pretend is all I can get from you. As long as I keep coming in second."

He jerked his chin to a place behind me. I followed his gesture to the table where Juliette was sulking, and Sam was wholly zoned in on the lit-up screen of his phone.

"Boyfriend—really?" His tone wasn't angry, it was hurt, and his eyes portrayed the same emotions when I twisted back to him.

"How did you…?"

I didn't know how he heard about that when I, myself, had only heard about it yesterday. But it ate at me to know he thought I solidified things between me and Sam. I didn't know what to say. The whole Sam situation was my own troubled predicament. I didn't want to sit and try to make a bunch of lame excuses.

He deserved more than that.

My lips remained sealed, even as Trey took my face in his hands and pressed his forehead to mine. "The shitty part is," he whispered against my skin. "I will happily accept pretend. I will take my place as second pick if it means you will have me. That is how stupid and pathetic you make me. I am nothing without you, May, and I will accept any crumbs of your affection you are willing to give me. Even if it is only pretend."

I was speechless, utterly dumbfounded by the boy who held my gaze, my face, heart and soul in the palms of his hands. I was so out of my league with him, and I couldn't seem to care.

Trey Turner deserved perfection, pure love, a beautiful clean life, but I was messy. I was a walking tragedy and I wanted him a part of my mess. I wanted him printed on my skin; I wanted his structured soul mixed in with the mismatched pieces that made up my own. I wanted him, every part of him, to know and understand me.

Trey wasn't second pick. He was far from second pick. He was the only choice, and that scared me because I was liable to mess it all up. To lose the most beautiful choice I could ever make, and it terrified me.

This was the moment in the night that I needed to speak. To expose my raw, unfiltered thoughts, but I was a coward when it came to this.

To being vulnerable.

I closed my eyes, and I twisted out of his hold. Then I ran.

I managed to hold myself together long enough until I knew I was out of sight of the tables and dancing couples. I tried to speed walk, but my heels were going to snap my ankles. Without a second thought, I kicked off the shoes, cheeks hot, head pounding. Stooping, I picked up the shoes and briskly escaped down the hall.

I didn't know how I found it, only that I was now sitting on the beginning steps of a staircase at the end of a dimly lit hall of the event center. Luckily, I was far enough from the banquet that no stragglers came anywhere near my secluded corner. I didn't know how long I sat there, with my fingers buried in the roots of my curls, gripping, and slightly pulling for some feeling.

A feeling to keep me grounded in myself as I thought back to Trey, what he said, and the shame that expanded to near bursting in my chest.

I needed to go home, to sleep, to walk and to think.

I reached around myself to grab my phone from my purse but was thoroughly disappointed when I realized my purse was still at the table.

"Kill me now," I groaned aloud, dropping my face into my hands.

"Always so dramatic, little Mason."

I lifted my head to find Williams, a smile tugging at his lips. He was swinging my abandoned, sparkly purse higher up his large shoulder.

"I'm not dramatic."

He snorted, taking the spot next to me on the steps. He dropped my purse beside me and rested one large hand on my knee as he let out a long sigh. "You, okay?"

I sidled up next to him and laid my head on his shoulder. "Yeah, just needed a breather."

"Same," he grunted while his thumb swept across the top of my knee. He inhaled deeply, then exhaled. "Trey left to take Juliette home. Is everything alright between the two of you?"

I didn't feel much better with that new information, but at least I wouldn't have to face Juliette the rest of the night.

"We're fine," I said, then remembered Williams wasn't supposed to be alone or here with me. "Where's your date?"

"I'm right here."

I turned with Williams. Cautiously approaching from around the corner, his date pushed her round glasses up the bridge of her nose.

"Hi, Maybelle."

I slanted a curious look at Williams, who was watching me with a sad smile. "Maybelle, this is Hannah Lacy. She went to high school with us."

"Oh," I exhaled, unsure of how to respond. "I—uh-sorry, I don't remember you."

Hannah smiled. "Don't be. And I'm sorry to interrupt. Noah left his phone at the tables." She held out the device and Williams accepted it, but not before taking her offered hand in his.

"Are you leaving?" he asked. Hannah nodded. "Can I take you out again tomorrow?"

Her smile brightened as she pushed her glasses farther up her nose. "Of course," she said before looking back at me, still smiling. "It was good to see you again."

"You too," I courteously said back.

And with one last wave to us both, she left.

"She didn't have to leave," I said, and Williams's smile grew, his focus still lingering on where Hannah last stood.

"Yeah, well, she knew you needed your best friend. She just wanted to make sure you were okay before she left."

I smiled, looping my arm with his. "I think Penny would try to fight you if she ever heard you call yourself that in front of her."

He vibrated with laughter. "Yeah, that may be true, but you and I both know I hold the spot of best friend."

I scrunched my nose. "I plead the fifth," I stated, snuggling closer into the big man. "But I'm happy for you. You and Hannah look good together."

"I think so too," he said.

A moment or two of silence passed before Williams asked, "Are you going to ask about your boyfriend?"

It took a few beats for me to register who he was referring to until it finally clicked. "Oh, no. He didn't.

Did he?"

He let out a deep chuckle, understanding my vague horror. "Oh yes. Sam announced the relationship status proudly in our living room just before you showed up this afternoon. Poor boy almost pissed himself with the way Trey was looking at him, though."

I grumbled as I squeezed my eyes shut. Now I knew how that information came about, and it twisted my stomach to think of Trey being blindsided with the news like that.

"So, when did that happen?" Williams prodded, and I wanted to throw myself off a cliff.

"It didn't happen. I didn't even know about the misunderstanding or whatever it was until yesterday when he called me his girlfriend in front of Chelsea. It was mortifying."

I really needed to talk to Sam and clear the air between us.

"I don't want to be with Sam," I whispered, not sure why I felt the need to bear myself to Williams at this exact moment. Maybe it was because of the already heightened emotions of the night.

Or that telling him was just one step closer to telling the person I really needed to bear my soul to.

"What do you want?" he asked, and the question had my throat burning.

No more pretending.

No more excuses and letting fear get in the way.

"I want Trey," I admitted on a deep breath, and Williams pecked the top of my head with a kiss.

"Good. Took your sweet time coming to that conclusion, but I'm glad you got there." He rose from his seat to his full towering height. "Your boy toy is waiting in the main foyer for you. If you want, you can talk to him before I take you home?"

I wanted to do no such thing. I wanted out of this dress and to be done with tonight, but Sam deserved an explanation before I bailed. So, I slipped my heels back on and rose from the steps.

"Let's go breakup with my boyfriend," I pronounced.

Williams offered his arm to me. "That's the spirit."

Dear best friend,

I met someone. His name is Trey Turner.

My family has officially moved to San Francisco. In the weeks preparing for our first semester of school in our new home, Liam has had football training all summer while I worked. At one point, he was gone at a football camp for an entire week, and I went to pick him up at the end of it.

At first, all was normal. I was in my blue pajama shirt, shorts and a lazy pair of sneakers with my hair tied crazily atop my head. Liam was normal. He gave me a quick wave before throwing his gear into our little family car. But something new with eyes of green and the sweetest smile I've ever seen on a face, followed at his heels.

He was so pretty. The sight of him stole the air from my lungs. Especially with that smile, splitting his face right in two.

Obviously, my first thought was, "oh, Liam made a friend" because that's what Liam does. He collects loved ones and new friends as easily as one would collect flowers from a garden.

And he always bundles up all the prettiest ones.

I expected Liam's new friend to help him pack up. To say goodbye and ignore me like everyone else but his eyes, those gorgeous, emerald eyes, were locked on me.

"Hi. My name is Trey."

And just like that, I thought for sure I was melting like sticky ice cream in the summer heat. All while this beautiful boy kept his eyes on me, and his hand outstretched.

I stumbled and could hardly mumble out a reply that resembled something like, "Hi, I'm Maybelle."

Then, as if my world wasn't already spinning off its axis, Trey Turner's smile grew wider as he took my hand and said, "You're very pretty, Maybelle."

My heart didn't just skip. It catapulted into my throat, then free-fell into my gut with an earth-shattering landing.

The comment was so simple, so gentle, but from this boy's lips, it was almost catastrophic. I'd never wanted to hold onto something so tightly yet run as far away as humanly possible. Everything around us had molded into a faded blur as I stared this boy in the eyes, warring with which instincts I wanted to follow.

My heart was pounding, scared, excited, curious.

My brain was racing, begging, screaming, running away. Terrified of pain, betrayal. Pleading that I would learn from the past and hide far away from any possibility of hurt.

But my soul… My soul seemed to know him. I can't explain it, but a deep feeling in my chest was drawn to him. It cooed and whispered with the relief that it found sanctuary and a place to heal and call home.

I, unfortunately, followed the warnings, the fear.

How could I not?

It hasn't been long since everything. I am far from healed and for the first time in years; I am safe. I am in a protected place where the past pains can't reach me, where that man can't touch me.

This bubble I've created for myself is lonely, but it is safe.

I can't just throw myself back out into the fire of uncertainty with only the hope that the shattered parts of me won't be charred to ash. I can't dive headfirst into the unknown with only a prayer that I will come out unscathed.

So, when that boy told me I was pretty, I gave him a curt smile and then I ran. It's been a few weeks now and Trey Turner has tried, oh he has tried to get my attention, speak to me, get to know me, but I just keep running.

I wonder if he will ever give up—I hope he won't.

Maybe someday I won't want to run. Maybe in the future, I'll have glued all my pieces back together and maybe—maybe I will tell him I think he's pretty too.

Maybe one day, he could be one of my picked flowers. Added to my minuscule bundle of gathered colors and smiles.

I hope. I really, truly hope.

Love,
Maybelle Mason

37

The Ambush

Maybelle

You really haven't talked to him in over a week?" Penny asked, sitting atop her bed, strung out on her stomach.

"Yeah. He's been avoiding me since the banquet," I said as I pulled my shirt over my head. Trey somehow managed to dodge me at the apartment and school. He did answer my texts with super basic replies but when I asked to see him, he left me on read.

At first, I was annoyed. Then I was hurt, confused, and frustrated—then I missed him. Trey's absence in my life was carving out a cavity I couldn't bear to leave hollow anymore.

And it had only been a week.

I hadn't realized just how much of my day-to-day Trey had integrated himself into and I into his. The random calls most nights to talk about our days, his hard practices or my most recent find in the school library.

Each morning walk was quieter, lonelier, not finding a smiling Trey waiting on the other side of my door for me. Which didn't help with my already paranoid feeling of being watched as I walked alone.

Trey Turner had woven his way into my heart and soul, and I was finally ready to accept it.

"But that all changes today," I said, sliding my sneakers on over my socks. "Bear is on lookout at the apartment. He said he'll text me when Trey gets home."

The cinematically timed ping of my phone had Penny grinning at me. "Game time."

In less than five minutes, I was at the apartment, powering over the stairs. I didn't knock when I reached the front door. I burst right in. Trey was in the kitchen, his bag in hand, as he looked at me with wide eyes.

Realization quickly donned, and he slanted a betrayed look at Bear. The big man was smirking on the couch, with Gracie by his side.

"Really?" Trey groaned.

Bear only shrugged his large shoulders.

Trey turned back to me. "What're you doing here?"

"I'm here to see you."

His eyes narrowed. "Why?"

"Because I've failed my last two math exams. I need you and your brain to teach me."

He watched me for a moment and in that moment, I genuinely feared he might turn me away. But to my sheer relief, he pivoted for the hall and huffed over his shoulder at me, "Fine. Come on."

I started down the hall after him but not before shooting Bear and Gracie a quick wink and thumbs up. I knew Trey wouldn't be able to turn me away when I needed help. It may have been a little manipulative of me, but desperate times.

I shut the bedroom door behind me, which earned me a sidelong glance from Trey, but he didn't argue. He dropped his bag on the floor while I kicked my shoes off. I jumped onto his bed with my bag, notebook, calculator, and pen in hand.

He didn't say much more than the bare minimum as he walked me through each problem. Which was fine. It was a good first step.

"Who thought it was a good idea to combine

numbers and letters?" I grumbled while writing out the wrong answer to a problem we'd been working through together.

He sighed, leaning close to scratch out my wrong answer and replace it with the correct one.

"How?" I demanded, and his lips sealed together as his eyes darted from me.

"The Father of Math, Muhammad ibn Musa al-Khwarizmi. You forgot to solve the equation in the parentheses first. Screwed up the entire process."

I tilted away, dropping a harsh cough into the crook of my elbow, then a barked "nerd" disguised as another cough.

Trey saw right through the charade. Again, his lips went tight, and I realized he was trying to hide his smile from me.

"Stop stalling and try again," he urged, and I obeyed. Not before I slid him one last dubious smirk.

Only an hour passed before we got through each math equation I claimed to struggle with. Even the few various questions I may have added to draw out the time. When we finished with the last one, Trey retreated from the bed.

"Good luck on your test. Close the door on your way out," he said by way of farewell before locking his bathroom door and turning on the shower.

Instead of leaving, I put my school supplies back into my bag then pulled out my little, black, leather-bound journal. I opened to a random page and began to read, because I refused to let one more day pass of wasted time between us.

I messed up not communicating the Sam misunderstanding with him earlier. I should've told him everything that night on the dance floor, but I didn't know how.

More like, I was scared to. When it came down to it, Sam was the last little hurtle between me giving myself to

Trey fully. He was the last obstacle and I let it sit there, carving out more space between us.

It wasn't fair.

When I was upset about the Juliette situation, cornered by mistrust, Trey hadn't let it rot between us. He wasn't afraid. He didn't allow me to continue believing he ever cared for her or would hurt me in that way.

He never ran from us or what could be.

Trey was always clear, honest about his feelings and intentions with me. While I… I ran away, pretended and locked my heart up.

He emerged from the bathroom. Steam wafted out with him on his exit and good god almighty, he was only wearing a towel.

Trey approached the dresser in the corner of his room, obviously missing me still strewn out on his bed. I gawked at the sight of his glistening skin, and his rippling muscles under bronze skin. I witnessed him in only a towel that day he was sick, but I hadn't gotten the opportunity to admire the way I could now.

I don't know why I was so startled when his towel suddenly fell from his hips, revealing every inch of his backside to me. But I yelped, dropping my face into the covers.

"Holy shit. Damnit, Maybelle!"

"Sorry!" The fabric muffled my hollered apology.

I could hear Trey's snorts of frustration. He rummaged through his drawers, then left with the sound of the bathroom door clicking shut.

I didn't move from my position of suffocation in the blankets. Even after he reemerged from the bathroom, I kept my face smothered.

"What are you still doing here?" he asked, not at all trying to hide his irritation.

"Are you modest?" I asked into the mattress.

"Maybelle." Trey's snipped tone had me lifting my

eyes to him. He cladded himself in armor meant only for me as his opponent. A skintight, black athletic shirt and black sweats that hung loose on his hips, revealing the band of his black boxer briefs.

"Why are you still here?" he asked again.

Despite all odds, I managed to breathe. "I'm not leaving until we're friends again."

His brows furrowed. "We *are* friends—I just don't want to talk right now."

I held up the journal. "That's fine. I have some reading to catch up on."

We were definitely going to talk, but I didn't want to push him just yet.

He studied me for a long moment. His green eyes narrowed at me before he plopped onto the bed. "Why don't you go hangout with your boyfriend?"

If I weren't trying to get on his good side, I would tease him for sounding jealous.

"I don't want to hang out with him," I said instead.

"Why?"

His eyes speared straight through my chest, making my lungs cave in as I breathed.

"Because I want to be with you." My heart hiccupped on the admission, but Trey didn't see it for the profession it was.

Instead, he tore his eyes from me and drove his hands through his wet waves. "Fine."

I returned to my journal while he pulled out his homework. I watched him from the corner of my eye, palms clammy with how easily that declaration had leapt from my lips. My heart rampaged against its cage like it could break out and run back to him, where it belonged.

The fan above us, the occasional creak of the bed from adjusting and the turning of pages filled the still moments. I peered up, catching him staring at me from the corner of my eye. When I faced him fully, he looked away. So, I stole glances, only turning away when he twisted to me.

Soon it became a game of quick stolen looks that turned into longing stares. I'd look at him over my book, and he'd peer back.

"What?" I asked, brows raised.

"Nothing." He shrugged, and we both went back to our tasks. But minutes later, Trey peeked over at me, and I met his green stare.

"What?" he asked softly.

"Nothing."

Both of us smiled as we returned to our homework and book.

I let the silence, our silence, carry for a few more moments before I finally whispered, "Trey."

He looked right at me, focus stripping. "Yeah, May?"

"Can we talk now?"

"I have nothing to say," he said, fast enough I felt the progress we made in the quiet fall apart.

"Yes, you do. We both do."

Groaning, he set his homework to the side. "Stop it, Maybelle."

"Stop what?" I demanded.

He sighed deeply, shoving his hands through his hair and gripping at the roots.

I waited a second, then two before adding, "I'm not leaving until we talk."

Turning from me, he slumped back into the pillows of his bed. "I'm not sure there's much left for either of us to say."

My heart sank. "What do you mean? I thought—"

I didn't get to explain, as he cut me off. "I know—I know I said a lot at the banquet. I just—I get it. You chose Sam, and I thought I could keep being your friend despite it, but damn it, May." He swallowed hard, his eyes darting from me as he stood. "I told you everything. I opened myself up to you and you—left. You ran away. You *keep* running away. You did it to me then and you're doing it to me now. I could handle it then, but now, with everything I know and everything between us... I want to wait for you. Hell, I *will wait*, but I can't be as close to you as I do.

"Date Sam. See where that goes. When you're done running, I'll be here. But if I'm going to survive until then, I can't handle just having pretend with you. I can't talk—or sacrifice more of myself until I have you."

He stared at me pleadingly. A begging look in his eye that asked me to stop the torture. To put him out of his misery.

I let the journal fall close on my lap, the wind in my determined sails sucked away.

What was I thinking? I couldn't bear my soul to this boy. All I was doing was hurting him. I needed to stop. I needed to get out, leave him be.

Packing up my few belongings, I kept the journal tied up in my hands as I stood from the bed. I avoided Trey's eyes as I strode to the bedroom door on wobbly knees. My fingers circled the brass knob. Just before I turned it to let myself out, I gathered my courage and looked back at him.

He was watching me. Pain in his eyes as he let me leave.

I was doing it again. Running away before giving him the full truth.

"I'm not dating Sam," I forced out. "I never was—I-I didn't choose him."

Trey's expression didn't change. He kept his jaw set, his body rigid, but his eyes tightened curiously. When he didn't speak, I reached back for the door. I was content, knowing I told him the truth.

That was enough for now.

But as the cold metal knob turned against my palm, I was torn off it, spun and pinned against the door. Trey's hands were twisting into the hem of my shirt, gripping me to him. My breathing was deep, quick. Each breath, each second and each pull closer had me pressing into his chest.

He seemed to notice too, as his green eyes fixated on how my body heaved with each inhale and exhale.

"Promise?" he asked, his grasp on my shirt going taut against my back, leaving absolutely no room between us. "It's over between you two?"

I gaped up at him, trying and failing to recover a semblance of coolness. "Trey—Sam and I never started. It was a misunderstanding, but I was *never his*."

With one hand, I latched onto the waistband of his sweats to stabilize myself. Feeling somewhat off-kilter, I inhaled and absorbed his spicy, cinnamon-sweet aroma. Unfortunately, my other hand still held my bag and journal.

The smile that spread across Trey's face was infatuating. One of his hands slid up my torso, brushing past my chest, to cup my cheek. "What does that mean, May? For me... For us?"

Caution coated his words, his movements. Almost like he wasn't sure what I was saying was real or pretend.

"It means I'm done running."

Eyes and smile going soft, he used his free hand to pull my things from my grasp, setting them on his dresser.

"Is this the point the couple finally gets together in those romance books of yours?" he asked, with both hands holding to me. Before I could respond, he nestled his nose into the exposed area of my throat.

My head fell back against the door as I sighed. "What would you know about the books I read?"

He pulled away, only far enough for me to make out the dark patches of forest green against the viridescent lighting of his eyes. "I know because any book I see you reading, I buy, and I read it too."

I eyed him, my fingers tangled with the material of his soft shirt. "Whatever. I snooped all over this room. I didn't see a single book."

Trey's eyebrows rose, but not out of surprise. They rose in a silent, *of course you did*, before he nodded to the nightstand next to his bed. The same nightstand I had, in fact, missed out on scouring because of Trey being sick and interrupting my search. "I have an e-reader. It's in the bottom drawer and believe me when I tell you, I've read every book you have."

"Why?" The question popped out of me.

His smile never faltered as he said, "Because I want to know you, May. I want to know the things you like, love, hate and dream about. I want to know what entertains you or gets your heart going faster. I want to know where your mind goes when it wants to get away. I want to know what makes you, you."

My mouth gaped wide open. I couldn't keep my cool now. I blushed and admired the man still drawing me in. This big, athletic boy had read every little smutty romance I had, merely because he'd seen me reading it.

"Okay, I'll admit, that's cute. But again, I have to ask, *why?*"

Those eyes were tearing into me again, returning with the tight, heavy feeling of the moment between us. Trey looked at me like I may be the only way to breathe as he held onto me and said, "Because I fell in love with you."

His words escaped him like a long held in breath. I wanted to kiss the words from his lips so I could know the genuine, passionate taste of them. I paused before giving into the unmistakable draw.

"You *fell* in love with me? You mean before—before I lost my memories?"

The answer to this question was essential, dire. I knew from reading my journal, from the stories and our friends that I was far from the same girl who originally fell asleep all those months ago.

Was Trey in love with a memory I didn't possess or the girl who woke up?

"May, I fell in love with you while you were sleeping," he said, then reached by me, grabbing and holding up my priceless journal.

"Before your accident, I liked you, but that is all it was. I hardly knew you. But after you fell asleep, and I stumbled upon this," he said as he shook the book for emphasis. "I fell in love with you, your mind, your heart. The more I got to know about you, the more I fell in love. I fall more every day because you woke up the woman I learned about through the pages of this book. I see you, May. You are a rarity that I want to continue to learn about, study and understand every moment of every day for the rest of my life."

I was spinning at unearthly speeds, flying above the clouds, and falling from dizzying heights. I may not have remembered loving anyone in my life. May not have remembered any past crushes or relationships, but in this moment... I knew without a doubt that I'd never been more seen or loved than the way Trey Turner saw and loved me.

And I loved him right back.

"I wasn't pretending, and you were never second pick," I quietly released into the slowly shrinking space between us. His eyes went wide with my honesty. "I'm yours, Trey. I've always been yours."

The deep, weight-relieving sigh he let out had him melting into me more as he murmured against my hair, "I've waited so long for this." His hands encircled me, and he molded me to him, our foreheads now resting against one another.

"I missed you," I breathed. "Especially for our morning walks. I hated walking alone."

His grip on my body tightened. "You weren't alone."

My eyes shot up to find his. "What?"

The coy chuckle Trey released was utterly delicious. "I waited outside your apartment every morning and trailed behind you like a freak."

That would explain the uneasy feeling of being watched. Shaking my head against his, I couldn't contain my smile. "Of course you did."

He sniffed, then took my chin in his fingers and made me look at him. "I made a promise that you would never walk alone again, and I keep my promises." His thumb found my lips, pressing into them like a gentle kiss.

"I'm going to kiss you now," he said, and I smiled as I tied my arms around his neck.

"It's about time."

Then he was kissing me. The act was languid. He was savoring it. Drawing out and appreciating every single second, every touch. Every new overwhelmingly beautiful feeling that sparked to life in the non-existent space between us.

His hands glided and explored up and down my waist, across my stomach. One of his hands effortlessly laced itself around the base of my neck while the other now gripped the back of my knee. He drew my leg up his thigh and hooked it around his waist.

Then I was in the air as Trey wrapped both my legs around his middle. He carried me to his bed and laid me beneath him.

He admired me as he lifted a hand to caress my temple and the framing curls of my hair.

"Let me show you all the things I could only dream of doing while I waited for you to pick me," he said.

In answer, I sat up with him, so we both knelt on the mattress. I helped him remove his shirt and then he was slipping off mine.

I followed his movements, where his eyes landed as I revealed myself to him. That emerald stare gripped my throat. It caressed the rise and fall of my breathing, intensified on the now bare expanses of my skin. His hands went to the waistband of my pants. He tugged me to him so he could more easily plant kisses along my jawline, down my neck and across my shoulders.

"Is this what you want, May?" he asked into my burning skin, and I shuddered. He stopped then to look me in the eye as he waited. I was speechless, breathing too heavy, body boneless.

"I want you, Trey," I began, not entirely coherent. "I want you to know me, all of me."

He crushed his mouth against mine and lowered me back into his bed. "You're so beautiful," he hummed against my stomach, as he slowly undid my pants. He stood from the bed, slipping my jeans off with ease. Then his sweats were on the floor.

Trey was back above me, fingering the strap of my bra. "Sit up for me, please."

I did, and Trey smirked as he undid the band. "So obedient," he chuckled, and I glared up at him.

"Enjoy it while it lasts."

His deep laughter rumbled through me. "Oh, I plan to."

Together we learned, taught, and received every blissful touch, feeling, and movement. As Trey promised, he loved and learned every bit of me. In a rhythm and intensity that had us both diving over the edge of pure satiated contentment.

I was home, cradled against him under the covers, feeling every bit of his body against my exposed skin.

"Mayhem," he said onto the back of my neck as he trailed a line of kisses along the tops of my shoulders.

"Hmm?"

He wrapped his arm around my waist, trying to pull me closer. "You're endgame for me," he breathed as he nipped at my ear.

"What does that mean?" I snorted.

He pressed a long kiss between my shoulder blades before lifting himself up on an elbow.

He hovered over me as he said, "It means I love you and I'll always love you." His forest green focus lined with glassy emotion as he brushed a stray hair from my face. "I've waited a long time to tell you that."

I put a gentle hand on his cheek, brought him to me and I kissed him. I kissed him like I could kiss away the past, all the heartache and loneliness he faced, and keep him here with me. Keep him in this blissful moment of peace in one another's embrace.

When we parted, I pressed my forehead against his and held him there as I whispered, "I love you too, Trey Turner. You're my endgame too."

38

Unforgettable

"You want to play some COD?" Williams asked in the doorway of my bedroom.

"Busy," I tossed over my shoulder as I folded my laundry and placed them into my dresser drawers.

"With what?"

"Maybelle's going to be here soon. I want my room clean before she gets here."

"You know," he sniffed. "I'm feeling extremely neglected by the both of you. Since you guys got together, there has been no time for me." He clapped me on the back, and I rolled my eyes. "Whatever happened to bros before hoes?"

"Watch it," I warned.

He let out a hearty chuckle. "Awe, my boy's the overprotective, touchy type," he teased. "Calm down, you know I have nothing but all the love and respect for little MandM."

I quirked a brow. "MandM?"

He smacked his lips together. "Cute, huh? Came up with it myself. Speaking of which. MandM has been chilling in the living room with me and Larson for the last ten minutes."

"And you're just now telling me?" I flung the shorts

I was folding haphazardly into the open drawer as I pushed past Williams, eager to see my girl.

I entered the living room. Williams trailed behind me, muttering something about me being whipped. Larson was on the couch, laughing at a video he was showing Maybelle.

She blatantly grimaced.

"Come on, May. That's some funny shit right there," Larson said, and Maybelle gave him a scrutinized side-eye.

"Mayhem."

She whipped her head to me. A beaming, beautiful smile overtook the scowl she had for Larson. I couldn't help but puff out my chest a bit more because of it.

I held my hand out to her. She immediately accepted, and I pulled her up, sat myself in her spot on the couch, then planted her on my lap. As she nuzzled up against me, I kissed the back of her neck.

"Alright jackasses, way to make me feel single as hell," Larson lamented, standing from the sofa. He grabbed Williams's shoulder as he joined him in the hall, leaning one arm against the other wall.

"Before I go to rot in my room alone, I've been meaning to ask. Did you guys hear about the new undercover security that's been hanging out outside our apartments?" He looked to Maybelle and me while Williams stared at us like he was really deep in thought.

"No," Maybelle said, responding for us both. "I haven't seen anyone either."

Larson pulled his phone from his pocket then and had a picture up on the screen as he handed it to Maybelle. "Fancy, huh? The school must have a new, fat security budget."

Maybelle took the phone and held it up for me to peer it over her shoulder. It was sort of blurry. Like the picture was taken from far away and zoomed in on. It wasn't super visible. But the image of a tall blonde man, dressed in a button up and slacks, leaning against a black, window-tinted vehicle with sunglasses on, just outside of Maybelle's apartment, was undeniable.

"How do we know he's undercover security?" I asked.

Larson shrugged. "Some sorority girls I know talked to him the other day. He told them he's a new hire. Real great at his job, though. Pretty sure he got every single one of those girls' numbers. I'd trust him to save my life."

Maybelle snickered, but her eyes didn't leave the screen of Larson's phone. "Enlighten me on how that qualifies him to save lives."

"Because a man who has the skill to get about eight girls' numbers in the same conversation is a hero in my book."

Again, she huffed a chuckle under her breath, but her eyes narrowed in on the picture. "He looks like someone I know," she uttered.

I straightened then, pulling her tighter into me so I too could look at the picture more closely.

"Who?" I asked.

She used her pointer finger and thumb to zoom in on the man's face. "You know Rick, the guy Penny told you about from my work?"

I stiffened further. "The guy with a staring problem?"

She nodded carelessly, then handed the phone back to Larson. "Yeah, that one. It kind of looks like him with the blonde hair and outfit, but it couldn't be. Rick only knows how to stare. I don't think he'd be able to have a normal conversation with one girl, let alone successfully flirt with a group of sorority girls."

Larson lifted from the wall, accepting the phone back. "Yeah, anyway, I thought it was cool. If you need me, I'll be in my room—wallowing. Good night." And he left, shutting and locking his bedroom door behind him.

Our attention turned to Williams then, who was smiling something devious as he said, "MandM, and

TNT! Damn, I'm good."

Then he too was gone down the hall with no further explanation, leaving Maybelle and I staring after him.

"You have some weird friends," she speculated, and I chuckled into her hair.

"*We*—we have some weird friends," I corrected. She smirked but didn't argue.

I took a tuft of her hair, winding it around my finger. "You got work off tomorrow like I asked, right?"

She shimmied her hips, and I flinched at the reaction my body gave her intoxicating movements.

"Easy, woman," I gritted out, and she giggled.

"Yes, I got work off and made sure all my homework got done for this surprise day you have planned. Are you going to tell me what this is all about yet?" she asked as she snuggled deeper into my embrace.

She leaned her head back onto my shoulder, tilting so she could place delicate kisses across my jaw line.

I stifled a groan as my hands inched up her waist. "If I tell you, that'll ruin the surprise."

Her hands joined with mine as she guided my caresses up and down her body to the places that got us both breathing a little harder.

"Please," she whispered against my ear and my body trembled with want.

I abruptly pushed her to her feet and tugged her toward my room. "Uh—what're you doing?" she asked, and I grinned like a giddy son of a bitch.

"You beg, I oblige," I said simply.

"That's not what I was saying please to," she sassed as I shoved her into the room and locked the door.

"You and I both know that's not true. Now, come here."

MAYBELLE

The next morning, I woke in Trey's arms, cuddled up

in his bed. He was already awake. He lifted himself up on an elbow to look down at me as he brushed my frizzy mess of bedhead out of my face.

"Good morning," he said with a dimple-framed grin that had my limbs melting to goo.

"Good morning," I said as I examined the way the sunlight broke through the curtains. How it lit up the highlights of his hair and the emerald green of his eyes.

His skin was smooth due to his recent shave. His smile was straight and bold. His hair toppled over his brows and the veins in his forearms bulged as he continued to play with the hair that cascaded around my face.

"You're so pretty," I whispered, and Trey chuffed before placing a gentle kiss on my collarbone.

"You think so?" he asked, placing a few more kisses down my chest.

"Mhmm," I breathed, as my back arched. It was like my heart was levitating against my ribcage, trying to meet his touch. Reaching out desperately to feel his bare lips and show him how it only beat for him.

"Trey," I nearly whimpered.

Instead of answering my pleas, he climbed back up my body, bringing us nose to nose as he smiled.

"Not yet. We have things to do today."

I glowered. "No—*you* have things to do. Things being me."

He pulled my legs up around his waist as he chuckled into the hollow of my neck. "Oh, I would love nothing more than to lay you out and have you for breakfast, but that'll have to wait. Just trust me?" he asked, and I conceded.

"Fine."

He grinned wider into my skin, then he was lifting off the bed. With my legs still wrapped around his middle, he carried me into the shower.

It wasn't until around early afternoon we finally

pulled up to a beach. Trey was being so weird. Actually, all of my friends were. Bear got up extra early to cook only me waffles with caramel syrup. Larson, obviously and painfully, bit back every sarcastic comeback in each conversation. And Williams was super touchy—like—he kept pulling me into a hug every two seconds, saying how happy he was that I was here.

Maybe I was dying, and Trey brought me to the beach to tell me? Even Penny was MIA, avoiding every single one of my texts and calls.

"You ready for our walk?" Trey asked as he pulled the keys from the ignition.

I narrowed my eyes at him and the sun dress I was wearing.

When I told Penny yesterday that I would be spending the day with Trey, she insisted on picking my outfit. I usually stuck to the neutrals, basic tops, and comfortable pants, but Penny vowed—for no particular reason—that I would want to wear something a bit more *girly* for the occasion.

Her words. Not mine.

She offered up a gorgeous, jade green, sun dress from the back of her closet. It had cap sleeves, a bodice that held snug to my chest and waist, then flared into a twirly skirt that stopped at my knees. I gratefully accepted because if Penny knew anything, it was fashion and how to drive a man wild with it.

"You want me to try walking through the sand in this thing?" I asked, gesturing to the dress.

His eyes tore at where the dress hugged my chest and flounced up my thighs. "I have so many things I would like to see you do in that dress, but for right now, yes. Just a short walk. You can hold my hand for balance if you'd like," he offered, grasping for my hand.

I let our fingers intertwine as I smiled at him. "Okay, fine. Lead the way."

Trey was opening my door and showing me down to

the beach within moments. "You know," he started, "you fight with me a lot less now. Why is that?"

"I don't know. I guess there's no point in giving you a hard time when you already won me over and made me yours," I said, bumping my hip into his as we stepped onto the sand.

"It's cute that you think there was a time that you weren't mine." He gave me a wry smile, wrapping his arm around my waist, graciously carrying most of my weight and balancing me out.

He led me to an area of sheer rock the waves clapped against and only a few miscellaneous people explored. I studied the leafy vines and pink flowers that climbed and wove themselves into the earth, and rock wall that cast a shadow onto the sand and—Penny?

Before I could ask or barely react, my best friend raced and collided with me. We staggered a few steps away from Trey, who smiled at the interaction.

"Oh, Belles! I'll get out of your hair, I promise! I just wanted to make sure I saw you today and got to tell you I love you and happy birthday!" she squealed, and I almost choked.

My what?

My eyes darted after her wide-eyed, to Trey, still wide-eyed, and then to the quilted blanket Penny had been apparently sitting with.

Atop the blanket was a picnic basket, fancy glasses, and what looked to be a bottle of cider. Then a gorgeous blue cake frosted to say *Happy Birthday* with one candle in the middle.

Penny squeezed me one last time. "Okay, I love you, have the best day!" She released me then launched herself at Trey, who caught her embrace with ease.

"Gosh, I love you two! Okay, I'm gone!" And she was. She skipped off to a parked vehicle, up the way, and drove off.

I finally looked to Trey, who grinned. "I asked her to

set this up for me and watch over it until we got here."

I turned slowly to the setup, my skirt catching in the salty sea breeze and my curls dancing across my face.

"It's my birthday?" I asked, not really knowing what else to say.

He grabbed the fabric of the dress at my waist, pulling me against him as he brushed back a curl. "Yeah. Are you upset I didn't tell you? I knew you've been busy and probably forgot, so I thought I'd surprise you. Was that, okay?" he asked, in all seriousness.

I paused, biting down on the inside of my cheek.

Was I mad at him? No, not at all.

What was upsetting was that I didn't remember my birthday. Just another reminder of how much of a stranger I was in my body. Another reminder that even after all this time, other people still knew more than I did about myself.

I shook my head.

"No, I like surprises. What's in the basket?" I asked, gesturing to the picnic set up, not willing to depress his efforts under my own personal drama.

His demeanor brightened as he led me to the blanket. I followed his lead taking a seat on the quilt, the basket and cake between us. He pulled out—pop tarts.

I glanced up at him, eyebrows raised.

"With how many of these you and Williams eat, I thought you'd want nothing more."

I shrugged. "Touché. Gimme." And I accepted a packet of pop tarts. "I didn't realize you were such a romantic, Turner."

I broke a chunk of my snack off and put it into my mouth. I studied Trey pouring us both glasses of cider with a tight grin on his face.

"Well, then, you aren't very observant. I'm very romantic and sentimental."

I continued to watch my cheery boyfriend, instantly recalling many accounts when he was romantic. For goodness's sake, he waited by my bedside for an entire year without hope that I would wake.

"Let me rephrase. I didn't realize you were so corny."

This earned me a sidelong glance.

"You like corny," he said as he handed me a glass, then took my other hand in his.

And that I did.

I took a sip of my bubbly drink, letting my fingers lace with Trey's and relished in the way the sun warmed my face.

Realization donned. I looked down at our hands held together, the sun glowing against our skin, and Trey watching me with unrestrained happiness.

Before I could acknowledge the importance of what he'd done for me, he moved onto the cake. He pulled a lighter from the bottom of the basket, lit the candle, then held up the cake for me.

"Alright, make a wish."

I studied him and the darling blue iced cake.

A wish. What more could I ask for? With Trey, Chelsea and all my friends, I had everything...

Except—one thing. I inhaled, then blew out the candle.

Trey plucked two forks from the basket, still beaming. "What did you wish for?"

I looked away, adjusting my dress. "Nothing, I have all I need," I fibbed, and he snorted.

"Yeah, okay. So, what did you actually wish for?"

This man knew me too well. I refused to make eye contact even as he handed me a fork.

"I have everything I could ever want, except my—my memories," I mumbled the last part.

His movements halted from what I could see at the corner of my eye. The world seemed to slow. Even the timing between waves crashing seemed to drag on.

After a few beats, I peered over at him.

He was watching me with the intensity I saw in him

when he was trying to solve a problem, usually my problem. It was the way he'd looked at me, the time he caught me with the bruise on my hip and that bookcase toppled over. And when I snuck out of the apartment, the first time I visited. He looked at me as if he thought long enough, he could come up with a solution that would keep me safe from anything and everything.

Sadly, this wasn't something he alone could fix. Nothing could save me from the harsh reality that was my circumstance.

"I didn't realize you cared or wanted your memories back. You seemed so content just moving on. Especially after learning about what happened to, you," he said as one of his hands moved to grasp the top of my knee.

"Eh—I didn't before. Especially because of the family I lost. Seeing how much Liam and Stephanie's deaths affected you all, I didn't want to know what that felt like. And, yes, the dark past intimidated me, but there's been a part of me that feels like a stranger in my skin. The other day, I noticed I have a scar on my thigh right here," I said, hiking my skirt up to show off a quarter's length, pale pink scar.

As if it was instinct, Trey's hand moved so his thumb could sweep across the mark.

"I had no clue where I got that. Luckily, I wrote about it in the journal. Some girl had acrylics on in a basketball game I played in. She went to swipe the ball from me but took a chunk out of my skin with her fake nail instead."

I pointed to a long, thin scar in my shin. "I don't know where this one came from, and I noticed an old scar above my brow right here." I put my forefinger to my head blindly. "It's so old I bet I got it when I was little. Maybe I fell downstairs or something. I wouldn't know, though."

I dropped my hand and turned to look out at the beach. Trey's fingers quickly pinched my chin, forcing me to look at him. He wasn't smiling half as much as before, but a slight smirk still tugged one side of his mouth up. Showing off the ghost of a dimple. His hand moved to cup the back of my neck, bringing me forward until his lips pressed into the aged scar on my forehead.

When we parted, he dropped his forehead to mine.

"I didn't even know my own birthday," I whispered, and the hand on my nape flexed.

"I know, May. I'm sorry," he breathed.

I shook my head and pulled away just far enough to look at him. "Don't you dare be sorry. You have nothing to be sorry for. You're perfect and one of the main reasons I have little to want. You make my life better," I coughed out on a half laugh, half cry, shocked by the sudden flood of emotions. "I just wish I knew more. That the last—oh god, I'm twenty years old, right?"

Trey chuckled and nodded in confirmation.

"I wish the last twenty years of my life weren't just gone."

He inhaled deeply before he relocated the items between us. He pulled me up next to him, his arm snaking around my waist and my head fell onto his shoulder.

"Well, Mayhem, my wish would be to give you those twenty years back if I could. If I could change the past. But my promise to you now is I will make the next twenty years and forever unforgettable."

I nestled into his embrace, wiping away the rest of my ebbing tears. "I know you will. You already are."

We held to one another, watching the horizon of sailboats and cruise ships bob about. Seagulls screeched, and a family of five made camp not too far up the beach from us.

Really, what more could I want? Especially in a moment like this, my best friend by my side, on this perfect day.

It was a weird feeling I couldn't quite explain. The incessant prickle of unease that I didn't have a known identity outside of the last few months since waking up. I wanted to know it all, to know myself.

But I would be okay without the memories, with the gift of my journal, and Trey helping me every step of the way. I could still live a happy and amazing life without them, and I would.

"Alright, enough of my depressing crap. Feed me cake," I demanded.

Trey chuckled and picked up the platter. He grabbed for his fork, scooping out a bite before holding it up for me. I moved to accept it, but he jerked the fork away at the last second. He smeared the frosting across my nose and up my cheek.

I gasped.

He bellowed with laughter.

In retaliation, I drug two fingers into the cake and streaked the blue sugary cream through his hair. Trey shot to attention, a challenge glinting in his eyes.

"Oh, you asked for it now, sweetheart."

I needed no more warning. I was up on my feet and trying to haul ass.

Another thing I could've wished for: functioning legs.

I didn't make it far before Trey was upon me and throwing me over a shoulder. I squealed as he trotted for the waves, splashing into the salty water as he plopped me on my feet.

I acted fast, cupping a handful of water, and splashing it up at him. He took it in stride. Shaking his head, his hair tossed the blue frosting away and the distraction was enough. I was too busy gawking to be ready for him grappling for me again. His large arm wrapped me up and pulled me deeper into the waves with him.

As the depth of the water grew, I had an uncomfortable realization. I latched onto him like a wet rat. "Uh, hey, just a thought, but I don't know if I know how to swim."

Trey stopped.

Granted, the water was only tall enough to reach his hips, but with the pursuing and pulling of the waves I didn't want to take any chances. He adjusted me around his front, so my legs encircled his waist. His hands held me up under the skirt of my dress, cupping the bare skin of my backside. The act was hidden by the dark blue of the rocking sea.

"Well, if it means I can keep holding you like this," he punctuated with a squeeze. "Then you'll never learn how to swim."

I swatted at him. The anxiety of drowning was soon forgotten as he held me above the waves and kissed me. A deep, gentle kiss that stole my breath, making me think that maybe drowning wouldn't be so terrible if it felt anything like this.

When our lips parted, the taste of salt and cream mingling on our tongues, I brushed my fingers through his hair. Then placed a chaste kiss on his forehead before whispering, "Thank you for giving me my perfect day."

Trey smiled. His eyes closed as he pulled me entirely against him and reconnected our kiss in a passionate flurry.

This wasn't just a kiss, but a promise.

This was a vow that I discerned as a guarantee that I would get a lifetime of perfect days. Hand in hand, the sun on my face, with the man I loved, with all my heart, by my side, for every single one of them.

39

Remember

Maybelle

Scoot, Belles, scoot! They close in less than five minutes!"

"I'm trying. We just need the cheese."

Catapulting myself across our shopping cart, I launched at the cheese sitting on the top shelf.

"Alright, package secured," I announced, and Penny snorted.

"Fall out then, before we get locked in here and have to build lives for ourselves like Natalie Portman in that *Where the Heart Is* movie."

I stopped right there, in the middle of the grocery store aisle. Another announced reminder over the loudspeakers saying the doors would close soon rang out. I ignored it to give my bestie a disgruntled look.

"That was such a beautiful movie based on a beautiful book, and that was main takeaway?"

Penny smiled too sweetly before she shoved me forward. "Nope, my main takeaway was to play safe with boys because they'll end up abandoning you in the middle of nowhere, anyway."

We were at a grocery store a little too far from home. Tomorrow Trey was coming home after he and the team had been gone for almost a week, playing back-to-back games out of town. In celebration of both wins, them coming home, and the semester ending, I thought I'd make Chelsea's famous lasagna for the boys.

Chelsea was a fancy gal, so, of course, her food was too. The lasagna called for specific ingredients that weren't available at any of the local shopping spots. So, Penny, being the best friend that she is, came on a little ingredient scavenger hunt with me. Luckily, we found everything I needed at this random grocer just before closing.

We both hustled toward the self-checkout line and halted as we got to an open machine.

"Things not going well with Daniel?" I asked as Penny handed me the groceries and I scanned them.

"What? No, things between us are great. Why do you ask?"

"I don't know. That was just a very pessimistic thing to say for a happy girl with a boyfriend."

She stopped handing me items to look at me. "Daniel and I aren't dating, Belles."

I abruptly stopped as well to look at my friend. "What? Since when?"

"Since forever," she said, handing me another item. "Danny and I are just friends."

"Hmph," I grunted, throwing the cheese into a bag. "Could've fooled me." We both went quiet then. I finished scanning, paid, and we walked outside into the balmy night.

"Don't get me wrong," Penny said, interrupting the rhythmic sound of our feet clicking against the pavement. "I do like him—it's just complicated."

Nodding, I adjusted the few bags in my hands up onto my forearm. "What's complicated about it?"

She sighed. "I don't know. It's just… Oh, oh no."

"What?"

She searched around herself, frantically checking her pockets. "Shoot. You wouldn't happen to have my phone, do you?"

Leveling a sarcastic smirk at my friend, I said, "You had it when we walked into the store. Did you leave it in the bathroom when you used it?"

Groaning, Penny spun back toward the front of the building. "I bet it's going to be a hassle trying to get them to open the doors for me. Ugh, I'll be right back."

I sniffed, continuing my approach of the vehicle that sat at the back of the vacant parking lot. Before Trey left, he had given me his car keys saying, "What's mine is yours".

Having been trusted with something as great as a car, I was overly cautious when I parked. Now, as I trudged the distance, I regretted trying to be extra safe with my boyfriend's car.

When I made it to the Jeep, I set the grocery bags down next to the rear wheel and knotted my hands around the cross-body strap of my purse.

The parking lot was void of life besides me.

Still... There was a fraction of my subconscious feeling extremely *twitchy*.

Straightening, still facing the car, I stretched my back out, digging in my back pocket for the keys. Heavy footsteps clunked behind me. I didn't think to look because I thought Penny was coming back—but I was wrong... I was so wrong.

"Maybelle."

Startled by the male voice so close behind me, I lost my hold on the keys and my panicked heart. I spun to find a tall, blonde man standing mere feet behind me. I didn't get the chance to look at him as my keys slipped from my clumsy fingers and clattered to the ground.

Right in front of his black dress shoes.

Chuckling, he stepped forward. "I'm sorry. I didn't mean to scare you."

I recognized his face instantly as he bent down. He maintained eerie eye contact with me as he picked the keys up and jangled them carelessly from one hand to the other. He wore the same high-priced business attire he'd always worn when I served him at the coffee shop. A white button-up, dress shirt, black slacks and a luxury watch on his right wrist that reflected the lone streetlight down the way.

"Rick," I breathed. "Wha—what are you doing here?"

Rick, my every-loyal coffee customer. The one that tipped me well and grabbed a coffee before silently taking a spot in the far corner of the shop. Where he sat and watched me go about my day-to-day tasks at work.

Warily, I extended a hand to accept the keys. He didn't react, he only watched me. It differed from the way he looked at me all those days while I worked. In the shop, his staring always seemed so absent-minded. As if he were daydreaming and his focus unintentionally fell on me, but not now. Now, his gaze, his studying dark eyes, ate at me, ripped at me and stripped me.

"Maybelle?" he said again, gently, with an unsteady step closer and I stilled. It was difficult to make out the entirety of him in the limited light. Except for the smile that was already sharpening his lips.

We were in the vacant parking lot of a store, in the middle of a town Penny and I hadn't recognized. It was far from campus and the coffee shop. With that being said, it was more likely for this meet up to be an act of divine intervention rather pure coincidence.

Or it wasn't an accidental run-in at all.

I should've run then. I should have left as soon as I saw his familiar face. I should've bolted straight for the store, for Penny when I had the chance, but I was glued in place.

"Yes?" I confirmed, shooting a quick glance at the still empty lot behind him.

Now that he was closer, I got a nose-full of a chemical, heavy smell that radiated from him. I couldn't name the specific notes of the scent. My mind was tangling with the details before me. It was warring with several instincts.

Numerous fears, reasons and facts twisted into an indiscernible mess.

All because of that one smell.

I didn't know why, but the smell made me want to cry—no, it made me want to scream.

My hand remained out, barely shaking, but ready to accept the keys as I studied him.

Rick was handsome, appearing as his usual clean-cut self. Except, as the distance between us continued to shrink, I saw a slight rumple to his appearance I hadn't yet witnessed. His hair was combed back, but a few stray blonde tufts fell out past his eyes. His clothes were neat if not for the rolled-up, uneven sleeves of his shirt that cinched around his elbows.

His choppy chuckle brought my eyes back to his. He was taking full inventory of my body. His languid perusal froze my bones.

"What're you doing here?" I bit out again, quickly growing uneasy with his creepy theatrics.

He took one step back, like I might've struck him. "Oh, Maybelle. Don't you recognize me?"

"Yes," I shoved out. "You're Rick. I serve you coffee where I work."

"Maybelle," he drawled disapprovingly. "My name is not Rick."

Goosebumps crawled a warning path up my skin. I was in danger and my body knew it before I could truly register the threat.

When I didn't speak, that sharp sneer melted into something akin to bitter amusement as he shook his head.

"You really don't remember me," he muttered.

I didn't care to understand what he was trying to say, what point he was trying to prove. Instead of paying his unsettling words any more attention, I stretched my hand out farther.

"Please give me my keys. I'm expected home."

He didn't flinch. That smile returned and kept growing, like an infection. He tutted as he pilfered the remaining safe distance between us with only a couple steps forward. I didn't try to step back. I was pinched between this man and the Jeep, leaving no room for me to retreat.

"Home?" he asked. His voice was soft, almost singsong like, but that smell… It was so strong, and it was invading my brain. Everything in my body was crying out in a million different, terrified voices for me to run, to hold still—to remember.

"Yes," I said breathlessly. "Home."

I continued to hold my hand out for the keys, but Rick refused to acknowledge my request as he held the keys to his side.

"Your home isn't here," he said lowly, the closeness allowing me to scent the alcohol on his breath. "Your home is with me."

I should've panicked at how close he was. I should've been scared of the way he watched me. Like I was a treasure he sought out and finally found. But I couldn't think past the ruckus of frantic thoughts banging against my brain with that damned smell.

Remember. Remember. Remember.

My vision blurred with trapped tears. I licked my lips, and his eyes sluggishly followed the movement.

"You've been gone for a long time. I missed you."

He was so close now, his breathing hot on my face, but his arms were hotter as they wrapped around my rigid body.

Remember. Run. Remember. Run.

My brain couldn't recall his real name right away, but my body knew his touch. Even though it never knew it to be gentle like this.

My joints locked up. My limbs paralyzed.

I was a child again.

A helpless, terrified, speechless child. I could feel it. The seeping in of recollections, the terror-filled memories that this man owned. Like each hit I'd ever been dealt was being struck against my skin at the same time.

I doubled over in his arms with the sudden overwhelming weight. I bit down on my chest-cleaving sobs, as every single moment I cried, cowered and begged came tumbling through my battered brain.

"Shh," he hushed, putting one hand in my hair and pressing my face painfully tight to his collarbone. "I've got you."

Bile burned the back of my throat as I remembered why that smell was enough to ruin me. It was his aftershave. He used the strong-smelling liquid to mask the persistent smell of alcohol on his breath. But they only combined to create a horror of scent that haunted each one of my waking nightmares.

The tears trapped in my eyes finally escaped down my cheeks as I trembled in Rick's—no, not Rick.

In Richard's hold.

"Good girl," he cooed, and I wanted to die. "That's a good girl. I'm here now."

My body had a mind of its own as I stood there, still as stone, with my hands fisted around the strap of the purse slung over my body.

Richard didn't need a gun or knife to persuade me to keep still. The fear and instincts that took over my body did the job for him.

He pulled back from me, cupping my face in both his considerable hands. His eyes were bloodshot, he had a shadow of stubble along his jaw and his shirt was undone at the top. He wasn't as put together as he had always prided himself on being.

And he was, without a doubt, drunk.

With hands holding either side of my face, pressing in on my temples, Richard stared at me. His drunken emotions overwhelmed his usually structured face.

"You have no idea how long I've been looking for you," he choked out. "I saw on the news that you'd been in a coma but woke up. I thought I finally found you, your mom, and your brother. I wanted us to be a family again. So, I ran straight to San Francisco. I had to see you."

He rocked forward and I couldn't help but rock with him as his hands held my head in a vice-like grip.

"But when I got to your hospital, they said your mom and Liam were…were dead." A strangled sob escaped him then, and I nearly buckled on my wobbly knees.

Stop, don't think about it now.

Stay focused. Think about them later.

He sniffed, and his grasp on my head constricted tighter. Closing my eyes against the pain, I bit down on my lip.

"Then they wouldn't let me see you, even though you're mine. You're mine, and they tried to keep you from me. It's okay though, I paid someone at the hospital to tell me where you were. I followed you to that house. Where the boy and woman took care of you. Trey and Chelsea, right?"

His tone was airy as he stepped forward. He pressed my back into the door of the Jeep, pinning me against the surface of the vehicle. "I waited for you. I waited and waited for you. I watched you sneak out at night when you lived there. I would follow you on those long walks you would take, you know? I was always there, watching out for my girl."

Pushing into me, Richard's forehead fell against mine, nailing my head to the car door.

"I watched you. I had to, because you're mine. Then I followed you to college. I visited you every day at work, every day, but you didn't recognize me," he grounded out the last part, his hands fisting my hair and pushing me against the vehicle. Hard enough to tear a whimper from my throat. "How could you not remember me? You're mine, and you didn't remember me."

"I'm sorry," I gasped out. "I'm sorry."

"Oh shh, sweet girl, don't cry, I'm here," he sputtered out, his hands detangling themselves from my hair and his fingers combed through soothingly. "I've got you."

Hold your breath, stay still, don't move.

"It's okay now because we found each other, and we can go home."

Survival was my only thought as I remained motionless in the hands of this monster and my body knew how to survive. It was the same routine, the same ritual my limbs and heart had performed through the years to keep me safe.

His hands cupped my face, making me look him in the eyes as he brushed at the hair sticking to my sweat-damp forehead.

"You look so much like her," he said as his thumb stroked my jaw. "My Stephanie." He kissed my cheek as he whispered, "Let's go home."

Hold still, keep quiet, obey.

There were no other thoughts, no other choices.

I nodded.

Richard, holding my hand, led me to a secluded, dark corner of the parking lot, where a black vehicle lay in wait. I let him pull me into that dark corner. I knew what happened in dark corners. I knew the dangers that stalked the shadows, but I didn't rebel against his lead.

As we approached the vehicle, he reached for another set of car keys from his pocket. His fingers fumbled with the clanking metal.

Coughing, I choked on my tears. I was going to die. Richard was going to get behind the wheel and I was going to die.

Finally, was the thought of a misplaced piece of me

that came crawling from my subconscious. *About time,* was the bitter whisper of a forgotten girl who'd been beaten and abandoned.

No one will care once I'm gone. No one will remember.

I violently shook my head against the thoughts I once welcomed and fed. That's when I saw red. Looking up, I could see Penny. She stood beneath a lone streetlight, face stricken, body still.

See, my heart screamed out to the ugly, festering words of my old, lonely soul; *I'm not alone. I won't be forgotten.*

I turned to Richard. He was still jumbling with the keys, groaning as he tried to unlock the car. I was going to die if I obeyed, if I went with him. Then my eyes fell back on Penny. I may not survive this night if I go with him, but if he saw Penny and got his hands on her... I would wish I were dead.

Because Penny Howell was my family.

She took a step forward.

I shook my head adamantly, mouthing, "Don't move."

I was so scared she couldn't see my silent warnings in the dark, but to my utter relief, she nodded and stayed put. I decided then. I knew what I had to do. To be done with this, this night, this man. I knew what I needed to do.

I needed to speak. For my family, I needed to speak.

"Richard," I squeezed out. I didn't think he heard me until his bloodshot, dark eyes rolled over to me. "I—I can drive."

His brows furrowed. "I want to drive."

It took everything in me to take a step forward, to extend my hand out and place it comfortingly on his forearm. So close to the keys and yet so far from peace.

"I know," I whispered. "But I can drive, l-let you rest."

His drooping eyes continued to scowl holes into my

bluff, and I was so sure he would ignore my request. I nearly buckled over with grateful sobs when the metal of his keys bit into my awaiting palm.

"Okay," he uttered, and I helped him into the passenger seat. I didn't let myself look at Penny until I had the passenger door closed. I rounded the front of the vehicle to the driver's side.

She looked ready to race for me. Her phone was to her ear as she mouthed to me, "Don't go."

I didn't respond until I threw the driver's side door open. I took only a moment to admire my sweet friend from afar. The girl who befriended me, invited me in and loved me.

"I love you," I silently mouthed back. Then I got into the car and sped down the road.

40

Fight, May

Maybelle

We'd only been speeding on the spacious, dark roads for a few minutes when Richard's hand reached over the middle console and gripped my knee. "Take the freeway."

I pressed down on the gas pedal.

His grip tightened. "Go faster."

The acceleration jolted us forward.

"Damn it," he bellowed, and I flinched. "Where are you going? You were supposed to go right!"

"I'm sorry," I choked out. "I got lost."

It was easy to fall back into that small place. To obey and keep quiet. Especially now, as I sped past rows of streetlights that exuded a pale glow in the night.

I knew what had to be done. Richard wasn't too drunk to know I was going the wrong way. I was supposed to take a right. Instead, I continued straight. As his hold on my leg screwed up into my skin, I yelped from the pain he tore from me.

"You never could do anything right."

The tears were no longer droplets dripping down my face, but a steady, defeated stream. Then his hand was in my hair.

"Useless," he gritted out.

I didn't listen to his vicious ramblings. I was too focused on the plan I decided on back in the parking lot.

My heart was racing, my limbs were trembling. I was so close. Almost there, just a couple more miles. Only a few more minutes until I reached our final destination.

There was a bridge I noted on mine and Penny's drive to the store. A bridge with easily broken guard rails by the looks of already caused damage, and a steep fall to dark waters.

The finish line was so close. I was so close to putting an end to the pain, to the fear, to the hellish monster that tortured me and my family for far too long.

I rolled the car to a stop at a red light and as we halted, Richard's fingers tangled into my hair, shaking my head by the roots.

Mentally, I ran away.

I retreated to a safe place in my subconscious, imagining I was in the safest place I found in my short, painful life. But it wasn't the beach I opened my mind's eye to.

I was with Trey. He was the one sitting next to me in the car, not Richard. I wasn't in pain as my imaginary Trey used his thumb to delicately stroke the tears from my face.

"I'm here, May," he whispered, and he was.

Trey Turner was by my side, always waiting and remaining with me, even in my last moments.

A pressure pushed into my side. I looked down to see the purse I still had strapped to my body, but a shape from inside was peeking out the top. The corner of a black leather cover poked my stomach. I didn't know how it got in there, but I held to the strap of the bag tighter as I blinked my eyes back up to Trey's.

"It's yours," I shoved out over my heart-wrenching sobs because if I had the chance to tell him one last thing, it would be this. "The journal. It's yours. It's always been yours."

His smile was kind. It was beautiful as his green eyes watched me. "I know."

Then my head cracked into the window.

"You ruined everything!" Richard screamed as he pulled my face from the glass, then shoved me back. "I lost everything because of you!"

I tensed, ready for the next blow, but soft hands caught my face instead. "Shh, Lovebug. I'm here. I've got you."

I squinted to see my conjured-up imagination of Trey was gone. Sitting in his place was—my mom, holding me to her. She felt so real, warm. The same as she had the night I lost her.

My head hit the glass again.

When Mom pulled away, her big, sea foam eyes watched me before she kissed my throbbing head.

"I'm so proud," she whispered. "*We* are so, so proud of you."

I didn't have to ask what she meant by *we*. I had a feeling I knew, and my heart caved in on itself. What a reunion that must've been. My mom finally running home to the love of her life.

I too would have that reunion soon.

She kissed my head again before she made me look her in the eyes. "Live, Maybelle. Take the leap and live."

"What?" I asked, hiccupping.

"Take the leap," she repeated before pulling me to her chest one last time. "You are Maybelle Mason, and you can do hard things."

I blinked. Hot liquid melted down my face. My vision was hazy, but despite that, when I blinked again, I saw my brother sitting in the seat next to me, clear as day.

"Fight, May."

My head and heart seemed to fissure as I made myself look at my twin brother.

"Fight. You have to fight," he repeated, and I felt shattered, hopelessly broken.

"I don't know how," I sobbed.

Liam's firm hands grabbed my shoulders and his misty blue eyes bored into me. "Yes, you do."

Hold still, keep quiet, obey.

It was the anthem my body sang to, now, and for all my life. For as long as Richard had a part in my fate, my body held still, it kept quiet, and it obeyed.

"I know," Liam said, reading my thoughts.

And he did. My brother understood this part of me. He shared in this heartache with me.

Except once.

My muddled brain was tired. It was lost, but the images, the feelings and the memories of that one night came crawling back.

That night he fought. That night my brother fought for me… because he saw me as something worth fighting for.

The world froze around me as I found myself back in the car with Richard. His hand was still in my hair, his breathing heavy on my face and my vision blurred him out of focus.

Tears streamed down my cheeks, mixing with the iron taste of blood spilling over my lips as I looked him in his dark eyes. The same eyes that looked at me, a child, and deemed me unworthy of human decency. The eyes that made me feel that I was not worth fighting for. That I was no more than a rug to tread on, an object to hit down over and over again.

I hadn't planned to survive this.

When I entered this vehicle, I accepted that I wouldn't get to tell Trey I was sorry for leaving our life together so early. That I wouldn't get the opportunity to thank him for loving me. For standing beside me through every phase of my life, even when he'd only been a book of empty pages.

Without realizing it, I chose to run. To escape. To take the empty path on the beach leaning right. But if I learned anything from these last months, absent of the scars on my memory. From my book, from Trey, it's that I too was worth fighting for.

I was not alone. And I wanted to live.

I screamed. I screamed with the volume and force of a thousand locked up cries for help that were finally let loose as I made my body move. I shoved Richard off of me. I lurched for the car door and threw it open.

I didn't make it far, though. His hands were quick as they laced themselves around my throat from behind and dragged me back.

"It's all your fault! You never could do anything right! Pathetic! You were always in the goddamned way. Worthless piece of—good for nothing—!"

He continued to seethe. More insults and vicious words pouring from him as his hands grew tighter. With my foot off the brakes, the car rolled forward into the empty intersection. My foot skidded along the asphalt as my body hung halfway out the open car door.

My vision and breaths were failing me, but I kicked, I thrashed, I scratched, and I bucked. I didn't stop. I continued to swing. I continued to fight. While my body shook from the loss of strength for the fight it finally won against itself, I thought of Liam.

"*I'm broken too,*" I had admitted to him on that beach all those long months ago. "*Maybe, from now on, we can try to talk more. Fix the broken pieces together?*"

In my mind's eye, Liam wasn't drunk as he swayed back and forth, nodding his agreement. He was standing tall with a brilliant smile on his vibrant face. Eyes bright and awake, he reached his hand out to me.

"*I'd like that.*"

I didn't see the semi-truck or its bright headlights. But I heard its blaring horn and its screeching brakes as it barreled into the passenger side of the vehicle.

I didn't see what happened to Richard as the whole world capsized. I didn't think as his hands fell from my neck, but I did what I'd been told.

I leapt.

I hadn't gotten much time to mourn my family's memory after remembering, but as my world turned white and I put my hand in Liam's… I didn't think I would be needing the time.

We had all the time in the world.

41

Come Home

Trey

Life.

For the most part, life and I were friends. At one point, I positively considered life a kind, worthwhile experience. Then my best friend died and the girl I loved fell asleep.

I felt betrayed by life. I thought we had a solid understanding of feasible hardships and meaningful rewards. But it took something irreplaceable to me.

Two people I loved and considered family.

Then when my trust was broken, and I was at my weakest, life tricked me into a false security. It gave me back the girl I remained patient for. I could handle the ups and the downs, the rejection and the back and forth because Maybelle was awake. That was the most important thing, that she was awake. She was alive.

Life was good in re-gifting me the presence of the girl I fell for through the words of a precious book. It was gentle in letting me hold her again, letting me keep her. But it was ripping my trust apart all over again by trying to take her back.

"Hang in there. We're close," Williams said from the back seat. Nodding, I held to the door handle of the truck, ready to dive out as soon as we arrived.

"What else did Penny say?" Larson demanded from

next to Williams. "Did the guy have a gun? Is that why she went with him?"

"No," Bear answered for me as he wove his truck through traffic. "She said that Maybelle willingly went with him."

Twenty minutes ago, I disembarked the plane home with my brothers after a couple of won away games. The moral was high. I was feeling really good, thinking I was headed home to be with the girl I loved.

Just as we exited the elevator into the parking garage, my phone started to ring. Penny was on the other line. She was in tears, and I instantly knew something was wrong with Maybelle.

My heart hadn't stopped dropping since. All rational thought left me. I was a problem solver. I fixed things. I protected. I was organized but as I listened to Penny sob on the other line… I was lost.

My mind scattered like water droplets on a searing pan.

Thankfully, Bear overheard the call. He explained to Williams and Larson, and they knew what I wanted— what I needed. In seconds, we were piled into Bear's truck and racing down the road.

"Turn left up here," Williams directed.

Bear obeyed.

"How far are we?" I managed to choke out.

Larson leaned up from the back, pointing past the windshield. "We're here."

The truck swerved up next to the closed off road. Red and blue lights lit up the night. Bear didn't park. He slowed, letting Williams and I jump out as he came to a stop.

I rushed forward, ignoring the signs, tape and vehicles, standing between me and my forever.

"Hey, you can't be here!" I heard someone holler, but I paid them no heed. Williams trotted up behind me. That's when I saw the wreck. There was a massive semitruck… and a small car. The right side of the smaller vehicle was crushed.

Not again, I thought as I sprinted past cops and paramedics.

"Trey."

I slowed as Williams jogged up next to me.

"Is that her?"

I followed his pointing. Three paramedics surrounded a gurney, raising it in through the back of an ambulance.

I took off.

"Maybelle." I lunged for the gurney, not sure what my plan was. The air was knocked from me as a hand caught my chest.

"What the hell are you doing?" A big man, a paramedic, judging by his uniform, pulled me away.

My mouth wouldn't work as I ripped his arm off me. In my head I was screaming. While on the outside all I could do was stare wide-eyed as they settled Maybelle inside and one of the medical personnel yelled, "Shut those doors. We gotta move."

"That's my girl," I finally got out over the chaos.

The man's eyes strayed from me to Maybelle then back to me.

My mouth formed the word, *"Please."* But I wasn't sure any sound came out.

Despite that, the paramedic asked, "Can you keep out of the way?"

I nodded fervently.

He gestured me forward, showing me a seat in the corner of the ambulance. "This one's family," he shouted but the others barely spared me a look. They were yelling stats and commands at each other.

Just before the vehicle doors closed, I caught sight of Williams.

"We'll meet you there," he said, and I nodded.

The doors clapped shut and the ambulance jostled off

with us inside. She was right there, just within reach, but I never felt so far away.

Blood painted her face. Her beautiful hair was matted, and her eyes were closed.

"We got you, sweetheart," one man said as he charted out on a clipboard. A woman rummaged around, pulling supplies from a side cubby.

I was helpless. Watching, waiting, praying.

Air evaded me as I stared. I lowered my head between my shoulders, desperately trying to pull breath into my chest. My eyes caught onto a purse sliding across the floor with the momentum of the ambulance. It shifted toward me and spilled out a small black book.

My journal…

I swallowed hard and grabbed at the book. My head rolled back against the wall behind me as I opened the heavily scribed on pages. I flipped past entries she talked about Liam. Entries, she cried. Entries she told stories and entries, she dreamed of a beautiful, love-filled existence.

I opened to the first page. The first page I read and the first page that changed my life. My eyes fell on the last words of that first passage.

My greatest wish is for you to love me as much as I love you.

"I-I do," I stuttered under my breath as I looked up at her in the gurney. "I love you that much and more," I admitted lowly.

A shrilling mechanical beep sounded through the space. The woman lunged toward Maybelle, checking lines and pulse points.

"Shit," she hissed.

My heart free-fell into my stomach.

"What's wrong?" I asked. Neither paramedic acknowledged me.

The man checked his papers, glanced at a handheld screen. "Start compressions," he ordered over the ruckus and wailing of the sirens.

Quick to answer, the woman climbed up over Maybelle, put her hands to her chest and began to pump.

I gripped the journal in both my hands. Kissing the cover of the book, I closed my eyes and held it to my lips as tears cascaded down my face.

"Stay," I whispered. "Stay with me, Mayhem," I prayed into the leather of the book.

I'd never prayed. Not to a god at least. But every word out of my mouth was filled with depths of my soul. It was fitting that the only prayer ever uttered from my lips be for her—to her.

"*Don't leave me*," I pleaded in my head, watching as the paramedics worked to keep her here.

"I can't get a steady rhythm," the man grounded out.

I dropped my forehead to the book. "*I can't do this without you. We had a deal.*"

"Let's shock her," ordered the woman.

"*I told you, 'No more walking alone'. I promised you I would walk with you every day. Morning, night, rain or shine. I meant that forever.*" I pulled back and swiped at the tears that fell to the leather of my book. "*Don't leave me to walk alone, please—please. I can't walk without you, May. I need you.*"

I dropped my head back against the wall, my tears streaming back into my hair while Maybelle's body jolted with each pump.

"*Stay, May. Please stay with me, baby. Please.*" I continued to beg into the void of my subconscious.

I was being devoured from the inside out. My hope, my faith, my joy was being stripped from me, and I was powerless to stop it.

Life was no friend of mine. It was a cruel reality, and I wasn't so sure I would survive it as I closed my eyes.

"*Come back, May. Come back home to me.*"

***

Beep. Beep. Beep.

I held to that constant noise like a lifeline. I settled back in my chair, eyes wandering over the sleeping girl in the bed.

"Trey?"

Peering over my shoulder, I saw Penny squeezing in through the half-open hospital room door. In her hands was a tray of food from the cafeteria.

"I thought you might be hungry," she explained in a hushed tone.

I couldn't eat. The adrenaline from the last several hours had hardened like a stone in the pit of my gut. But when I looked back at the golden-haired girl asleep in the bed, the weight eased a fraction.

The doctors said she was a miracle. They insisted she was fine. That she should wake any minute now. I wasn't sure what I believed, what I could trust. I knew I wouldn't feel sure until I saw those beautiful blue-green eyes look at me.

It'd only been a couple hours since we arrived. Maybelle slept but she was stable. Apparently, she'd been awake earlier, but I missed her. I was preoccupied with an officer.

I had white-knuckled Maybelle's journal in one of my hands as the police officer explained to me who took her. My eyes fell to her neck. Discolored fingerprints marred her skin.

Luckily for that bastard, Maybelle was the only one to survive the crash.

Penny placed the plate on the small table next to Maybelle's bed.

I mustered up a smile. "Thank you."

She nodded. Her eyes weren't on me though; they were on Maybelle. Maybelle was beautiful. Even with a large bandage across her forehead, the bruising around her neck and her pallid complexion.

Penny cautiously perched herself on the edge of the bed in front of me, her eyes still studying our girl.

"I'm so sorry, Trey."

Tears fell then, and she swiped at her eyes. "I keep replaying what happened in my head." Her hands fidgeted together, and her eyes trailed back to Maybelle. "I should never have listened to her when she told me not to move. I should've run to her. I should've done something." Her head bowed. "I'm so mad at her for leaving, for not letting me help, but more than anything, I'm furious with myself. She needed me and I didn't move."

My heart cracked, and I reached for Penny, putting a hand on her knee. "Penny." She didn't look up at me as she continued to cry. "You did nothing wrong. You're not to blame for what happened."

When she continued to look elsewhere, I finally said, "Penny, look at me." When she did, tears stained her cheeks.

"This is not your fault," I reiterated.

Squeezing her eyes closed, she nodded, sniffling as she twisted to Maybelle. "I just wish I could've done more."

I had never related with anything more. This feeling of complete helplessness. This uncertainty and lack of ability to do anything was enough to drive me mad with grief.

"I understand."

She shook her head and placed a hand on Maybelle's, that rested at her side. "I wanted to wait until she woke up but—Daniel is here to pick me up."

"Good," I said. "You should go home, get some rest."

She still didn't tear her eyes from Maybelle as she asked me, "What about you?"

There was no me without Maybelle.

"I'll be fine."

She stood, leaning over the bed to place a kiss on Maybelle's brow as she whispered into her skin, "I love you too."

Penny wasn't the only one who had sat here with me and Maybelle. Earlier, my brothers had been here. My eyes turned to the side table and bundle of forget-me-nots Larson had insisted on picking up for Maybelle.

After I called and updated them on the situation, they showed up

It was odd and remarkable comparing this time to last. Maybelle wasn't in a coma, but it wasn't just me waiting for her to be okay. There was a whole family waiting and hoping.

I rubbed my fingers over the worn book in my hands. Thankful for answered prayers.

***

I startled awake.

I didn't remember falling asleep, but that's not what startled me. It was the empty hospital bed in front of me that had me shooting up. My eyes scoured the room, but they quickly found her. She stood in a hospital gown on the other side of the unlit room. Looking out the window that peered over the city and the darkly lit sky.

Speechless, I remained in my chair beside the bed, watching the girl that admired the twinkling city lights. Her face was solemn as she studied the sights below, and her hands were folded to her chest. Her hair was a mess of tangled coils falling down her back. Her skin had more color to it from what I could make out against the limited light reaching in through the window.

She was like an angel, glowing in the dark of the night. My heart was racing in sporadic, life-threatening rhythms as I waited and watched. Unsure if my grief had broken my ability to see reality or if this beautiful miracle was mine to keep.

Tied up in the hands she had pressed to her chest was the book I'd been clutching to for dear life. Maybelle held to the journal like I had, like it was the only way to breathe.

When her eyes finally slid to me, I couldn't read the expression in them. She was quiet as she took a couple of cautious steps toward me.

My whole body was screaming at me to throw myself at her. To touch her, make sure she was real, that this wasn't a dream, but I held still in my chair. I didn't know all that happened to her after she got into the car with Richard.

Besides the accident, I sensed that those long moments in the vehicle took much from her. I hadn't been able to be with her then, but being with her now, there was one thing I had the power to give her.

I wanted her to have the choice of what would happen next. I wanted her to have the control here.

Maybelle stopped at the foot of the bed, her blue-green eyes piercing into me with a thousand emotions. Relief soothed the tension in my shoulders at the sight.

"Trey," she rasped.

"May."

She sighed, hugging tighter to the book as she said, "Can you take me home?"

Joy had me leaping from my chair to her. I was ready to cradle her in my arms all the way home. Except Maybelle fell back a step, halting my approach entirely.

"Sorry," I whispered, and that had her body loosening with tension and my heart aching. "Of course I can take you home. My mom will be happy to see you," I said, trying to soothe her.

"No," she said in a barely audible voice. "I mean, my home."

My heart ceased pumping. My soul caved in on itself. "You—you remember?"

Maybelle pulled the book from her chest. Again, I couldn't discern the look in her eye as she answered, her attention locked on the journal.

"I remember everything." When she looked back at me, silver lined her eyes. "Take me home, Trey. Please."

42

Can I Hold You?

Maybelle

Trey.

He'd been the first thing I felt, saw, and smelled when I woke up. But just like last time I woke up in a hospital bed, my head hurt, my body ached, and the confusion was almost unbearable.

Except this time, I had time to collect myself. I could take in my surroundings, remember the last moments before unconsciousness took me and... Everything else.

Each memory, detail, dream and nightmare were back in their designated files.

Then I saw the book.

My precious journal in Trey's hand. It was important to me before the return of my memories. I understood the sacredness of its contents, but now it was like being reunited with an old friend.

I held to it desperately as Trey and I snuck out of the hospital. We didn't think the hospital would actually bar me from leaving. Trey took me not wanting to talk to people and my desire to be home as soon as possible very seriously. So, he decided that sneaking me out was the best option.

Before running, he mentioned it would be best if I wore something other than the open-back hospital gown.

I agreed. He offered his hoodie, that skated past my mid-thigh. It was all we had in terms of modesty and disguise.

Trey was timid when I asked him to help me remove the gown. He softly undid the ties and made an extra effort not to touch my skin with his. As the gown slipped from my limbs, I noticed his eyes were deliberate in their focus to land on anything but my body.

When I was finally standing in only my underwear, I didn't shiver against the chill of the room. I didn't cower with embarrassment when his sad green eyes finally met mine. I mechanically followed the way he guided his hoodie over my head. Then let him pull the hood up to hide my face from the hospital staff.

I knew I scared Trey when I retreated from him. I knew I made him unsure of what to do or how to act. But I needed a moment. I needed time because I was struggling to differentiate between fiction and real-life. I remembered jumping from the vehicle when that semi-truck crashed into us.

But I could also remember many moments after that.

Blissful, perfect, precious moments I didn't have the right words to explain.

Then I was awake. I was here.

My mind felt like a mess, my body ached, my skin burned where it had been viciously gripped, and my heart felt hollow.

Honestly, I think my heart was just unsure it had the strength to feel, the courage to let everything in all at once. I needed time and what helped me not feel guilty for taking that time was that I knew Trey wanted me to take it. It was obvious in the way he was cautious with me, gentle in the way he spoke. He was gifting me the space and ability to choose without pushing his needs on me.

"Follow me, May."

He beckoned me forward, out to the parking lot and through the front doors. He didn't lead me to the Jeep though. It was Chelsea's car I recognized in the parking lot.

"Where's your—" I started, then remembered the keys I was trusted with and the chaos that later ensued.

"Oh, I'm sorry," I mumbled.

Trey's smile was soft, but it didn't reach his eyes. "You have nothing to be sorry for. I'll get new keys soon."

I hopped into the passenger seat of Chelsea's car, and Trey buckled my belt for me. I still hadn't put down the journal I had clutched in my hands, and I think he wanted to make sure I didn't have to.

This journal acted as my life raft, my anchor in the storm of my childhood. Now it felt like it was the one thing keeping me afloat. Like if I let go, I would sink and drown under all the feelings and memories.

I was desperately trying to allow them in as a steady trickle and not the tirade of chaos it had the capacity of being.

The drive to San Francisco was long and it was silent. Even at pit stops, we didn't talk, but the silence was the same as it always was with him. It was safe.

I was safe.

I woke up from my short sleep in the early evening. I even had the chance to watch the sun in its descent behind the horizon. When we finally reached my home, the California sun was still asleep, hiding behind the smoggy blanket of stars.

Trey didn't have his keys Liam had gifted to him, but I remembered where we kept an extra key. Atop the red door frame, just below the black and white sign that read, *Mason*. A sign I finally understood. A sign that welcomed me home. A signal to all weary souls who lost their way that they finally made it back home.

When we opened the door, I had to bite back the emotion that ached in the back of my throat. My mother's beautiful home was dirtied with neglect. The home she built for her children. A haven she created to help heal her babies from a lifetime of hurt.

The smell was still the same, though. Almost as strong as if mom had just lit a scented candle of citrus, cinnamon, and vanilla. Letting it burn away the scents of our past.

I cautiously stepped into the house with Trey right there with me.

"I want to clean it," I whispered as I turned to him. "Will you help me?"

He didn't hesitate. "Of course."

We didn't sleep that night or that day. We didn't speak either. We cleaned and cleaned and cleaned.

Trey started out on the opposite side of the house, keeping his distance as he tidied. I kept to my area, mentally working through the last couple days with myself. I let that trickle of feelings flood through me.

I had to keep reminding myself that I was safe. That no monsters could come crawling from the dark corners of the world. My demons were gone. I defeated them.

I fought in the battle, and I won.

The memory of vengeful hands ceased plaguing me. Instead, I held onto the one thought I had when I jumped from the car. The same thought I had as I took Liam's hand, teetering on the edge of one life and the next.

I want to live. It was a new anthem my body, my mind, my heart and soul sang to with renewed vigor. I can't explain the experience I had after I accepted Liam's hand and leapt from the car. All I knew was my mind hadn't been so dark or quiet those hours I rested. And the company that was with me understood the hopeful song my being sang to.

I want to live.

I want to live.

I want to live.

If I listened long enough, I wasn't alone in my singing.

If anything, I knew without a doubt that I would never be alone again in this life I vowed to love—to live.

After a long while of recovering my home, I found myself drifting closer to where Trey was hard at work. He was so focused on his area. He didn't speak to me. But I noticed the subtle glances at me from afar.

When I looked back at him, he didn't immediately tear his gaze from mine. Instead, he smiled. I smiled back. Then we returned to work.

At some point in the next day, when the sun had already grown bright in the sky, breaking through the windows, I watched him.

Trey's lips were tight as he concentrated on wiping down a countertop layered in dust. I studied those lips. The lips I had kissed and the lips that kissed my—my everything. I had seen that body that ripples and swells against the confines of his clothing. Trey Turner, in all his glory, had seen every single inch of me, had worshipped and caressed every bit of my skin.

The skin that was now on fire as both my worlds collided before me, leaving me breathless.

"Mayhem?"

My focus tore up from his grinning lips as I looked at him. I couldn't help the twitch of a smile at the corner of my mouth as my eyes met his.

I really, really liked that nickname.

"Trey," I answered.

His smile grew a smidge more. "Are you okay?"

I nodded. "I'm a little hungry," I admitted, and his small grin grew into a full smirk.

"I have some snacks out in the car," he offered.

"Pop tarts?"

"Of course."

We silently dined on pop tarts after that. Smiling when we made eye contact, but we didn't talk again, not until later that night. When we both stepped back from our work and admired the clean home before us.

It was like I never left. Like Mom and Liam could walk back in through the front door at any moment. The cherry on top was the candle Trey salvaged from a storage closet and lit with a lighter he found.

It smelt of soft flowers, tart oranges and a little like… hope.

"May," he said, and I turned to him.

I was no longer dressed in his hoodie. Earlier I spilled water all down the front of it when I was readying to mop. I changed myself into a lightweight pair of shorts and a soft, blue, cotton tank. Then I braided my hair back into a long rope down my back.

"Yes, Trey."

He wore jeans and a fitted navy-blue tee, his tan skin a beautiful color against the fabric. He took a step toward me, and my breath caught.

"Are you okay?" he asked me again.

He was nervous.

The Trey Turner was nervously talking to me, but he knew me, every bit of me. He had read my journal. My beautiful journal I safely stowed in my old bedroom, waiting for the moment I was ready to gift it back to the man who stood in front of me. My blush became scorching as I recalled him claiming that journal was his.

That *I* was his.

I couldn't keep up with the molding of my life before the memory loss and after. It was all a lot.

He took another couple of steps forward and was now very close.

Kissing distance close.

"Maybelle."

My eyes snapped up from his lips back to his eyes and a half smile pulled at his features. Being this close, I finally noticed the bruising of exhaustion under his eyes. The weariness of his smile. This poor boy had gone through hell and back in the last couple of days. I could see every bit of the pain and trepidation in his movements as he spoke.

"I'm okay," I whispered.

It was dark now that the sun had vanished behind the night sky. We hadn't turned on the house lights. The only source of illumination was the candle he lit and the feeble glow of the full moon glancing through the windows.

He didn't move as he watched me, only nodded. "Do you want to talk about it?"

I did, and I didn't. I wanted to tell Trey everything. One day, soon, I would tell him about it. Tell him about how I ran, tell him about how I fought, and about Liam, but not tonight.

Tonight, I just wanted to be with him.

"I do," I answered lowly, meeting his steps with my own. Our bodies were so close they nearly touched with each deep breath. "But not tonight."

He nodded, his eyes searching mine.

"Can—can I hold you?"

His question was so soft, a breath that almost blew me away into oblivion. I couldn't speak, I couldn't function normally, but I managed to bob my head once.

He didn't hesitate. He closed the remaining distance and grappled me against him. His hand cradled the back of my head while his other arm encircled my waist.

"God, you scared me," he said. His breath warm against my ear.

"I'm sorry," I tried but squeaked. Trey held me tighter.

"May." The timbre of his voice shook with his rising emotions, and I gripped the collar of his shirt in my hands. "You have nothing to be sorry for. Nothing. I'm just happy you're okay. I don't know what I would've done with myself if—" he trailed off, pressing his words into my hair. Then he cupped my face with both of his hands. "I'm afraid my heart is just too vulnerable when it comes to you, Maybelle Mason."

I smiled at the use of my words on that beach all those

long months ago. When we'd both been so young, so scared, and so naïve to what our future offered us.

I needed to speak, but words evaded me. So, I responded the way Trey would've on the beach that night before we were interrupted.

I kissed him.

The kiss was gentle, but it was deep and so full of feeling. It wasn't a fleeting, subconscious show of affection. It was a finally. A coming home. A deep breath and a morning in bed after the longest sleep.

His thumbs stroked my jaw. Then cautiously they moved down, skimming over my neck. His body was magnetic and a force I had no other choice but to hold with all my strength to.

I tilted my head back, pleading for more.

I missed him.

I missed his hands, his heat, his gentle touch. And the desperation in which he held to me like I was the only way to breathe. Trey's hand laced around the back of my neck, tangling with the curls at the nape. He parted from me then, watching and waiting.

"Talk to me, May. Tell me what you want." His voice was strained. Like it was painful for him to stop, but he did.

I licked my lips, tasting the slightly swollen feel of them. My grip on his shirt flexed, then my hands flattened on his chest as I realized this pause pained me as well.

"Trey," I breathed, testing my voice.

It was as unsteady as I anticipated, but his eyes only softened as he continued with patience. I lifted my hand to his cheek, swiping my thumb near the corner of his mouth. Like I could coax that heartbreaking smile from him. The hand at my waist palmed my hip and I could feel the rapid beating of his heart under my fingers.

"I know you," I whispered. "And I love you."

He sighed into me, his forehead falling against mine.

Like my declaration broke a dam of anxiety in him, allowing relief and stability to flood him. I looked up into those deep depths of green, whispering, "I need you."

And he was kissing me.

His kiss shifted from reverence to hunger, pure need as his hands found my thighs and lifted me. I wrapped my legs around him. My fingers tangled with the silky tufts of his chocolate and caramel curls.

Trey was walking, but I couldn't breathe, couldn't think about where he was taking us. I could only feel, think, inhale, exhale, and taste him.

He lowered me onto my feet, the back of my knees meeting with the bed in my small bedroom. He peeled himself from me, his hands back to holding my face as he studied the scene. His gaze devoured the sight of me, the bed behind me, and I trembled with the need to have him on top of me.

"I just need a second," he said through a tight breath and my brows rose, surveying him.

"Is something wrong?" I asked, and he chuckled deeply.

"No, everything is perfect," he assured, his eyes gleaming with wonder. Then his mouth dropped to the base of my throat, trailing tender kisses across the exposed skin.

"The teenage boy in me is over the moon right now. It's been a dream of mine to kiss you in this bedroom— in this bed." He smiled into the skin of my shoulder, as his hand lifted to slip the strap of my tank top away and down my arm.

I giggled, half-gasping when he sucked at the skin under my collarbone.

"Well, I'd be lying if I said it hadn't been a dream of mine to be kissed by you whenever or wherever you wanted."

My mouth quickly snapped shut.

Wow. My life.

I was confidently flirting with—my boyfriend, Trey Turner, while he kissed the skin beneath the neckline of my top.

His amusement vibrated against my skin, sending a rush of feeling and goosebumps all over. He was a drug and I the addict. There was no rehabilitating me of the obsessive addiction.

"Sit, May."

I perched on the edge of the bed. Then he knelt in front of me, reaching for the laces of my shoes. He made quick work of them, slipping them off and then my socks.

He reached over and gave the hem of my shorts a tug.

"Stand for me, love."

I smirked. "Make up your mind, Turner."

But I obeyed, my knees buckling as I stood in front of him on his knees. Trey's grin was devastating as he smiled up at me.

"There's that attitude I love so much."

His face leveled with my sternum. His large hands tickled up from my exposed calves. They moved up behind my knees to cup the back of my thighs, pulling me flush against him. He nuzzled his face into the bare skin between my rising shirt and the falling waistband of my shorts.

His hands latched onto the bottoms of my shorts. He shimmied them down my legs, as he kissed the newly revealed skin of my hips, then my thighs.

My shorts were pooled at my feet. Pausing, he looked up at me from where he knelt, his eyes glazed over with so many emotions, wants, and needs.

"I am going to kiss every square inch of you, and I am going to take my time," he breathed, and I nodded, not sure if it was a request or a warning. He spun me so I faced the bed. He pressed his deviant smile into the skin of my lower back.

"I love you. You're perfect."

Trey pulled my tank top up as he kissed up my spine, standing with the climb. My shirt was off, and he tugged at the end of my frizzy braid. He removed the hair tie, combing his fingers through the long-crimped coils. When his fingers knitted through my loose hair, I followed his gentle pulling. My head rested back on his shoulder, allowing his mouth to find mine.

This kiss was crucial—pivotal as his other hand splayed out across the bare plane of my stomach. I was shattering in the best ways for him.

He knew my skin, my hair, my fingers, where to kiss me.

But I wanted all of him. I wanted his skin.

I twirled in his grasp, facing him fully and fisting the fabric of his shirt, tugging up.

"Off," I demanded, and when he quirked a brow, I sweetened the command with a soft, "Please."

He chuckled, kissing me as he worked to pull his shirt over his head. "Yes, ma'am."

Trey stood before me in his black briefs, pulling me toward him. I let my finger pads trickle across his chest, travel down the valleys and hills of his large, warm arms.

His intense, heavy stare followed my every move, my every caress along his skin, but his hands and body were still. He let me do my own amount of feeling and exploration of him. I kissed, I admired, I touched and learned the body that I loved, the body I knew.

It was different now, though.

The intimacy between us was warm, buzzing with the infatuation of my crush from before. From when I only adored from afar, and my deep resounding love for him after, *now*.

"I love you. With my whole heart and soul, I love you," I gasped.

All my life, I'd been running away, trying to escape. But as he pulled me in tight, I never wanted so badly to stay. To be kept by this beautiful, safe man.

He laid me out on the bed, and he kissed me.

He kissed my knees, my inner thighs, the places that we both wanted to touch and be touched. He wasn't timid nor cautious. He was praising, driving, consuming.

He was home.

I was home in his arms, engulfed by his touch. He hovered over me, deliberate and gentle, as he loved me to the pinnacle point of sensation. As I free-fell from the heights we'd flown together, Trey lowered himself to my ear.

His heavy breathing was a welcome constant as he whispered, "I need you too, May. You are my whole heart and soul. You're my end game."

43

Peace

Trey

I had died and gone to heaven.

That was the only explanation for the angel that laid across my chest in the morning sunlight. Maybelle's golden curls were a fluffy mess across her bare back, her skin glowing and freckled.

My body melted into the mattress with relief and gratitude that my girl was home, safe in my embrace. She was no longer alone, and neither was I.

I prayed that I could stay here, watch her sleep. A wish I never ever thought would tempt me. But seeing her like this, in this bed, in my arms, snoring only slightly—it was all I could ever want.

I'd gotten so close to losing everything. So, fucking close it made me sick. After this hellish week, I doubted I could ever breathe normally outside of her presence again.

Maybelle's nose scrunched. She sniffed, then blinked as her arms stretched out. Blue-green framed by a curtain of thick, light lashes was all I could see.

"Hi," she huffed, and it was officially the loveliest thing I'd ever heard.

"Hey, Mayhem," I breathed, and to my surprise, her

cheeks pinked. My eyebrows rose and she quickly averted her gaze. So, I pinched her chin between my fingers and brought her focus back to me.

"May, sweetheart, are you embarrassed?" I teased, and her cheeks got redder.

Her smile was tight and coy as she whispered, "I just really like that nickname."

I chuckled, pulling her up my body so we laid nose to nose with her still atop my chest. "Good. I don't plan to stop using it."

She nuzzled into my neck, and I tangled my fingers through her curls.

"May, what're you doing?"

"Hm?" she hummed.

Her face was buried in the space between my jaw and shoulder as she placed kisses in tender spots. It felt so good. She felt good. Her soft full lips nipping and caressing up my neck, and along my jaw.

She placed a lingering kiss against my Adam's apple and the gentle pressure had me hissing. My hands found her naked hips.

She was irresistible to me, and she knew it. I rolled us, pinning her to the bed beneath me as I claimed her mouth with mine in a searing kiss. When Maybelle gasped, I broke the kiss, smirking at her under me.

"What do you think about us moving this to the shower?"

Her small smile was answer enough.

I rose from the bed, pacing across the room. My hands raked through my hair as I glanced back at her. She pulled the blankets over herself and looked me over with snarky amusement.

Winking back to her, I opened the door to the bathroom and started up the shower. When I returned to the bedroom, she had shrunk under the sheets, her face rosy.

"You coming?" I asked, approaching the bed and the

beautiful woman in it.

Her cheeks were a fiery crimson now as I tugged at the blanket she took refuge in.

"Oh, May, don't go getting shy on me now," I taunted as I ripped the blankets off.

She squealed, but I snatched her up in my arms. I carried her to the shower, kicking and giggling.

After our shower, I'd gone out to get us a real breakfast. As much as we loved pop tarts, we needed real food. I brought it home for us. We ate it in the kitchen. We talked about old memories. Like that morning I woke to her singing. We laughed and reminisced.

I thought for sure I'd never been happier.

I then took a few minutes to call and message our family and friends. I let them know we were both alive and well. Which was quite the dramatic ordeal with certain individuals.

Let's just say, I had a lot of apologizing to do to calm Williams, Larson and Bear.

And no, they were not concerned in the slightest about my whereabouts or wellbeing. It was all about Maybelle. How she was doing, when they could come see her, if she would be well enough to hop online and play teams on COD soon.

And a bunch of other bullshit I could only laugh at.

Despite the three of them being a collection of worrying idiots for the girl I loved, I'd never been more thankful to call them my brothers.

Now, I was in only my black boxers while Maybelle had wrapped herself in a fluffy pink robe. We cuddled together in her bed. She laid on my chest while I held our precious journal up for us both to read as we tangled together in the sheets.

"Trey," she whispered.

We were skimming over an entry about Liam. How he helped a young Maybelle build an elementary science fair project.

"Yes, May?"

She pressed in, placing a kiss to my bobbing throat, sending a shudder through me.

"What do you miss most about Liam?"

"His big heart," I said, not needing to think long on it. "He was the best supporter, constantly cheered everyone on. You know he talked about you all the time?"

She twisted into me so our eyes could meet. Her light brows quirked.

"Really?"

I nodded. "Yeah, he constantly talked about you. Especially when we were doing something fun, he would say he wished you were there. He also showed me your old highlight reels from when you played basketball."

Those vivid blue-green eyes widened. "He showed you what now?" she demanded, sitting up and shattering the close intensity between us.

I chuckled, sitting myself up with her.

"Yeah, he showed me your best games. He was very proud. You were quite the superstar."

The light flush creeping up her cheeks made me want to nip and kiss her skin. Which I planned to do until her palm landed on my chest, stopping my approach.

"Hold up. When you and I chatted in the kitchen graduation morning, you said that you didn't know I played sports."

Now I was blushing. I grasped her hand, bringing it from my chest to my lips. I placed a soft kiss on her palm before admitting into her skin, "I lied."

She gasped in mock disbelief. "Trey Tory Turner!" she exclaimed, and I tackled the tantalizing woman back to the bed, pinning her down with my weight.

The darling, pink robe slipped, revealing more of my favorite expanse of skin. I trailed praising kisses from her collar bones down and around to all the exposed places while I spoke.

"What can I say? I had a big crush on you, May." I nibbled the bare skin above her navel. "I would've done anything to get you to notice me for just a moment. Speak one sentence to me. Spend a second of your time with me."

A kiss against her inner thigh, gliding up to her knee.

"Then that morning you were talking to me. I was willing to do anything to keep you with me."

I rose back up, kissing the underside of her jaw. Then I whispered my lips along the shell of her ear.

"Even tell a small lie."

When our eyes met, noses touching, the grin on my face was tight, full of cramping cheek muscles. Maybelle's smile was sweet, innocent. It made me want to tease and taunt the sexy woman until her sassy, infuriating side came out to play.

Thankfully, I didn't have to do much to persuade as her eyes narrowed.

"You really are obsessed with me, aren't you?"

I kissed her because yes. Yes, I was.

I pulled away, smiling uncontrollably. "That would be the understatement of the century." I lay down, my head resting on her chest, her arms snaking around, drawing me closer to her.

"Trey," Maybelle said, her arms pulling tight, allowing no room for escape. It was perfect.

"Mayhem?"

"I need you to take me somewhere."

"Anywhere, love."

***

The sky was a blazing sunset of oranges, pinks, and yellows when I put the car in park. Maybelle was quiet, but it was a good quiet.

We were going to see her family for the first time in almost two years.

Opening her door for her, I took the flowers from her hands. Allowing her to step out of my mom's car onto the plush grass of the local cemetery.

I took her hand and glanced behind me.

"Come here," I said as I hugged my mom into my side.

Mom smiled at me then smiled at Maybelle. Maybelle's eyes were still glossy from their reunion.

"Thanks for being here, Chels," Maybelle said, and Mom reached around me to squeeze her arm.

"I wouldn't miss this for the world."

Hand in hand, I led Maybelle down the pathways of tombstones. The quiet peace created a sanctuary in the field of resting souls. I tilted my head to glance at the girl dressed in a white tee and jeans. I couldn't ignore the clog of emotion in the back of my throat.

She was glowing.

My mom must've sensed my blooming emotions because she hugged me tighter.

A harsh intake of breath from Maybelle had me looking ahead to see a man standing before of our intended destination. The man was tall. He wore a black shirt, dark jeans. His skin was tan. He had black, straight hair with white highlights. There was a disheveled amount of facial hair along his jaw and a slump to his shoulders that I once related to.

"Xavier," Maybelle breathed, and the man spun.

His dark eyes widened at the sight of her. Without another word, Maybelle was striding from me to the stranger—Xavier.

He held his arms out to accept her. They met in a heart-wrenching hug. Maybelle was crying, and so was he. They both grasped to one another, with only their tears, nearby birds and far off traffic to fill the silence.

Mom sniffled beside me. I twisted to her and she smiled up at me with tears in her brown eyes as she pointed. "Stephanie told me about him."

Maybelle pulled back, the two of them still embracing as she giggled through a sob. "You've gotten old," she said, running her fingers through the patches of white hair.

Xavier guffawed through his tears.

"And you talk," he pointed out. They both embraced once again, their laughter combining into a merry melody.

They parted from one another, and Maybelle's smiling eyes turned to Mom. "Xavier, this is Chelsea."

He shook Mom's hand with a courteous nod.

Then Maybelle's eyes found mine. "And this is Trey. Liam's best friend and my—my boyfriend."

The adorable flush to her cheeks had me stepping up next to her, hooking an arm around her waist.

I locked hands with Xavier in a firm shake.

"Yes, I think we've met," he said, and the pieces clicked into place.

"Tacos?" I asked, and the man grinned.

"Yes, I served you and Liam once or twice in my parents' restaurant."

I nodded, remembering a few nights Liam dragged me to his favorite taco shop after a wild party or two. Where Xavier would leave the restaurant open for us, feeding us all the free tacos and water, he could get us to eat.

My laughter was a ruckus of humiliation as I remembered the time I barfed in the restaurant bathroom. All while Liam and Xavier laughed their asses off at me.

"Damn it, Sir. You might have the most humbling stories to tell about me. That being said, you're not allowed to give a toast at our wedding so I can keep hold of at least an ounce of my pride."

Xavier's smile grew. Maybelle slanted me a sidelong glance. Mom beamed.

"No promises," he remarked with a wink, then turned

to Maybelle, smile still bright. "Wedding? How exciting for you two. When is it?"

Before Maybelle or Mom could open their mouths, I quickly cut in with a promising, "Soon."

Again, Maybelle was giving me a curious side-eye, but I didn't turn from the man in front of us.

Xavier's chuckles were deep as he clapped me on the shoulder. "Well, I'll keep my schedule open for the near future." Then his dark eyes fell to the two partnering stones in the grass.

Stephanie Anne Mason
Mother
Cherished friend
And confidant

Liam Mason
Son
Brother
Friend
And Captain

My vision went misty, just as it always did when I spent time here. It got easier, but it'd been a while since I returned because of the busy schedule I happily let Maybelle take over.

Being back here, with her, brought on a whole new rush of feelings.

"I like to come here Sundays and talk to them—well, mainly her," Xavier admitted. "Liam was never a good listener. So, I hang out with him but Steph... She always listened. Always accepted everything a person was as more than enough."

At his words, Maybelle stepped in close to him, her eyes glued to the stones as she laced her fingers in his.

"You know, she cared for you. She would've said yes to you the first time you asked her out if she didn't have us to worry about."

His watery eyes turned to Maybelle. "I didn't mind the waiting. It's knowing she finally said, 'yes' that keeps me going."

Awareness, understanding and a thought crept in as I watched Maybelle squeeze Xavier's hand.

Love. It's a crazy, stupid thing and I don't think I truly comprehended or knew the words to describe it until now.

Love is patient. I think Xavier and even I would know that best. Love can be painful, but love is worth it. It's a passionate, trusting, enduring, and multilayered phenomenon.

It's a complete leap of faith.

I watched the girl I loved smile sweetly. The girl who radiated life and what it should be at its core. I learned something new as I watched her.

Living teaches us how to love. How to be brave enough to accept it, acknowledge it, nurture it, want it, and be a conduit for it.

"She really, really liked you," Maybelle said.

Xavier's eyes screwed shut as his chin fell to his chest. A beat, then two passed before he cupped Maybelle's face in two large hands.

"You are not alone. The Fernandez family is in your corner. You're welcome home to us whenever you need. You hear me?" he insisted, his eyes piercing hers as she nodded.

"Good," he said.

He threw one last look to Stephanie before stepping out towards the path to the parked vehicles. He called back over his shoulder, "And since you're a Fernandez, you get the family discount so free tacos forever. Visit soon, my mama misses you!"

Maybelle's laughter was contagious as she hollered back, "I will! Thank you!"

***

Sprinkled stars peeked through the smoggy clouds. The near winter night chill was a welcome as we sat with Liam and Stephanie. While Maybelle and I huddled together under a thick blanket, Mom sat on a nearby bench with her eyes turned to the sky.

We hadn't done much talking, but I think Maybelle did. In her heart as she sat and hummed, tracing the carved words across the headstones with her fingers. I didn't think she cried or spoke as we sat with her family because I didn't think the time, she spent unconscious was lonely.

I had a feeling Maybelle had time to pick up a few of the pieces between her, her mom and her brother. I believe she got the reunion she needed to carry on. One day she would tell me about it, and I looked forward to hearing it.

But for now, she needed no words as she sat with her family. Finally, all of them, at peace.

44

Forever Races

Trey
Eight months later

Are you ready to eat dirt, Mayhem?" I challenged, jogging back from the finish line to the starting line I traced in the damp sand.

The sun was finally showing signs of life in the early morning hour with the glowing horizon. The streaks of light set Maybelle's frizzy curls ablaze. She didn't pull them back this morning. She thought this was going to be a chill morning walk on the beach, but I had other plans.

My Maybelle was going to sprint today.

Her easy jogging was smooth, graceful even. She'd been trying so hard the last few weeks to sprint without losing balance.

"I don't know. You saw me last week. I literally ate dirt and had to gargle water three times before I wasn't crunching down on the sand hiding in my teeth," she whined, but I knew she was capable of anything, except turning down a challenge.

She would do it; she just needed a push.

"Sounds to me like you're scared," I jabbed, and she popped a hip. "Come on. We go back to school next week. How awesome would it be to start the school year having accomplished this?"

The mention of school already starting back up had my insides twisting. After winter break last year, Maybelle and I went back to school together. She wanted to finish out the year and be with me while I finished my second season of football. I think it helped her to be with our friends in the wake of the return of her memories and the accident.

Once the year ended, though, Maybelle and I retreated to the Mason home. We hid out there for the last few summer months, relishing in the secluded alone time.

We, of course, visited Mom multiple times and her new boyfriend, whom she finally introduced us to. Surprise wasn't a good enough word to describe what I felt when Doctor Nathaniel Brown entered my mother's living room.

Apparently, the two of them had really *bonded* while taking care of Maybelle during her coma.

As caught off guard as I was by the pairing, I couldn't help but be happy for my mom. She seemed over the moon in love and if she was happy, so was I.

Maybelle and I had also taken trips back to school for my football training together. We spent multiple nights with Penny and Williams when they stopped by to visit, but the rest was just us. We started routines living together, habits and a life. It was a reality I was not willing to let go of so soon.

"Fine," she groaned, readying herself at the makeshift starting line. "Loser does dishes."

I winked at my competitive girl before also readying myself at the line.

"Deal."

And without warning, Maybelle was off, cackling like a deranged woman.

"Cheater!" I hollered, hustling after her, but I didn't catch up as fast as I previously would've.

Maybelle's short muscular legs were pumping, racing, sprinting and she was flying. Her movements were steady, deliberate, purposeful as she crossed the finish line.

She did it—and I fell to my knee.

Her back was still to me as she bounced with excited squeals. "I did it! I did it! I did—" Those blue-green eyes blinked rapidly as they found me down on one knee. Then to the velvet box I held with a gold band and solitaire diamond glittering in the sunlight.

Her hand flew to her mouth.

"Maybelle Mason," I breathed, and she took a step toward me.

"Trey."

My throat constricted as I choked out the words I practiced multiple times in the mirror and recited to Williams over the phone.

"These months of spending every waking moment with you, doing real life with you, have been the happiest days of my life. Every chore, the amazing nights in bed together, meals, and everything in between have been perfect with you."

She nodded, continuing her approach as I spoke. Her glossy eyes never leaving mine.

"I thought about asking you to move in with me, because I can't spend one more night without you in my bed or in my arms. Knowing that what I really wanted to ask you was for your hand in marriage. And I'll admit it… I am so obsessed with you."

She snorted, and I sniffed.

"I love you, May. I see you. I know you. I want to keep knowing you, learning about you, living with you. You are the life I want to live."

Choking, I coughed on the emotions that threatened to turn me into a blubbering idiot.

"So—Maybelle Mason," I quickly shoved out. "Marry me."

She ran to me. She crossed the sandy space between us, veering left. Kicking up sand as she tackled me in a fit of giggles and squeals, Maybelle planted frantic kisses all over my face.

"Yes. Yes. Yes. Yes," she exclaimed between each kiss, her arms linking around my neck. Soon, each kiss was drawn out, and each excited "Yes" whispered more reverently as she molded her body into mine.

I let my hands glide up the backs of her thighs, my fingers dipping in against the thin fabric of her leggings. With a roll of her hips and the languid glide of her tongue, I gripped tightly to her waistband.

"May, sweetheart."

"Hmm?" she crooned, the vibrations against my lips setting my nerves on fire.

My hands were now exploring up her shirt, a mind of their own. "If I don't get you home now, you're going to be cleaning sand out of your hair for a week."

Her round, peachy lips turned up, pressing into me.

"Well, then, my dear, future husband. Take me home."

Author's Note + Acknowledgements

Hey y'all. First off, thank *you* for reading. It's truly an honor to have my book on your shelf, in your hands, and playing out in your mind.

This story has had many faces.

It started out in the hands of a young girl, starving for connection in a big world. It grew in the mind of a high schooler, who just couldn't find the silver lining to so many dark clouds. In the end, it was melded into a universe of its own. Structured into a mess of emotions and love in the hands of a community built by a girl who refused to lose her hope.

I'm baffled that we've made it to this point. What an incredible adventure this book has taken me on. I can't wait to see where it goes and the hearts it touches.

Over a decade ago, I started writing in a journal dedicated to my future husband. I was a lonely kid that really sucked at making friends.

So, I made friends with the man I would one day marry.

The idea to write was built off this need to hope that I could not only trust someone to love me the way I deserved but that I could let myself love and be loved without fear. Over the years, I fell in love with the idea of someone who befriended me and saw me as an equal.

That being said, I want to start off by thanking my best friend and husband, Brendan. We wouldn't have this story if it wasn't for him. He was the first to cheer me on and encourage me to get the story out into the world.

I want to thank my real life, Stephanie Mason. Thank you, Mom. Thank you for holding me on your lap while I cry (even now) and thank you for being an example of resilience.

I want to thank those who loved the book when it was scraps. Thank you to my aunts, Sharon and Heidi. Thank you for loving and supporting the most. I want to thank my amazing Beta readers. I specifically want to thank Elizabeth, Brook, Kinley and Emily for reading, loving and supporting this book. Y'all are fabulous. Thank you for helping me fall back in love with this story.

Lastly, I want to thank Meg Rosenthal, fellow author and friend. Thank you for helping me turn this story into something worth reading.

Photo taken by Scarlet Economou

About The Author

Taryn is a proud, undying fan of romance books, and an obsessor of emotionally deep, traumatic, beautiful fiction. When she's not writing out random, heartbreaking stories, poems, or an array of books in progress, she's either trying a new restaurant with her sweet husband or on a drive exploring their home in Utah. She's also a content creator, and host of The Wannabe Author podcast. A platform where she interviews traditionally and independently published authors about their journeys. She also invites industry professionals to talk about the world of publishing. If you want more of Taryn and updates on future projects, you can connect with her on social media or sign up for her Substack to get more of her ramblings.

Scan the QR to find more
of Taryn and her books